NORFOLK COZY MYSTERIES

COMPILATION: BOOKS ONE TO THREE

KEITH FINNEY

Keith Finney - Author

1
AN INVITATION

Welcome to your invitation to join my Readers' Club. Receive free, exclusive content only available to members including short stories, character interviews and much more.

To join, look out for the link towards the end of book three and you're in!

BOOK ONE

DEAD MAN'S TRENCH

1

IN A HOLE

Alan Fairchild's blood pressure wasn't in a good place. Getting the head of archaeology at Cambridge University to meet Stanton Parva's history group was a coup.

Why on earth turn out if they won't listen? Alan fumed in his thoughts. Did no one care that he'd sweat blood to secure a private tour of the dig, which he knew to be of national importance?

"May I emphasise again," said Professor Pullman, as heads swivelled and old friends chatted. "On no account interfere with the excavations you will see this morning."

It was an unequal battle. The gentle waters of Stanton Broad, glistening in the morning sun, had much more appeal than a dusty academic. Add in a golden carpet of Norfolk reed swaying rhythmically in the breeze, and the result was inevitable.

"Our hypothesis is that this vast Roman villa complex was wantonly destroyed. All the signs point to Boudica, queen of the Iceni Tribe. In around AD 60 she led a revolt against the Roman legions. Also..."

The professor's words failed to impress one section of

the group as they soaked up the latest village gossip. First amongst equals was Phyllis Abbott, a sprite eighty-two-year-old whose loss of hearing caused her to shout then accuse others of not speaking the queen's English.

Alan tried a flanking manoeuvre to work his way around the rebels so he could get close to Phyllis, who was in deep discussion with her best friend, Betty.

Phyllis was lamenting the post office's move from the village shop, which she'd run until age seventy-one, to the petrol station on the outskirts of Stanton Parva.

"Modernising the post office is what they call it. How come making things worse can be better for the customer? And what Her Majesty must think about it, well, I just don't know. What do you think, Betty?"

Betty nodded as she attempted a reply.

"Well, yes... I suppose..."

Phyllis was having none of it.

"There's no supposing about it. How do I get to Flatley's petrol station with my leg? Then there's the price of a first-class stamp. Shocking, that's what I say."

By now, Alan had sidled up to the pair and knew from Betty's scowl that she'd given up any hope of challenging her friend's views on the subject.

"Shush," said Alan, a wobble in his voice letting slip that his nerves were getting the better of him.

Phyllis shot Alan a cold stare.

"Who are you shushing, young man? Just like your mother, you are."

The old woman dismissed Alan with an imperious wave of her hand before turning back to Betty.

"And you know what?"

"No. What, dear?" offered Betty, pleased to be asked her opinion.

"When I went to pay for my Jiffy bag, that stupid boy asked which pump I was using. Well, I thought he was talking about the thing Dr Bridlington prescribed me. I told him to mind his own business. Then..."

The rest of the group were torn between Boudica chasing out the Romans and Phyllis' medicinal pump.

Alan had had enough.

"Er, excuse me, Phyllis, but I'm sixty-five, and my mother's been dead for fifteen years."

Half turning, she switched conversation from Betty to Alan without missing a beat.

"I remember you when you were in shorts. They called you snot sleeve, didn't they? And your mother still owes me for a pint of milk," said Phyllis, before once more engaging Betty in the thorny issue of Jiffy bags.

Alan withdrew, trying hard to act as if his run-in with Phyllis hadn't happened.

Keen to regain a measure of control, he turned to the professor.

"May I ask if the villa's location had anything to do with the expanse of open water?"

It was a question to which he already knew the answer, but anything was better than another rebuke from Phyllis.

"Ah," replied the professor, pleased once more to be the centre of attention. "In fact, the Broads weren't dug until the twelfth century when the growing population needed peat for cooking and heating."

Alan's relief was palpable as the academic gave a positive response to his question.

Professor Pullman waxed lyrical about the abandoned peat diggings being filled over time by rising water levels to form the Broads, until the manic laughter of a Minions mobile ringtone interrupted his flow.

Alan strained to see where the sound was coming from and meandered through the group until he came across Angela Simms, who was rummaging through her enormous shoulder bag to silence the din.

"Can you manage?" asked Alan, sensing Angela's embarrassment.

"Never you mind this lot. They can tut all they like."

Alan shook his head in admonishment at two male members of the group.

"You can moan all you like, but just think, what if someone was trying to get an urgent message to you? Until you take the call, you don't know why they're ringing, do you?"

The two men half turned from Alan, shrugging their shoulders like two naughty schoolboys.

Alan turned back towards Angela just in time to see her retrieve the mobile and scurry from the group, her face etched with concern.

As Professor Pullman seized his opportunity to round off his introduction to the site, he turned from the group, lifted his right arm, and urged the assembly to follow as he set a blistering pace towards a small mound in the middle distance.

It took a couple of minutes for Alan to realise Angela hadn't rejoined the group. Fearful she had received bad news, he scanned the field to see where she might be.

A hundred yards or so to his left he noticed the young woman standing ramrod straight, frozen to the spot.

Alan quietly backed away from the group and ambled towards the woman, not wanting to draw attention to himself—or to Angela.

As he neared, he noticed Angela held both arms to her sides. Her phone hung limply in one hand.

Oh Lord, he thought.

"Is everything okay, Ang?" said Alan in a low, quiet tone, keen not to startle her.

She didn't respond.

Alan slipped the mobile from her hand and raised it to his ear. Angela offered no resistance. He turned and walked a few paces back towards the distant group.

"Ang, are you still there? How's the signal? Can you hear me?"

Alan spoke into the handset, trying his best not to alarm the caller.

"Hi, she's fine but tied up for a minute or two. I'll get her to give you a ring back. Is that okay?"

Alan didn't wait for a response. Instead, he ended the call, switched the mobile to silent, and slipped it into his shirt pocket.

Retracing his steps towards Angela, both now stood at the edge of a deep excavation.

Alan saw what she saw.

The body of a man.

2

THE WALLED GARDEN

The eyes were open, face drained of colour. A trickle of congealed blood puddled in the dusty ground to the side of his head.

"I knew that bugger would come to a sticky end one day."

Alan, startled at the sudden sound of voices, turned to see Phyllis at the head of a small group of club members, who had wandered over, curious at Alan's earlier departure.

The old woman showed no sign of shock. It wasn't the first time Phyllis had observed violent death. War service had seen to that.

Alan instinctively moved closer to Angela, who hadn't moved a muscle.

He looked across to Phyllis admiring her composure but puzzled by her comment.

"What do you mean?"

"Well, they don't... or should I say, didn't, call Fred Collins 'Narky' for nothing. He was a bad-tempered bully, that one."

"Mrs Abbott," Alan responded, not sure how to finish

the sentence. Simultaneously, he turned Angela away from the horror. She offered no resistance.

"It's true," Phyllis continued, her voice quiet now yet still lacking any trace of sympathy for the dead man. "He always picked on the young 'uns from the 'big house.' He knew they couldn't answer back."

Alan returned to the edge of the excavation. He shook his head.

"What a waste."

Phyllis fumed. "Waste? What do you mean? He thought he was God's gift to women. Always trying to paw them. I've seen him do it. Given him a piece of my mind more than once, I have."

Phyllis kicked some loose earth into the trench, watching it settle like unwanted confetti on the dead man's exposed cheek and shoulder.

Alan recoiled, at last summoning the courage to challenge the old woman.

"For the love of God, Phyllis. Show some humanity, will you? No one deserves to die like *that*."

The old woman tilted her head upward and sniffed the air, dismissing his show of sympathy for the dead man.

She pointed a spindly finger towards the corpse.

"Seen this in the war. Men who lord it over other lads. Try it on with their girlfriends. When a jealous man gets his blood up, he can do anything. And from what I know, plenty had it in for that fat sod."

Before Alan could respond, he noticed the remainder of the group approaching and headed them off before they reached the excavation.

"There's been a terrible accident," said Alan. "We need to call the police. I'll try and get through on my mobile, but to make sure we do, I need someone to run over to the big house and raise the alarm."

All eyes descended on Rod. He was the youngest by decades.

"I'll do it," replied Rod, making off at a sprint towards Stanton Hall.

* * *

ENJOYING the solitude of the Hall's walled garden, Anthony Stanton filled his lungs with a riot of heady scents. As the dew lifted into Norfolk's big sky, the effect seemed all the stronger.

This place is about as far from work as I can get, he thought.

Anthony kicked a spray of gravel from the pathway, cutting its way through blazing beds of late-summer flowers.

He flopped onto a rickety, cast-iron bench and tilted his head backwards. A warming sun had the desired effect.

For the first time in a long time, he pushed painful memories to the back of his mind.

The quiet didn't last long. Reacting in an instant to the sharp crack of a rusty gate latch lifting, he hunched over as if to make himself as small as possible, his attention focused on a dark outline filling the gate opening.

Anthony squinted at the silhouetted figure of a woman.

"Excuse me, this area is private."

The voice was assertive. He expected compliance.

Ignoring his words, the woman continued to close the distance between them.

"So it's true. You're back, Anthony... and in one piece too. Lucky for you they couldn't shoot straight."

He recognised the voice. Using the long form of his first name was a giveaway. She always did that to provoke him.

He chose not to react.

"Military training has its uses."

"Hello, you," said Lyn.

"Hello, you," he replied.

The ease of their exchanges had all the familiarity of a long-married couple relaxed in each other's company.

"Still breaking the rules, Lyn. Just like at school... and the Hall still isn't open to the public today."

Lyn smiled, unmoved by his halfhearted rebuke.

"Just as well I'm not Joe Public, then, isn't it? And as for school, we couldn't all be the class swot, could we?"

Lyn's barbed comment rolled back the years to a time when they were at Stanton Primary together.

He gave a throaty laugh. Time had passed, but the constant ribbing he got from his classmates had stayed with him. He'd always seemed to come top in exams, but it wasn't the only reason he stuck out. Ant spoke differently and lived in "the big house."

His smile widened as he recalled how she was the one who controlled the others. A talent, he suspected, Lyn still possessed, judging by the confidence in her voice and the way she held herself.

"Wasn't my fault my parents bought in to that swinging-sixties hippie thing, and sent me to the local primary school for oiks instead of public school."

Lyn gave him a sideways look and shook her head in that dismissive way only she could get away with.

"Playing the victim doesn't suite you, Ant, and anyway, you wouldn't have suited pinstriped trousers or a straw boater. At least your parents spoke to each other in words with more than one syllable and lived in the same place."

"Things any better now?" Ant responded.

Lyn let out an almost inaudible sigh.

"Let's put it this way, at least Mum has stopped throwing things at Dad. Mind you, living at opposite ends of the village helps."

Ant didn't pursue the point and broke eye contact knowing the damage went deeper than Lyn would ever admit.

"Anyway, I popped over to drop off a chocolate cake to your parents. It's their favourite, you know. I bring one over every Saturday."

Ant smiled as Lyn flopped next to him on the bench.

"I didn't think you'd come back after Greg's death."

Ant rolled his head as if to make sure his exposed skin captured every ray the sun had to offer. His arms hung across the back rail of the bench. Lyn didn't try to avoid contact as she settled back.

"I didn't intend to stay away for so long. At eighteen you think your parents will live forever. I'm still not sure if I'm back for good, even though…"

Ant faltered. He shuffled his feet in the gravel.

Lyn stared into the distance, looking at nothing in particular.

"A flying visit, then? Your brother's been dead a long time, and the estate seems to run itself from what I can see."

Ant gave a short, sharp laugh.

"That's just the problem, Lyn. You know better than me how frail Mum and Dad are. To tell you the truth, it was a shock."

He stopped, sensing Lyn's reaction.

Another telling-off coming.

"For heaven's sake, Ant. They're both in their eighties, and the man had a heart attack a few months ago. What did you expect?"

Ant shrugged his shoulders and changed tack. It was

easier than thinking about his parents not being around forever.

"The thing is, Lyn, the estate's in a right mess, and I'm not cut out to fix it."

Lyn sensed his unease.

"That was Greg's job. And what happens? He flips his car into Stanton Broad, and goodnight Vienna."

"Sounds like you're feeling sorry for yourself again, Anthony."

There she goes again.

"Not at all," replied Ant. "I'm just stating a fact. It was Greg's inheritance, not mine. Turns out the estate income has been slipping for years, and the Hall is in a hell of a state. You've seen the water damage. Dad's tried, but it's too much. To make things worse, people paid to look after the place just haven't done their jobs."

Lyn's expression softened.

Ant settled back into the bench, his head once more falling backwards as the sun bathed his face.

"Isn't it strange, Lyn. You know, when you're a kid, you look up to your parents and assume they know it all. Then whether it's poor health or just getting older, you realise they're not invincible after all. You must see it all the time."

Ant opened an eye and squinted into a bright Norfolk sky.

"Dad mentioned you started as head teacher at our old school in September. Spooky or what!"

He let out a throaty laugh.

"Come to think of it, it's kind of strange dealing with stuff in classrooms I sat in as a child," replied Lyn. "But you're right. I see kids affected by things at home. There's a familiar look in their eyes when voices are raised—*a rabbit caught in the headlights* type of look. Despite working like stink, sometimes we can't fix things. But we try. That's all anyone can do."

Ant sensed her sudden nervousness and could have kicked himself for making her remember her own childhood traumas.

"Sorry, Lyn. Didn't mean to do that, I know you had it tough at home."

After a few moments of uneasy silence, Lyn gave Ant a sideways glance as she playfully pinched the skin of his arm between two fingers.

Ant winced in mock pain but made no move to distance himself from the attack.

"That's something else you did in class, remember?" said Ant. "I never understood why."

Lyn smiled.

"Let's just say it was my way of toughening you up," she replied.

Ant had to admit Lyn had got him out of several sticky situations with Jezza, the class bully.

"Of course, there's another explanation."

Lyn gave Ant a puzzled look. She was at risk of overacting.

"And that would be?"

"Affection, Lyn. I asked my father once why you kept hitting me when you spent most of your time fending off Hillier and his thugs. Dad was clear about it, and seeing as I didn't have a better explanation, I believed him!"

Lyn waved at Ant dismissively.

"In your dreams, Anthony Stanton. My older brother used to pinch me, so I took it out on you. One snotty boy was just the same as any other to me. Anyhow, you sat next to me and were daft enough not to fight back."

Both laughed, the interlude having served as a convenient pressure valve for less-happy memories.

"Right. Time for a piece of chocolate cake and a cup of tea with your parents."

As she spoke, Lyn sprang from the rickety bench and launched herself towards the gate.

"Haven't I endured enough pain for one day without being exposed to your baking?" moaned Ant as he sprinted to make up the distance between them.

"Remember that nut caramel toffee you made with salted peanuts in year four? Yuck!"

Without stopping, Lyn bent down, scooped a handful of gravel and tossed it over her head.

"And before you say anything, if I'd have wanted to hit you, I would have. You're not the only one who's a crack shot."

The levity didn't last long. As Lyn reached out to lift the latch of the gate it moved towards her at speed, causing Lyn to cry out in pain as the heavy construction smacked into her.

"Oh, er... sorry, miss. Only..."

Ant's instinct was to shout at the lad. The look of panic on the youth's face stopped him from doing so.

The boy didn't wait for either a welcome or reprimand.

"It's your land agent, sir. He's, er... sort of... dead."

Ant felt a swell of frustration at the youth's nervous ramblings.

"What do you mean, 'sort of'? Either someone is dead, or they are not dead."

Ant glimpsed Lyn's look of disapproval and knew he'd gone too far.

Rod looked no less frustrated as he tried to make himself understood.

"Up at the dig site. He's in a ditch. They told me to fetch the police."

Ant pointed towards the elegant columns fronting the imposing entrance to the Hall.

"The phone's in the hallway. And you'd better ask for an ambulance."

3
OIL ON TROUBLED WATERS

Lyn dismounted Ant's quad bike with care, relieved to have arrived at the dig site in one piece.

"Please, Ladies and Gentlemen," Alan pleaded, "come away from the trench. The police will be here soon. They will not think well of you tramping all over a possible crime scene."

Ant knew Alan had a point. The force's first action would be to secure the scene and protect possible evidence.

Lyn watched as Ant's bearing changed from chillaxed companion to military commander. She winced inwardly as he barked a command.

"We've a few minutes before they arrive, so let's get organised."

Lyn moved into head-teacher mode striking the perfect balance between assertiveness and mother hen.

"Come along, you lot. Let's get you over here to gather your thoughts. I expect the police will wish to take statements from you all."

A quick glance at Ant told Lyn she had his approval.

"Over here" amounted to a pile of soil about fifty feet from the trench.

The prospect of being interviewed by the police did the trick in getting the group's attention.

"Murdered by a jealous husband," said Phyllis.

"I think it was Jed. He was always arguing with Narky," offered Betty.

"Nonsense. He was a drunk, and I reckon he tripped and fell—stupid man," chipped in Graham Drake, known by all not to have been a fan of the deceased.

"You never liked him, did you?" shouted Melvyn Green from the edge of the group. "Be careful what you say when the bobbies arrive, or they'll have you."

Graham Drake looked less than impressed with Melvyn, but then he'd never got on with him either.

Lyn had had enough.

"You'd all better be careful what you say to the police. It's not a murder mystery weekend you're on, you know. Whatever you say, the police will check."

Lyn's mild rebuke did the trick as she watched several heads drop a little with eyes fixed on the ground like naughty schoolchildren. Except Phyllis.

"Are you suggesting we keep quiet when the cops come?"

Lyn chose not to rise to the elderly woman's bait.

"I'm suggesting you tell them what you know and what you saw, not what you would have liked to have heard or seen... and Phyllis... cops? Really?"

***

"For God's sake, young man. Can't you do anything right?"

"Professor. It slipped. Anyway, it was only a..."

Ant watched the academic explode with anger.

"It was only what? Are you trying to tell me what is, and what is not, historically important on my dig?"

Simon Hangmead froze as he surveyed the shattered fragments of a Roman oil lamp, which formed a neat arc around his feet.

"What's the matter?" asked Ant as he looked up from the bottom of the trench to see the professor launching into a terrified-looking, young man.

Shaking his head in frustration, the professor broke off eye contact with his student, turned towards the voice, and bent forward to peer over the excavation.

"Lord Stanton, I…"

"That's me. Now, what can I do for you?"

The professor looked troubled, though not about the dead man.

"My excavation. Please, may I ask you to refrain from—"

Ant cut off the professor.

"Which is on my father's land, Professor." Ant worked hard to stifle his emotions.

Did this stupid man not care a man lay dead, possibly murdered?

Ant could tell from the professor's irritated look that he was unused to being interrupted.

"As you say, er, your family's land."

The academic's apparent submissiveness failed to impress Ant whose steely eyes made plain who was in control.

"You see, the university insist I bring a certain number of undergraduates on each dig, irrespective of ability. All in the cause of widening participation, whatever that's supposed to mean."

What a snob, thought Ant.

His silence compelled the professor to keep digging a proverbial hole for himself.

"Anyway, this young man has destroyed the remains of a valuable artefact. It might be argued that such items are common on villa digs, but that's not the point. It is the context which matters and what the discovery may have meant for the dig as a whole. Note I use the past tense, since the item is no more: it no longer exists."

Sounds like Monty Python's *parrot sketch to me*, thought Ant as he watched the professor's face flush in response to his widening grin. Ant could see the academic was tempted to bite back, but the thought of offending his benefactor wisely prevailed.

"Well, in the scheme of things, a broken lump of baked clay isn't too important at the moment is it, Professor?"

Unable to take his ire out on Ant, the professor turned his attention to the undergraduate, who had just finished picking up all the shards he could find.

"Take them to the finds tent. Record location, material, and design in the prescribed manner. I assume even you can do that?"

Ant watched the young man narrow his eyes then quickly lower his head. As he did so, the neck cover of his canvas desert cap rippled in the light breeze of a warming day.

Dismissing the interlude with the professor and his errant student, Ant returned his attention to the body that lay at his feet. He surveyed the scene, just as he had done too many times on active service.

He still found it distasteful.

"With all due respect, might I suggest you leave that to the police, Anthony?" said the professor, his voice indicating his subordinate position in their relationship.

Ant continued with his work as if no words were spoken. After judging sufficient time had elapsed to reinforce the pecking order, he lifted his gaze to the bespectacled head peering over the trench.

"Could it be you are more interested in me not damaging your excavation than any sympathy you might have for this poor soul?" Ant's intonation was flat.

The professor chose not to reply; there wasn't any point. Instead, he withdrew without comment, leaving Ant to ponder the quietness and odd contrast of a cloudless sky overhead and death at his feet.

Within a minute of the professor leaving, Lyn reappeared. She looked down on Ant with a mixture of sorrow and admiration.

"Rooting around a corpse is not my idea of a fun day out."

Ant rolled his shoulder back so he could glimpse his friend without moving his position over the body.

"At least this one is fresh—and in one piece."

He could see Lyn was shocked at his matter-of-fact description of the body.

Before either had chance to pursue the topic, the harsh sirens of police cars approaching at speed startled both friends.

Hell, it's happening again, thought Ant as he curled up at lightning speed and clasped a hand to each ear.

"You okay?" said Lyn, her concern obvious.

Ant ignored his friend. It took him the best part of a minute to unfurl himself from his foetal position. He deliberately chose not to offer Lyn any eye contact. Instead, he stepped away from the body and climbed out of the trench. A spray of dust gave his presence away to a fast-approaching policeman.

"What are you doing in that trench? Viscount Stanton, is it not?"

The voice was authoritative.

Both turned towards the man.

Not from around here, thought Ant.

"Detective Inspector Riley," said the man, his voice laced with irritation.

"You're not local?" said Lyn.

The detective glanced into the trench before turning his attention back to Lyn.

"Correct. On detachment from Suffolk. Not that that's any concern of yours, miss."

Riley emphasised the word "miss." His taunt failed to trigger any reaction from Lyn, much to the detective's annoyance.

"And as for you, sir?" enquired Riley. "It may be your family's land, and in a way your professional territory, but why did you find it necessary to contaminate a possible crime scene?"

He's done his homework, thought Ant.

Aware he was on thin ice, Ant trod with care.

"You're right, Inspector. I should have known better, but I thought I saw movement and wanted to check if there was anything we could do for the poor chap. He is... or was... one of my father's employees. Noblesse oblige, and all that, you know."

It was all Lyn could do to stop herself from laughing. She knew Ant was playing with the detective.

"I see," he said, scratching his head. "Then perhaps the gracious Viscount Stanton could indulge a humble policeman and give him the benefit of his wisdom. Is the gentleman in question dead? Or is he afflicted? Perhaps derived from the strong smell of whisky in the air, which prevents him from closing his eyes when looking directly at the sun?"

Both looked skyward.

Ant adopted an exaggerated look of angst, varying his gaze between the body and the detective.

"Inspector. I think I know where you're coming from. No one, not even a drunkard, could look at that sun without blinking, could they?"

Riley wasn't impressed.

Ant continued his act.

"He's dead. That being the case I need to cancel the man's tenancy as of today. This will allow me to get his tied cottage ready for a new occupant."

He hadn't finished with Riley yet.

"And in future, please endeavour to use my correct title. As a courtesy to my father's title I am addressed as Lord Stanton."

He turned from the policeman and sauntered back towards his quad bike.

Lyn followed without comment.

Riley looked on as the pair left, unsure if his view of the aristocracy had been reinforced, or he'd been the butt of Ant's peculiar sense of humour.

Either way, he didn't like it.

4
WALK THE TALK

Unsure whether to laugh or scold Ant for the way he'd treated the detective, Lyn leant forward and shouted into Ant's right ear as the quad bike roared over the open grasslands of Alder Meadow.

"What was all that guff about tied cottages and tenancies? You sounded like a toff from *Downtown Abbey*."

"Sorry, can't hear you. What did you say?" shouted Ant as he revved the bike's engine.

Lyn responded by flicking the back of Ant's neck. Her perfectly manicured nail made its presence known. Unwilling to risk a second stab of pain, he brought the machine to a gradual halt on the crest of what passed for a hill in Norfolk.

"What was that for?" protested Ant, as he dismounted the bike while rubbing his neck.

It was now a competition to see who would break eye contact first. As usual, Lyn won.

"That fool Riley knew who I was. He's also aware of what I do for a living. If he had issues with either, it's not my fault, is it!"

Lyn half turned and feigned interest in a wherry sailboat gliding along Stanton Broad.

"And you're happy to play the arrogant, rich chap from the big house, are you?"

He smiled.

She frowned.

"Look, I'll play any role our detective friend assigns me. It suits my purpose for him to think me an inbred aristocrat. With luck, he'll leave us in peace to get on with things."

Lyn's frown deepened.

"If you're not careful, you'll stick like that," said Ant. "Remember what they say about frightening horses and children—and you deal with a lot of children!"

Lyn held up all ten fingernails as a friendly warning to Ant.

"Okay, I surrender. I'll do you a deal. You keep those nails to yourself, and I'll tell you what I found."

Lyn blew air across her fingers as she preened a nail tip.

"I think I've made my point, but what the heck are you on about?"

Unable to resist the temptation to keep Lyn waiting, he helped her off the bike and led her down to the edge of the Broad. They watched the wherry as it sailed around a bend. Soon all they could glimpse was its sail peaking above the reeds.

"Do you remember the times we spent on the boat when we were kids?" he asked.

Lyn smiled at the memory.

"I see now why your father called her *Field Glider*. You know it hadn't occurred to me until this second. Just look at the canvas float through the meadow. Wonderful sight, don't you think?"

A few minutes passed as the pair watched the slow-flowing water and pond skimmers dancing across its glinting surface.

"Come on, Ant. Get on with it," said Lyn.

He lay back on the baked grass, closed his eyes, and drank in the sun's warming rays.

"The land agent. It wasn't an accident. I'm sure of it."

Lyn waited for more. Instead, only silence.

"But he was drunk. And the stone... He landed on it, didn't he?"

Again, he made her wait.

"Well... yes... and, er, maybe. Or to be more exact, no and yes. I mean maybe."

"What?"

Lyn's tone warned Ant it was time to explain.

"Well, as for the whisky, yes, it was all over him, and I mean *over* him. But not the slightest whiff from his mouth?"

Lyn shook her head in exasperation.

"But you told the inspector he—"

"I played the part the man wanted me to play. As for the stone, yes, it caused his death, but he didn't fall onto the thing. Someone gave him one hell of a clout then placed it beneath his head once he was in the trench."

Lyn was having none of it.

"Hang on. I could smell the whisky even from where I was standing, and I heard what you said to the inspector.

Ant nodded his head in agreement.

"Yes, but he, or she, made a mistake. The bottom of that excavation was as clean as a whistle from the work the university bods had done. Why was that particular stone left? The murderer was too clever by half. Yes, the stone used to kill him was placed correctly; even the blood spatter matched Narky's head injury."

Lyn's mind was racing.

"Perhaps in the scuffle he knocked it into the trench then fell onto it, I suppose."

Ant shook his head.

"Good point, but why only that stone? No lumps of soil. No other rubbish in the bottom of the trench. No, believe me, he was poleaxed, and down he went like a sack of spuds. Then the killer placed the stone to make it look like Narky fell onto it."

Ant watched Lyn frown as she weighed up both theories.

"You see that stone sat on top of the soil? No depression, no movement from where it may have been originally. It just sat there. Fair enough if the thing had been half buried with the sharp end sticking out of the ground. But that wasn't the case. Now, if a bloke as heavy as Narky fell the best part of five feet, wouldn't you expect the stone to shift at least a little, or create a slight depression in the surface of the soil?"

Lyn nodded. It was time to concede, at least for now.

"Come on, Sherlock. Let's walk back to the Hall while I demolish your theory. I'm sure you can get one of the estate workers to bring the bike back."

Lyn waved a loose arm at the machine as she spoke.

Ant took little persuading.

"You're on. Come on, last one to the top of the hill makes the tea."

Reaching the crest of the small ascent Lyn raised her arms in triumph.

"You need to get yourself fit, mate. I thought the army were the best of the best."

Ant arrived a few seconds later shaking a hand in disagreement.

"As usual, you cheated. You started running before I'd finished talking."

Lyn laughed.

"I've heard everything now. At least you didn't say you let me win like you did when we were kids."

Ant lifted his chin and sniffed the air.

"I have nothing more to say on the matter, except, look at that. Isn't it beautiful?"

Ant's attempt to change the direction of the conversation worked as Lyn turned to join Ant looking down and into the mid distance.

"You're right. The Hall sits so wonderfully in its landscape. And to think your family has owned it for over two hundred and fifty years. Astonishing!"

Ant let out a gentle sigh.

"But for how much longer, I wonder?"

Lyn gave one of his arms a gentle stroke then playfully pushed him sideways with her shoulder.

"Come on, misery pants. No more of that. You may be many things, Anthony Stanton, but a quitter you are not."

Ant picked up on Lyn's encouraging smile. It was enough to lift any momentary doubts he had about the Hall's future.

"Oi! That hurt," replied Ant as he returned her smile and hurried to catch up with her.

"Oh, do shut up, and stop being a softie. Now let me get this straight. Narky wasn't drunk; someone perfumed him with spirits. He didn't fall; the same person clobbered him and pushed him into the trench. Then they went to the effort of making it look as if he'd fallen in a drunken stupor and hit his head on a small rock. Why? It makes no sense."

Ant nodded as the pair sauntered toward Stanton Hall.

"I agree, Lyn, but there are murderers who panic and leave clues all over the place. Others are more cunning, calculating. Almost fastidious in what they do."

By now the pair were approaching the west gate of the Hall. Ant had a surprise for his friend.

"And to prove my point regarding the meticulous murderer, there's this."

Ant slipped a small, folded piece of paper from his trouser pocket and handed it over.

"Careful, it's evidence."

Lyn unfolded the object as if it were a sheet of gold leaf.

"Good Lord."

"I know, but just read it," replied Ant.

I KNOW what you're up to and have the proof. If you don't leave us alone, you'll get what's coming to you, understand? Back off, or else.

"WHO DO you think wrote it? Where did you find it?"

Ant took the note back.

"Scrunched up in one of Narky's hands. It took a lot of working loose, let me tell you: rigor mortis and all that."

Lyn conjured up a mental picture of the scene. She didn't like it.

"As for the author, well, it's on estate-headed paper. And see these blotches? If you whiff them there's just a hint of methylated spirit."

Ant held out the note so that Lyn could see, or rather smell, for herself.

"Suppose so," she said. "So who's your painter?"

Ant shook his head.

"Not a painter, Lyn. Unless I'm mistaken, methylated spirit is a key part of French polish, and Glen Dawson has been renovating bookcases in the library."

Lyn couldn't hide her admiration for Ant's deductive skills, though she would have cut her right arm off rather than admit it to him.

"Isn't he the estate carpenter?"

"Yes, which means I have a responsibility towards him."

Lyn stared at Ant in disbelief.

"But he may be a murderer. It's not a game we're playing here. We need to tell the police before they find out and come after you for obstructing a police enquiry."

Ant grinned.

"Don't worry, I'll turn on the charm."

"Charm? Riley thinks you are an upper-class twit. It never worked with the class bully; remember him? It won't wash with that bully of a detective either. He's no fool, you know."

Ant accepted the admonishment, pushing the open palms of his hands forward.

"Mea culpa. I'll take the risk, Lyn. I won't let the police near Glen until I've made sense of this mess. And before you go off on one again, you'd do the same if it was one of your ex-pupils, and don't tell me any different. I know you too well."

"You mean *we'll* take the risk."

"As you say, old girl."

Ant waited for the fuse he'd lit to go off before sprinting forward and escaping through an open doorway before Lyn could land the wallop heading his way.

* * *

THE EARL SAT in the oak-panelled library of the great house as he bit into Lyn's cake. He lapped any filling that escaped and congratulated himself on consuming every morsel.

Outside in the corridor, Ant and Lyn continued their discussion as to who might have murdered Narky.

"Anyway, one thing is for sure. We need to crack on before Riley comes sniffing around here. Better bring Dad up to speed. Come on, he'll be in here."

Ant turned a large brass knob and pushed the heavy oak door open.

"I see you two have met up again. I also see you are still daft as brushes when you're together."

Ant and Lyn exchanged an embarrassed glance before increasing the distance between them.

"Afternoon, Dad. I see you've found Lyn's cake. Any good?"

Ant gave Lyn a sideways glance. As he expected, she didn't think much of his comment.

"Careful, Son. If you want any of Lyn's excellent cake you need to watch out. Right, Lyn?"

"Absolutely. Sharp tongues are likely to go without."

The nearest Ant came to admitting defeat was to cut two slices of cake and offer one to Lyn.

"I'll take that as an apology, then. Shall I?"

The earl laughed, spitting bits of cream into the atmosphere as he did so.

"Mum will kill you, Dad."

The earl held a finger to his lips and gave them both a wide-eyed smile.

"Anyway, to what do I owe the pleasure of your company this fine day?"

Ant's demeanour became more serious. It was time to break the bad news and spent the next ten minutes explaining the events of the morning.

"What next, then? I assume you will not leave it to the police."

"Spot on, Dad. I'm heading over to Glen's place. Are you coming, Lyn?"

She was ahead of him.

"No. I want to take another look around the dig site. You never know what might turn up."

"Okay, but make sure you don't trip over the police tape and end up in that trench yourself. It'll be a giveaway to Riley that you've trampled all over his crime scene."

Ant noted Lyn's dismissive smirk. He winked at his father.

The earl gave each an affectionate smile as he gestured for them to get on with their investigation.

5

A BETTING MAN

I love September, thought Lyn as she strolled back to the dig site.

The busy landscape of farmers gathering in the harvest and tourists larking around on their hire boats made her heart race as she recalled the happy times of her early childhood racing across cropped fields and waving innocently to smiling holidaymakers as they sailed by.

A mosaic of fields ranged in colour from the deepest green to vivid yellow. A scattering of flint-faced churches and brick windmills pierced the flatlands, the latter now without their sails but no less glorious.

The scene triggered painful memories too. It was to this place that she came as a teenager when her parents' constant squabbling got too much.

Lyn thought about her early relationship with Ant. She smiled as she crossed a field of barley, their ripened ears tickling Lyn's knees as she waded through the golden crop.

What a pair we made. Me escaping my parents arguing, Ant trying to make sense of his privileged background.

When Lyn reached the excavations, all was quiet, other

than the sound of two muffled voices coming from the professor's tent.

Careful not to make her presence known, Lyn detoured around a cluster of temporary buildings. Within sixty seconds she'd reached the trench Narky was found in.

Tempted, though she was, to duck under the police tape and jump into the excavation, she resisted.

If Ant found nothing else of interest and the police cleaned it out, I guess I won't uncover any new stuff either.

Instead, Lyn concentrated on an area around a nearby spoil heap. She reasoned the murderer might have hidden behind it then jumped Narky.

Her plan proved fruitless. She was about to call it a day when something caught her eye. On the ground, midway between the excavation and the spoil heap, a small object stood proud against the sandy-grey colour of the compacted earth.

It was black with jagged edges.

Part of a thermos flask cup? Lyn thought.

Lyn studied the odd-shaped item, applying a level of care the professor might give to a precious find.

No, the radius of the curve was too big for a cup, but what else might it be? she thought.

Then a clue.

"VK."

On the outside of the curve, Lyn could make out two large letters. A maker's mark, perhaps? No, the letters had been hand painted and not by the hand of an expert.

The owner's initials, perhaps? thought Lyn.

* * *

"Ah, Glen. Glad I've caught you. Could I have a word?" said Ant as he shuffled over to a man tightening the handle of a yard brush.

Surprised at the unexpected visitor, Glen Dawson laid the broom against a nearby water butt.

"Mr Anthony. They said you were back. Nice to see you."

Glen's voice was friendly enough, but it didn't conceal his nervousness.

"Nothing wrong. I was in the area and just wanted your advice on something, Glen."

Ant picked up on Glen's agitation.

Perhaps he had something to hide? thought Ant as he extended his hand.

"Oh, er, well, happy to help if I can, Mr Anthony. Please come into the house."

Glen shook Ant's hand then half turned towards a chocolate-box-looking estate cottage.

"I wish you would call me Ant."

Glen smiled nervously.

"Now, Mr Anthony, you know I've worked on the estate all my life, as did my grandfather and father before me. They taught me how to address the gentry."

Glen's response caught Ant off guard. He'd forgotten the effect a sudden visit by his father or him had on some of their long-standing tenants. Ant knew it was his responsibility to put Glen at ease, not the other way around.

"Sorry, Glen, that was tactless of me. Listen, whatever makes you feel comfortable, okay?"

Ant's touch of humility did the trick as he watched the hint of a smile spread across Glen's face and his shoulders drop.

"Oh, I see. Well, if you say so, er, Ant, but what Grandfather would say, I don't know."

Glen shook his head and lowered his gaze.

Ant knew he needed to move the conversation on without appearing to disrespect Glen's close family.

"Dad had told me what a fine chap your grandad was, and I know your father served the estate all his working life, but times change, Glen. And a good thing too. Wouldn't you agree?"

Ant's acknowledgement of his family's loyalty to the estate did the trick as he watched Glen's eyes meet his, together with a small, almost indiscernible, nod of the head.

Glen gestured for Ant to enter the open front door of his cottage. He shouted to Ruth, his wife.

The woman had none of the restraint her husband had shown. Instead, she welcomed Ant and offered to make refreshments.

Although Ant still suffered from the after-effects of eating too much of Lyn's chocolate cake, he was too much of a gentleman to refuse the woman's hospitality.

"Thanks so much. A cup of tea would be great. White with one sugar, if I may?"

Ruth smiled and disappeared into the kitchen, leaving the two men standing in the middle of the small room, its height made all the lower by an open-beamed ceiling.

"Please, Ant, take a seat. Now what's this advice you're after?"

Conscious he'd put Glen at ease under false pretences, Ant trod carefully. He'd undertaken enough interrogations to know how important it was to gain trust. That way he stood the best chance to get the information he needed.

"Well, you may think I'm being daft, but I had an argument about French polish with a friend the other day, and—"

"French polish?" Glen interrupted.

"Yes, I know, sounds silly, but I think white spirit is an important part of the mixture. My friend said I was wrong."

Glen shook his head and smiled.

"You know, a lot of tradesmen think that. The truth is, it's methylated spirit."

Ant feigned disappointment.

"Blast, that's cost me a tenner."

Ruth walked through from the kitchen holding a tray of tea.

"What's cost you a tenner?"

Ant shrugged his shoulders as Ruth handed him a delicate bone-china cup with matching saucer.

"A gift from your great grandmother, they were. It has been handed down the family and very proud to have them we are too."

Ant saw the pride with which she handled the precious objects and made sure he treated them with the greatest care.

"Well, Ruth, thanks to your husband, I've learnt to my cost about French polish and methylated spirit!"

Ruth scrunched her face up at the mere mention of the sticky concoction.

"Yuck. Can't stand the smell of that stuff. Glen's been doing work up at the big house, and it's been all over his clothes every day for a fortnight. Isn't that so, Glen?"

Her husband looked sheepish knowing he was in bad books with his wife for all the extra washing he'd caused.

Ant scrutinised Glen's reaction. It was playful. He observed no anxiety at the mention of meths.

Now it was time for Ant to show his cards. He hoped they'd forgive him, whatever happened.

"Bad do about Toby Collins, isn't it?"

The atmosphere changed in an instant. Glen tensed.

Ruth placed her cup back into its saucer with a clunk, not checking to see if she'd caused any damage.

"Narky, you mean. Yes, a bad do all right, but he was a bugger, Mr Anthony."

The reversion by Glen to formality told Ant he was onto something. He pressed his point home.

"The police are saying he fell in a drunken haze. Stank of whisky."

"Whisky?" replied Glen, his voice tinged with surprise.

"Not Narky," said Ruth. "That sod stuck to beer. Never touched spirits as far as I know. Every time he came round here he reeked of—"

Glen sprang from his chair to stand beside Ruth, taking her hand as he did so.

"Ant doesn't want to know about that, Ruthy. Let's not talk ill of the dead, eh?"

For the second time during their meeting, Ant felt uncomfortable. This wasn't like work. It was too close to home and involved people for whom he felt responsible.

"It's okay, Glen. I've been made aware of what he was like with the ladies. I'm sorry, Ruth. If my father had known what the man was like, he'd have sorted it. I promise you."

Ruth's hard exterior slipped. Her eyes glistened with emotion.

"There was nothing we could do without causing a fuss. None of us wanted that. Instead, us girls learnt how to handle the creep."

The show of raw emotion threw Ant, but he knew he had to get the truth out of Glen before the police picked up on the gossip.

"Glen. There's something I have to ask you, and I understand why you—"

Glen cut across Ant.

"You mean did I kill Narky for bothering Ruth? No, and that's the truth. Some of us lads hated the man, but as far as I know no one touched him."

Ant watched as Ruth gave her husband a look he'd often seen his own parents share. Proof of an unbreakable bond and a deep love in no need of words to explain it.

"The thing is, Glen, there's this..."

Ant handed over the piece of paper he'd taken from Narky's corpse.

Glen accepted the unwanted gift without surprise. Instead of reading it, he raised the note to his nose.

"Methylated spirit. That's why you came. You didn't lose a bet, did you, Mr Anthony?"

A coldness now permeated the room. Ant's hosts shot him the hardest of stares.

"It's true, Glen. I'm sorry. As you say, there was no bet. But I found that note in Narky's clenched hand—before the police had chance to crawl all over his body."

The pair separated and looked at each other in panic. Ant thought he was about to get a confession.

"I told you not to put anything in writing, Glen. Now look what's happened. When the police—"

"But nothing happened, love. "I know it was stupid to write the letter, but I didn't know what else to do. I did not kill that nasty sod. You have to believe me, my love."

Ruth glared at her husband.

"Tell that to the police, Glen. See what they say."

Ant intervened.

"Look, the police aren't coming, at least not yet. But Glen, you must tell me what happened."

Glen slumped back into his chair and stared down onto the footworn stone floor.

"He was blackmailing us. That's the truth of it."

Ant glanced at Ruth then fixed his stare on Glen.

"But why?"

Glen looked towards his wife. She nodded without saying a word.

"He wanted me to get involved in his scam. He found out Dad has a gambling habit, and we were desperate for money to pay his debts."

Glen lowered his head.

Ant struggled to make sense of Glen's explanation.

"Scam... What scam? And your dad?"

"Dad's got a dodgy kidney. The silly old bugger's drunk like a fish all his life, and he's bedbound now. Hates not being able to get into his garden. Anyway, he played bingo on an old laptop we had hanging around for a couple of years. I didn't even know he knew how to work the damn thing. It was only pennies a game at first. We didn't know anything about it. Then the bailiffs arrived. Narky overheard me telling a mate in the Wherry Arms and collared me. He said if I countersigned false invoices to the estate he'd generated from fictitious building contractors, he'd pay off Dad's debts."

At least he now understood why the estate was in such a financial mess.

"And before you ask," Glen continued, "no, I didn't. I refused, point-blank. So he came to the cottage bothering Ruth. I wrote that note saying I'd tell your father if he didn't stop. We wanted him out of our lives, but I didn't kill him. Honest to God, I didn't."

The room fell silent, with only the sound of an ancient long-case clock making its presence known. After seconds, which felt like hours to Ant, he responded.

"Glen, I believe you, and the police won't hear any of this. They don't know the note exists, and that's the way it'll stay. Now who holds your father's debt? Give me the name of the company and I'll sort it."

"But—" he said.

"But nothing. And if the police turn up, tell them about Narky pestering Ruth but nothing more. They'll have picked up the same response from around the village, so they won't have any reason to dig further, will they?"

6
SPEAKING IN TONGUES

Lyn finished pouring herself a generous glass of Prosecco before wandering onto the patio to take in the early evening breeze.

The old schoolhouse was a building she passed on her way to class every day as a child. She always wondered what inside might be like. Now she owned it.

It had been a struggle, but the borrowed view onto farmland at the end of the back garden had swung it.

Strange how life turns out, she thought.

Things couldn't be more different now. Instead of acting as a gofer between her mother and father, she was in charge of her life.

Sure, it was a small village and impossible to do much without someone noticing, but Lyn saw no reason to move.

The foibles of village life soon melted away as Lyn settled into a comfy recliner. She placed her drink on a low glass tabletop and picked up her book of the moment.

Nothing better than a good historical romance, she thought.

But try as she did, the events of the past twenty-four hours kept niggling.

She knew the reputation Narky had, although she'd never met the man. No matter how he behaved, she knew no one deserved to die like that.

Doubting she'd make much progress with her book, Lyn popped it back on the table and picked up her wine. As she sipped from a tall glass and gazed out across the meadow, she noticed a group of people in a huddle.

Curiosity having got the better of her, Lyn returned the Prosecco to the table and passed into the meadow via a low gate in the hedge.

"Found anything interesting?" she said, engaging three metal detectorists and explaining her own interest in history.

"I'm Lyn, by the way. I live in the house just over the hedge."

The three strangers looked over Lyn's shoulder towards the old schoolhouse before returning Lyn's friendly smile.

"I'm Sid, the oldest and most intelligent of our little band, and the daft-looking one to my left is young James. We're here for a weekend rally just up the road, and the organiser got us permission to detect the meadow."

Lyn shook Sid's hand before turning her attention to the teenager.

"Let me guess, he's your father?"

Lyn picked up on the twinkle in the lad's eyes.

"Thought so."

Sid pointed at a young woman wearing what Lyn assumed to be the obligatory uniform of detectorists, comprising of camouflage jacket and trousers, stout boots, and oversized bobble hat.

"And finally, we have Sandy. She's just dug an Eddy One, silver hammered, lucky sod."

The strange terminology baffled Lyn.

"Hammered Eddies? What on earth are you talking about!"

The detectorists looked at each other then laughed. Lyn just looked puzzled.

"Well," said Sandy as she pulled a small plastic box from a hip pouch, "look here." Lyn watched as the woman delicately picked out a small silver disc with gloved fingers and placed it into the palm of her free hand.

"This is a silver penny. Struck in Winchester in the reign of Edward the First, I'd say. That would make it thirteenth century. Isn't that amazing?"

Lyn couldn't help but notice Sandy's face light up as she explained her find.

"And the 'hammered' bit?"

"They were made by placing a disc of silver on a metal die, with its matching pair placed on top. Then—wallop! A big bloke with a good swing 'hammered' the die to stamp the design and make it legal tender."

Lyn smiled.

"Ah, I see, makes perfect sense. Could I ask you a huge favour? Would you like to show off your metal-detecting skills to the kids at my school sometime? They'd love it."

"Your school?" said Sid.

"Sorry, I should have said I'm head teacher at Stanton Primary, and I'm guessing the thought of finding treasure will more than keep my young charges' attention."

The detectorists exchanged glances with no need to discuss the request.

"Great idea, as long as you have a go first!" Sid replied.

Before Lyn had chance to answer, he slid the headphones over her ears and handed over the metal detector.

"That's it, swing it slow and low. Good technique; you're a natural!" he exclaimed as Lyn ambled forward, her ears filled with beeps and grunts as the machine distinguished between different types of metal.

Lyn was in her element, and before long she'd picked up a high-pitched, bright-sounding signal.

"Let me listen," said Sid as he cupped an ear to the earphones. "You've got something all right."

A few minutes of digging in the rock-hard soil produced a neat hole, at the bottom of which something glistened. Lyn knelt and scraped around the small object. Finally, the ground gave up its hostage.

An aluminium ring pull.

"Congratulations on your first find. Circa last year, I'd say. Don't worry, we find more of this stuff: bits of old iron and bullets rather than coins, let alone gold and such like!"

Lyn examined the shiny object as if it were a rare medieval treasure.

"Here, let me help you untie yourself," said Sid as Lyn handed back the headphones and undid the arm strap that held the detector in a comfortable position.

As Sid retrieved the machine, she glimpsed the armrest properly for the first time.

That's it, she thought.

The broken shard she'd found at the dig site matched the shape of the support.

"What an amazing coincidence," said Lyn. "I found a piece of one of these the other day." She pointed to the armrest.

"Do you know anyone with the initials 'VK'?"

The trio looked puzzled for a moment, then it dawned.

"Vikki King. She's in our club," said Sid.

Lyn knew she was chancing her arm.

"Any chance of putting me in touch with her? Just something I want to talk to her about," said Lyn.

"We can beat that. Vikki's with us on the rally. We've got a BBQ later tonight. We'll introduce you if you fancy a soggy beef burger!"

* * *

THE FIELD WAS HEAVING with detectorists as Lyn pulled onto the campsite. Making her way through the throng, she strained her eyes to see any of the trio she'd spent a pleasant thirty minutes with earlier in the evening.

"Lyn, glad you could come."

The voice was hard to pinpoint above the hubbub, but a friendly hand on her shoulder made her turn. Sid's smiling face greeted her.

"Hi, I'd never have found you in this lot. I didn't know metal detecting was so popular."

Before Lyn could continue the conversation, she reached for her mobile. It was Ant. The din and poor reception made it impossible to hear him, other than something about new information. Then nothing. She tried ringing back twice. His news would have to wait.

Breaking through the crowd, Sid came to a halt in front of a woman standing by a burger bar.

"Vikki, there you are. This is Lyn, the lady I mentioned earlier."

Lyn sensed the woman was nervous.

"Thanks for agreeing to see me. Did Sid explain why I wanted to meet with you?"

The woman failed to take Lyn's extended hand.

"I've done nothing wrong. We all have permission to be on the land. Not everyone likes metal detectorists, you know. I assumed you wanted to have a go at me."

Lyn smiled.

"Do you think I'd mix it with you lot if I wanted to have a go?"

Lyn waved her arms at the throng to make her point, still smiling.

Lyn could see her acknowledgement of the busy camp had helped Vikki relax.

"Suppose not."

The two spent a few minutes talking about safe subjects. Lyn, about how her pupils would love to try their hands at detecting, and Vikki, about getting sore feet and swollen knees digging the hard ground. Lyn tried to judge her next move, knowing Vikki might take flight.

"You know, when I was at the dig site yesterday, I found something. I think it was a piece of a metal detector. It had the initials 'VK' on it—"

Vikki cut Lyn off midsentence.

"That's why you're here." Vikki's nostrils flared as she looked in vain for Sid who was now lost in the crowd.

Lyn tried hard to calm the young woman, but she was having none of it.

"Look, I'm no nighthawk, okay? I told you, we all have permission to be on the land."

Lyn looked confused. She'd never heard the term.

"Nighthawk? What in heck's name is that?"

Vikki folded her arms as if defending her private space.

"Illegal, so-called detectorists who work the fields for finds after dark. No permission, no insurance, and they don't belong to a professional body. We hate them cos they get us all tarred by the same brush. It's not fair."

Lyn could see Vikki felt strongly. Emotions were running high, and she needed to reassure the woman.

"Listen, I haven't a clue what you're on about, and I'm not accusing you of anything. I just need to find out how that piece of plastic ended up near the spoil heap, that's all."

Vikki's arms remained tightly folded.

"Two of us were asked to check the spoil heap again by that professor bloke, to see if any metal artefacts had slipped through. My mate didn't show up, and since I was already there, I detected alone."

Lyn sensed now was the time to push things.

"What happened? I can see from your expression that something upset you."

Lyn watched as Vikki scanned the crowd as if playing for time. *Why the hesitation?* thought Lyn.

"I swiped him one, okay?" Her eyes bored into Lyn, nostrils flaring.

Lyn wasn't sure how she felt. Elated? Scared?

Was Narky's murderer standing right in front of her?

God, what now? she thought.

"Who did you swipe, Vikki?" was all she could muster.

Vikki's eyes widened.

"I can tell this is upsetting for you, and I'm sorry. I just want to help. But to do that I need to know what happened up there."

Lyn sensed Vikki's dilemma. She knew from her own experience of the need to talk when something bad happened. Vikki wanted, needed, to tell someone what she had done.

Vikki started to shake. Lyn's instinctive reaction was to hug her. It worked.

"I didn't hang around to find out. All I know is a bloke came at me. I didn't hear him at first because of my earphones. I swung my metal detector at him, and he fell. Then I legged it. It was only after that I discovered I'd broke the armrest."

"I hope he's okay. I didn't mean to hurt him, but he scared the life out of me."

Lyn tried to reassure Vikki, but her expression must have given the game away.

"He's not, is he? Are you the police? Is he in hospital?" Vikki blurted.

Lyn released Vikki and pulled back a little. She tried to pick her words carefully, but there was only one way to say it.

"A man died up there on Saturday morning, Vikki. I'm sorry."

As she spoke, her mobile rang again. Lyn fumbled in her jacket pocket and tried to silence the phone.

When she looked up, Vikki had disappeared.

7
LUNCH FOR TWO

Sunday morning introduced itself with a heavy layer of low cloud and the threat of rain.

Bet it throws it down today. Why does it always seem to rain on a Sunday? Lyn thought.

Even the pleasure of sipping the first strong coffee of the day did little to lift her mood as she looked at the leaden sky through her kitchen window.

At least my parents can't chuck me out in the garden anymore while they argue, she thought.

It seemed the more successful Lyn's career became, the more her thoughts turned back to her childhood. She knew one day she'd have to confront her demons.

* * *

"Are you seeing Lyn today, Son?"

His father had a glint in his eye as Ant pushed the wheelchair through a tall pair of French doors and out onto a paved terrace.

"The gardens are looking good, Dad," said Ant as he surveyed the formal lines of box hedges and dense planting of lavender.

"It's September, and the lavender is going over, as you well know. Stop trying to change the subject."

Ant knew his father would refuse to be distracted by his sudden interest in horticulture and pondered the knack parents had in turning their adult offspring back into children.

He tried to deflect the question, though he didn't know why he felt the need to do so.

"Dad, you've been trying to marry us off since we were eighteen. It's not going to happen. What sort of chap falls for a girl who was his security detail at school? A bit embarrassing, don't you think?"

The elderly gentleman chuckled, so much so that his shoulders heaved as he coughed.

"See what plotting does for you," said Ant as he bent over to check his father wasn't in any real distress.

"Don't worry, Anthony, it's not another heart attack. You're safe for now. Anyway, bodyguards come in handy no matter what age you are. You, above anyone, should know that."

Ant knew that in one sentence his father had made light about his own health, the estate's future, Ant's military service, and his relationship with Lyn. That was his father's style. Ant admired his brevity, even if the Earl of Stanton's words made him uncomfortable about his past and future.

"I see you haven't lost your enthusiasm for mapping out my future, Dad. I understand my responsibilities, and I'm not talking about Lyn. She's an adult and knows her own mind."

"Well, one of you has to, I suppose," replied Ant's father, his face beaming.

Ant shook his head in playful response as they spent a few minutes taking in the open landscape that surrounded Stanton Hall.

Interrupting the silence, Ant asked the question that was the real purpose of his visit.

"That was a bad do up at the dig site, wasn't it?"

Ant's father nodded.

"Have you found anything out yet? I'll lay a bet it's not just those metal detectorists who are doing some digging. Come on, tell me what you've discovered."

Ant's smile dissolved.

"I found out that our land agent had been fleecing us for years, Dad. Did you know?"

Ant watched his father hesitate and play for time by jabbing the armrest of his wheelchair with his index finger.

"I knew something was wrong but couldn't put my finger on it. The accounts seemed to balance, and he always behaved impeccably to your mother and me. I assumed he was a good sort of chap and loyal to us. However, year after year, cash went out faster than it was coming in, and I just couldn't understand it. I had intended to speak to you, Son."

Ant sensed his father visibly shrink in his wheelchair as the truth dawned.

"The truth is, the more I find out about Narky, the more unpleasant and calculating a thug he turns out to have been. It seems he found a way, or stumbled across, a means of siphoning off cash from the estate and intimidating anyone who got in his way, or whose compliance he needed. He was the one in control of events, Dad, so he could act any part he wanted in front of Mum and you, so don't be too hard on yourself. We'll find a way of putting this place on a firm footing."

Ant's father rallied as he listened.

"And recent events have rather dealt with the matter, don't you think?"

Ant knew his father had picked his words with care.

"That's one way of looking at things, Dad. But I need to be sure certain people are telling me the truth. Otherwise, Narky's death may remain unresolved and the estate's future in danger."

Ant's father nodded then shocked his son by doing something he'd never done before.

"Give your father a hug."

Ant instinctively bent over the earl and gently folded his arms around the elderly man's delicate shoulders until their heads kissed each other's cheek. After a few seconds, his father patted Ant's back as a signal he understood well.

Sitting on a curved stone bench to the side of his father's wheelchair, Ant sensed the earl wanted to say something to him.

"Is everything all right, Dad?"

His father frowned and looked earnestly at Ant.

"I know this probably isn't the moment to raise the subject, but truth be told, Anthony, it's all getting too much for your mother and me." The elderly man gave his armrest one last stab with his finger before adding, "There. I've said it."

Relaxing back into his chair, having spoken the words he'd needed to voice for a long time, his agitation eased.

Ant's shock at finally hearing the words he dreaded was no less for it actually happening.

Why do we think our parents will live forever? thought Ant.

"I hesitated all this time because of the pressure I knew

you would feel in sacrificing your military career and having to return home. And for what? A life mending dilapidated buildings and fending off the day when the estate might have to go over to the National Trust: lock, stock, and leaking roof. And on top of that, this Narky business and all the damage he's done to us."

Ant pushed the wheelchair back through the French doors and into a spacious drawing room without responding to his father's admission. He had just heard his father admit, perhaps for the first time in his life, that he couldn't cope.

The rich décor and family portraits that hung on each wall hit home as Ant reflected on his privileged background and the responsibility that went with it.

"But the main thing is, Anthony, that we get an expert in to help run things. Don't you agree?"

Ant's father didn't give him chance to respond.

"Now, let's have that cup of tea before you shoot off to see Lyn, and you must take back her cake tin." The Earl of Stanton spoke in a matter-of-fact way. Head buried in a book, his eyes anywhere but on his son.

Ant knew this wasn't the time to prolong his father's distress. At such times in his family, he knew a touch of light-hearted banter was called for. It was easier than confronting truths.

"My plans do not include seeing Lyn today, as you well know, Father. But seeing as you want that blessed cake tin returned to her, I will, indeed, take it."

Ant's father nodded, all the time pretending to read his book.

"As you say, Anthony. As you say."

* * *

"All right, all right, I'm coming," moaned Lyn as she made her way from the kitchen to the front door.

"My father said you wanted this back." Ant held out the cake tin. "And I wanted to check your telephone."

"Good morning to you too, Ant," replied a bemused Lyn, relieving her visitor of the tin. Since when have you been in the telephone maintenance business?"

Ant followed Lyn down the hall and into the kitchen.

"Since you stopped answering your phone. I wanted to fill you in on my meeting with Glen."

Lyn glanced at the handset on the granite worktop next to the fridge. It was flashing.

"Ah," said Lyn, before attempting to change the subject, "and I've got something important to tell you."

"Ah," replied Ant, as he perched himself on a bar stool.

Enjoying seeing Lyn squirm, he pushed home his advantage.

"Seeing as I made the trip over here just to bring the cake tin back, do I get lunch? Anyway, where were you last night? First you cut me off on the mobile, then you don't answer your home phone."

Lyn threw a well-aimed tea towel at Ant as she bent down to open the oven and retrieve a cottage pie.

Ant didn't bother ducking. Instead, he caught the towel, folded it into a neat square and hung it over the stool.

"So how does your news trump me seeing the carpenter? For all you know I could have found our murderer."

"Place mat," urged Lyn as she pointed to the worktop so she could put the piping-hot dish onto the dining table. Task accomplished, Lyn slipped off a pair of oven gloves and sat opposite him.

"Because I've found our murderer, that's why," she announced, trying hard to control her excitement.

Ant raised an eyebrow.

"You need not look so surprised, you know," she said, irritated he didn't take her news with the seriousness it deserved.

"Not at all," replied Ant. "You may well have, but don't forget Glen."

Ant explained the conversation he'd had with the carpenter and his wife.

"We know Narky was a bad lot, and although Glen's explanation seems plausible, I've one or two scars on my back from believing people I *wanted* to be innocent, so we shall see."

Ant could see Lyn's frustration as she realised there was a contender who might scupper her own theory. She lost no time in telling Ant about Vikki King and listed the case against the detectorist.

"She was there on the night Narky died, had a motive because she feared an attack, and Vikki *admitted* hitting 'someone.'"

Ant rose from the table and walked the short distance to the coffee machine, gesturing to Lyn if she'd like a drink.

"No thanks. Well, what do you think?"

Ant took in the rich aroma of the fresh coffee and took a sip.

"Not bad. Not bad at all. Where did you get it from?"

He watched as Lyn's face flushed. He knew what he was doing.

"Joke," he added to head off Lyn's fury.

"On the one hand a good defence lawyer will argue self-defence. On the other hand, a good council for the prosecution will press the jury for a guilty verdict on the basis that Narky was unarmed and drunk as a lord. Nevertheless, we need to speak to her, pronto. The police aren't far behind us, and they'll have a field day with the evidence you found."

Lyn began to draw imaginary sketches on the tablecloth with her finger.

"Is there a problem? I know when you are trying to avoid saying something."

Lyn withdrew her finger and looked over towards Ant.

"There's a slight problem. Vikki has disappeared."

"Clumsy of you, that," teased Ant. "Do you think she'll still be in the area?"

Lyn wasn't sure whether Ant was being sarcastic or asking a genuine question.

"I don't know, and I'm loath to tell Inspector Plod in case he messes it up."

Ant nodded.

"I'm with you on that, old thin—" he started.

Lyn picked up the tea towel, making ready to flick a corner at Ant.

"I've said before, don't you call me old... anything."

"Okay, okay, point made. Anyway, I'm agreeing with you, aren't I? So no more threats of violence, please."

Ant put on his best "little boy lost" look for added impact but could see Lyn remained unimpressed.

"All I'm saying is that we'd better get a move on if we want to catch up with your mysterious Vikki. That's if she's still around. The rally finishes in about two hours, you know."

A look of panic spread across Lyn's face as Ant's words hit home.

"Come on," said Lyn as she zipped across the kitchen and towards the front door. "Your car or mine?"

Ant looked crestfallen.

"Er... what about the cottage pie? I'm starving."

Ant pointed at the steaming food nestled in a gleaming Pyrex dish.

Lyn had already opened the car door.

"It'll keep," she shouted. "Slam the door on your way out; it sticks.

8

THE RACE IS ON

It was fortunate that Mini Clubman cars tended not to take up much space on the rural roads of Norfolk.

Any faster, and she'll have us in a ditch, Ant thought and considered themselves all the luckier for not having met a tractor coming the other way. Harvest time meant the huge machines hunted in packs. Ant held on for dear life and tried to banish memories of his brother's car accident.

Lyn's excited voice broke his depressive train of thought.

"There she is."

Lyn jabbed her finger towards a figure in the middle distance as the car approached the rally site.

"For the love of mercy, woman, slow down," Ant shouted as he grabbed a plastic handle just above the passenger door and braced himself. The vehicle shuddered as it completed a sudden swerve to the left.

"I've felt safer in a Challenger tank under fire than with you."

Lyn gave Ant a dismissive glance as she leant forward into the steering wheel.

"Made it," squealed Lyn as she brought the Clubman to a sliding halt within an inch of her target.

Ant took a few seconds to summon enough courage to open his eyes. As he did so, he noticed a crowd of onlookers dusting themselves down from a soil-laden vortex of air caused by Lyn's energetic driving.

"Thank you for such an uneventful ride, Lyn. Remind me to get the bus back, will you?"

It took Ant a little longer to loosen his grip on the handle above his head.

In front of Lyn's Mini, a startled Vikki King leant at a curious angle into the boot of her own car. She looked as though she was unsure whether to jump into it for safety or run for cover.

"Vikki, glad we caught you. This is my friend, Ant. It's his land you're on, and well, we want... that is, er, need..."

In her excited state, Lyn's words tumbled into one another.

Sensing she was in danger of doing more harm than good, Ant intervened.

"Hi, Vikki. What Lyn is trying to say is that she was so sorry to have lost sight of you last night, and could she have another word. Isn't that right, Lyn?"

Lyn didn't take to his tone, and Ant's failure to note her sternest head-teacher look further inflamed the situation. She could see his intervention had spooked Vikki as she watched the detectorist play with the shoulder straps of her backpack and avoid eye contact.

Lyn sensed it was time for everyone to take a breath and begin again.

The brief silence worked.

"About last night," said Vikki.

Lyn's eyes widened. She hoped for a confession.

"Sorry," Vikki continued, "Jed Bridges grabbed me. He's organised the rally and wanted to get pictures of my finds. When I got back, you were gone. I tried to find you but assumed you'd got fed up waiting for me."

Lyn's excitement faded as it dawned on her Vikki's explanation was plausible and that she might not be the murderer after all.

Why would the woman have hung around if she had intended to give me the slip last night?

The more Lyn mulled things over, the more ridiculous she felt. Catching Ant's glance, she knew he had already come to the same conclusion.

"And have you found anything of interest?" Ant asked in a well-practised manner.

Vikki let go of the backpack.

"Two Henry's. One hammered, a jetton, and a cut half. Oh, and a John one. So not bad for a weekend on hard, dry ground. Not much resistance for the detector to work on, you see."

"A what and a what?" replied Ant, baffled at Vikki's stream of gobbledygook.

She tried again.

"Well, a hammered is—"

Lyn interrupted.

"I'll explain later, Ant. Let's just say not a bad haul of handmade silver coins around eight hundred years old and a seventeenth-century French gaming counter. Now what about that man who attacked you at the dig site, Vikki?"

"Impressive or what," said Ant. "Been watching *Time Team*, have we?"

Vikki nodded. "Spot on, Lyn. Except that jettons were never official legal tender, more like—"

"Yes, yes, I know," replied Lyn, irritated at being corrected in front of Ant.

Lyn could see Ant enjoyed the moment and awaited further explanation, hoping she would make a mistake.

"No, I haven't watched that Tony Robinson bloke, I mean. And yes, I know all about jettons. A couple of Vikki's detectorist friends gave me a quick introduction to the hobby yesterday."

"Well, fair play, anyway. Then again, as a teacher, I suppose you're used to catching bits of information and presenting it back to your pupils as if you're a world expert." Ant's response was light hearted, but it hit the spot.

Lyn gave Ant one of her special stares reserved for only the worst behaved of her pupils.

They continued to exchange the barrage of insults only good friends can get away with without exchanging blows. Around them the hubbub of vehicles being loaded and driven off the field intensified.

In between giving and receiving playful insults, Lyn noticed Vikki was keen to join the exodus and had closed the boot of her car and belted herself into the driving seat.

She broke off from squabbling with Ant.

"Ah, you're keen to get away, I suspect. Have you far to drive?"

"Four hours if there aren't any holdups."

"Just a quick question, Vikki," said Lyn as she gathered her thoughts. "Is there anything else you can tell us about the man who attacked you? Anything at all?"

Vikki shook her head as she lifted her foot from the clutch pedal and pressed the accelerator.

"Sorry," she replied as her car started to move. "He came at me so fast I didn't see him. He was like a whippet."

With that she drove off, leaving the pair shrouded in a whirling mist of dry clay.

"Well, that's that. Now what do we do?"

Ant cleared the last of the dust from his lungs with a throaty cough and cast his eyes across the horizon. Lyn watched for some pearl of wisdom from her more experienced sleuthing partner.

"I think that the cottage pie you cooked should just about be the right temperature for eating, don't you?"

Lyn frowned.

"A murderer on the loose, and all you can think about is food."

9
REFLECTIONS

Ant crouched and covered his head with a soapy hand as Lyn dropped a Pyrex dish. It crashed onto the stone floor of her kitchen.

"That's the second time in three days you've reacted to a sudden noise like that," said Lyn. She tried hard not to show alarm.

Ant didn't answer at first. Instead, preferring to pick up individual clumps of soggy potato and mincemeat that had splattered all around them.

"I defy anyone not to jump when one of those shatters," replied Ant, having used the time before speaking to calm himself. "And you always were the clumsy one."

Lyn was having none of it.

"Don't change the subject, Anthony Stanton. Jump, yes. Cower, no. Now what's going on?" Lyn wasn't in the mood, and she could tell Ant knew it.

The pair continued to do the dishes in silence. Lyn washing. Ant drying.

Lyn had decided she wasn't going to let the matter drop.

After placing the last of the dried dishes in a pine plate rack, Lyn pressed the point.

"Come on, let's sit down."

She led her friend by the hand to the dining table.

"Now, please, talk."

Lyn studied his face closely as she sensed him struggle to find the words.

"Ant, look at me."

He did as he was told. She watched his eyes fill with tears, and he fought for the right words.

"PTSD. That's—"

Lyn gently interrupted and raised a hand to his cheek by way of reassurance.

"I know what post traumatic stress disorder is, Ant. Why haven't you said anything before?"

She moved her hand to wipe away the faintest of tears from the corners of Ant's eyes.

Ant didn't move an inch except for fiddling with the salt cellar until Lyn covered his hand with hers and brought the circular movement to a halt.

"Not the sort of thing a military intelligence officer admits to, is it?" He offered no resistance to Lyn's hand restraint.

"Why are you being so hard on yourself, Ant?" replied Lyn, her gentle tone doing its job in helping him relax. "I don't know what you've seen on active duty, but if the news on the telly is anything to go by, I can imagine."

Ant let out a short, sharp laugh as he threw his head back. He tried to stifle the sound. He didn't mean to offend.

"Imagine? You've no idea. Only *we* know." Lyn guessed his response conjured up images he'd rather not recall.

She had no answer to offer but sensed his unease was returning.

"It's okay, Ant. You're safe here."

Ant brought his head forward and met Lyn's eye contact.

"When I report back to the barracks, the shrinks want to assess me before they'll let me rejoin my unit. If things go belly up, you might be seeing a lot more of me. That means Dad's problem with running the estate will be sorted. Two birds killed with one stone, you might say."

His tone was more pragmatic now.

"If I sound a tad angry, I'm sorry. It's just I'd have preferred to pick my own time for packing the military in."

Lyn studied her friend. She didn't detect anger. In fact, just the reverse. He looked calm now, almost matter of fact. Lyn suspected he'd wanted to have this conversation for a long time.

Now it was her time to share.

"You know, when I was training to qualify as a teacher, they put me in a tough inner-city comprehensive in Hampshire. I got to know a teacher who'd worked there for over thirty years and had seen it all. He loved his job. The other teachers bribed the kids with treats to keep them quiet but not Graham. He went into the classroom, got on with his job, and do you know what? The kids loved him."

Ant put the salts down with the lightest of touches.

"So you're telling me a fairy tale about a superb teacher that every child in the world loved? What's that got to do with the price of fish?"

"Nothing," she said. "He told me that as a young teacher, he'd hit a brick wall after about twelve months in the job. He felt he couldn't live up to his own expectations and developed panic attacks. Then one day, for no particular reason, he sat on the floor in a corner of the classroom, put his head in his hands, and cried like a baby."

Ant cocked his head to one side.

"So was he a great teacher or a lousy one?"

"Neither," said Lyn. "It took six months on sick leave for him to accept what had happened. Then it clicked. He hadn't failed at anything; he got out of teaching for a few years and did other stuff until he felt ready to go back. Now he's in control. He deals with things as they are, not what might have been, or could be."

"And your point?" said Ant.

"Go with the flow," she replied as she slowly picked up the salt and tipped a gentle trickle of the white crystal onto the table.

Had anyone else said that he would have told them to stop patronising him. With Lyn, it was different. He had nothing to prove to her. He'd always acknowledged she knew him better than anyone.

"Look at the mess you've made," said Ant, his mood lifting in the safe company of his trusted friend.

"Maybe you're right," replied Ant as Lyn watched him carefully gather the salt into the palm of his hand. "But one thing's for sure. Sitting here won't find our killer, will it?"

Ant threw the salt he'd collected over his right shoulder and stood up. Lyn returned his broad smile. Her chair made a scraping sound as she moved it backwards over the stone floor.

"Time to visit the crime scene again, yes?"

* * *

"LORD, that fool of a detective is milling about up there. Better keep out of the way until he's gone," said Ant as Lyn brought her car to a stop on the edge of the dig site.

"You'd better move the Mini through that gate onto the farm track." Ant was pointing to an ancient, wooden structure held together with twine that nestled between two great elm posts. "If he comes back this way, he'll see us and will want to know what we're doing."

Get a move on, man, thought Ant as he watched the detective wander around the dig site kicking clods of earth, first with one foot then the other. *Looks like he's lost a pound and found a penny,* mused Ant as he looked at his watch. A further ten minutes passed before the policeman gave up, dusted himself down, and returned to his car.

"Do you think he found out about the broken metal detector?" said Lyn.

"Not a chance." Ant shook his head. "He'd have come for you quicker than a rat up a drain pipe if he'd cottoned onto anything like that."

Within a few seconds the detective's car had disappeared from the field.

"Better safe than sorry," said Ant as he leapt from their hiding place, clambered over a rickety wooden stile, and made off, leaving Lyn in his wake.

"Thank you for helping."

Ant gave a quick look over his shoulder. "Equality and all that. You can't have it both ways."

Lyn huffed.

Ant sensed he would pay for his comment at some point.

Seconds later, the pair stood over the trench, that until a few days previously, had cradled the body of Narky Collins. Now empty, Ant might have convinced himself that nothing had happened at all.

Then from behind, a muffled noise.

He went into automatic pilot. Hunching his back to make himself the smallest target possible as he made his way to the side of the spoil heap.

Ant gestured for Lyn to follow. She needed no encouragement.

Out of the gloom, Ant made out the shape of a tall, young man.

"Sorry to startle you. I'm Simon. I'm part of the team from the university."

Ant's shoulders dropped as he heaved a sigh of relief.

"Good God, man, you gave us the shock of our lives. What are you doing up here on a Sunday? It's almost dark."

Simon repeated his apology.

"I'm trying to get back into the professor's good books by seeing if any artefacts have made their way onto the spoil heap. It sometimes happens, you know."

The man's voice trembled. Ant could see he looked terrified.

"Hello, Simon," said Lyn. "No need to be scared. Not of us, anyway. As for your professor, well, that's another story. It's okay though. We won't tell."

Lyn's calming words did the trick. Simon's demeanour changed.

"It's so hard, you see. To get a full-time job in archaeology, I mean. I thought if I could make up for my mistakes, it might stand me in good stead, you know, with the professor."

After a few minutes of gentle conversation about what the university hoped to learn from the dig, Ant brought matters to a conclusion.

"Well, all I can say is, that based on what we've seen here this evening, the professor needs to know just how committed you are to your career."

Ant's words of encouragement had the desired effect. The young man smiled as he turned to leave.

"Oh, did you find anything?"

"Find anything?" replied Simon. Er, no. Not this time."

Then he was off with the neck protector from his cap fluttering in the light breeze.

Ant suggested they take a minute to reflect on the case so far.

"So we have a carpenter that threatened to expose Narky for trying to blackmail him but who seems to have a rock-solid alibi."

"And we have a metal detectorist up here that night who admits clobbering someone who, how did Vikki put it, 'ran at me like a whippet.'"

Both fell silent for a few seconds.

Ant broke the impasse.

"Back to basics. Let's see what the villagers have to say. Somebody must know something. This is Stanton Parva after all: the gossiping capital of East Anglia!"

Lyn laughed.

"In the meantime, I have the small matter of work to prepare for school tomorrow. Speaking of which, would you like to visit your old alma mater to catch up on the world of education?"

Ant groaned. "Must I?"

"I'll even throw in a free school dinner for you," added Lyn as she sped off back towards her car.

"Yuck," replied Ant, well out of earshot as he made up ground to catch up with his companion.

10

A CLASS ACT

Lordy Lord, doesn't everything look small, thought Ant as he wandered around the space in which he'd spent the first year of his school life.

"Wasn't sure if you would turn up, Ant." He watched Lyn as she strode in with a confident air about her and a cluster of children in her slipstream.

"Their teacher will be a few minutes late, so I'll just get them settled, then we can go over what we've found out so far."

Ant nodded as Lyn welcomed each child to the classroom and directed them to their seats as each gave Ant a curious stare.

"This is an ex-pupil, children, and this was his classroom when he was a little boy," Lyn explained.

Ant felt as though he were that little boy again and was certain he would sit on one of the miniature chairs if instructed to do so by the head teacher.

"Good morning, Joe. Did you have a good weekend?"

"Yes, miss," replied Joe as Lyn welcomed in the next child with a similar greeting.

Ant could see Lyn was in her element directing one child to hand out the exercise books, checking another had brought their gym pumps, and reminding a third to tie her footwear.

"We don't want to hit our head again, do we, Charlotte?"

"No, miss," replied the girl, bending down to tie her shoelace.

A few minutes later a dishevelled-looking young man tumbled into the room making the children giggle.

"Oh dear, my car broke down again, and I didn't have enough money for the bus, so I had to walk."

The teacher's explanation caused the children to giggle all the more as Lyn handed over the keys to the room and winked at the teacher.

Ant almost felt sorry for the man. However, the chance to escape the noise and general air of chaos tempered his sympathy as he followed Lyn down the corridor like a little boy about to be put into detention.

"He seemed a bit disorganised, don't you think?"

"Don't be taken in by the act. Dicky Summers is one of the brightest young teachers I've got. The kids love him, and his little antics keep their attention."

After a short walk, the pair passed through a solid-looking door adjacent to the front entrance of the school to be met by the pained expression of Tina Broughton, Lyn's secretary.

"Sorry, Lyn, it's the Cummings. They're in your office. I couldn't stop them."

Lyn winced.

"Not again? What's it about this time?"

Ant watched as Tina handed Lyn a note. Her reaction said it all.

"They're saying Tim's spelling isn't coming on quick enough."

Ant glanced at the note.

"It's not just their son's spelling that needs attention," chipped in Ant before watching Lyn fold the scrap of paper and slip it into her jacket pocket.

Lyn noticed Tina giving Ant the once-over.

"It's Anthony Stanton, isn't it?"

"Correct," replied Ant. "But—"

"Never forget a face, no matter how much age changes it," interrupted Tina without the slightest hint of sarcasm.

Ant's mouth remained half-open from his unfinished sentence as he tried to recall the woman.

"I was a dinner lady here when you two were kids. Always getting into trouble, I recall."

Lyn laughed; Ant blushed. Tina nodded her head towards Lyn's office.

"The sooner you're in, the sooner it'll be over, Lyn. I'll have a mug of strong coffee waiting for you."

Lyn let out a quiet moan before turning to Ant.

"Sorry. Looks like we're not going to get time to talk things over. Catch up with you later?"

"Don't apologise; I'm glad to escape. I'll use the time to ask around about Narky and catch up with you tonight. Don't forget, you're dining with us tonight. Mum and Dad can't wait to get us together!"

Lyn had already disappeared before he'd finished speaking.

"Don't worry. I'll remind her," said Tina as she showed Ant out of her office with a gentle pat to the small of his back. As he made his way to the exit, Tina called after him in a quiet voice.

"Be careful, Anthony. Narky has... mean had, some nasty

mates. It they think you're after them, they won't wait for you to knock on their door."

Ant noticed Tina nod in a conspiratorial fashion as if to emphasise her point.

Hmm, this chap gets more sinister by the day, thought Ant.

* * *

"I will not tell you again, Lord Stanton. Keep out of my investigation, or I'll arrest you—and the schoolteacher."

The Wherry Arms fell silent as the detective let fly at Ant.

Unconcerned with the verbal assault, Ant turned from the bar to face his tormentor.

My dear Riley, you really do need to calm down. If you take blood pressure tablets, they don't seem to be working. Your cheeks are quite flushed."

A quiet laughter filled the small space as the locals enjoyed the spectacle.

Nothing better than winding up plod, especially this one, thought Ant as he took a sip of his drink and placed the pint glass carefully back on its beer mat.

"The thing is, Riley, I have an obligation to those who use my land, and..."

"And I'm telling you that owning a bit of land and having a fancy title doesn't entitle you to compromise a police investigation."

Ant's expression didn't change as the detective attempted to belittle him.

"I'd hardly call owning five thousand acres a bit of land, Detective, and as I told you previously, I couldn't have known the man was dead until I physically checked. I really do think I acted reasonably, don't you?"

The cackle of laughter from their engrossed audience continued with each exchange.

"Interfering with police evidence is a serious offence, Stanton. I won't tolerate it. Do you understand me?"

Ant took a second sip of his beer, winking at the barman as he lifted his glass.

"My dear detective—"

Ant's point was cut short by one of the barmaids handing over a phone that had been ringing for the last few seconds.

"It's for you."

Riley fumed as he waited for Ant to continue.

"Are you free? Where are you? Thank the Lord the morning's over. Now, where did you say you were?"

Ant held lazily on to the receiver as he watched the detective turn puce in the face before replying.

"I didn't, and well, I'm sort of free."

"What on earth's the matter with you? You're talking in riddles. Are you in the pub?"

"Yes."

It took Lyn two minutes to walk from the school to the village centre.

"Let me tell you one last time. I don't care if it's your land. And the same goes for your young lady. Leave it alone," barked Riley as he strode out of the bar, brushing past Lyn as she entered.

Lyn looked at Ant with bemusement as a round of applause broke out around them.

"Let's just say the dear inspector would rather we minded our own business. Not that he's getting anywhere, judging by his mood."

"Would you like another drink? And the young lady?" quipped the barman.

"Don't you start, Jed," replied Lyn. "Young lady, indeed."

She looked at Ant for his reaction before quickly looking away as Ant made eye contact.

Soon, the bar had returned to its normal gaggle of disparate conversations. Meanwhile, Lyn had seated herself next to Ant and placed her shoulder bag on the floor.

"I'm guessing it's not the usual," shouted Jed. You know, since you're at work and all that."

"Better just be a shandy, then, Jed," said Ant as he smiled at Lyn.

He could see she wasn't impressed.

"What," said Lyn as she glared at Ant. "Single lady likes to drink in a village pub?"

Ant smiled, savouring Lyn's flaring nostrils.

"Oh, shut up and just drink your beer."

The more Lyn bristled, the more Ant enjoyed the moment.

Ant hesitated just as he tasted the first of his new pint. Returning the glass to the table, Ant stared at its contents, transfixed by the amber liquid.

"Have you missed Fen Bodger pale ale so much you need to check it's still there?" said Lyn in a quizzical tone.

She was pleased to no longer be the source of his amusement.

"Jed," Ant shouted as he looked towards the barman. "Was Narky Collins a beer man or a shorts man?"

Ant could see Jed didn't need to think on the matter as he dried a glass with a towel that had seen better days.

"Too tight for shorts, that one. Guzzled beer like the rest of the lads."

Lyn caught on straight away.

"Interesting, that's what Glen's wife said," commented Ant.

As they digested the implications of Jed's response, Professor Pullman made his way over to the bar.

"I'll have a large bottle of your finest to take out, my man. Glen Stuart if you have it."

Jed's face beamed as he relished the sale of his most expensive whisky.

As Ant watched on, he was tapped on the shoulder from behind. He turned to see a familiar face.

"Hi, Alan. How're things with the history group. Found any more bodies recently?"

He watched Alan smile as the man entered into the spirit of things.

"Funny enough, we... Actually, no. But you never know, do you? Anyway, how are your investigations going?"

Ant smiled back at Alan then winked an eye at Lyn.

"Funnily enough, things are beginning to get rather interesting."

* * *

LYN'S THOUGHTS wavered between the humdrum of her busy day at school and the confused matter of Narky Collins as she strolled the mile from home to Stanton Hall. Lyn knew Ant's parents were always pleased to see her. It was as if she provided a tangible link to Ant when he was away on active duty.

Turning a corner on the roadway with deep ditches on either side, so typical of rural Norfolk, Lyn smiled as the Hall came into sight, its clever landscaping hiding it from view until the last minute. Built in the fifteenth century, the profile of the building was a mixture of medieval, half-timbered façades, and later Georgian stonework with symmetrical windows.

What she hadn't expected to come across was a young woman sitting against a tree, staring at a mobile phone. As Lyn closed the distance between them, she heard a quiet whimper as the girl wiped tears from her cheek.

"It's Wendy, isn't it?" asked Lyn. She spoke in a soft, soothing tone calculated not to alarm the young woman.

The girl shifted her gaze from the phone to Lyn.

"Yes, but how do you know my name?"

"Oh, don't mind me. I'm a teacher, and it's a trick we learn along the way. You must have heard of word association?"

Lyn's question seemed to snap the girl out of her misery. Meeting Lyn's eyes, she settled back against the trunk of the magnificent oak.

"Suppose I have, but—"

"You're one of the professor's undergraduates up at the dig, aren't you?" interrupted Lyn. "You were talking to one of your colleagues when I passed the other day."

Lyn smiled as she spoke. It proved to be momentarily infectious.

"Oh yes, I see," replied Wendy before all trace of her grin disappeared.

By now, Lyn had reached the girl and perched next to her on the steep bank in which the giant tree stood.

"Want to talk?" asked Lyn as she put a comforting arm around the girl's shoulders.

Eventually the girl responded.

"He had a go at me for being late."

"Who did?" replied Lyn, "Your boyfriend?"

"No, no. The professor. But he told us the wrong time. He's always doing it. He's so disorganised. Then he blames us." Tears fell as she spoke.

Lyn summoned up all her years of teaching to put the girl at ease.

"Well, it's not the end of the world. From what I hear, that professor of yours seems to shout at everyone. Try not to take it so personally, and you'll be okay."

Lyn's words had little effect on Wendy.

"Now he won't answer his mobile." Her sobs became louder.

"Who, the professor?" replied Lyn, knowing her intervention was inadequate.

Wendy shoved the phone into her pocket before freeing herself of the tree.

"No, no, my boyfriend. Oh, you don't understand. It doesn't matter. I need to go."

Before Lyn could utter another word, Wendy walked away and rounded the corner, disappearing from her line of sight towards the village without saying another word.

* * *

"That was a lovely meal. Thank you, Gerald." Lyn's fulsome thanks to Ant's father for supper were genuine. She'd had a soft spot for the Earl and Countess of Stanton all her life. They'd offered a friendly space as a young teenager when her parents were arguing and she'd had enough.

"Brings us a cake every week, you know, Anthony. Chocolate's my favourite, isn't it, my dear?" The earl looked at Lyn then to his wife to whom he gave the gentlest of touches to the side of her cheek. Her eyes lit up as she smiled at her husband.

Ant had heard this story, like all the others many times,

as had Lyn. Both smiled and paid attention as if hearing it for the first time.

Lyn sensed her host's sudden change of mood.

"We've told Anthony he mustn't come back on our behalf. We know he's doing important hush-hush work. Isn't that right, my dear?"

Lady Stanton nodded, displaying a fragility that shocked Lyn.

She glimpsed at Ant and could see he looked uncomfortable at the sight of his elderly mother.

Thirty minutes passed until Ant's parents decided it was time for bed. Lyn waited patiently, and Ant spent a further ten minutes to check they were safely in bed.

"What do they say, Lyn? Once an adult, twice a child. God help us all; that's all I can say."

He shrugged his shoulders as he picked up an After Eight mint.

Lyn changed tack by telling him about the girl she'd met earlier.

"Then just as I thought she was talking about the professor, she cut me off and said 'boyfriend.' Strange, don't you think?"

Ant smiled and wagged a finger at his companion.

"Our little investigation is making you jump at shadows. Think about it. Young woman is upset and in her own world. Young woman is confronted by nosy stranger. Young woman does a runner. Hardly puts our dear professor in the firing line for murder most foul, does it?"

Lyn scowled at Ant, certain he wasn't taking her seriously.

"Stop it. You know what I mean. If you don't want me to help in this case, just say so."

She watched Ant's face drop but was in no mood to let him off the hook.

Ant opened his right hand and patted his chest with an open palm.

"Mea culpa, mea culpa—my fault."

Lyn raised her eyebrows.

"I know what the Latin stands for. It's not just for public-school boys and the Mafia, you know."

Lyn watched Ant frown as she made a rare reference to his teenage years at Eaton. She knew her comments had hit home and regretted the reference immediately.

"I'm sorry, Ant, I..."

"It's okay, Lyn. I was out of order. It's just that boyfriend/girlfriend stuff is a crazy thing to understand."

Lyn's eyes flashed at Ant as she suddenly felt uncomfortable.

Stupid man, she thought.

"Let's just say she did mean her boyfriend. She probably meant he had done the dirty on her or stood her up. That's all I'm saying. I tell you what. Why don't we track him down and see where it leads us—if you can get that Wendy girl to dish the dirt."

Lyn gave a slight nod of her head as she stood up, extended a hand, and brushed Ant's shoulder.

"It's getting late. Let's see what happens, eh?"

She crossed the spacious sitting room and opened the wide panelled door. Looking back at Ant, she could see he was lost in his own thoughts.

Perhaps we pushed each other too far tonight, she thought.

11

MORNING ASSEMBLY

Tuesday morning started like any other at Stanton Primary. Lyn, in her office working through the post, which as usual, Tina had opened and laid out in four neat piles:

Urgent
Can do later
For reading
File in bin

Lost in her thoughts about the previous evening, Lyn didn't hear the secretary enter.

"Best get going now, or you'll be late for morning assembly." The secretary was pointing at the clock on the wall in front of Lyn.

"Hell's bells," replied Lyn. "Nine o'clock already."

Lyn shot past a smiling Tina and took the twenty yards to the hall at a canter.

As she entered the room, the excited chatter of 200 five-to-ten-year-olds subsided as they caught sight of the head teacher.

All was in order. Children seated on the floor, legs and

arms crossed, their teachers and classroom assistants lining the side walls. Front and centre stood a wooden lectern, the day's prompt sheet having already been put in place, courtesy of Tina.

Twenty minutes later, Lyn was heading back to her office to begin the day's work.

"Coffee, yes, please," said Lyn as she re-entered her office and sat down opposite her secretary to go through her diary for the day.

"You say it every day as if it's the first time I've made you a coffee," replied Tina. She smiled as she gave her boss the gentle reproach.

"After keeping two hundred kids amused for twenty minutes, it feels like every day is the first time I've tasted coffee," Lyn joked.

The two women spent the next ten minutes exchanging gossip and confirming the running order for the day. This day would be like most other days: full, varied, but always challenging. It was just how Lyn liked it.

"Oh, by the way, those metal detectorists have confirmed they'll do the demonstration you asked for, tomorrow afternoon. I've phoned the professor, and although he's not happy about it, he's agreed they can use a strip of land just outside where he's been digging."

Lyn smiled.

"Heavens, they were quick. I didn't think for a moment they'd agree to it. Okay, tell the class teachers of those on this list it's a go, and let's make sure we get parental permission."

"Will do," replied Tina.

Alone in her office, Lyn again reflected on how Monday evening had ended.

I shouldn't have bitten like that, but he drives me nuts sometimes.

Lyn picked up the telephone receiver and dialled a familiar number.

Damn, that stupid answer machine, she thought. *Bet he's out and about cracking on with our investigation while I'm stuck here with loads of pointless paperwork and dealing with wonks from the county council.*

* * *

ANT WAS ENJOYING his morning driving around the estate on his quad bike. The endless landscape of the Norfolk Fens never ceased to amaze him.

He stopped for a moment to enjoy the sight of a kingfisher as it surveyed Stanton Broad from its favourite perch.

Now and then it would take to the skies then plunge into the Broad making hardly a ripple on its surface. Sometimes the bird would resurface empty mouthed. More often than not, its efforts were successful.

Ant's thoughts drifted to what he had been missing all these years. His joy was tempered with the responsibilities he knew went with coming back permanently.

Soon will be time to decide, he thought as he revved the quad's engine and made off towards a figure in the far distance.

"Thought it was you, Glen. Never-ending job mending the fences, I suppose."

The estate carpenter dropped his claw hammer to the grass and wiped a bead of sweat from his brow.

"You can say that again. Thousands of acres and open access for the public to most of it. Keeps me in a job, that's for sure."

A brief silence fell, and Ant sensed Glen wanted to say something but was hesitating. He guessed what it might be.

"How's your dad coming along, Glen?"

Ant's question helped the carpenter overcome his embarrassment.

"He's doing all right, Mr Anthon... er, Ant. That is, except for having the laptop taken off him. I've told him, no more bingo, that's for sure."

Ant smiled, which was the signal for Glen to give himself permission to laugh.

"He wasn't pleased at first, mind you. But the threat of the bailiffs lifting his prized Welsh dresser did the trick."

"Talking about bailiffs, Glen, is everything okay on that front?"

Glen nodded.

"That's all sorted. I can't thank you enough, Ant."

Ant nodded, reaching over and patting Glen by way of reassurance.

"Got to look after each other. Isn't that right, Glen?"

"All the same, thank you. I won't forget it."

Ant raised a hand and pointed towards the dig site.

"Talking about not forgetting, something I meant to ask you yesterday. I'm trying to track Narky's movements in the days running up to his death. You didn't say when you last saw him, Glen."

Ant watched Glen's reaction carefully. The carpenter's cheek betrayed the slightest of twitches as he formulated his response.

"Oh, er, sometime early last week, I think."

Ant didn't push the matter any further but took note of Glen's hesitant response.

I hope Glen's telling me the truth, thought Ant and made a mental note to check out his story.

"That's great, Glen. I just want to get things clear in my head. Now I must be off. Best of luck with the fence."

Revving the engine with a flick of his right wrist he turned the machine and roared off into the distance not waiting for the carpenter to respond.

12

FIELD SURFING

"Love this time of evening, don't you, Lyn?" said Ant as he let loose the final mooring rope of his father's boat, *Field Surfer*.

Lyn nodded her agreement and took in the lazy sunshine of a quiet Tuesday evening.

Free from its ties, the vintage vessel glided away from its mooring as Ant jumped aboard and allowed the craft to drift into the middle of the Broad.

Ant busied himself setting the wherry's distinctive triangular sail.

"Take the tiller, will you?"

Lyn did as Ant asked, practising a skill she'd used many times before on their outings on the wherry.

"Now that we have some peace and quiet, shall we go over our investigation? I'm worried that Riley will get to the murderer first, and that wouldn't do at all."

Ant finished tying off the rigging and deftly walked towards the stern.

"I'd forgotten how competitive you are, Lyn."

She eased the tiller to the left and guided *Field*surfer around a gentle bend in Stanton Broad.

"But you're right; if we don't crack on, that stupid policeman will beat us to it. That said, from what I'm hearing around the village, he's still treating the death as if it were accidental."

Lyn shook her head.

"He may have had a go at you in the Wherry Arms, but if he thinks that, he hasn't spoken to Jed, has he?"

Ant nodded, indicating he agreed.

"Lyn, if there's one thing I know about our dear constabulary, it's that once the investigating officer gets an idea into their head, the whole team runs with it; they've no choice. Riley is convinced Narky fell into that trench in a drunken stew and poleaxed himself when he landed."

Ant warmed to his theme.

"Let's take a step back and look at what we know about Narky. He was a bully and thirsty for cash. Perhaps Glen wasn't the only one he was trying to screw for money."

Lyn gently pushed the tiller to her right to keep *Field Surfer* in the centre of the Broad.

"Without knowing what he had against other men in the village, we could be looking at dozens of suspects, none of whom we could put under suspicion until we'd have spoken to them. After all, what did any of them have that needed a favour from a brute like Narky? It's just not a logical avenue for us to go down, Ant."

He detected the spark of inspiration from Lyn as she finished speaking.

"Yes?" said Ant.

"Wait a minute. What about... the professor?"

He smiled and gave a single clap of his hands.

"Spot on, Lyn. Think about it: the prof needed access to

the land, and Narky controlled that. Perhaps, as the dig produced more finds, the professor wanted extra time, and Narky threatened to close the site down if he didn't pay up?"

"And we've seen how short tempered the professor is when he doesn't get his own way, and we also know he's a whisky drinker."

"Right again, Lyn."

Ant could see from Lyn's expression that she had enjoyed the compliment and acknowledgement of her contribution to the investigation.

Got to make more effort on that front, he thought.

Lyn pointed towards the unfolding landscape ahead.

"You know, it still gives me a thrill every time I'm on the Broads. There's something about the calmness and space that gets to me."

Ant smiled as he recalled their adventures on *Field Surfer* as children.

"What, even when Dad was barking orders and moaning about us mucking up his prized mahogany decking with blackcurrant juice and the like?"

Lyn laughed.

"It certainly was the love of his life, wasn't it?" Lyn replied. "He spent years renovating her. Oh, and by the way, you were the mucky one, if I remember."

Ant returned Lyn's smile as he watched the boat slide effortlessly along the water making full use of the following breeze.

He scanned the horizon as the Broad opened out into a wide basin, its banks obscured by swaying stands of Norfolk reed. Overhead, set against the reddening sky and setting sun, a heron patrolled its territory on the lookout for an opportunistic meal.

"Just to confuse things, what if Narky was bumped off by

that girl you came across last night—or at least someone she knew? After all, what was she doing by the Hall at that time of night?"

Ant's sudden switch back to their investigation caught Lyn by surprise.

"What do you mean?"

"Well, think about it. Perhaps whoever killed Narky thought we were getting too close; what better way to find out what we're up to than keep watch on us?"

Lyn shook her head in disbelief.

"Isn't the idea of covert surveillance that you hide, not stand by a tree on a quiet country road wailing your eyes out?"

Ant thought for a moment and allowed his hand to brush the water, his fingers causing a tiny ripple in its surface.

"Hmm, I think what you are saying to me is that I've lost the plot."

He noticed a look of irony spreading across her face.

"To paraphrase your good self: got it in one."

The point wasn't lost on Ant. He changed the subject.

"You know, being stuck on the A47 from time to time makes me think that moving freight by water again might not be such a bad idea."

Lyn protested.

"What, and spoil all this?"

"Can't be any worse than summer tourists in their hire boats causing havoc and almost decapitating themselves on our low bridges, can it?"

The banter tailed off into silence as the wherry continued its sedate progress.

Two glasses of white wine later and a dimming light

indicated it was time to turn the wherry through 360 degrees and make for home.

"Watch out for the boom, Lyn."

She pulled the tiller hard and watched the sail flick from port to starboard. Having learnt from bitter experience, Lyn ducked allowing the boom to swing from one side of the boat to the other without hindrance.

"And before you say anything, my trusty deckhand, it wasn't my fault you fell in when we were nine."

Lyn signalled her disagreement.

"I beg to differ. You told me to fetch you the rope, knowing I'd have to stand up just before you tacked. Even your dad said it was your fault."

Lyn's concocted glare defied Ant to argue the case.

He still tried.

"As a matter of fact, I remember Dad saying it was just as much your fault for being daft enough to fall for my little jape."

"Ha ha. You admit it. You were to blame!"

Irritated at being manipulated into an admission of guilt, Ant gave the boom a push causing the wherry to jink to the left. This time Lyn was ready.

"I'm not nine anymore, Admiral Nelson."

Ant watched as a wry smile crossed her lips as she corrected the tiller to counteract Ant's attempt to catch her out.

As the vessel neared its mooring, the land sloped upward. On the horizon, the outline of dig site tents stood out against the fading sun.

"Here, grab this and tie her off," said Ant as he threw a hemp rope in Lyn's general direction.

As the familiar sight of the village green came into view, the pair veered to the left and made for the pond. They leant against a rusted rail and watched the ducks gather expectantly in front of them.

"What about your carpenter? Could he have anything to do with it?"

As she spoke, she fidgeted in her pocket for remnants she'd fed the throng with earlier in the day.

"I want to believe he's innocent, but there's something nagging at me that I need to get to the bottom of."

"Worried your loyalty to a long-standing tenant family is getting in the way of your objectivity?"

Ant turned to look at Lyn.

"Something like that."

The pair broke off eye contact to watch half a dozen ducks scurry for the crumbs on offer.

The conversation fell quiet again. The lights of the Wherry Arms flickered across the village pond. Familiar sights and sounds of a full pub filled the air. The only other noise involved Phyllis berating Betty on village gossip as they scurried home from the shop. From what Ant could deduce, Betty continued to survive their friendship only by taking every opportunity to agree with whatever it was Phyllis was saying.

Ant pulled away from the railings and pointed towards the pub.

"Your round, yes?"

"Not so fast, matey. We need to agree what we do next. Your pale ale can wait."

Lyn's rebuke made Ant focus.

"Okay, I'll catch up with the professor tomorrow then check out Glen's alibi. Now, time for that drink. Remember, you're paying."

Ant was across the narrow road and through the door of the pub before Lyn had much chance to respond.

13

A GOLDEN AFTERNOON

"Well, you did the landlord's takings a power of good when you bought that whisky," said Ant as he ambled across to Professor Pullman.

The academic didn't acknowledge Ant at first; instead, he concentrated on zipping the entrance to his tent shut.

Ant watched as Pullman slowly turned in the general direction of his voice.

"Ah, yes, Mr... or is it Lord... Stanton. Never got the hierarchy of the English nobility into my head, I'm afraid." Pullman let out a brief, nervous laugh.

Ant studied the professor as the trace of a snigger spread across the man's face.

Not impressed, matey, thought Ant.

"A little surprising, Professor, given you live in the past, so to speak?"

Ant didn't give Pullman an opportunity to respond. Instead, he watched his cheeks flush and eyes narrow.

"Given my father is the Earl of Stanton, as his eldest surviving son, it accords me the courtesy title of Lord, though actually, if we're being precise, as I know you like to be, our family name is Norton-D'Arcy, so if you wish to be formal about it, you may address me as Lord Anthony Norton-D'Arcy of Stanton."

Ant was enjoying goading the academic and could see from the man's pursed lips how well his remarks had hit home.

"But let's not stand on ceremony, Professor. We are all friends here, aren't we?"

Ant's upward inflection at the end of his comment, together with deliberate pause, invited a response from the professor. Once again, Ant didn't give him a chance to respond.

"Listen, why don't you call me Anthony. We're not ones for standing on ceremony around here, at least not amongst friends." Ant knew he had put the professor back in his box and exposed the academic's befuddled routine.

Professor Pullman turned from Ant to check the tent zip for a second time.

Ant knew the man was playing for time.

"Yes, yes, quite right, er, Anthony."

His efforts to distract attention from his stupidity didn't divert Ant's unblinking stare. Point made, Ant took the temperature out of their dialogue, if for no other reason than he wanted something important from Pullman. Information.

Not yet the time to press home my advance, thought Ant.

"Glen Stuart is a favourite whisky of mine too."

Ant could see that his change in tone had thrown the professor.

"Oh, I see. Is it?"

"It is, Professor. Scotland's finest. Though not cheap, as you know. But well worth the price."

Ant watched as the professor's demeanour changed. Suddenly he looked nervous.

"As I was saying, Professor."

"What, yes, indeed. The landlord at the Wherry Arms was, as you say, most grateful for the sale. And please forgive me for not saying hello in the pub, by the way, but the detective inspector seemed rather keen to speak with you."

The professor pulled himself to his full height and relapsed into his more usual cocky tone.

The man's renewed confidence didn't impress Ant. From memory, he recalled that by the time the professor was at the bar buying whisky, Inspector Riley had left.

"It was an emergency," continued the professor. "You see, I was replacing a bottle stolen from my tent."

Pullman half turned and nodded towards his accommodation.

Ant's eyes followed, his brain racing to make sense of the professor's unexpected response.

He could see that the man was studying him closely and worked hard not to show any reaction to the professor's explanation.

"Always happy to help our wonderful police force," replied Ant, trying to throw Pullman off balance. "They asked about my drinking habits. I imagine they've asked you too?"

Ant watched the professor for signs of agitation. There were none.

"No, no. In fact, I've seen little of the police. Not since that terrible day. Why should they be interested in an elderly academic's habits?"

It was Ant's turn to think on his feet.

Slippery fish, this one, thought Ant.

"Oh, no reason, or at least none they mentioned to me. You know the police. Information is power and all that."

The professor shrugged his shoulders.

"Glad to say I have little to do with the police. Not much call for them on archaeological digs... unless we find human remains less than two hundred years old, that is."

Ant allowed the professor to play his little game.

"And until the discovery of that unfortunate man, I had seen neither hide nor hair of the police."

As the pair took measure of the other, Ant broke his eye contact to survey the dig site. An area of around five acres, he could see the land was punctuated with several slit trenches and spoil heaps. To one side stood a large temporary building where, from its open entrance he could see, all artefacts came for cleaning before being catalogued. Next to this stood a cluster of smaller tents Ant guessed housed the undergraduates and other academics involved in the project.

"So has it been worthwhile?"

The professor hesitated.

"In the main, yes. We knew an extensive villa complex existed here. And as expected, we discovered a hypocaust used for the underfloor heating to the complex. A bonus was the smaller buildings. Servants' quarters, we think."

Ant nodded then pointed to two trenches that joined at right angles.

"Why excavate like that?"

"Well, we had a hunch that the complex met a violent end, and we've found evidence of burning. Given the owners were clearly of high status and wealthy, we were surprised not to find any precious metals."

"Perhaps they left in a hurry. You know, if they were being attacked or something?"

Ant watched as the professor gesticulated with his hands pointing first at one part of the excavation then another.

That's got him going, thought Ant.

"Yes, we think an attack by Boudica. But that's the point, you see. In such circumstances, precious items are often buried in haste. The theory is that owners hoped to retrieve them at a later date. But here, nothing. Also... what the... Blast."

The professor's words trailed off as he spotted a group of people on the far side of the dig site.

"Problem, Professor?"

"You might say so. That silly school asked if they could bring a group of children up here so that irritating metal-detecting group can show them how their infernal machines work."

Ant could see the academic fizz as he watched the gaggle of excited children form a circle around half a dozen adults. Pullman marched towards the group, his hands waving in all directions.

"Not too close. I told that woman. Only on that side of the tape, if you please. Don't you understand English?"

Ant smiled as he followed the academic, soon spotting Lyn at the centre of the group. As usual, she was directing operations, which he acknowledged was no small task when dealing with excited youngsters.

Ducking under the red-and-white, plastic tape that indicated the dig boundary, Ant came within listening distance of Lyn's group. He could see four detectorists demonstrating their machines and explaining what the different tones meant. Meanwhile, Lyn and her secretary circled the children like a pair of sheepdogs, watching out for stragglers.

The professor stood, arms folded, eyes peeled for any incursion onto his precious dig site.

"Children, who wants to have a go at finding treasure?"

Ant recoiled from the volume and pitch of screams coming from the children. They volunteered as a pack.

Hell's bells, I've known quieter battlefields, thought Ant.

"Settle down," said Lyn in a calm, assertive voice. "Everyone will get their chance. Now, James, Carol, Nick, Chloe. You four first."

The youngsters stepped forward, brimming with pride at being, in their eyes, first amongst equals. The rest let out a collective moan.

Ant watched as the professionals explained how to work a metal detector. He also noted that the professor intensified his gaze, watching for any infringement of his agreement with Lyn.

"His voice doesn't half grind," said Ant as he joined Lyn watching the excited youngsters.

"He does shout rather a lot, doesn't he, and so disorganised. Apparently, he's always forgetting stuff. At least that's what the undergraduate said I came across. You know, the one—"

"Yes, yes."

He had no wish to be reminded a second time he'd not been listening when Lyn told him about the distressed girl. "Perhaps he's just your typical academic. Bright as a button without an ounce of common sense. Or perhaps that's what he'd like people to think?"

His train of thought was interrupted by yet another increase in noise from the children as a detector let out a bright, sharp sound. Ant watched the attention the signal got from the four professional detectorists. Silence descended as one of the detectorists helped a young student turn a clod of soil with a short spade.

"Found a hoard, have you?" asked Ant, a broad smile spreading across his cheeks.

As he spoke, the child got up from his knees and held something to the light. The artefact glinted in the sun.

A gold coin.

The professor attempted to snatch the coin from the child.

"You must all vacate the dig. This land is an important archaeological site, and its history must not be disturbed by amateurs."

An embarrassed silence descended. Ant filled the void.

"Professor, as you know, this is my family's land and not yours. I will decide who, and who does not, access it."

Ant watched as the professor wasted no time in protesting.

"An artefact of historical importance has emerged. I demand that—"

Ant had had enough.

"You demand nothing, Professor. Now, shall we all enjoy the find by having a good look at it, children?"

Pullman's chastened reply disappeared beneath a collective cheer from the children.

It took only a few minutes for the children to tire of examining the coin.

Might as well have been a bottle top, thought Ant, before noticing Lyn trying to catch his eye.

"Lyn, time to get this lot back to school before they scatter all over the place. Professor, I suppose you might want the coin?"

Ant could see Pullman didn't need asking twice. He

snatched the precious artefact and made off at pace for the finds tent.

That just left Ant and the four detectorists looking at the hole left from digging the coin up.

"That reminds me," said Ant as he watched the detectorists pack away their beloved machines. "Can you ask Vikki to get in touch. I'd like to speak to her again. You've all been so good with the kids. The least I can do is buy her a new machine—but don't tell her why I want to see her."

Ant immediately saw how pleased her colleagues were with his offer.

As they were leaving, one of the group turned back to Ant.

"Funny thing is, it's not the first time that hole has been dug."

Ant looked puzzled.

"What I mean is, whoever first dug that hole knew what they were doing. We have a special way of doing it, you see, so that when we put the loose earth back, we leave as little damage as possible. Farmers don't like a mess being left that might hurt their beasts."

Ant nodded.

"I get what you mean; beasts with broken legs are not a pleasant sight."

The detectorists nodded in agreement.

"So you're saying that someone who knows what they are doing goes to the trouble of digging a great hole. And to cap it all, they leave a gold coin that a child manages to find?"

"That's my point. I don't think it was so much not finding it, rather leaving it behind. Perhaps they were in a hurry?" replied the detectorist.

Ant looked back at the hole.

"Are you saying there's more down there?"

"I'm saying it's likely there *was* more than one coin down there."

The detectorist held a shard of unglazed pottery in front of him.

Ant examined the fragment of baked clay.

"What is it?"

"We think it's part of the pot that contained a hoard. From its diameter of this bit, I'd say it was huge. Look, there are more remnants scattered around, so I'm sure we're right. We're just surprised the professor didn't pick up on it."

Ant's suspicions intensified.

A professor who plays the fool, a detectorist who claims she suffered an attack, and a would-be blackmailer.

Time to try out a few theories, thought Ant.

14

GIFT HORSES

"Wow, a great place you've got. Beats my studio flat," said Vikki as she strolled along the marble-columned entrance and into Stanton Hall's oak-panelled morning room.

Ant's eyes followed Vikki's gaze up to the high ceiling decorated with gilded plasterwork. At its centre hung a glittering crystal chandelier.

"An accident of history as it happens. Believe it or not, one of my ancestors won it on the turn of a card. Fortunately for the family, the guy died before his luck at cards ran out and he lost it again."

Vikki smiled, shaking her head in disbelief as he gave her a potted history of the Hall.

"And one thing the male line paid particular attention to was marrying well. Hence, we're still here."

"Not earned wealth, then?"

Ant looked at Vikki, his eyes narrowing in playful rapprochement.

"Do I detect the merest hint of disapproval? Perhaps

you're right, but we do our bit to use the estate to help the village economy."

Vikki laughed again.

"Yeah right, I bet you do."

Ant led his companion through to the great hall and into one corner. Behind an ornate Georgian sofa stood two old, red leather fire buckets, on which faded traces of the family coat of arms remained just visible.

"Alas, they're not needed in case of fire. The opposite, in fact. When it rains, we have these all over the Hall; it's one thing to own a grade-one-listed building. Quite another having the dosh to keep it going."

Ant was impressed as he watched Vikki look closer at the fabric of the building with what looked to him like a keen interest.

Perhaps she does understand, he thought.

On went the tour, room by room, until they arrived at the library.

"Dad's favourite room," said Ant as he made his way over to a large mahogany reading table on which rested an oblong box with a picture of a metal detector on the side.

"Here, for you."

Vikki's cheeks flushed.

"This is so generous of you... and I'm sorry if—"

"Not at all, it's a perfectly reasonable reaction. I thought much the same myself growing up here. That was until I realised how many villagers rely on the Hall for their living."

Ant sensed Vikki relaxing, which given the real reason for his invitation, he knew to be important.

"As for the detector. You deserve it. Your club has done so much for us, both on the dig, and in working with the kids."

Before either could continue with their conversation, a quiet knock on the heavy oak doors interrupted their flow. In walked one of the day helpers with a tray of tea and shortcake biscuits.

"Great job, Tim. Thanks for that."

The immaculately dressed young man placed the refreshments on a side table next to an unlit fire.

Vikki had a "how did he do that" look on her face as Ant handed the perplexed woman her tea, courtesy of a delicate bone-china cup and saucer.

"Not magic, Vikki. I arranged for Tim to bring us drinks when he heard us enter the library. Milk and sugar? And how about a biscuit?"

Vikki declined the sugar and nabbed two biscuits as she accepted his invitation to sit.

Several minutes passed as they exchanged views on securing access to land by detectorists and the scourge of nighthawking.

Ant turned the conversation to more pressing matters.

"It certainly was a nasty business up at the dig site, wasn't it? I mean someone going for you like that. Then there's the dead bloke."

Once again, Ant watched Vikki's body language to see if his gentle probing had any giveaway signs of defensiveness.

Am I on the money, or is two and two making five? he thought.

He could see Vikki looked uncomfortable.

"Please, forgive me. I didn't mean to bring back memories of something I quite understand you'd rather forget."

"It's okay," said Vikki, her voice shaking. "You're right. It was horrible. But at least I'm still here. The one thing I can't get out of my head is what if..."

Vikki's voice tailed off as she gazed into the blackened fire at the back of the stone hearth.

Ant allowed the silence to continue until he judged she'd gathered her composure.

"Best not to think about the 'what ifs.' You're here; you're safe. That's what matters, Vikki."

Ant could see that his guest took comfort from his words.

Now or never, thought Ant.

"The thing is, Vikki, the killer is still out there, and you can help catch whoever murdered Narky."

Vikki's eyes began to veer away from the hearth and towards Ant. Her hands gripped the lionhead armrests of her chair.

"How? I've already told you everything. I was up there with permission. A man jumped me. I walloped him and ran—and I didn't see a body."

He watched as her eyes burned into him. Her tone exuded defiance.

Ant nodded his head as she spoke. His intention was to show empathy.

"Something is nagging away at me. A conundrum, you might say. I don't believe someone as committed to metal detecting as you, having paid almost two thousand pounds for your machine, would just leave it where you dropped it.

"What do you mean? I told you I killed no one. I didn't know a man had died until your friend told me, so—"

"But that's my point," Ant interrupted. "I accept you were not involved. And so you had no reason to believe the man who attacked you would still be there later that night."

Vikki broke off eye contact. Her head dropped. She slumped into the safety of the thick leather, button-back chair.

"So you see. If I had been you, I'd have gone back to collect my metal detector. That's what you did, wasn't it, Vikki?"

She half turned her head to look at her interrogator.

He sensed the words she wanted to say wouldn't come.

She nodded her head.

Ant raised himself from the chair and crossed the few feet that separated them. He crouched beside the woman and took hold of her hand. His reassurance worked as he felt her white-knuckle grip on the chair arm loosen.

"I went back on Friday evening. Like you said, I assumed no one would be up there, and I wanted my detector back. But as I got to the top of the slope, I could hear two voices. Two men arguing."

"Yes, go on," interrupted Ant in a low, quiet voice.

"They didn't see me... and I sure as hell didn't want to get involved. I assumed they were nighthawks. You know, like I explained before, detectorists that dig land when it's dark without permission and steal whatever they find."

"But why?" he asked, his voice quiet and non-judgemental.

Vikki grimaced.

"Bad lot, they are. We all get tarred with the same brush."

Ant could see, almost feel, the depth of her hatred she felt for such people.

"I get you. But let me ask again. Why did you think they were detecting?"

"Because the fat one was on his knees digging at something. The other one, the thin one, was standing over him shouting his head off."

Ant could see the effect the recollection was having on Vikki.

"I know it's hard, but can you remember what the thin bloke said?"

Vikki's eyes scanned the books lining the surrounding shelves as if she were searching for the words to use.

"Look. While they were arguing I saw my detector, grabbed it, and ran like hell before they cottoned on I was there."

She pulled her hand away from Ant's reassuring embrace as if to confirm the interrogation was over and she intended to leave.

Ant sensed he had only one more chance to prise further information from her.

"Listen. I know you had nothing to do with Narky's murder. Do you hear me? You have done nothing wrong. But if there's anything more you can remember about that night, it might just help catch the killer."

By now he had clasped Vikki's hand again. His voice deep and quiet. His eyes not allowing Vikki to break eye contact.

She closed her eyes as if running a film tape, turning her head like a downhill skier practising the twists and turns of the course before leaving the starting gate.

"'Leave it. Leave it down there.' That's what the thin one said... or something like that. Yes, I'm sure that's what he said. At least that's all I heard."

Ant worked hard to hide his excitement.

Now we're cooking with gas, he thought.

"Vikki, you've been so brave. Thank you. Who knows, you might just have helped clear this mess up and get a killer off the streets."

* * *

IMPATIENT TO TELL Lyn about his evening's work, Ant picked up the 1970s-style phone at the bottom of the hall staircase and dialled her number. Frustrated at not getting an answer he left a breathy message.

15
ABSENT FRIENDS

"At least you picked my message up this time," said Ant as Lyn shut the front door, and he followed her into the kitchen. "I thought you didn't like mess."

Lyn shrugged her shoulders as she looked upon the scene of general dishevelment with heaps of student exercise books scattered around the worktops.

"This is the result of just one member of staff going off sick. Dozens of the stupid things to mark, and a Rubik's Cube of a puzzle to redo the staff timetables."

Ant headed over to the coffee percolator and grabbed two mugs.

"Then I guess you could do with one of these?"

As Ant handed Lyn the steaming drink, he folded the timetable planner in two with his free hand.

"Don't think you'd appreciate me spilling coffee all over your new staff rotas."

Lyn didn't need to answer. Ant could see her look was enough.

"What's so important you needed to stop me working out how to cover my classes tomorrow?"

Ant could see she hadn't the slightest interest in his unexpected visit.

"You know. Narky's been dead for almost a week now, and the police, as far as I know, are nowhere near finding out how or why he ended up in that ditch. That's because…"

"That's because Riley thinks there's nothing to investigate."

Ant waited for Lyn to finish then left several seconds before continuing for added effect.

"That's because Riley's lazy and looking for a quick fix."

Lyn shook her head as she again focused on the piles of student work awaiting attention.

Ant followed his friend's eyes around the room.

"What if I told you Vikki King holds the key to this whole thing?"

Lyn's eyes flashed, her attention on Ant restored.

"Remember, it was you who thought she killed him all along, and—"

She interrupted again.

"And?"

Lyn placed her mug of coffee on the table.

"If you would let me finish," said Ant, his voice tinged with frustration at having his flow curtailed. "I have an idea how we can prove she did, or did not, do it."

Ant watched Lyn play with her mug, turning it on the spot by its handle.

"Well, Sherlock, what's your plan?"

Ant smiled. He'd known his friend long enough to know when he was being goaded.

"I refuse to rise to that," he said, acknowledging Lyn's smirk.

Ant explained his meeting with Vikki earlier in the day.

Lyn listened, examining every word to see if it reinforced her belief she'd been right about "VK."

"But that doesn't move us on much, does it? Yes, Vikki's admitted she went back for her detector and saw a thin bloke standing over a fat bloke digging. What if they were nighthawks after all? We'll never find them, let alone prove either had anything to do with Narky's death."

Ant once again made his way over to the coffee percolator and topped up both mugs before resuming his chair.

"There were no nighthawks up there that night." Ant spoke with a certainty that surprised Lyn.

"How can you be so sure?" The dig has been on regional TV several times, so plenty of people knew of its existence. Also, I'm told the detectorist club advertised the rally in at least four specialist magazines plus loads of detectorist forums. If I was inclined to do a spot of midnight treasure hunting, I'd have known where to be. After all, I'd be one of a hundred comparative strangers roaming the place swinging a detector."

Ant nodded, acknowledging the logic of Lyn's argument.

"I know because I checked," replied Ant. "In fact, there has been no nighthawk activity in this part of Norfolk for six months. Not since the police nabbed three blokes in April near Wells-next-the-Sea. They won't be out of prison for a year or two yet."

Lyn held her coffee midway between the table and her lips, waving a plume of steam away from her face.

"Checked? I thought you couldn't stand the police?"

Ant risked overacting as he folded his arms and elevated his chin.

"That's a terrible impression of Mussolini. And that didn't end well for him, did it?" chided Lyn.

Ant's hurt look amused Lyn. His pride pricked, he resumed without the folded arms or puffed-out chest.

"Intelligence work comes with its perks, Lyn. I do not need to trouble the likes of our beloved Riley when I need information, if you get my drift."

"Don't be so pompous, Ant. It doesn't suit you," quipped Lyn, determined to ground her best friend.

It was Ant's turn to play with his coffee mug now.

"Anyway, you were telling me about what Vikki said to you before she left. Come on, let's have it, Sherlock." Lyn spoke with a renewed interest, having bested her friend.

"Hmm," Ant replied, not at all pleased Lyn had won round one in the "who's the boss" stakes.

Deciding not to dwell on the verbal beating Lyn had given him, Ant erred on the side of brevity.

"Vikki told me the thin one said, 'Leave it down there.'"

Ant watched as Lyn thought for a moment and looked over to a pine plate rack hanging on the wall to her right, her eyes dancing as if she were counting its contents.

"What if the fat one was Narky, and he'd found something the thin one wanted?"

"Or he went to retrieve something the thin one had already discovered? And what if the thin one was the one who jumped her earlier that night?" said Ant.

Lyn jumped up to retrieve a scrap of paper from the sideboard in the hallway.

"I drew this last weekend when I was trying to make sense of what happened the night Narky was murdered."

She laid her sketch out on the tabletop.

"So here's the trench where Narky was found. And here's the spoil heap." Lyn's finger moved over the sketch at a feverish pace as she shared its contents. "Over here are the archaeologists' accommodation and the finds tent."

The only area not marked was where Vikki said she saw the two men arguing.

Ant filled in the missing information.

"It was here, given the position she must have been in as she came up the slope. This must be it."

He pointed to a position on Lyn's sketch then marked it with a pen taken from his breast pocket.

Both studied the document, moving fingers across its surface as they conjectured what might have happened.

"Hang on," said Lyn as she tapped a finger on the map. "That's around the position one of my pupils found the coin."

Ant noticed her eyes widen as the connection she'd made hit home.

He paced around the dining table without once taking his eyes off the sketch.

"So," he began, "let's assume the fat one was Narky Collins. We know he was hungry for money. To end up in a trench with his head caved in must mean he was trying to relieve someone else of a great deal of cash—"

"Or something worth a lot of money?" Lyn interrupted.

"Yes," replied Ant. "The question is, who was he stealing from?"

He could see Lyn was deep in thought, her eyes fixed on the sketch.

"Lyn?"

"I wonder," she said.

Ant decided not to ask the obvious question; instead, letting his friend follow through in her own time.

"You know the girl I mentioned to you. The one I came across when—"

"Her again? Wendy, wasn't it?"

"Well, I spotted her going into Hammond's Bakery at

lunchtime when I was travelling back to school from a meeting. Turns out she bought a tuna bap. Not my cup of tea, but..."

Ant couldn't hide his exasperation at the needless detail.

Lyn ignored his protest.

"So I took the opportunity to sit with her under the old buttercross and have a chat. She was a lot calmer than the other night, I can tell you. In fact, she apologised."

Ant frowned.

"And...?"

Lyn sighed.

"Well, it turns out someone wasn't where they should have been. With Wendy, I mean."

Ant understood at once.

"The question is, if they didn't meet Wendy, where were they last Friday night?"

"Got it in one," replied Lyn, her face mirroring Ant's in their growing anticipation at having cracked the case.

"I've got an idea," said Ant, as he leant into the table and pointed at a small circle on the sketch.

"Meet me here at ten tomorrow morning. And I need these people with you. All of them. I don't care what you tell them; just get them up there."

Ant scribbled several names on the back of Lyn's sketch before passing it to her.

"Good job I've a good deputy head. Friday can be a hell of a day at school, you know," said Lyn as she glanced at the list.

16

HATS OFF

Hope Lyn got everyone there, thought Ant as he ran through how he intended to unmask Narky's killer. He rehearsed what might go wrong. Above all, he didn't want to make a fool of himself in front of Detective Inspector Riley. Ant knew his pride shouldn't come into it. But...

Not going to happen, he thought.

"What's all this about, Anthony?" asked the professor, as he spotted his patron approaching.

Ant held his hand.

"Nice to see you, again, Professor. The place looks busy today," replied Ant, ignoring the academic's question.

Professor Pullman shook the hand, his grip firm.

"That head-teacher woman wishes to dragoon me into a meeting in the finds tent. She's already press-ganged a number of my staff. Said you wanted to talk to us all about something important?"

Ant could see Pullman's response laid bare his irritation at being told what to do. He played with the academic.

"Come, come, Professor. It sounds like you don't like being ordered around by a woman?"

He led Pullman to the finds tent, pleased that Pullman bit as he bristled at Ant's implied accusation of misogyny.

Ant deployed a well-trodden management trick, guaranteed to cement his position as top dog between the two.

"Don't be so defensive, Professor."

Pullman fell for it and gave Ant the response he'd anticipated.

"Defensive. I'm not, I—"

Ant purposely interrupted the professor.

"You are, Professor, but not to worry; we're here now."

Ant knew his tactic to be a cheap shot, but he knew its effect would be important in forcing the professor onto the back foot.

That worked a treat, thought Ant.

Ant pulled aside the entrance flap of the finds tent, which rippled in the strong breeze that had wafted across the dig site all morning.

"Please take a seat, Professor. Here, let me help you," said Ant as he cleared items of clothing from a vacant chair. He gestured for the academic to sit.

"Good morning, Detective Inspector Riley. Thank you for coming. Of course you know the professor. Not sure if you've met Glen Dawson, who is our estate carpenter, Also, Vikki King, a local metal detectorist?"

Ant pointed to the two individuals in turn.

"By the way, you two. Thank you for responding to Lyn's invitation so positively."

The police force's representative was less content with unfolding events.

"We passed the time of day while waiting for your gracious arrival," replied Riley.

"I suppose you think you're clever?"

Ant smiled as he watched Riley take out his pocketbook with an exaggerated flourish.

"Wasting police time is a serious offence, you know."

Ant purposely turned away from the detective before the man had finished speaking.

"Wasting your time is the last thing I wish to do, Riley."

Ant could see his ruse had worked as the policeman stiffened, clearly taking umbrage at his tormentor's attitude. Ant knew Riley was all the angrier for having to put up with treatment he'd accept from no one but his superiors.

Point made; Ant continued.

"It's about Narky Collins. Now I know that you, Detective Inspector, and your team have tried your hardest to solve the case, but—"

He could see Riley was spitting feathers to interrupt his nemesis.

"Solve *the case*? What do you mean, man? The matter is closed. That unfortunate man fell into the trench in a drunken stupor, hit his head, and died. That's an end to it; do you hear?"

Ant saw Riley looked self-satisfied putting his interrogator in his place. The three other guests also relaxed on hearing the detective's conclusions.

Ant pressed a finger to his lips, frowned, and tilted his head forward as if in deep thought.

"Well," said Ant, raising his head and looking towards Riley, "what if I told you how Mr. Collins *really* met his end? And what if I could prove murder and hand the killer over to you this morning?"

"What are you talking about, man? Are you mad? Proof? What proof?"

As Riley finished speaking, two figures entered the tent.

"Ah, Lyn, good to see you both. Simon, thank you for coming. Take a seat," said Ant.

The detective's confused state reached new heights as the pair occupied the two remaining chairs.

"And who may I ask is this young man?"

The detective gave Simon a withering stare.

"Oh, he's one of my undergraduates, though I'm as baffled as you as to why he's here."

"All in good time, Professor, Detective Inspector," said Ant.

Ant watched the colour drain from Pullman's face.

"This gentleman, Detective, likes to be in charge. In fact, he insists on everything being done his way. Isn't that so, Professor?"

Pullman uncrossed his arms and brushed imaginary mud from his trouser knees, trying hard to look in control.

"If you mean I insist on my staff being professional at all times, then I plead guilty." Pullman puffed out his chest and wafted a hand at Ant as if to bat away his accusation.

"Quite right, Professor," replied Ant before continuing. "You have a heavy responsibility that requires a firm hand. That's true, isn't it… Simon?"

The undergraduate froze at being singled out.

"Don't worry, Simon. I'm not asking you to criticise the professor. I know how important he is to your future. But all the same, he's not treated you well, has he?"

Simon gazed at the floor. Ant guessed he wished he was anywhere except in this tent.

Ant turned back towards the policeman.

"Did you know the professor is a whisky drinker, Detective Inspector?"

Ant could see Pullman was showing signs of panic.

"Look here. I had nothing to do with that nasty man's death. I—"

Ant interrupted.

"How did you know he was a nasty man, Professor? After all, it's not as if you're a local, is it?"

Ant could see the detective's eyes darting between the professor and him, unsure where the conversation was going. He guessed Riley was kicking himself for not checking the academic's drinking habit during his investigation of Narky's death.

"You may think we academics live in ivory towers," replied the professor, "but we see; we hear. I observed him in the pub and the way he treated people."

"Then you had a reason to dislike him?" said Ant.

Pullman glared at his interrogator, at one point rising from his chair, before thinking better of the idea.

"Don't be ridiculous, man. How might dislike morph into murder? And what about motive?"

Ant smiled. He had achieved his purpose.

"As you say, Professor. What motive might you have had?"

The academic settled back into his chair, unsure whether his interrogation had concluded or merely been paused.

"And talking about motive," said Ant as he turned towards Glen Dawson.

The carpenter froze at the unwanted attention.

"But Ant, I thought you believed me when I explained—"

Ant held an open palm towards Glen.

"The thing is, Glen, when we last met, you told me you hadn't seen Narky in the week leading up to his death. Isn't that so?"

Ant watched as the carpenter looked towards the tent entrance.

"No help out there, Glen."

Ant moved to his left, blocking any attempt the carpenter might make to bolt.

After a few seconds of silence, Glen responded.

"I admit it..."

Ant watched as Riley fumbled in his jacket.

Going for the handcuffs already, thought Ant.

"I confronted the nasty bugger in the Hall's stable block. I told him I'd had enough, and he could bugger off. I said I was going to shop him to you for fiddling all those invoices."

Ant closed the space between the carpenter and himself, looking down at the hapless man.

"But why didn't you tell me that before, Glen? Don't you trust me?"

He watched as Glen began to break down. It wasn't a sight he liked to watch.

"I was ashamed and thought you might think I'd done him in if you knew we'd been arguing. The day before he died, Narky got in such a rage, screaming and shouting. I thought he was going to clobber me. I think I might have threatened him. I can't remember, but I was scared. I ran out of the yard, and that's the last time I saw him, swear to God."

Ant allowed the carpenter to compose himself before addressing Riley.

"Detective Inspector, did you know Narky Collins was blackmailing Glen, and who knows how many other men in the village? One for the ladies was Narky, whether they wanted the attention or not."

Inspector Riley adopted his now all too familiar bemused look.

"The reason for the blackmail isn't important, but—"

"But perhaps, a motive for murder," shot back Riley, gaining confidence he could take things from here.

"Mr Dawson, where were you on—"

"No, no," said Ant, cutting across the detective. "Glen didn't kill Narky Collins. I invited him here today only to show you just what a bad lot Narky was. Glen, like a few other men in the village were, I suspect, not too upset to hear of the man's death. But did he murder him? No."

Ant smiled at Glen, who he noticed was fidgeting with a toggle on his coat.

"Ant, I don't know whether to laugh or throw up. Are you telling me you believe me after all?"

Riley began to stand up, handcuffs in hand.

"Not so fast, Detective."

He turned back to Glen.

"Yes, I do believe you. As luck would have it, someone witnessed that argument."

Ant watched as Glen once more began to get tearful.

"I asked estate staff, who normally come across you, if they'd seen you with Narky. As it turns out, Graham, the stable lad, heard a kerfuffle as he was cleaning out my father's mare. I have to tell you it didn't look good for you... until he said he'd also seen you the next evening going into your workshop at the back of the stable block. He added you were making a hell of a din with your machines, by the way. So you see, if you'd told me when I first mentioned Narky to you, I could have checked your alibi out and informed the good detective here. As it is, you're lucky I asked around, aren't you?"

Ant approached Glen again, this time patting him on the shoulder as he watched the man visibly slump into his chair.

Riley sat down again, pushed the handcuffs back into his

pocket. It looked to Ant as if he were watching a man losing his bet on what he thought was a sure thing.

"I will check to see if your alibi stands up or if this is a fairy tale. Do you understand, Mr Dawson?"

The carpenter nodded. Ant could see he was exhausted by events.

"However, Detective Inspector, someone in this tent *did* commit a violent act the night Narky died."

Ant turned towards Vikki.

"Isn't that so, Miss King?"

The woman frowned as Ant turned towards her.

"A person who kept the fact secret, and which might have condemned her, until Lyn and I dragged the truth out of her."

All eyes fell on the detectorist.

Ant watched as her anger grew.

"But... but, I told you, I... You've been so kind. Why are you—?"

"Please do not confuse a single act of kindness with belief in your story, Miss King."

Ant could see he was unsettling the woman as she shifted nervously in her chair.

"And what have you to say about Miss King, Detective?"

Ant turned to the policeman, urging him to respond.

"But we interviewed dozens of them at the rally."

That one hit home, thought Ant, as he watched the detective do up then undo the buttons of his jacket.

"That may be so, but this lady hit a man that night and brought him to his knees. Isn't that correct, Vikki?"

She panicked and tried to run for it. Riley reacted in an instant and grabbed the terrified woman, restraining her arms while retrieving a pair of handcuffs from his jacket pocket for the second time.

"Vikki King," the inspector began, as he clamped the hard iron restraints on the woman's wrists. "Can you explain—"

"That won't be necessary," said Ant, cutting across the detective.

Ant knew he had again succeeded in angering Riley as he watched the detective's frustration bubble to the surface.

"Although Vikki did, indeed, clobber someone that night, it was self-defence. Isn't that right... Simon?"

Ant had managed, in one sentence, to confuse everyone in the tent. A brief silence was broken by the sound of Vikki gently crying, her eyes glistening with tears.

"Please, Detective, allow the young lady to resume her seat. She is not our murderer, as I shall explain in due course."

Ant touched a hand to his chin and looked at the floor.

"Now, what was I saying. Yes, that's it: Simon, you attacked Vikki, didn't you?"

The undergraduate failed to react to the resumption of Ant's interrogation. Instead, he concentrated on fiddling with his iPhone.

"Isn't that right, Simon."

This time Ant raised his voice, simultaneously wrestling the gadget from the young man's vice-like grip.

Simon avoided Ant's eyeline for several seconds.

"Specifically, Detective Inspector, this young man attacked Miss King last Friday night. Correct, Simon?"

He's a cool one, thought Ant as he watched the young man stare at Vikki then Detective Inspector Riley as if dumbfounded as to why anyone might accuse him of such a thing.

"Did you attack this lady, Mr Hangmead?" asked Riley as he released Vikki from the wrist restraints.

Ant broke off from Simon and searched the caller list of the undergraduate's mobile.

"Please don't do that. It's private."

Ant ignored the young man. He scrolled down the screen, stopping at one particular entry. He smiled as his thumb rested on the name he had been searching for.

"Leave it!" shouted Simon. His demand startling everyone, except Ant.

"It's him," said Vikki, her tone strong, angry, resolute.

This time the inspector's job involved restraining Vikki from lunging at the undergraduate.

Simon stood between attacker and target.

Relative calm restored, Ant handed the mobile to Lyn and resumed his interrogation.

"Do you have a receding-hair problem, Simon? I know a lot of men can be self-conscious about such things."

He watched as the young man first glare then smile dismissively and shake his head.

"Then why are you so wedded to your hat? Every time I've seen you, you've been wearing it. Even when it's dull. In fact, there's a distinct lack of sun in here, and yet there it sits upon your head."

Simon raised a hand and adjusted the visor as if checking it was still in place.

"Never give it a thought. It's just something I always wear. What's wrong with that?" he said, his voice giving away his growing nervousness.

"Oh, nothing," responded Ant casually. "It's the neck cover that intrigues me. I'm sure you'd feel better without it in this stuffy tent. Why not take the hat off? Here, let me help you."

As Ant neared, Simon stiffened.

"No, don't."

Ant reached forward to lift the hat from Simon's head.

"There we go. Now, isn't that better?"

The undergraduate placed a hand over the back of his neck.

"What do we have here, my friend?"

Simon bristled. His nostrils flared.

"Let's show these good people what you've been hiding," said Ant as he spun Simon 180 degrees.

The manoeuvre exposed a two-inch gash, red raw with a flap of scabbed skin covering the injury.

"Bloody hell," said Vikki. "It was you who jumped me. That's where I hit you with my detector. Git, you could have killed me."

Simon struggled against Ant's firm hold.

"More like you could have killed me. I thought you were a nighthawk stealing from the dig site. All I was doing was protecting our work, that's all," replied Simon.

Ant watched the professor smile at his undergraduate, proud that a member of his staff had proved his loyalty to the team.

His indulgence didn't last long.

"Oh, if only that were true," said Ant, his grip tightening as Simon struggled. "Vikki was nowhere near the dig area, at least not the official one. But she *was* close to an area you wanted for yourself. You didn't know she'd left her detector after fending you off, only to come back later to retrieve it. It was then she saw a tall, thin man standing over a fat bloke. Also, she's just identified you as the man she heard shouting 'Leave it down there.'"

Simon ceased his struggle as he attempted to gather his thoughts.

"But she couldn't have seen me later. I was with my girlfriend. I can prove it. How could I be in two places at once?"

Across the tent, Lyn flicked the screen of the undergraduate's mobile phone before glancing in Ant's direction. She offered an almost imperceptible nod of her head.

Good, you've seen that name too, thought Ant.

"You can come in now, Tina."

Ant spoke just loud enough to penetrate the tent's canvas structure.

Lyn's school secretary entered, followed by a young woman. Ant watched Lyn smile at Tina, acknowledging a job well done.

"This, Detective Inspector, is Wendy Jones. She is also one of the professor's undergraduates… and sometimes girlfriend of Mr Hangmead. Isn't that right, Simon?"

Simon threw Wendy a menacing look. She turned away.

"Simon is right in one sense. He *should* have been with this young lady. But he didn't show up, did he, Wendy?"

Simon attempted to intervene.

"Wendy… tell them…"

The young woman concentrated her eyes on Riley.

"We should have met, but he didn't show. The next day he told me the professor had called an urgent meeting he had to attend. Stupidly, I believed him."

Professor Pullman shook his head as Riley looked at the academic for confirmation.

"I later checked with a few of the other undergraduates. There was no meeting. I thought he was cheating on me like he has before, so when Lyn came across me that night I… I…"

Ant took the opportunity to focus their attention back on the angry, young man.

"So what happened, Simon?" asked Ant in a quiet but determined tone that required an answer.

Simon looked around before sitting down and casually crossing his legs and his arms.

"I don't know what you're talking about. I've done nothing wrong except stand up my girlfriend for—"

"For what, Simon?"

Ant cut across the undergraduate hoping to throw him off guard.

"A village girl I met weeks ago. Very obliging, you know, these locals."

Lyn caught Ant's attention.

"May I have a word with Casanova, here?"

Ant held an arm out towards the young man.

"I thought you might." He smiled as Lyn stepped forward.

"Two-timing a girlfriend is never a good idea, chappie. It always comes back to bite you. But for the sake of our general amusement, let's play your little game, shall we?"

Ant was intrigued where Lyn was about to take things.

"Of course, you know I am the local head teacher, don't you? That means all the local children go through my hands at some point in their lives. Not only that, but I like to keep tabs on my charges as they grow, and as you say, this is a small place. So do tell me the name of your latest conquest, Simon?"

Ant watched the undergraduate's smile fade as he narrowed his eyes. It was the same look he'd seen the young man give the professor when being told off for questioning the importance of a find he had dropped. This time Ant could see the man was having trouble controlling his anger.

Better get ready to get between these two, he thought.

"I can't remember," replied Simon, brushing Lyn's question aside with disdain.

Better be careful, young fella. She's onto you, thought Ant.

"Really? You'll have to do better than that for the detective, here."

Ant flicked a glance at the policeman. He appeared pleased to have been acknowledged.

"Felicity. Her name was Felicity—"

"Do we have such a lady in the village, Lyn?" interrupted Ant.

He watched as his friend's face lit up like a candle.

"Ah yes, I know Felicity. Such an unusual name, Simon. In fact, we have just one Felicity in the village."

Ant turned his attention back to the undergraduate. He was clutching the sides of his seat so hard his knuckles had turned white.

"Now unless our Felicity, or Flo as we know her, has turned into a cougar, she wouldn't be your type, Simon."

Ant was joined in a throaty giggle by Glen.

"You see, Flo is a ninety-three-year-old."

The laughter increased with Ant leading the chorus.

"Now you've got me intrigued, Simon. Do tell us more."

The undergraduate's shoulders slumped for a moment. It wasn't long before he regained his composure.

"So, her name wasn't Flo... or whatever. It was..."

"Stop it. Stop it now, and tell the truth. Just for once."

Ant, like everyone else, including Simon, was startled by Wendy's anguished intervention.

The occupants of the tent fell into complete silence. Ant watched as Wendy's eyes burned into Simon's expressionless face.

"Let's drop the charade, Simon. There was no other girl. There was no urgent meeting with the professor. You were too busy doing more important things as you saw it. Is that not the case?"

Ant studied his foe's body language closely as he spoke.

"I've only met you a few times, and fleetingly at that, and yet I watched as your anger almost got the better of you. Now let's say you had a deal with Narky, and he tried to double-cross you. Perhaps on that particular night you couldn't hold your temper and hit out. It might even have been self-defence. But either way, your actions resulted in that man's death. Isn't that so?"

Ant half expected Simon to erupt and allow his bubbling anger free reign. Instead, the undergraduate's demeanour slowly, imperceptibly at first, began to change. As he relaxed back into his chair he began to smirk.

"He got greedy. Stupid, ignorant thugs always do." I found a hoard of gold coins. All my own research. It took months of trawling through archives. The professor thinks I'm stupid. Well, look who found the gold."

Professor Pullman blinked as he took in the enormity of Simon's confession and the consequences for his professional reputation.

"Anyway, that stupid fool somehow found out. Don't ask me how. He came sniffing around and said he would tell the professor if I didn't give him a cut of the money."

Ant put his hands into his pockets and spoke in a calm, measured voice.

"So, you murdered him?"

Simon glanced at Ant who watched as his smirk broadened into a smile, shrugged his shoulders, and swung his crossed leg up and down as if maintaining the beat of a favourite music track.

"I told you, he got greedy. I agreed to pay him to keep him quiet, but then I came across him excavating the hoard. He must have been watching me for days. Anyway, he got what he deserved. His fault, not mine. Simples."

Ant could see the casualness of Simon Hangmead's

confession appalled everyone, except him and Riley. They'd listened to such excuses for murder many times.

"So you killed him and staged the scene?" said the detective inspector.

Simon laughed.

"He took some getting into that trench, the fat sod. But yes, I found a piece of a detector and couldn't believe my luck when I saw her initials on it. Then I found that note from him." Simon pointed to Glen. "I stuck it in the dead bloke's hand and closed his fist around it then put the stone under his head. Job done. Oh, except for the whisky. I think that was a great touch, don't you?"

Even Ant now flinched at the cold-heartedness with which the young man spoke.

"Except, Simon," said Ant, "Narky Collins didn't drink whisky. If you had used beer, you might have got away with it, except you aren't as clever as you think, are you?"

The undergraduate's smile vanished.

The tent fell silent, except for the quiet weeping of Wendy as she realised her gentle, well-mannered boyfriend was, in reality, a callous murderer.

EPILOGUE

"Lord Stanton," said Detective Inspector Riley as he slipped into the passenger seat of the police Jaguar. "You were right about Simon hiding the hoard in that spoil heap. However, next time I'll arrest you for obstruction and concealing evidence. Do we understand one another?"

Ant raised his right hand to his forehead as if doffing an imaginary cap.

Riley turned to glare at Ant as the police car sped from Stanton Hall in a cloud of dust.

"Let me guess," said Lyn as she linked arms and strolled into the walled garden with her best friend. "I'm thinking he wasn't inviting you to the station Christmas party this year?"

"Er, no. But I got a 'thank you.' At least that's how I take not getting myself arrested, anyway. And another thing—would you believe he almost got my title right!"

Ant felt the gentle squeeze of Lyn's hand on his arm. Both laughed.

"So our dear detective inspector knows you're a real lord!"

"It would seem so, Lyn."

There followed a cry of pain as Ant reacted to Lyn pinching the soft flesh of his exposed arm.

"What was that for?"

"To prick that pompous ego of yours."

"Joking. I was joking."

Ant attempted to massage out the pain and offered Lyn sight of his injury.

Lyn giggled.

"All the same, you need reminding."

Ten minutes passed as the pair strolled along the meandering gravel path of the enclosed garden. From time to time, one or the other would extend a hand to catch the top of a rose or line of lavender. They reached the bench they'd last sat on one week earlier.

"So what will you do?" asked Lyn, her tone serious.

Ant knew what Lyn meant. He hesitated. Instead, he tracked a flock of geese as they flew over the great house.

As the seconds ticked away, he knew Lyn expected an answer.

"I report to my commanding officer on Monday morning. After that, a medical assessment. Then we'll see."

Lyn swayed to her left and gently body bumped Ant. It was her way of letting him know she understood.

"The thing is, Lyn, whether they pass me fit or not, there's Mum and Dad to think about, let alone this place."

Lyn turned to look at her friend.

"Sounds as if you've made up your mind?"

Ant returned her look before cricking his neck to catch the last of the geese disappear.

"Perhaps you're right. If you think about it, who needs a battlefield with murders to solve around here?"

"I'll tell you what," said Lyn. "You solve the murders and fix the Hall's roof, and I'll keep the chocolate cakes coming for your mum and dad and do my Dr Watson act on you. Deal?"

Ant smiled.

"Are you asking, or telling?"

END

GLOSSARY

UK English to American English Glossary

- **Bap:** Bread roll
- **Bobby:** Cop
- **Broad:** A stretch of water formed from old peat diggings. Common in Norfolk and Suffolk regions of the UK. Can take the form of narrow stretches of water like canals, or open water like small lakes.
- **Buttercross:** Medieval term used to describe a standing cross, or open-sided small building, where foodstuffs and other goods were exchanged, usually in villages or small towns.
- **Car bonnet:** Hood
- **Car boot:** Trunk
- **Collared:** Slang word for catching or getting hold of or catching a person. Sometimes used in context of the police; "He was collard and taken to the police station. Also e.g. "My friend collard me and talked for ages".

- **Cottage pie:** Traditional dish cooked in a dish comprising a beef base (mincemeat) and mashed potato topping. Can include carrots, onion, celery and other vegetables to hand.
- **'Daft as a brush':** Friendly admonishment for being behaving in a silly way.
- **Gobbledygook:** Something that doesn't make sense. "You're talking gobbledygook, Jim." Normally used in a friendly, informal manner, rather than as an insult.
- **Jezza:** Short-form 'slang' for male first name 'James'.
- **Jiffy bag:** A padded bag used for shipping fragile contents.
- **Long-case clock:** Grandfather clock, for example
- **Meths:** short form for methylated spirit
- **Mobile phone:** Cell phone
- **Oiks:** Rude or unpleasant person. Sometimes used lightheartedly, e.g. "Hey, behave, you little oik."
- **Plod:** nick-name for a policeman or "the police"
- **Primary school:** Elementary school
- **Public school:** A school were all fees are paid by the student's parents/guardians (as opposed to a state school, which is free).
- **Straw boater:** A traditional flat-topped hat with a wide brim and decorative ribbon. Now mainly used by people attending sailing regattas.
- **Tenner:** Colloquial term for a ten-pound note (UK currency)
- **The Big House:** Often used by village residents to describe the local manor house. In Scotland

- the term is sometimes used to describe a local prison.
- **Tied Cottage:** An old fashioned landlord/leaseholder arrangement not often used now but historically common in farming and mining. The landowner built the house (often of poor quality), rented it to his employee, but when the farmworker or miner left their employment, the family would HAVE to move out of the cottage.
- *Time Team*: A popular UK TV show that sets a team of archaeologists the challenge of digging and interpreting an historical site or feature over three days.
- **Toff:** Slang word for upper-class or rich person generally seen to be "looking down" on other people.
- **Wallop:** To hit someone, 'I gave him a good wallop'.
- **Wellies or Wellingtons:** Rain Boots. Footwear that extend to just below the knee. Usually used for walking or country sports in poor weather. Said to have been named after the Duke of Wellington.
- **Wherry:** A traditional sailboat used for carrying goods and passengers on the Norfolk & Suffolk Broads

BOOK TWO

MURDER BY HANGING

1
THE HANGING TREE

Sally Evans struggled to keep with up her jogging mate, Jessica Brownlow, on the muddy forest track.

"It's okay for you, Jessica. You're not the one with a passenger on board."

As Sally leant forward, with a hand resting on each knee to catch her breath, she glimpsed her friend feign indifference.

"It's more likely that second double latte from Baldwin's has done for you. I told you to take it easy."

Sally wafted a hand in playful defiance and chose not to acknowledge the mischievous smile spreading across Jessica's cheeks.

"Anyway, you're only twelve weeks gone! And you were the one that insisted on doing this route. We could have done the old railway run in half the time."

Sally straightened her torso, and hands on hips, took a deep breath.

"I said we could do this route if *you* wanted to. You belted across the village green tout suite, which by my reckoning, settled the matter."

A score draw now established, the pair took in the quiet beauty of Stanton Woods. A heavy frost coated the bronze-tinged leaves in a white coating of crystalline ice. Backlit by the low morning sun, Sally thought the effect was breathtaking.

"Crisp winter mornings are magical, aren't they?"

Jessica nodded as a shaft of sunlight pierced a gap in the tree canopy, hitting the ground at a low angle just ahead of them.

"Beats making the beds and washing dirty socks. Talking of which, we'd better get a move on. Tell you what, the first to the clearing gets to choose which track we use back to the village," said Jessica.

Keen to gain the advantage, Sally set off before her friend had finished speaking.

She turned to see Jessica hanging back, kicking aside frosted leaves from the track and guessed her friend didn't want to push too hard in case she fell and injured the baby.

Thought so.

Before long, Sally arrived at the clearing to claim victory knowing Jessica had engineered the result.

About to let out a whoop of victory, her attention was suddenly grabbed by the dreadful sight ahead.

She wanted to scream; no sound would come.

She stood rigid, her head cocked to one side and tilted upwards.

"Good God."

Sally hadn't noticed her friend arrive. At her feet lay a wide, short log on its side resting on the thick carpet of leaf mould.

"Come away," said Jessica as she placed a comforting arm around her friend's shoulder.

"Nothing we can do for him now, poor devil."

The limp figure slowly swung from side to side in a gentle breeze.

"How does someone end up desperate enough to do that, Jessica?" Her hushed tone and extended arm reinforced the point.

"He must've been so cold and lonely. By the looks of things, he's been there all night. See the frost on the rope? Heavens, it's awful."

Sally accepted Jessica's guiding arm in turning her away from the body, towards a fallen tree on the opposite side of the clearing.

"Take the weight off your feet. We need to get the police up here. Will you be all right if I go for help?"

Sally nodded, dusted a coating of frost from the fallen tree, her back towards the body.

"I'll be fine. Just be as quick as you can."

* * *

LYN BLACKTHORN, head teacher of Stanton Parva Junior School was, as usual, late as she drove out of the village towards Norwich.

The agenda for the monthly meeting of heads didn't inspire her. But at least it was a chance to catch up with old friends and have a communal moan.

Good to get a bit of group therapy.

Keen to make up time, Lyn pressed the accelerator of her Mini Clubman, entering open countryside only too aware of the dangers posed by the narrow lanes and unkempt drainage ditches.

They left little room for error.

Rounding a shallow bend to the right, Lyn reacted in an instant to a figure standing on the verge, waving her arms.

Once stopped she wound down the window. She recognised the woman, concern etched on her face.

"Jessica, what's the matter?"

"Lyn, thank heavens it's you. There's a body; we need the police."

Lyn's mind raced as she made sense of Jessica's breathless words.

"A body? Has there been an accident?"

Jessica shook her head as she turned back in the direction of the clearing.

"An accident? No, I don't think so. He's hanging from a tree."

Lyn's expression turned to shock.

People don't hang themselves in Stanton Parva.

Her momentary lapse of concentration passed and reverted to type, focusing on what needed doing. Taking her mobile from the dashboard she pressed the emergency services shortcut.

"And Sally, she's pregnant... and..."

Lyn frowned.

"Sally? Pregnant? What's that got to do with—"

She allowed Jessica to interrupt.

"Oh dear, I'm sorry. I mean, well... We were jogging and..."

Lyn nodded.

At the same time her call connected.

"Police and ambulance please. I think there's been a suicide by hanging."

After giving the operator their location, Lyn turned back to Jessica

"I get it. Jessica, is..."

Yes, she's in the clearing with the, you know..."

* * *

"Sally, how are you? Jessica has told me what happened."

"At last. Thought you'd got lost."

In truth, less than ten minutes had passed.

Lyn turned towards the tree and walked with a measured pace until she stood just in front of the man. His facial features distorted, but she still recognised him.

"It's Ethan Baldwin."

Her two companions stared wide eyed at the lifeless figure.

"Ethan? No, it can't be. I saw him just the other day; he seemed fine. It's awful... and we didn't even recognise the poor man."

Lyn gestured for Sally to retake her seat.

"I'm afraid so, Sally. You're both in shock. Why would you recognise him? Look at the state he's in."

Lyn noticed her unwitting invitation for the pair to once again view the corpse had an unexpected calming effect on Jessica and Sally. She sensed looking at the body helped them accept what had happened.

Lyn encouraged the women to talk about their memories of a man the whole village knew and respected as their church warden.

The interlude didn't last long.

Lyn heard the rustle of leaves from behind. She turned to see a familiar figure.

Lord, what an irritating man you are.

"You seem to make a habit of finding bodies, Miss Blackthorn," said Detective Inspector Riley.

As he spoke, he gestured for two police constables to tape off the patch of ground surrounding Ethan's corpse.

"Please step back, ladies. I won't have the scene contaminated."

Lyn bristled. She found Riley's tone officious and lacking emotion, save for his own self-importance.

She refused to be baited. Normally respectful of serving officers, she had little time for this one.

"That will be Ms Blackthorn to you, Detective Inspector."

She knew he detested women getting the better of him. Lyn also knew Riley hated being told to use the noun because he couldn't say it without sounding like a bee with anger management issues.

Now there's a man in need of a polyp removal surgery if ever I saw one.

The mental image of an assertive nurse removing streams of cotton wool packing from Ryley's swollen nostrils after the operation appealed to Lyn's sense of humour.

Riley ignored her instruction.

"And no meddling this time. And that goes for your man friend."

Lyn watched as Riley crossed his double-breasted overcoat in an exaggerated fashion and did up fake horn buttons against the chilly breeze.

Lyn smiled and pressed another of Riley's buttons.

"I presume you are talking about Anthony Norton D'Arcy, the Lord Stanton?"

Her assertive tone caused Riley to wince as her expert shot found its target.

"Whatever," said the detective, making no attempt to disguise his petulance.

Lyn pressed home her advantage.

"Well, Mr Riley. You can be sure that if Lord Stanton, or

I, find anything of interest, you'll be the first to know about it."

She guessed her friendship with the Earl of Stanton's son fed Riley's inferiority complex. She could also see her use of the detective inspector's civilian title added to his already bad mood, not helped by the stifled chuckle of the two constables on the other side of the clearing.

"Get on with your job, you two," barked Riley.

Lyn watched his face turn puce. His subordinates attempted to stifle their laughter. They turned around and made themselves busy adjusting the police tape for no other reason than to break eye contact with their superior.

There stands a man only a mother could love, thought Lyn.

* * *

"Hi. Listen, Tina, can you give my apologies to the heads' meeting. Just say something came up, and I'll contact them later to explain."

"Okay, I'll sort it, but it must have been important for you to pull out? Are you all right?"

Lyn conjured a mental image of Ethan's hanging from the tree.

"Yes, yes, I'm fine. Let's just say it's been a difficult morning, Tina. Anyway, yes, on my way back. I'll tell you all about it then. See you in about twenty minutes."

Lyn terminated the call without waiting for a response, brought the Mini to life and roared off, laying a trail of mud from behind the front wheels as she transitioned from soil to tarmac.

As she entered Stanton Parva, Lyn noticed half a dozen locals huddled around the entrance to St. Mary's, the church where Ethan had served as warden for decades.

Suppose I'd better break the news to the vicar.

Lyn pulled into the small gravel car park separated from the ancient graveyard by a low flint wall. Locking the Mini, she made her way to the waiting locals.

"Don't suppose you've seen Ethan," said Mary Chadwick, a longstanding member of the church choir.

Oh no, what do I say?

She deflected the question, her teacher training coming in handy for once.

"I was just going to ask you the same question about Reverend Morton. Is he around?"

Lyn's measured informality did the trick in sidestepping the parishioner's question.

"Wouldn't be waiting in the cold if he'd bothered to turn up on time," said a man with a red nose and watery eyes.

"The reverend should have arrived half an hour ago. It's not at all like him to be late," another added.

Great, a dead church warden and a missing vicar, thought Lyn.

2

MEMORIES

Lyn strolled from the dining room of Stanton Hall and into the conservatory with her closest friend, Lord Anthony Stanton.

She knew his title was only a courtesy designation because his father was the Earl of Stanton but sounded impressive to her nonetheless.

"Lovely supper, Ant. Now that your parents have gone up, there's something I want to talk to you about."

Lyn watched her best friend tense. She realised immediately he'd got the wrong end of the stick. About to rephrase her sentence, Ant got in first.

"The assessment, you mean?"

Lyn hadn't meant to get him to talk about that just yet. Nevertheless, she could see he needed to.

"So how did it go?" From your expression, I'm guessing not too well?"

Lyn watched on as three deep furrows creased Ant's forehead.

"Officially, it's a medical discharge. Unofficially, they're letting me go but have put me on the reserve list for any special-operations stuff that might come up closer to home. As usual, the army wants it both ways."

Lyn made for her favourite wicker chair and looked out over the rolling pasture sloping gently down to Stanton Broad.

"Well, you either have post traumatic stress disorder or you don't. What do they want from you?"

Turning to face Ant, her voice betrayed simmering anger at the way the army had behaved towards him.

"They reckon that while I can't cope with battlefield conditions, I am capable of undercover stuff in the UK. Simple as that."

"And your parents?"

She noticed Ant take a sharp intake of breath.

"Problematic, that one. I've decided to keep quiet for the time being. I don't want Mum and Dad to think they've forced me into it."

Lyn cocked her head to one side.

"Forced you into what?"

He took several seconds to respond.

I'm coming back for good to manage the Hall and estate. Someone's got to sort the mess out, and I'm not having another estate manager ripping us off, like Narky Collins."

The mention of Narky set off a tangle of emotions as she recalled their recent investigation into his murder and discovery that he had been generating false invoices for years, bleeding Ant's parents dry.

Distracted for a few seconds, Lyn finally turned her attention back to Ant. She surmised from her friend's determined tone that discussing his future helped bury less-palatable memories of his military service.

Lyn's eyes widened at the prospect of having him home. *At last*, she thought.

"When will you tell them?"

Lyn worked hard to keep her excitement in check.

"In a day or two. You could see how knackered they both were at supper."

Lyn smiled. She admired how he fussed over his parents and contrasted it with the difficult relationship she had with her own mother and father.

"But there will have to be changes. We have to get this place paying for itself if it's to have any future."

Lyn let out a throaty laugh.

"Tell me about it. I got soaked when I brought over the chocolate cake I baked. Your stupid porch roof leaked water all over me."

"My point exactly!"

Lyn watched Ant laugh and assumed he was visualising the bedraggled state she had arrived in.

"Your mum and dad will love it. You know how long they've wanted you back but wouldn't have put you under pressure by saying so..."

Lyn hesitated.

"Especially because you're... the only one left?"

Neither needed to speak further on the matter.

"Anyway, what have you been up to today? You said you had something to tell me. Not more boring school stuff, I hope?"

Lyn rested back in the wicker chair and lazily wagged a finger at him.

"Well, if you're not interested..."

Ant returned Lyn's gesture.

"None of that head-teacher stuff from you, young lady."

Lyn refused to rise to his tease. Instead, her smile broadened as she gestured for him to sit on the chair opposite.

She recounted the discovery of Ethan's body and the curious case of the missing vicar.

"And to cap it all, Riley's certain it's suicide and had the cheek to warn us both off."

* * *

"The thing is, Ant," said Lyn as they inspected the tree Ethan had hung from, "Ethan was crippled with arthritis. There's no way he could have strung a rope over that branch, let alone haul a heavy stump, climb onto it, and kick it away to hang himself."

Lyn watched as Ant took in the scene. He stood behind a cordon of blue-and-white, plastic tape with the repeated message: Police Do Not Cross.

"It certainly must have taken some effort; I'll give you that. He must have been, what, three feet off the ground?"

She noticed Ant give the fallen tree stump, Ethan had used to stand on, a backwards glance and frown as he walked to the far side of the clearing. He turned, crouched, and fixed his gaze on the ground six feet from where the church warden's body had hung. She knew he was in battlefield detective mode as he forensically surveyed every detail of the scene.

"That's interesting."

Lyn looked on, knowing from past experience not to interrupt his train of thought.

"Look at this."

Lyn obeyed his direction to join him.

"See those two faint lines?"

Lyn followed Ant's pointing finger but saw nothing. Closing one eye then the other to get a different perspective made no difference.

"Nope. Don't see anything except mud and leaves."

Lyn almost fell backwards in surprise as Ant clapped his hands.

"Exactly, but not all leaves are the same, you know. Do what I do, and you'll see it."

Lyn watched as Ant moved his upper body and head from side to side while keeping his feet fixed to the spot.

"If you catch the light you can just see two narrow lines leading out of the clearing towards the main road."

Ant pointed to emphasise his point.

Lyn copied Ant's technique. It worked.

"Good Lord, yes, I see. So you agree it wasn't suicide?"

Ant was already following the tracks.

Thirty seconds later, Lyn looked on as Ant studied a small patch of mud.

"What?"

"Bald tyres, Lyn. Poor maintenance I'd say. But it could be anything that's been down here. Not proof of murder."

Continuing along the track, the pair soon came to a gravelled area accessed off a main road from the village.

"It's used as a car park now. Nothing official or anything, but the landowner has never had any problem with the locals using it."

Lyn broke into a broad smile as she finished speaking.

Ant laughed. It was his family's land.

"Shame the kids don't appreciate it though," replied Ant.

Both looked up at a line of broken branches.

"I seem to remember us doing much the same when we were kids, Lyn."

She remembered happy summers larking about in the woods with Ant and his older brother.

Seems like half a dozen lifetimes away.

Lyn looked at her watch.

"Oh Lord. Great times, Ant. But if I don't get back to school for year-six choir practice, my secretary will have my guts for garters, to say nothing of the kids. Come on, Ant."

With that she was off heading at pace back to the Mini.

"I'll make my own way back to the village, Lyn. It'll save you time not having to drop me off."

"Talk later, then, Ant. We can decide what to do next, yes?"

* * *

MEMORIES of his brother Greg and the sight of the church sparked a need to pay his respects. He spent five minutes in quiet contemplation in front of his older brother's headstone.

I wonder if the church has changed much since...

Pushing open the medieval oak door of the east entrance kept in place by ancient iron-strap hinges, Ant paused to admire the faded flags hanging from nave walls. He knew each represented a regiment that had fought during the World Wars. As he walked forward, lost in his own world, his attention was drawn to the diminutive frame of a young woman sitting in the front pew.

He quietly passed then turned around to face her. Ant noticed the young woman's pale complexion and watched tears make slow, quiet progress down her cheeks.

Ant readied himself as she looked up at him. Before he could introduce himself, she spoke.

"He was always nice to me. Why would he do that?"

Her voice started to break.

Ant guessed who she was talking about. Nevertheless, he didn't want to get it wrong.

"Who?"

Ant studied her face.

No older than eighteen, I'd say.

Ant watched as she lowered her gaze until it was fixed firmly on the burnt-orange-and-cream-glazed floor tiles.

"Ethan."

He hesitated for a few seconds.

"Ah, yes. I heard. So sad. Dreadful thing to have happened."

Ant made no attempt to press the matter. He didn't need to.

"We could talk to one another about whatever we wanted. Even though he was a lot older than me. But lately he was strange. I think he was worried about something. I think someone was giving him grief. Wanted something he had. He wouldn't tell me. That wasn't like Ethan. Do you think they hurt him?"

Her assertions took Ant by surprise.

Why was she thinking that way? More to the point, why would she be opening up to a stranger in an otherwise empty church?

Ant watched on helplessly as she broke down. She sobbed, tears streaming down her flushed cheeks.

Poor girl. What the hell do I do now?

A voice came to Ant's rescue.

"Samantha. It must be awful for you, but the church is here to provide comfort."

Ant turned to see the reverend walking towards them.

"Anthony, how good to see you, though it has been some time since we've seen you on a Sunday, hasn't it?"

The vicar spoke quietly. Ant thought his gentle Irish lilt fitted the moment perfectly. But he wasn't sure how to respond. He'd never been one for religion even though he felt something that seemed to help when Greg died, without quite understanding why.

Wish I knew what to believe.

As the vicar took a seat next to the teenager, Ant seized the opportunity to escape.

Best leave it to the professionals.

As he walked down the narrow tarmac path towards the road, he heard a commotion coming from the church car park.

A familiar figure stood in the near distance.

Detective Inspector Riley.

"I want to talk to you," Riley shouted.

Ant smiled. He could see the redoubtable Phyllis had other ideas.

"Don't you ignore me, Sergeant. You splashed Betty and me when you came screeching across the path. In my day, bobbies had respect for people. The only thing you seem to care about is getting to the chippie before it closes. Disgraceful."

Ant watched in amusement as Riley tried in vain to escape his tormentors.

"Madam, I..."

Ant grinned and reckoned the icy stare Phyllis gave the hapless policeman could freeze the life out of a snowman.

"Don't call me madam. Such a rude man. I'm a respectable married woman not the owner of a knocking shop."

Her lifelong companion, Betty, nodded. Ant knew she always agreed with Phyllis because it made for an easy life. Emboldened, she started to speak.

"But Phyllis, your Albert's been dead these last twenty yea—"

"Never mind that now, Betty," interrupted Phyllis

without looking at her friend. "So what are you going to do about my dirty tights, Sergeant?"

Ant sensed Riley had had enough, which served only to increase the comedic value.

"Madam, I made no such accusation, and I am not a sergeant. In fact, I am a detective inspector, and what exactly do you expect me to do about your tights, wash them myself?"

Ant knew Riley was now in for a fall and could easily predict Phyllis' response.

"You dirty, dirty man," shrieked Phyllis.

Yep, thought so.

By now, a small group of curious onlookers had gathered.

"Keep your hands off my tights. What a horrible little sergeant you are. Let me tell you…"

Ant watched as the tirade continued with Phyllis threatening the hapless Riley with her sizable handbag then seized the moment and slipped from the policeman's clutches, while the detective was otherwise engaged fending off a fake-crocodile-skin battering ram. Waving at the policeman, he observed Riley almost bursting with frustration in his unsuccessful effort to placate Phyllis and stop him escaping.

3
A FISH SUPPER

Restoring vintage cars came close to an obsession for Ant. One make dazzled him in particular: a Morgan. Tonight he was ably assisted by his mechanic friend.

"Amazing machines aren't they, Fitch?"

The two men, each dressed in a blue overall that had seen better days, stood side by side as they admired the sorry remains of a once majestic 1936 4/4 Roadster.

Ant knew that to an outsider, the mangle of bits and pieces scattered around the barn floor might seem fit only for the skip.

He ogled the treasure with the wide-eyed amazement of a true believer. To him, the unkempt mixture of metal and wood represented the best of British engineering.

Ant knew Fitch felt the same way.

"You're not wrong."

Ant savoured each of the threadbare components.

"Hard to imagine these cars are still made by hand, isn't it? I imagine some people have tried to persuade Morgan to automate production: you know, just in time, multiskilled assemblers and all that stuff."

Ant noticed Fitch rolling his eyes.

"What?"

He threw an oily rag across the exposed framework of the car.

Ant watched on as Fitch caught the stained fabric with a flourish of his hand.

"You sound like one of those consultants that steal your watch and sell you the time for six hundred quid a day. And here, you can have this back."

Tilting to the left, Ant dodged the blackened fabric, watching as it shot past and landed in a limp heap on the rough concrete floor.

"You know, like someone always banging on about forward planning and pressing the pedal to the metal. Now who might that be? Oh, I know. You!"

Ant smiled as his friend placed a finger to his lips, widening his eyes in fake surprise.

To a stranger, it might seem as though their verbal sparring could lead to fisticuffs.

Ant knew he could trust Fitch. They thrived on sharp banter, each calculated barb further reinforcing the already strong bond between them.

Ant was keen to change the subject now that he'd failed on the sarcasm front.

"Where's that half-inch spanner?"

Fitch obliged by gently throwing the tool, its trajectory aimed with care to force Ant into a full-stretch catch.

"Glad to see you still can still put your cricketing skills to good use."

Ant smiled before both men returned to their respective tasks, absorbed in the motoring history that lay before them.

Fitch was the first to break the silence.

"It'll be great to see her on the road again."

"You're right there, matey. A Morgan isn't something you see around here every day, is it?"

The mechanic nodded.

"Funny you should say that. There's a stranger running around the village in Morgan's latest Plus Six model. One of the Moonstone first editions. Must have cost him a packet. I tell you, he looked a right chav in his designer T-shirt and shades plonked on his head."

Ant's ears pricked up.

"Shades? This time of year? Bozo."

"Precisely, Ant. Seems he's intent on building some posh houses on that plot of land behind poor Ethan's place. It seems he can't develop the site without getting his hands on Glebe Cottage and demolishing it."

* * *

Looks like it's going to be a frosty one again, thought Lyn as she gazed at the jet-black sky and clear, full moon on her evening stroll around Stanton Parva.

She marvelled at the silhouetted rooftops of the higgledy-piggledy, thatched cottages.

I do love this place.

Lyn passed half a dozen teenagers pressed like sardines onto one of several wooden benches around the village green. She remembered doing the same thing on the same benches, only without the smartphones, when she was their age.

"Hi, miss," said one.

"Hi, Lyn," added a second, more confident girl.

She smiled. Lyn knew each of them. A few had siblings

at her school. Others because she'd taught them as a student teacher.

"Keep safe, you lot."

Lyn enjoyed the company of young people. She never ceased to be excited by even the small part she and her staff might play in helping them make the best of the opportunities that lie ahead of them. It was why she went into teaching and enjoyed watching young minds soak up new ideas and information.

I love it when kids think they are the first people in history to be their age, and only they can change the world.

None of the group responded. Instead, they smiled. Lyn sensed they had retreated back into their own world, from which adults were strictly excluded.

Not all Lyn's memories were pleasant ones as she skirted the village pond and looked over to a neat row of flint cottages.

Shoehorned between the butchers and the old post office, stood Lime View.

Lyn frowned as she remembered looking out of the window of her tiny bedroom as a nine-year-old. Downstairs, her parents would be quarrelling. It was usually about money or rather the lack of it. She'd hated having to tell the tally man *"Mum said can we leave it this week,"* and the angry look he'd give her.

At least I escaped to university.

A light breeze washed across Lyn's face as she rounded the corner into High Street and with it the seductive aroma of fried cod.

That sorts supper out.

Watching her step, Lyn navigated the raised threshold of Sid and Carol's fish and chip shop.

"Now then, stranger. We've not seen you in a while."

Sid spoke in his usual friendly tone. Lyn felt his jocular voice precisely fitted the rotund frame of a man in his late fifties too fond of his own cooking.

"It's only been two weeks, Sid. Glad to see you miss me."

They laughed as Carol walked through a connecting door holding a tray of fresh fish.

"Hi, Lyn. Who's a stranger, then?"

Her laid-back voice resonated around the white-tiled walls of the old shop.

Lyn smiled.

"Your husband thinks I'm neglecting you too."

She pointed a friendly finger towards Sid.

"Cod, chips, and mushy peas, please, Carol."

The slender woman looked at the empty, glass-fronted compartment above one of the fryers then at her husband in well-practised admonishment.

"Old fool," was all Carol had to say.

Lyn watched as Sid winked at her while taking the tray of fish from his wife.

"And remember, not too much beer batter this time."

Lyn looked on as Sid sighed and dipped the fish into the creamy mix before wiping the excess coating off, with an expert flick of his wrist against the side of the stainless-steel container. Finally, he lowered the cod into the bubbling oil between forefinger and thumb.

"Only twenty-two years I've been doing this, Lyn."

She held her arms up and stepped back from the counter as if in retreat.

"Don't involve me in your domestic tiffs."

"My darling husband, it's twenty-four years, if you must."

She turned to Lyn.

"Then again, he never remembers our anniversary either. I don't know why I bother."

Lyn directed a "tut tut" at Sid.

"I ask you, Lyn. What sort of husband gives his wife a birthday card for her wedding anniversary?"

Carol looked Sid full in the eye.

"If I were you, Sid, I'd be offering to make your wife a nice cup of tea."

Lyn could see Sid had clocked onto her strategy of side-stepping further embarrassment.

"Well, at least you get a card. I never get the same number of socks back that I put into the wash basket."

The two women laughed as the image of Sid walking around in odd socks sank into their collective consciousness.

"Fish will be out in a minute, Lyn," said Carol as she moved the cod around the fryer with a long-handled pan skimmer. "Awful what happened to Ethan, wasn't it?"

Lyn thought for a split second how she should answer. Perhaps Carol might have picked up something on the village grapevine that could prove useful.

"Yes, dreadful."

Lyn took note of Carol's reaction. The woman looked thoughtful as she gave the pan skimmer another swish around the fryer.

"And finding a new church warden won't be easy. Reverend Morton can be a funny devil when he wants."

Lyn raised an eyebrow. Carol let out a short, sharp laugh having realised she'd just compared a man of God with Satan.

Lyn continued with her cautious approach.

"I suppose we can all be a bit funny when the mood takes us, Carol."

The woman nodded as she busied herself wiping away

the excess oil from the edge of the fryer with a spotlessly clean cloth.

"That's true. But from what I saw the other day, those two weren't getting on."

Lyn's intrigue intensified as Carol continued.

"I was only saying to Sid this morning that I stumbled across them in the church going at it like two ferrets in a sack after evensong. Red in the face, both of them, they were."

I wonder what that could have been about?

Lyn frowned as she rested her elbows on the stainless-steel counter and leant forward.

"I see. I wonder what that could have been about?"

Lyn watched as Carol submerged the skimmer into the oil and lifted the newly fried cod into the heated storage shelf above.

"Sid thought it was something to do with the collection. Maybe the warden accused the vicar of pinching some of it."

Lyn shook her head in disbelief.

"Surely not. After all, he's the vicar!"

Carol mirrored Lyn's movement and leant forward, whispering so as not to be overheard.

"From what I could make out, Ethan told the vicar he would report him to—"

Carol suddenly straightened up and turned her attention to a new customer entering the shop.

"Mrs Oldsworth. Nice to see you again. You've come with the Girl Guides' order, have you?"

Lyn finished putting salt and vinegar on her supper, scooped up the tray, and after exchanging goodbyes, made her way to the door.

I need to talk to Ant about this.

4
SCHOOL DAYS

Ant smiled as Lyn's secretary closed the door behind him.

"You're lucky. She who must be obeyed is between meetings.

He knew what a good gatekeeper Tina was at keeping distraction away from Lyn and considered himself lucky to be granted an audience.

"How's your week been, then? Ant knew his enquiry would ensure he stayed in her good books.

"Oh, you know. Usual stuff, patching kids up, and keeping disgruntled parents away from Her Majesty." Tina pointed towards Lyn's office. "And it's Wednesday, so it's an evening at Cinema World in Norwich for me."

Ant warmed to the theme. "Anything good on?"

Tina's eyes lit up. "You betcha; it's only the director's cut of *The Thing from Another World*'. Speaking of which, I suppose I should announce your arrival."

"I've an odd-looking bloke wearing a scruffy, waxed, shooting jacket and mucky boots slouching in front of me, who insists he knows you. Should I send him on his way, or do you want to see him?"

The intercom clicked as Tina pressed the receive button.

A few seconds of silence followed, which Ant assumed was for dramatic effect.

"That'll be Ant, I suppose? Send him in, but tell him to wipe his feet first."

Ant knew Lyn's white painted office was immaculate. The sterile space always made him feel as if he were about to undergo root-canal treatment.

"The head will see you now."

Tina smiled.

Ant guessed she was enjoying the moment.

"Will she now?"

He raised an eyebrow and waited to be shown through.

"Oh, and I don't know why you bother with that inter-thingy. I could hear her through the door, you know."

Ant nodded his head toward Lyn's office.

"I heard that," said a voice from the other side of a half-glazed door.

Ant smiled at the secretary.

"I rest my case."

"Whatever," said Tina as she opened the connecting door, stood to one side, and allowed Ant to pass.

"Coffee?"

Lyn looked up from a heap of papers.

"I'll have my usual. The scruffy one will have an Americano with two sweeteners."

"Will I, indeed?"

Ant lifted a moulded steel chair from one side of the small room and sat opposite Lyn.

"You know you're not supposed to have sugar, so I'm looking out for you. That's what mates do, isn't it?"

His friend had too much of a twinkle in her eye for Ant's liking.

"You wouldn't believe how much paperwork there is in this job. Just look at it."

Lyn swept a hand across the desk to emphasise her point.

"This lot is just about health and safety. See that pile—finance stuff. And that," she said, pointing to a thick document, "is a Department for Education consultation, due in next week."

Ant sniffed and looked at a small rectangular landscape photo on one of the bare walls as if disinterested in his friend's woes.

"I wondered what you got up to all day. After all, it's only a tiny school, isn't it?"

He watched as Lyn's mouth opened and prepared himself for the onslaught.

"Sounds like you're both ready for a snack," said Tina as she entered the room and placed a tray holding two coffees and four chocolate digestive biscuits on the desk between the sparring partners.

Ant pointed at the biscuits.

"No added sugar, I hope?"

Tina wagged a finger as she retraced her steps to the door.

"Watch it, you."

The next few seconds passed in silence as the two mates savoured the coffee and dunked their respective digestive biscuits.

"So what have you been up to, Ant?"

She dipped the tip of her index finger into her mug to retrieve a small piece of her snack from the hot liquid.

Trying not to smirk, he watched Lyn wince in pain from a scalded fingertip.

"You do that every time."

She savoured the piece of soggy digestive while shaking her hand as if to eject the pain from her pinked finger.

"Can't waste any, can I?"

Ant shook his head and smiled.

"To answer your question, I've been doing my Morgan up with Fitch and—"

"Boys and their toys, eh?"

As she spoke, Lyn peered into her coffee to ensure every morsel of the biscuit had been rescued.

"And we're making good progress replacing that sliding axle—"

"I thought an axle's job was to revolve, not slide all over the place?"

Ant gave Lyn the crushed look of a man having his most treasured possession trashed. He slouched into the angular frame of the uncomfortable metal chair, only to quickly sit up again due to a sudden pain in his coxis.

"Lynda Blackthorn, you know full well that the sliding axle is part of the front suspension of the Morgan. You helped my father enough times when we were kids and know almost as much about these cars as I do."

It was clear to Ant that Lyn intended to keep her council even though his use of her full name was meant to provoke. Her knowing smile displayed all he needed to know.

I'll get the better of you one day, thought Ant.

Lyn brushed a hand across the piles of paper again.

"Anyway, why are you here? I'm rather busy, you know."

Ant looked indignant.

"You were the one who said we needed to catch up. But

if you don't want to know the stranger, that's all right. I'll follow up on the lead myself."

Ant knew the mention of a new lead would whet Lyn's curiosity.

He watched as she placed her coffee on the desk and looked at him expectantly.

"You mean you *do* think Ethan was murdered?"

"Well, let's not get ahead of ourselves, but Fitch told me about a property developer who's been sniffing around the village. Apparently, he wants to build a dozen or so 'executive' houses on the field behind Glebe Cottage."

Lyn returned her second biscuit to the plate instead of dunking it.

"But what has that got to do with Ethan?"

Ant lifted a blank piece of paper from the edge of Lyn's desk and picked up one of several coloured pens scattered across the desktop.

He drew a rough sketch of the field, Glebe Cottage, and the main road in front of the house.

"Do you see? That developer can't build without owning Ethan's place and knocking it down. It's the only access from the road onto the field. Without Ethan's place, that development will not happen."

Lyn's eyes widened as the details sank in.

"So you're saying that one way or another the stranger with the posh car needed Ethan out of the way?"

"Got it in one."

Ant scrunched the scrap of paper, taking careful aim, then lobbed it with the deftest of touches into an empty wastepaper basket.

"Hole in one."

Irritated at Lyn's lack of interest in his party trick, Ant

watched as she sat back in her leather swivel chair, swinging it from side to side.

"Well, Anthony, you're not the only one with a scoop."

Ant involuntarily raised both eyebrows as he reacted to the increasing excitement with which Lyn spoke.

"I was in the chip shop last night and—"

Lyn's train of thought evaporated as the door opened.

"Your eleven o'clock is here," said Tina with just the upper part of her body appearing around the door. Ant realised that her facial expression made it clear that 11 a.m. meant 11 a.m.

"Tell you what, Lyn. Why don't we catch up in the Wherry Arms tonight? In the meantime, there's something I want to check out anyway."

Ant watch Lyn as she prised herself from the chair and smoothed the fabric of her pencil skirt and jacket.

He was impressed with her sudden switch to head teacher mode in preparation for whatever her meeting involved.

"That's fine, Ant. See you tonight."

He could see she was already mentally in another place.

Leaving Tina's outer office, Ant glimpsed an agitated woman, her glare fixed on Lyn.

Glad I don't have to deal with parents looking to punch my lights out, he thought.

***

The Wherry Arms was quiet for a Wednesday evening as Ant and Lyn settled into the tiny snug of the ancient hostelry.

"Well," said Ant as the pair sat around a small, circular table. "Ethan did not commit suicide: no doubt in my mind now."

He watched as Lyn took a sip of her lemonade spritzer, her eyes now fixed on his.

"You had some doubt, then?"

Ant savoured his pint of Fen Bodger pale ale.

"I know Riley insisting it was suicide is enough to think the opposite, but I wanted to be sure. Well, now that I've seen the autopsy photographs, I'm certain."

Lyn almost choked on her drink.

"You've seen what? How on earth—"

"Told you before, Lyn," said Ant, interjecting, "the job I do, or should I now say, did, has its perks. Turns out the pathologist is an old mucker of mine from the army. We worked together on…"

Ant's words faded as he recalled the circumstances of their previous cooperation while on active duty.

He gazed into his pint glass watching the bubbles making their way to the surface. He knew Lyn had cottoned on. He found her awareness reassuring.

"Come on, Ant. Snap out of it. Tell me about the photos."

Ant reacted positively to Lyn's abrupt approach. It worked, though he knew he would need help sooner rather than later.

"There were two rope burns around Ethan's neck. It took some finding, but there's a distinct, but narrow line of bruising buried beneath the rope used in Stanton Woods. It looks as though—"

"Wait a minute. Are you saying someone strangled Ethan, and he was…" interrupted Lyn.

Ant saw the look of disgust spreading across her face as she struggled to complete the sentence.

"Still alive when he was strung up?"

He reached over the table and cupped Lyn's hand.

"I'm afraid it's quite likely, Lyn. If there's one saving grace, he'd have been unconscious, if not already dead, by the time he was strung up, poor chap."

Ant loosened his hold on Lyn's hand and instead gently stroked the freckled skin to give some reassurance.

"The thing is, Ant, if that developer bloke *was* involved, I don't think he was working alone."

Ant frowned.

"What brings you to that conclusion?"

Lyn swilled the remains of her drink around the tall glass in a slow, circular motion.

"I don't want two and two to make five, but remember this morning when I started to tell you about the fish and chip shop?"

Lyn retold the conversation she'd had with Carol.

"And that was on Sunday, the day before Sally and Jessica found Ethan."

Ant watch Lyn as she took a final swig of her drink, emptying its contents in one go and placed the now empty glass back onto the table, rotating it between her hands.

He followed suit by tipping his glass at a sharp angle and demolishing the final third of his pint.

"Okay, this is what we'll do," said Ant as he gathered the two glasses and got to his feet. "I'll track down the developer. Can you sound out the vicar without tipping him off to what we're up to?"

"Love to. The only thing is, I'm covering for a sick colleague tomorrow, so it's fractions and spelling with year four all day for me—yuck!"

Ant smiled. He suspected her pupils hated that stuff as much as he had.

"No worries," replied Ant. "I'll sort it, and let you know how I got on."

5

MORNING PRAYERS

Thursday morning broke with a clear blue sky, which framed a corn-yellow sun in all its late autumn glory.

What a great place to live, thought Ant as he walked the two miles from Stanton Hall to the village. He scanned an uninterrupted view of Stanton Broad and its floodplain. The ancient landscape was so different from the manicured gardens and open parkland of the Hall but no less breathtaking.

Ant glimpsed a wherry moving serenely along the Broad and figured the owners were taking a late season holiday.

The skipper's doing well to catch what little wind there is, he thought as he watched in wonderment while the triangular sail rippled in the light breeze.

Within twenty minutes, he was on the outskirts of the village: his gaze once more drawn to the church.

This is the second time in two days I've sensed the need to go inside. What's going on?

He entered the already open door and slipped silently onto the pew nearest the exit. He watched Reverend Morton look down the nave of the church. Ant assumed the six other parishioners were regulars for the morning service. None of them, it seemed to Ant, were under seventy.

"Just a few announcements before I finish."

Ant watched as the vicar's scattered audience began to fidget.

Perhaps they're competing to be first out the door.

Lyn had mentioned to Ant that the vicar had a reputation for roping the unwary into some "voluntary" task or other as he shook their hand at the end of the service and wished them a good day.

"We have just said prayers for the soul of our dear brother Ethan. To celebrate his life, I wish to announce this morning that we will be holding a special service of thanksgiving. It will take place a week on Sunday. I ask you all to spread the word so that as many villagers as possible have an opportunity to join us."

Ant watched as the proposition was met with general approval, apart from Phyllis and therefore Betty. He surmised the pair positioned themselves towards the rear of the church to better see who was in the church, who was sitting next to whom, and if any salacious gossip was to be had.

I bet they beat the vicar to the door to escape getting roped into anything.

Busy criticising the poor show of flowers, the two women prattled away to each other. Ant guessed they heard little of what the reverend had to say.

"Gladys Bircham never was any good at flower arranging," said Phyllis. She pointed to a dismal display of hellebores drooping from a vase next to the pulpit. "Remember at school when she brought that deadly nightshade in and almost killed us?"

Ant knew that Betty may have wished to respond but

realized there was little point since Phyllis would only cut her off midflow.

"Nineteen thirty-eight, that was," continued Phyllis, "and what did she end up as? A flaming nurse. I ask you."

Ant watched Betty bristle at the use of intemperate language in church. He knew what the problem was: she lacked the courage to rebuke her lifelong friend.

"Have you a question, Mrs Plumstead, or are we just gossiping?" asked the vicar.

Ever the diplomat, Reverend, thought Ant.

His question threw Phyllis off guard. It had been so long since anyone in the village had used her married name. Although Archie had died over two decades earlier, she still missed his quiet contentedness, particularly his habit of coming home from work and dozing in front of the fire each night after tea until bedtime.

"Me, Reverend? What makes you think I have anything to say?"

Ant smiled as Betty looked at the floor and pinched her little nose in, which he assumed was a well-practised routine to stop herself giggling. He could see that the remaining parishioners felt no such need for restraint.

The more agitated Phyllis became watching several sets of shoulders rising and falling in unison, the more amusing Ant thought the scene.

Ant gave credit to the vicar for having made his point not pursuing the matter further.

I imagine he's ready for his coffee and a tot of brandy.

"Go in peace," added the reverend after leading his congregation in a final prayer.

Within seconds, he disappeared into the vestry. Ant knew the clergyman needed to make a quick dash around the outside of the church to appear at the entrance and catch his parishioners on their way out.

Although Ant was nearest the door, he waited until everyone else had left, nodding to each as they passed in turn.

Things didn't quite go as Ant had planned. As he exited the church, he saw that the vicar was deep in conversation with a parishioner.

It was plain to Ant that the reverend was eager to evade the woman's clutches, and from the bit of conversation he could overhear, avoid what seemed to be a regular invitation to Sunday lunch.

As Ant drew nearer and caught the vicar's eye, the reverend seemed to grasp his opportunity.

"Ah, there you are, Anthony. Mrs Redwood, thank you so much for your kind offer, but there is a matter on which I must speak to this gentleman."

Ant couldn't help but notice the forlorn body language the woman had adopted. She passed by with a look that left little to Ant's imagination.

"Oh dear," said Ant as he acknowledged the vicar's awkward smile.

"It's uncharitable of me to say, I know, but you've saved my digestive system from a dreadful fate. Still, I'm glad you've called by. I wanted to thank you for your wonderful contribution to the church bell restoration fund. Such an important cause, and your family are, as always, such generous benefactors."

The compliment threw Ant.

I guess Dad must have signed the cheque.

"Think nothing of it."

He tried to hide his ignorance of the matter.

"The village owes such a lot to the church, and by extension, to you."

Ant was pleased that it was now the vicar's turn to blush.

"Not at all," replied the reverend.

"It was a good service. Very thoughtful subject matter today."

Ant watched as the clergyman frowned and raised his arms outwards before allowing them to free fall back to his sides with a thud.

"Yes, but God's words touch fewer and fewer people as each season passes. What to do? That's the question. What to do?"

Ant was keen to probe the vicar about Ethan. He still had his reservations, despite his military training, to exclude no possibility, no matter how fantastic, from any investigation. But could the clergyman really have been involved in the man's murder?

He turned to look across the graveyard that surrounded the church. An imperfect pattern of headstones tilting at crazy angles gave testament to a thousand years of sacred history.

"Not to put too fine a point on it, Vicar. You now have one less parishioner."

Let's see where this takes us, he thought.

The vicar bridled at Ant's sudden mention of the late church warden. Ant knew he'd hit a nerve but wasn't sure if it was genuine remorse he was observing or an involuntary defensive reaction.

"Very sad. Such a gentle-mannered man. Never a bad word to say about anyone. Do you know, Anthony, I don't think I ever heard Ethan raise his voice in all the time I knew him."

Time to push. That's not what Carol said she'd seen.

"Except with you, Reverend." Ant fixed his gaze on the man.

Ant noticed the clergyman stiffen.

"What do you mean, Anthony? My relationship with Ethan was always cordial. The only—"

He hesitated.

"But you *did* argue with Ethan recently, didn't you?"

The reverend's eyes began to glisten with tears.

Is this about regret at being rumbled, or grief?

"It's true. We did argue. And now he's dead. Lord forgive me."

Ant moderated his tone. He saw the effect of whatever had happened between the two men take hold in the vicar's mind.

"About those falling congregations, Anthony. That also means less money from collections and bequests. The archbishop has threatened to close St Mary's if things don't improve."

Ant was not a religious man, but the thought of a place of worship his family had been involved with for generations ceasing to exist appalled him.

Can't let that happen.

"But what's that got to do with Ethan, Vicar?"

Ant observed the man's body language as he retrieved a pristine, white handkerchief from his vestment. The reverend carefully unfolded the material before cupping it around his nose for a second or two.

"I wanted to remove the pews so that we could use the space more flexibly. You know the sort of thing. Hiring the church out for events and suchlike."

"Sounds a logical approach to try."

"I thought so too, Anthony. But Ethan…"

Ant sensed the vicar hesitating as his emotions got the

better of him.

"Ethan opposed the move. He said it was going against the Christian tradition and would have none of it."

Ant allowed Reverend Morton to compose himself before pressing the point.

"Could he have stopped you?"

The vicar shook his head.

"No, but he could have made things very difficult. He was so well respected in the village. Do you know that pews were only used on a regular basis in English churches after the Reformation? I told him that, but he wouldn't listen. Instead he threatened to get up a petition."

Ant shrugged his shoulders.

"But, Vicar, you could just have told the villagers about the archbishop's threat."

"That's the point, Anthony. The archbishop forbade me to say anything to anyone until he'd made a final decision. What was I to do?"

The vicar's dilemma caught Ant off guard. Did he just happen to be a man in the wrong place at the wrong time when he was overheard by Carol? On the other hand, he had a motive and the opportunity to murder Ethan. But was he a killer? And how could he have strung the man up?

Stranger things have happened, thought Ant.

The vicar looked at his inquisitor with alarm.

"You don't think I killed Ethan, do you? For goodness' sake, Anthony."

His voice began to break.

Not the time to ease off.

"It doesn't matter what I do or don't believe, Vicar. It just doesn't look good, does it? When Detective Inspector Riley gets hold of you, he'll think it's Christmas."

Ant sensed the vicar beginning to panic.

"Don't worry, he doesn't know about you arguing with Ethan. At least not yet. But I need your help. Was there anything else bothering the warden?"

He could see the relief washing over the vicar's face.

"Anything at all, Vicar?"

"Ethan hadn't been himself for weeks. I'm sure that's why he argued with me. It just wasn't like him."

Ant placed a hand on the vicar's lower arm.

"What do you think was going on?"

The clergyman's eyes flickered as if processing a Rolodex for information.

"He was such a private man, Anthony. But there was one thing he said some weeks ago. Now I come to think about it, his mood changed around that time."

"Go on," urged Ant.

"Grindle. His name was Grindle. Something about land. But it didn't make any sense to me."

It does to me, thought Ant.

6
THE BUTTERCROSS

"What are you looking so flustered about?"

"Flustered? You know I have to be back at school for a governor's meeting within the hour. What kept you? I've got you a bacon bap from the tearoom. Might just about still be warm."

Ant smiled expectantly as he retrieved a crumpled, brown paper bag containing his lunch from Lyn's outstretched hand. His nostrils flared as the warming aroma of the honey-roast snack wafted over him.

"Did you remember to get brown sauce?" asked Ant as he peered into the simple packaging.

"Don't push it. Lord or not, you can like it or lump it."

Ant stretched to catch a paper napkin Lyn had thrown in his general direction. The shot fell just short so that Ant was forced to bend down in order to retrieve it.

"I take it that bowing before the school head teacher is my penance for getting above myself?"

He saw immediately that his tongue-in-cheek remark had failed to cut it with Lyn. Ant winced at being on the receiving end of her harshest head-teacher stare, gesturing with a crooked finger for him to join her on the buttercross steps.

"Why are we eating out in the cold when there's plenty of room in the tearoom?"

He pointed at the near empty establishment on the opposite side of the street. Ant's enquiry met with indifference.

"Never mind that; anyway, fresh air is good for you. Now how did you get on with the vicar?"

His expression exposed his disagreement with Lyn's view on the efficaciousness of the chilled environment. And he wasn't just thinking about the weather.

Fresh air, indeed. It's starting to flaming snow.

Accepting Lyn had refused his plea for a cosy chair by the open fire in Dotti's Coffee and Book Emporium, he recounted his meeting with Reverend Morton.

"I suppose you could say his explanation for the fallout with Ethan is plausible, but—"

Ant wasn't best pleased to be cut off midsentence.

"Oh dear. I think we're about to get the third degree." Ant's eyeline followed Lyn's index finger in the direction of a police Jaguar. The car's deceleration and blinking left indicator confirmed their worst fears.

"He's clocked us, Lyn. If we'd have eaten in the damned tearoom, Inspector Plod wouldn't have seen us. And I haven't even finished my bacon bap."

The pair watched as Riley rolled out of the police car and strode towards them, a finger pointing for added dramatic effect.

"I told you two to keep your noses out of this case, didn't I?"

"He's not happy, is he?" muttered Ant to Lyn as he scoffed

down the last of his snack, spraying bits of bread on Lyn's coat in his haste not to be cheated out of lunch.

He watched as Lyn shot him an icy stare and brushed the lapel of her coat.

"Do you mind, you mucky pup?"

Ant shrugged his shoulders and offered a weak smile like a naughty boy caught scrumping.

Ant, concluding that discretion was the better form of valour, averted his gaze, and instead, concentrated on the pathetic figure of the detective now standing a few feet away.

"You look a little flushed, Inspector. Do you have a problem with blood pressure?"

Ant adopted his most assertive pose as he awaited an answer and watched a white skull cap form over the policeman's thinning hair.

"Do come under the canopy; all that snow on your head cannot be good for either your blood pressure or follicles, although I have read some scientific evidence that intense cold can stimulate hair growth. What do you think, Inspector?"

Ant's tone of faux concern served only to enrage the already agitated policeman.

Ant noticed that although it was Riley's choice to close the gap between them, he appeared intensely uncomfortable being so near another human being.

"I neither have a problem with blood pressure nor thinning hair." Riley hesitated for a second or two before continuing. "Anyway, so-called 'cold therapy' doesn't work. In fact, it just gives you a headache."

Ant almost choked on the last crumbs of his bap as he watched Riley blush all the more as it dawned he'd confirmed having the very problem he'd just denied.

Ant could hear Lyn chortling behind him. He nudged her arm by way of telling her to stop.

He felt her lean into him.

"That hurt," was all he heard before he felt himself being propelled into Riley.

Ant was unsure who now felt the most uncomfortable as the two men disentangled from each other, each giving a manly grunt and looking at the snow-covered ground.

Ant threw Lyn a scowl then turned back to Riley and observed displaced ice from the policeman's scalp slithering down the detective's purple cheeks.

"Would you like a tissue, Detective Inspector? That must be uncomfortable," said Lyn. She stretched her right hand out, a paper napkin pinched between two fingers. "It's only got a little bacon fat on it, but I'm sure it'll do the job just fine."

Ant watched Riley snarl but grudgingly hold out his hand to accept Lyn's gift. That was until mention of the bacon fat.

Not as daft as I thought, mused Ant.

"Thank you, but no," replied Riley, stiffening his gait. "You may think us stupid in tolerating meddlesome members of the public, such as yourselves. This does not mean, however, that our patience is without limit."

Ant noted the growl with which the detective spat his words and considered the man had decided that attack was the better form of defence.

"You spoke to my pathologist, didn't you?" said Riley.

Ant gave the man a look of disdain.

"Do you own him, then?"

His response left no room for confusion about his dislike of the policeman.

"I thought the days of serfdom in this country had long gone?"

Ant could see Riley was unsure how to respond. Here was a member of the aristocracy lecturing him about serfdom. What to do?

Eventually, the silence was broken.

"You would know more about such matters than me, Lord Stanton."

Ant smirked, allowing the detective to think he'd put him back in some imaginary box, however, and semblance of reasserted authority vanished from Riley as the last remains of snow on his scalp started to move. The white carpet slid past the detective's left ear and hit the floor with the dull thud of a snowball hitting its target.

"There, now. That must feel better," quipped Lyn.

"Hope you don't feel too light-headed," added Ant.

Denying Riley time to respond, Ant pressed on.

"Oh, we did away with all that serf stuff in 2010. We all have to change our ways, Detective Inspector. You know, a bit like the police not being on the take these days. Or perhaps some are. What do you think?"

He watched as Riley's eyes narrowed. Ant had done his homework and knew suspicion had followed the detective for years. The force's response was to move him around the country.

Out of sight, out of mind, eh?

"And how are you liking Norfolk? Where was it you served previously? And before that?" It was not a question to which Ant expected an answer. He'd made his point. Riley's reaction confirmed as much.

"Anyway, you were talking about the pathologist. You know, the one it seems you own? Well, you may wish to know Quentin and I served Queen and Country together. I heard on the grapevine that he was working in Norwich, so I toddled off to the big city and said my hellos. Nothing wrong with that, is there?"

Ant sensed Riley had become distracted.

"Are you listening, Detective Inspector?"

Fed up with having a damp scalp, Riley produced a crumpled tissue from his coat pocket and dabbed his forehead. Ant guessed it gave him a chance to think of a response to his deliberate baiting.

"I've told you both. Ethan Baldwin committed suicide. There are no suspicious circumstances. No mysterious cult hanging people by the full moon. No celestial beings venting a vengeance from heaven on one of their own."

Ant cut Riley's self-congratulatory response short.

"Careful, Inspector. That's blasphemy and is absolutely uncalled for."

Ant knew his riposte would unnerve the detective. After all, how was he to know the son of an earl didn't have connections in the church or wider establishment that had the power to harm his career?

Satisfied his ploy had worked, judging by Riley's slumped shoulder, Ant went in for the kill.

"Anyway, Detective, let's not get bogged down in theology, and of course you'll know all about the tiff between Ethan Baldwin and the vicar, won't you?"

Ant's tone was measured in the extreme.

He watched the detective.

"Never mind what I do, or do not, know about the vicar and Mr Baldwin."

Well done, Detective. You didn't fall for that one.

"Let this be a final warning. If either of you get in my way again, I'll nick you. Do you understand?"

Ant turned to Lyn as the detective retraced his steps to

the Jaguar.

"That was fun."

"Anthony, you are a tease, and you'll come undone one of these days, young man. Anyway, do you think he knows?"

Ant laughed and pulled Lyn by the hand as they walked gingerly across the ice-covered cobblestones towards Dotti's place.

"You bet he knows. It was written all over his face. Look."

Ant pointed at the Jaguar roaring out of the village with an icy spray spitting from its rear wheels.

"He's heading for the vicarage."

"Never mind the car. You'll go too far with him one of these days. Like it or not, he can make both our lives a misery if he wishes to."

Ant didn't react. Instead, he looked into the now empty paper bag which had contained his lunch, blew into it, and scrunched it closed. With a swift thump with his free hand he exploded it, which resulted in an almighty bang.

He watched Lyn, who had been looking the other way, jump with shock.

"You always do that, fool."

He could see she was far from pleased.

Ant's schoolboy smirk signalled his contentedness with recent events.

"His chief inspector knows Riley's an idiot. He doesn't want him here anymore than we do."

Lyn snatched what remained of the paper bag.

"And you know this for a fact, do you?"

Ant's smile broadened.

"You might say so. I couldn't possible comment."

His tone was meant to intrigue.

Lyn busied herself picking bits of bap from Ant's collar. He made no attempt to stop her.

"So why did you tell Riley about the vicar? Haven't you just dropped him in it?"

Ant shook his head.

"As I said, he must have suspected him already. I just wanted him to know that we knew, to wind him up. If the vicar *is* up to something, Riley will frighten him to death, which may flush the man out for us."

Ant brushed a thin layer of snow from Lyn's shoulder.

"So you think it's worth keeping our eye on Reverend Morton?"

Ant nodded.

"As we've both admitted, he has a plausible explanation for the argument with Ethan. Nevertheless, I sense there's something going on in the background he doesn't want anyone to know about. Let's hope it's not covering the tracks of a murder."

He watched as Lyn's mood darkened. He could have kicked himself for overlooking the obvious.

Mustn't forget how close Lyn is to the church.

"Enough of the sad face," said Ant, keen to lift his friend's mood. "Are you still in touch with that old boyfriend of yours? You know, the one in the planning department in Cromer?"

He watched as Lyn gave him a world weary sort of look.

"You know quite well I see him from time to time, so don't be so obvious. What do you want me to do?"

Ant pulled ahead of Lyn, keen to reach the coffee shop as sanctuary against the worsening weather.

"Oh, just wondered if you might ask your sweetheart a question or two, strictly for the good of our investigations, you understand."

Ant got no more than five paces before Lyn's well-aimed snowball caught his exposed neck.

7
PAPER TRAIL

Friday morning prayers progressed in their usual efficient way. Today, like every day, Reverend Morton led his dwindling flock in contemplation and thanks.

Except today it was a troubled vicar who trudged back to the vestry.

He stowed the medieval chalice and silver plate back into the safe before undoing and hanging up his vestments. The vicar then slumped into a simple wooden chair, which fitted to perfection in its frugal surroundings.

It took less than a minute to count the collection and enter the total in the church ledger.

The archbishop's words swirled around his head.

"Sort the finances out, or I'll deconsecrate the church."

He thought his superior's words harsh for a senior cleric.

Whatever happened to charity? reflected the vicar.

The stillness allowing the vicar to ponder his dilemma did not last long. His mobile started to dance across the table, its screen illuminated with a name he knew well.

Swiping the screen to the right with his thumb, the vicar heard a familiar voice.

"Yes, I know we agreed," he responded. "There's something I must do first. I'll be with you as soon as I can."

Reverend Morton didn't wait for a response. Instead, he ended the call and slid the phone into the inside pocket of his jacket.

Locking the vestry door, the vicar walked to the front entrance of the church. He then turned left to walk through the old graveyard. Staring at one grave after another, he kept seeing the same surnames crop up. He was aware some locals were able to trace their families back hundreds of years.

I just can't allow this sacred place to close.

In the near distance he saw Glebe Cottage, its name picked out in white lettering on a piece of carved wood fixed to the ornate wrought-iron front gate.

Reverend Morton reflected on what "Glebe" stood for. It meant a cottage, and the land the building stood on had once belonged to the church.

If only we still owned it, the church's financial future would be secure.

Seconds later, he stood at the back door of Ethan's home. It had been unoccupied for just a few days. Already it looked forlorn waiting for its owner to return.

The vicar looked over his shoulder checking to see if anyone was about.

Soon he concentrated his gaze to a small, glazed earthenware planter by the door. It had been there for as long as he could remember. Stooping down he tipped it on its edge and retrieved a key. He'd warned Ethan many times not to leave it under the jar. Now he was glad the warden had failed to heed his advice.

Crossing the kitchen, he made his way into the hallway; the vicar took care not to touch any surfaces. A pair of delicate, white gloves he used for polishing the church silver served their purpose as he turned a Victorian brass doorknob.

The vicar was keen no one should know, at least not the police, that he'd been in the cottage.

As he entered the front room, he felt as if Ethan had just nipped out to collect his morning paper and would be back at any moment. On the dining table rested a half-drunk cup of tea. In the saucer, the remains of a wafer biscuit.

Reverend Morton tried hard not to notice the ordinariness of it all.

He shuffled through the tidy row of lever-box files that lined an alcove next to the chimney breast. He opened one then another as he searched in vain for the vital document.

His frustration surfaced as he thumbed the final cardboard container. The vicar prised back the sprung plastic arm that held its contents secure with so much force that it snapped into several pieces, each fragment flying in a different direction.

Convinced his mission had been a failure, he turned and made his way back towards the door. In doing so, he knocked a crossword puzzle book from the arm of Ethan's favourite chair. Bending down to retrieve the publication, he noticed a sheaf of paper nestled between its pages.

"Thank the Lord." Such was the relief that he couldn't help speaking out loud to an empty house.

The vicar leafed through the pages held together at one corner with a paper clip.

He had found what he'd been looking for.

As the adrenalin rush subsided, he became increasingly aware of the precarious position he now found himself in.

How would he explain being in Ethan's cottage?

In his haste to exit the building, he decided to save a few

seconds and leave by the front door instead of his planned route to keep out of sight via the back door and through Ethan's vegetable garden to the church.

It was a mistake.

"Good morning, Vicar," quipped a relaxed voice.

Reverend Morton looked up from the stone paving slabs, with a start. He hadn't expected to come across anyone.

"Ah, er, Tina. How are you this morning?"

In his agitated state, the words tumbled over one another.

He watched in terror as the school secretary smiled.

"Thank you, I'm—"

"Good, good," he said, not waiting for Tina to finish. "Can't stop. God's work will not wait." As he spoke, he pushed the sheaf of papers into his cassock.

* * *

"So, at the moment, Anthony, there's not too much to worry about."

Ant was thankful for the reassurance as he showed Dr Thorndike into the library of Stanton Hall. A thermos flask of coffee rested on a small table just inside the wide double doors of the exquisite book-lined room.

"Please, do take a seat. Coffee?"

Ant pointed to a leather carver to one side of the roaring fire.

"Just the job for this snowy weather. I suppose logs are something you have plenty of."

Ant watched as the doctor dropped into the deep pocketed, leather seat and leant forward, rubbing his hands together before the yellow-and-blue flames, licking the soot-covered, iron fireback.

"You should see what the garage is charging for a bag of logs these days."

Ant's face began to flush.

"It bears no relation to what we sell them to the garage for, I can tell you," replied Ant as he handed a steaming cup of coffee to the medic.

He noticed the doctor's amused look.

"Ah, I see. So you supply—"

Ant returned the physician's smile.

The two men spent the next few minutes exchanging views on the long-range forecast for the winter and amazement at how early in the season snow had fallen. All too soon the doctor returned to the subject of Ant's parents' health.

"As I said earlier, there is no immediate danger. However, heart failure is a debilitating condition. While your father is currently the stronger of the two, we should take nothing for granted."

Ant now understood that the doctor's lighthearted banter was his way of preparing the recipient to receive news of something less palatable.

Ant's background meant he wanted to get on with things.

I can deal with things I know about.

"Your prognosis?"

Ant couldn't take his eyes off the doctor as he once more turned to the roaring fire.

Let's have it, Doc.

"This cold spell will do your parents no good, whatsoever, so it's important that your father isn't allowed to gallivant around the estate."

Ant gazed into the remnants of his coffee.

"You know Dad as well as me, so fat chance of keeping him indoors."

Dr Thorndike rose from his chair.

"Yes, I know. But there is no option if we are to keep him with us for the longest time."

The words struck Ant like a thump to the head. He knew the reality of the situation. He just didn't want to hear the words.

"I suggest we occupy your father by getting him to tend your mother. You know, reading to her and so forth."

Ant looked up at the doctor and let out a throaty laugh.

"What? They'd kill one another. Mum's worse than Dad is when it comes to being nursed. You know how independent they both are."

The doctor nodded.

"I do, Anthony. But you should know this. If you fail to slow your father down, he may not live to see the summer. On the other hand, if he behaves, well—"

Ant shook his head, the small movement almost undetectable. He acknowledged that Thorndike had no need to finish his sentence.

"Not sure Dad has ever looked at life in those terms, Doctor. I'm certain he's not going to do so now."

The two men shared a look without the need to discuss the matter further. However, Ant sensed Thorndike wanted to ask him something. He guessed what was coming.

He felt the doctor's right hand coming to a gentle rest on his shoulder.

"And how are you doing, Anthony?"

Ant didn't react to the physical contact nor did he meet the doctor's concerned stare.

"You've heard, then?"

"Your father told me. He—"

"Dad? He doesn't know."

"I can assure you he does, Anthony. I doubt you're the only one who has military contacts, eh?"

The implications of the revelation appalled Ant. He'd wanted to keep it from his father until he felt ready to talk about it.

"You know your father. He's old school. He'll wait until you're ready to tell him. But there are two things I want you to bear in mind."

Thorndike had Ant's full attention.

"Your father cannot wait too much longer for you to say something."

Ant's eyes glistened as the doctor's words sank in.

"And you will pay a high price if you delay treatment for your PTSD for very long. But you know that already, don't you?"

Ant felt the doctor's gentle touch morph to a tight grip and immediately understood.

Delay on either front was not an option.

Ant nodded.

"I'll sort it, Doctor. And thank you. I guess I needed to hear that."

Ant nodded as he met the doctor's steely, but reassuring, look.

"Good. I'm here to help when you're ready. Speaking of which, I understand you've got together with Lyn again, so to speak?"

Ant bristled at the comment, though he didn't understand why.

"Well, I wouldn't say—"

"Doesn't matter on what basis you're seeing her, Anthony. Don't underestimate just how important it is to have someone you can trust to turn to. Do you understand?"

Ant had no need to reply. The look between them was enough.

"Anyway. I'll say goodnight."

The doctor slipped on his overcoat as Ant showed his visitor back into the cavernous hallway and opened the heavy entrance doors to the hall.

"Drive with care," shouted Ant as the doctor crossed a patch of snow-covered gravel towards his car.

"I will. With luck, the vicar is off the road now. The blighter almost killed me on my way over. He was driving like a madman. In a hurry to get somewhere by the looks of things."

8

THE OPEN ROAD

"I thought you said this thing was, how did you put it, 'in fine fettle.' It sounds ready for the scrapyard to me."

Lyn's words stung as Ant worked hard to keep the Morgan going despite the engine misfiring.

He was still feeling down after Dr Thorndike's visit. To top it all, his beloved Morgan began to misfire.

"I'll pull over to check. I'm certain it's nothing serious."

He could see Lyn looked far from convinced as he coaxed the stuttering car into a paddock at the top of a small rise. The sorry state of the Morgan was at odds with the stunning view over Stanton Parva.

"Well, it sounds serious to me, Ant."

Certain the engine was about to fail, Ant turned the engine off and glided the vehicle to a silent stop. Ratcheting the handbrake as far up as he could pull it, Ant depressed the clutch and put the car into first gear.

"You always do that. You know you're not supposed to leave a parked car in gear."

Ant chose to ignore his friend's criticism.

"Oh, I forgot. Since it's broken down, the car isn't going

anywhere, is it?" added Lyn. Her inflection delivered a withering verdict.

Ant removed his back-to-front peaked cap and unfurled a thick wool scarf from around his neck.

"And as I tell you every time, that's the way Dad taught me to drive. Funnily enough, I haven't had a parked car run away on me yet. Unlike someone I could mention."

Ant gave Lyn a knowing look.

"You know full well the handbrake was faulty that day. The garage said so. Anyway, nobody got hurt."

He enjoyed the sight of Lyn in full displacement mode, removing her wool bobble hat and undoing the zipper on her winter coat for no particular reason other than to not look at him.

Ant let out a belly laugh.

"That's if you don't include Arkwright's vegetable display stand. Not to mention the squashed tomatoes. Looked like the scene from *Apocalypse Now.*"

The more Ant laughed, the more annoyed he knew Lyn was becoming. He also knew his friend would bide her time since she clearly wasn't retaliating. Ant was the first to acknowledge Lyn had the measure of him since they were at school together as children.

Silence fell as the two friends took in their surroundings. Having the soft top of the Morgan stowed away meant they were able to take in the Norfolk night sky in all its majesty.

"Strange old world, Ant. No matter what mess we cause down here, everything up there seems to remain the same."

Even though Ant wanted to scrutinise the Morgan's instrument display for an explanation of the car's bad behaviour, he matched Lyn's gaze scanning a thousand shimmering stars.

"I guess you're thinking about Ethan too, Ant?"

He looked across at her.

"Yes, I am."

"Have we got it all wrong? Could he have killed himself?"

Ant shook his head.

"We both know he didn't commit suicide. Let's think about what we *do* know. He was too frail to have got himself off the ground. Then there's the argument we know he had with the vicar."

He watched as Lyn's eyes widened. She was suddenly animated.

"Speaking about the vicar. I think your idea of using that daft detective to flush him out may have worked."

Ant's curiosity went into overdrive.

"What do you mean?"

"Well, Tina saw him coming out of Glebe Cottage. She said he looked as if he were trying to hide something from her. When she tried to engage him in conversation, he did a flit, pronto. Strange behaviour for a man of the cloth, don't you think?"

Ant nodded.

"More than strange because the doctor told me the vicar almost ran him off the road: said he was driving like a madman."

"Thorndike. Why have you been speaking to him?"

Oh dear. Now I've put my foot in it, thought Ant as he picked up on her concerned glance.

He reacted quickly to divert Lyn's line of questioning.

Not ready to discuss the topic yet.

"Er, what? Oh, I'll tell you later."

Ant took the opportunity to escape further questioning by opening the driver's door and climbing out.

"Strange name for a cottage, 'Glebe,' don't you think?"

As he spoke, Ant undid a leather strap holding the bonnet in place then lifted the cover to expose the full glory of the machine's engine.

"And I thought you liked history," responded Lyn as Ant's head disappeared into the engine compartment.

Thank heavens Lyn's not pushing the Thorndike thing.

Ant knew Lyn well enough to tell his reaction to the revelation was enough to stop further discussion on the matter: for the present, at any rate.

"Glebe refers to land owned by the church, Ant. Back in the day, the vicar was able to get an income from it to supplement his stipend from the church diocese."

Ant lifted his head from the engine, catching it on the bonnet as he did so. Massaging his scalp by way of checking for blood, he straightened himself and turned to Lyn.

"Who's been swallowing a dictionary, then?" Ant made no attempt to hide his sarcasm, although he could see it had no effect on Lyn.

"I did some village history with the kids a few weeks ago. One of the children asked about it, so I researched the subject. You know, like teachers do."

Now who's being sarcastic.

"Ant, what if the vicar thinks he still has a claim on the place? Perhaps he was looking for evidence when Tina saw him."

Ant leant on the open door of the Morgan, his interest engaged by Lyn's developing theory. "And don't forget that property developer. I think his name is Grindle. He certainly had a motive for wanting Ethan out of the way."

"Why?" replied Lyn.

He could see she was none too pleased as Ant seemed to cut across her theory about the vicar.

"Does the term 'ransom strip' mean anything to you, Lyn?"

From her facial expression, he guessed it didn't.

"It's when someone owns a piece of land that a developer needs before they can finalise a construction deal. In this case, the land Glebe Cottage stands on is the only access point onto the land Grindle presumably owns. If he doesn't secure Glebe Cottage, he can't develop the land. So you see, whoever *does* own the cottage can hold Grindle for ransom, so to speak."

Ant watched as a smile returned to Lyn's face.

Now the penny's dropped.

"You're saying that either the vicar or Grindle may have murdered Ethan? You know, so they could get their mitts on Glebe Cottage and demolish it? Perhaps they were in it together?"

Ant shook his head.

"No, I don't think the vicar murdered Ethan. It just doesn't fit."

He hesitated for a few seconds before continuing. "Then again, if he *did* find proof the church still owns the cottage and the land it stands on, then happy days, except—"

Lyn broke in.

"The vicar may be Grindle's next..."

9
SAINTS AND SINNERS

The frosted surface of Norwich Road glistened like a carpet of diamonds in the low morning sun as Ant drove to the village.

At least the Morgan's behaving, he thought as its engine purred beneath the bonnet.

Ant revelled in the village's laid-back Saturday routine. One minute he'd be slowing down to give a horse rider safe passage, the next, giving way to the postie on her rounds.

Love this place.

Two minutes later, he pulled into the forecourt of Fitch's Motor Repairs.

"Looks like you're busy," said Ant as he glanced around the cluttered space. A hotchpotch of vehicles filled the uneven, compacted earth and gravel yard.

"Always am, Ant. I keep my prices down and give top-notch service. Works for me," replied Fitch, while wiping his hands with the proverbial oily rag. "How's she running?"

Ant looked forlornly at the Morgan.

"Behaving for now but a sore point, and sort of why I'm here."

Ant watched as Fitch gave the car a quick once-over with his practised eye then shrugged his shoulders.

"It's not my company you're after, then," teased Fitch. "What's the problem?"

Ant reached into the passenger's seat and pulled out a wet towel.

"Ah, so you've been using the car as a portable shower, have you?" said Fitch.

Ant didn't see the funny side, a reaction he knew made Fitch enjoy the moment even more.

"Something like that. The thing is, I'm in Lyn's bad books. We went out for a drive last night. You know, soft top down, starry night, that kind of stuff. Then out of nowhere, it rains cats and dogs. I put the soft top up. Job done, you would think. Unfortunately, Lyn got soaked as I drove her home."

Fitch inspected the seam of the canvas covering, running his index finger along the soggy material.

"I don't want to say, 'I told you so,' but I told you so!" Remember me saying it needed waterproofing?"

Ant held his hands up in capitulation.

"Yes, yes, all right. Fair cop, guv. So have you got a can of that waterproofing spray stuff so I can fix the stupid thing or not?"

Ant knew his tone was bordering on the desperate.

"I have, but you'll have to wait for the top to dry or you'll be wasting your time. Anyway, serves you right. You know as well as I do that roaring around pitch-black roads in an old car is hardly Lyn's idea of a night out. You should have treated her to a meal or whatever romantic types do these days."

Ant frowned.

"That's enough of that. There's no boyfriend, girlfriend

stuff going on with Lyn. What are you thinking, mate? I mean—"

Fitch interrupted.

"What did that Shakespeare bloke say? 'He doth protest too much, methinks.'"

Ant cocked his head back and sniffed the air.

"To be strictly accurate, Fitch, I think you'll find Shakespeare talked about 'the lady,' not a 'he.' Anyway, moving on," said Ant without the trace of a smile. "What are you working on currently?"

Ant followed Fitch across the yard.

"There's a jammed tail lift on this van. It belongs to old Wilcox, and it's in a right old mess." Ant could just make out the faded name sign on the side of the box van:

Wilcox Removals and Storage.

Just then the sound of a car door banging caught both men's attention. A well-dressed man was leaning over his Morgan just outside the entrance to the garage.

"Do you know him, Fitch?"

The mechanic strained to see around his friend and glimpse the suited stranger.

"That's the bloke I was telling you about. His name is Stephen Grindle."

"Ah, yes. And that's his new Morgan Sports he's driving. Beautiful beast, isn't it? Must have cost a pretty penny. So he is our mysterious property developer, then."

Ant turned back to Fitch.

"It most certainly is; there must be a shed load of money in property to afford a car like that."

You're not wrong there, mate.

"Spot on, Fitch. Listen, I'll be back in a minute. I want a word with our friend. Let's see what he knows about Ethan's place."

Ant moved towards the yard entrance without waiting for a response from Fitch.

"Yours, is it? She's a beauty, no doubting that," said Grindle, pointing to Ant's car.

Ant looked back at his vintage Morgan.

"Yes, she is, and judging by what you're driving, I assume you're a fan too?"

Ant studied the stranger closely trying to get his measure. He knew the man was, in return, sizing him up.

"I've loved Morgan cars since I was a kid. Promised myself that if ever I made it, I'd buy one."

Ant watched Grindle stroke the front wing of his car as he spoke. It was if he were petting his favourite cat.

"Whatever you've made it in, it didn't take you long."

Can't be more than thirty, thought Ant as he silently admired the man's car.

"They're still handmade, you know."

Am I really that transparent?

"Have you done the factory tour?" he added. "Fascinating stuff. The café isn't half-bad either. I can recommend the cappuccino and lemon drizzle cake."

Grindle offered a thin smile. Ant could tell the stranger liked to be in control. He had come across such personalities many times. Bold front, brittle underneath.

Time for some fun, I think.

"No, I haven't. I've been meaning to go for years, but work and stuff always seems to get in the way."

He observed that Grindle's smile had slipped.

"Work? What does that mean to you?"

Ant noted the none too subtle change in Grindle's demeanour.

This is good.

"What do you think I do for a living, then?"

Ant's voice had an edge intended to tease.

"I doubt telling your servants what to do up at Stanton Hall takes much out of your day."

He's done his homework, but why so bitter? thought Ant.

He examined his opponent's expression. Grindle's cheeks twitched, indicating pent-up aggression.

He knows he's not reacting well. One more push, I think.

"Ah, I see. Another class warrior. As you say, instructing the servants on their daily duties does not take long."

Ant had adopted the same pantomime character he used on Detective Inspector Riley.

"The thing is, it leaves much more time for my other job. I don't do it for the money, you understand."

He watched as Grindle flushed. His nostrils began to flare.

"Other job?"

So he has trouble keeping his emotional intelligence in check under stress, does he?

"Oh, I dabble in land and related stuff. Now, what did you say you do?"

Ant's tone displayed a deliberate air of disinterest.

"Well, you've got enough of that. Land, I mean."

Sensing his opponent thought there might be a deal for the taking, Ant went in for the kill.

Got you.

"Oh no. You misunderstand, Mr Grindle, eh, Stephen, isn't it?"

Grindle nodded. Ant could tell the man was confused as to how he knew his first name.

"You see, I don't buy or sell land. The estate has been in the family for centuries, and well, we don't need the money, if you know what I mean?"

If only you knew the truth.

"When I say dabble, what I mean is that I specialise in planning anomalies. Fascinating topic, you know. I can't tell you how many shifty characters I come across who try to shaft some poor person out of their little house or whatever. Believe it or not, there are some people who will just stop at nothing to get their own way. Can you believe that, Stephen?"

Ant's domination of Grindle was complete.

"And what of you, Stephen? What did you succeed in so young to deliver this sort of wealth?"

Ant waved a hand in the general direction of Grindle's spotless Morgan.

"Property development. But—"

Ant purposely cut across Grindle.

"Oh dear, old chap. I do apologise."

He knew he was in danger of overacting but couldn't resist the temptation.

"Please forgive me speaking in such general terms. I didn't mean for a second to tar you with the same brush as the nastier elements of your profession. You do understand, don't you?"

Ant placed a hand on one of Grindle's elbows by way of reassurance. In fact, his intention was to reinforce his dominance.

He noted that Grindle tried to recoil from the physical contact.

A brittle personality indeed.

Within seconds, Grindle had regained his composure. Ant observed the first signs of the man's arrogance reasserting itself even if his eyes told a different story.

"No offence taken. After all, you weren't to know what I do for a living. Oh, and for the record, I conduct my business by the book."

Ant smiled to himself at Grindle's overemphasis on the overt reference to lawful trading.

"I'm sure you do," replied Ant as he extended his right hand.

Grindle reciprocated.

Handshake completed, the men parted company.

Ant watched as Grindle slid into his Morgan and marvelled at the low, masculine rumble of the exhaust as he disappeared into the distance.

"What was all that guff about you specialising in, what did you call it, 'planning anomalies'? And what about those bloody servants? You do talk a load of—"

Ant cut Fitch off, holding an open-palmed hand up to reinforce matters.

"As I've told you before, Fitch, look someone straight in the eye; talk with enough confidence, and they'll believe whatever you tell them. As for the servants, well, you're my mechanic, aren't you?"

Fitch made as if to doff an imaginary cap before retrieving the sodden towel from the forecourt floor.

"I believe this belongs to you, sir?"

Ant ducked as Fitch let fly.

Too late.

"Round two, I think, Fitch."

A split second later, Ant was pursuing his quarry at full pelt around the yard with the dripping towel flying between the two friends at regular intervals.

The chase ended when Ant's mobile rang.

"Do I have to?"

Ant watched Fitch stop in his tracks and noted he had the look of someone expecting to be tricked. The man had his arm out in a defensive position as if expecting his opponent to launch another attack with the filthy fabric.

"I will, yes: half past seven."

Ant pressed a key on the mobile to terminate the call.

"Bad news?"

"You could say that. Lyn's making me go to the quiz tonight at the village hall."

Fitch roared with laughter, made all the more enjoyable by a hardened military officer receiving orders from a head teacher.

"I don't know what you're laughing at. She said you have to come too."

10
QUIZ NIGHT

Ant walked at a brisk pace as he crossed High Street and held his collar up against the chilly evening wind. He turned the corner into Long Lane and walked down the narrow stone path that traced its way past an assortment of thatched cottages.

Two hundred yards ahead stood the village hall. Ant could see an array of multicoloured lights providing a welcome distraction from the leaden sky.

As he neared his destination, he caught sight of a strangely familiar figure.

Samantha. I wonder if she's feeling better now.

"Hi, good to see you again. How are you doing?"

Ant chose his tone carefully after seeing her so upset in the church.

He quickly realised that in the semi-darkness, Samantha hadn't seen him. Instead, the girl had her head down as she locked the wire-framed gates of Wilcox Removals and Storage.

"Oh, okay, thank you."

Samantha spoke hesitantly as she half looked at Ant

while turning the key in a heavy padlock. "It's kind of you to ask."

"Are you coming to the quiz?"

Ant checked himself realising how insensitive his question might appear.

He sensed Samantha was looking through rather than at him.

"Sorry, no. I need to get home. Dad will be waiting and…"

Ant's embarrassment grew. He wanted no repeat of the church situation.

"Of course. Of course. Do forgive me."

She smiled.

"Please. There's nothing to apologise for. Are *you* going to the quiz?"

Brave girl, thought Ant.

He admired her composure after her recent loss of her friend, Ethan.

"Yes, I am, although I hate quizzes. I always get the answers wrong. Let's walk together until I get to the hall, yes?"

Samantha didn't answer. Ant noticed the beginnings of a smile as she joined him.

The two walked in silence for a few seconds, neither looking at the other. Ant wasn't quite sure what to say.

It's either the weather or hobbies.

He opted for the latter.

"I don't suppose there's much for a young girl to do around the village, is there?"

It was the best he could come up with.

Samantha shook her head. It was what he'd expected since he'd felt the same at her age.

"No. Although there's the Sea Cadets I go to sometimes. They do some interesting stuff."

Ant worked hard to show interest. Anything to get her talking. He was pleased that her mood seemed to lighten as she explained the complexities of a sailing ship's rigging.

All too soon they reached the village hall.

"Well, I'd better get in, or my teammates will be after my scalp."

"And my dad will be expecting his tea," replied Samantha.

For the first time in their few minutes together, she gave him eye contact.

Ant took a step back, smiled, and gestured for the young woman to pass. Seconds later, he crossed the small car park of the village hall to see Lyn standing at the door making an exaggerated arm movement to look at her watch.

"Thought you'd got lost."

"Someone needed a bit of company." He didn't elaborate, and Lyn didn't enquire further, although he knew she'd seen him talking to Samantha.

"You're here, then."

Ant could just about hear the familiar voice above the general hubbub of the small space, having politely pushed himself through a throng of villagers. Turning to face Fitch, he saw Tina was with him. Ant acknowledged both with a friendly smile.

"Seems so."

Ant patted himself down as if checking all was present and correct.

"So this is our team, is it? Heaven help us. A retired soldier, a useless car mechanic, and a bossy head teacher. That just leaves you, Tina. At least you can spell and are used to organising a rabble."

Ant wore a look of mock resignation on his face.

"Speak for yourself," replied Lyn as she also strained to make herself heard above the noise.

Ant strained to look around the small hall. He knew the drill and shared everyone's irritation at being corralled at one end, since they were only allowed to take their allotted table on command of the quizmaster.

He could just about make out Jack Valentine, host for the evening, as he struggled to make his way onto the tiny stage. Ant, like everyone else, sometimes bridled at the man's officious manner but readily acknowledged that without him events such as tonight wouldn't happen.

"Testing, testing, one, two, three," said Jack. He then blew into the microphone for good measure, giving a passable impression he was suffering a bilious attack.

"Why does everyone who picks up a mic go through the same stupid routine?" protested Ant.

"Think it's as much about nerves as anything else," replied Tina.

"Do you remember that comic who built his whole act on pretending the microphone kept cutting out?" said Fitch.

Ant looked as puzzled at the other two.

"Is that one of tonight's questions?" joked Ant.

"Got you," replied Fitch. "It was Norman Collier. He was a great comic, wasn't he?"

Before Ant could reply, the sound of Jack's voice boomed around the wooden building.

"Ladies and Gentlemen, if there are any, that is. Please find your tables. The quiz is about to start."

Makes the same joke every time, thought Ant.

The hall erupted into a frenzy of movement as people scurried first one way then the other to locate their team's base.

As Ant neared their table, he felt a hand on his shoulder. Turning, he was surprised to be met by a smiling, young woman. For a split second he was unsure of who she was.

"Sally. Great to see you. Are you feeling better after your shock? And the baby?"

Ah, now I know who you are.

"It's been a hard few days for you, hasn't it? said Ant without letting slip he'd been momentarily confused, pleased that she hadn't seemed to have noticed.

"I'm fine and thanks, both of you. I know you're working like stink to find out what happened to poor Ethan. Oh, and yes, the baby, Dr Thorndike says he… or she… is absolutely fine. Thanks for asking."

Ant glanced at the two women who were exchanging contented smiles.

Well, that's all right, then.

A semblance of order soon returned as the noise level reduced to a low buzz as heads bent towards the centre of team tables to finalise tactics.

Responsibilities allocated and pencil checks completed, the assembly readied itself for battle.

Jack's tone changed as he asked the first question. He spoke in a low, serious voice, as if he were about to deliver a four-minute warning of impending doom.

"Your first question. Which British general met his end at Khartoum?"

Ant took careful note of a player at the next table.

"I know this. It's Gordon Ramsey," said the excited man.

He noticed Lyn giving him the eye.

"You're not serious, are you? For heaven's sake, Ant, you're a military man. You should know this."

Above the hubbub, he attempted to defend himself.

"Don't be daft. She's talking rubbish. It's Alf, not Gordon Ramsey."

Ant looked mystified as he watched his teammates almost fall off their chairs laughing. He gave Fitch a particularly hard stare.

"What?"

"Ant, you're nearly right... and very wrong. The former is a chef, but the latter was England's football manager at the 1966 World Cup."

Ant wore a perplexed look as he plundered his brain for the military history that had been drummed into him at Sandhurst.

"Give up?" asked Fitch.

He continued before Ant had time to react.

"The answer is Charles Gordon. You know, 'Gordon of Khartoum.'"

Ant thumped the centre of his forehead with an open palm. He could see Fitch had a look of expectancy.

"What do you want, Fitch, a *Kinder Surprise*?"

"You can keep your chocolate egg, Ant. It means the first round of drinks are on you."

* * *

"THANK HEAVENS THAT'S OVER. My head hurts."

Ant massaged his temple for emphasis as the first part of the evening came to a welcomed end. He shivered in the chilled air as he and his three companions gathered just outside the rear door of the hall. They had a job to dodge the fog of tar and nicotine from a huddled group of middle-aged locals standing opposite.

I hate second-hand smoke.

Ant frowned at the smokers and gave an exaggerated

cough. No words were exchanged, but his acting skills were enough for the offenders to move away from the door and shuffle farther onto the car park like a waddle of penguins bracing themselves against a blizzard.

"Reminded me of those horrible school spelling tests," said Fitch.

Ant nodded, raised an arm above his head then brought it down as if striking something.

"You're not wrong there. Remember our English teacher, Stinger Cumberland, and that stiff leather strap he hid up his jacket sleeve?"

Ant watched Fitch shudder, Lyn laugh, and Tina frown.

"Called it his 'stinger,' didn't he?"

Ant pointed to the back of his left hand.

"Too right he did. You got a whack across here for each spelling you got wrong. Flaming hurt, that strap did."

"And never on the right hand so you could keep writing. Can't imagine that happening now."

"It does not, Fitch. Anyway, it didn't work since both of you are still atrocious at spelling. Am I correct?"

Ant looked at Fitch as they both broke out into laughter.

"No, and I still hate the smell of leather."

"My point exactly, Ant. Not the leather bit, of course," said Lyn, trying to make a serious point. "Corporal punishment, I mean. Just useless and wrong."

Ant looked at his other two companions as a combined smirk broke out.

"Now then, Head Teacher. You're quite right. We're only winding you up, even if I do still bear the scars."

He glanced at the back of his left hand and pulled a faux sad face.

"Hmm," huffed Lyn. Ant watched as the expression on her face changed from mate to headmistress. The more severe her look became, the funnier he and the others found it.

"Ladies and Gentlemen, if there are any," said the quizmaster.

His stale joke met with a universal groan. "Part two will begin in three minutes. That's three minutes. I thank you."

"Why does he always have to be so precise. It drives me nuts."

"His father was an accountant, Ant. I think that might have something to do with it," said Fitch.

The others gave Fitch a bemused look.

"What?"

"Fitch, his dad was a bookie who went bankrupt, which in my mind has to be a first."

Ant winked at Lyn and Tina, who were already ahead of him. He then placed a reassuring arm around Fitch and ruffled his friend's hair with his free hand.

"Come on, we'd better go in for the second half. Look, the throng is almost upon us."

Ant pointed to the smokers who were taking a synchronised final drag on their cigs, and a crush of villagers headed for the open entrance.

Ant raced ahead with Fitch. He had no intention of taking a pummelling from Phyllis, Betty, and the other formidable elder stateswomen of the village. He was wise enough to know they were not to be messed with.

"Did you manage to fix that van you were working on earlier, Fitch?"

His friend opened both arms as if describing the size of a fish he'd caught.

"Yes, but you wouldn't believe the damage a piece of old hemp that size could do."

Ant nodded, though he didn't quite understand Fitch's

point. He struggled to hear his friend over the frenzy of excited villagers as they took their seats and waited for the quizmaster to do his thing.

* * *

STEPHEN GRINDLE PARKED his Morgan outside Glebe Cottage. In the darkness he peered at the lonely building. Shadows danced across the flint wall like backlit glove puppets acting out some crazy slapstick routine.

He waited as his car's hands-free telephone system played the call tone.

Grindle tapped the steering wheel with both hands and played an imaginary drum riff as his frustration grew.

At last the call connected. He didn't wait for the other person to finish speaking.

"I'm sat here doing nothing, that's what. Where are you?"

His tone was angry, his patience exhausted. He'd had enough.

"We need to meet and sort this deal out once and for all. I've too much money sunk into it to let it go now. Do you understand?"

11

SUNDAY LUNCH

"I'm sorry the chocolate cake is a day late," said Lyn as she handed Ant her coat.

Walking across the oak-boarded floor, her steps fell silent as she crossed onto the lush pile of a hearth rug. She stood behind two occupied dining chairs in their prime position in front of the warming, open fire.

Lyn placed a hand on each chair back and leant forward before planting a warm kiss on the Earl of Stanton's cheek. She turned and landed an affectionate peck on Ant's mother's cheek.

"Not to worry, you do spoil us with your wonderful baking, my dear," replied the earl, his voice bright as a button. "Nice you're able to join us for Sunday lunch, and we now have our sweet!"

Lyn watched the earl's face light up with delight.

"Hope you don't mind us eating in here instead of the dining room. As you know, this used to be the drawing room in the old days. It's much cosier than the other room."

"I think it's a great idea. There's nothing better than a

roaring fire that you can feel on your cheeks on a day like this," replied Lyn.

She'd listened to the same story about the origin of the room by the old lady many times. It didn't bother Lyn in the slightest.

"I'll serve."

Not waiting for a response, Lyn opened the hostess trolley and accepted Ant's offer to help dish up the piping-hot meal.

"Such a good idea, those warming cabinet thingies, aren't they?" said Ant's father. "It was the cook's idea and means she can prepare food for us without having to hang around while we old duffers shuffle our bones."

* * *

A PITILESS WIND blew off the North Sea, courtesy of the Russian Steppes. Keen to escape its ravages, Ant and Lyn took full advantage of the shelter offered by the walled garden.

As they walked their lunch off, both were in a reflective mood.

"Your mum sounded tired, Ant. Gerald looked a bit distracted too. Is everything all right?"

Ant pulled the few remaining leaves off a rose bush overhanging the gravel path.

"You know Mum and Dad. The doctor tells them to take it easy, and what do they do? Dig over a new flower border. In their mid-eighties and thrashing about with spades. I ask you."

Lyn's gaze followed Ant's finger as he pointed to a tiny patch of newly cultivated earth.

Lyn picked up on Ant's intonation in a heartbeat.

"So that's what Dr Thorndike's visit was all about."

She watched as Ant stopped his impromptu hand pruning and pivoted his head towards her.

"I didn't say he'd called when I mentioned him to you the other day."

She knew he was being defensive.

Lyn fixed Ant with a look he was unable to ignore.

"You didn't need to. I know you better than you know yourself sometimes."

Lyn's smile, and the sincerity in her voice disarmed Ant.

It always did.

They continued their stroll as each reminisced about childhood certainties and always having parents around.

Except as grown-ups, they knew these things were an illusion.

"But they're as happy as Larry, you know, Lyn. Apart from Dad's war service, they've never spent a night apart. Can you believe that? I dread to think what will happen when one of them goes."

Lyn could see how Ant struggled with the thought and watched as he fell silent for a few seconds.

"And your parents, Lyn?"

Lyn shrugged her shoulders. "Do you know, they still can't spend more than two minutes in each other's company without arguing. Why one or the other doesn't move out of the village is beyond me."

"Parents. We moan about them when they're here. Can't bear to think about losing them, Lyn."

Lyn turned towards Ant, exchanging a look that needed no further explanation.

"Right, enough of this depressing stuff. Let's talk about murder," said Ant.

Lyn couldn't help but laugh at the irony.

"I love your idea about what's depressing and what isn't, Ant."

Lyn followed her host into a small summer house in the far corner of the walled garden.

"Heavens, thank the Lord it's warmer in here out of that easterly," said Lyn.

The pair strolled to one end of the rickety, wood-and-glass structure.

"I have a confession, Ant. I often come in here after I've dropped your mum and dad's chocolate cake off on a Saturday."

Ant cocked his head to one side and reached down to retrieve something from the floor.

"I know you do."

A quizzical look spread across her face.

"How?"

She looked on as Ant held up the item he'd retrieved from the herringbone-patterned brick floor.

"I only know one person who eats black-and-white, mint humbugs around here." He held up an empty sweet wrapper.

"Heaven knows how you manage to eat those things without pulling your teeth out."

Lyn worked hard on her guilty look as she snatched at the empty wrapper.

"I admit it, you've caught me red handed. As for preserving one's molars—secret is to warm them in your pocket first."

Lyn pointed to her cheek to emphasise the point.

"I didn't know you wore dentures?"

His smile gave away his intentional misinterpretation of Lyn's words.

"Clever clogs. You know what I mean."

She tossed the empty wrapper at Ant, who, failing to duck in time, felt the wrapper tickle as it bounced off his forehead and returned to the floor whence it came.

Lyn's smile broadened with the satisfaction of knowing her aim remained accurate.

"Speaking of clever clogs, have you spoken to your boyfriend yet, Lyn?"

Lyn bristled, which was the reaction she knew Ant had intended to elicit.

"You know full well I haven't seen him since Noah was a lad."

A scowl spread across Lyn's face.

Ant shrugged his shoulders, raised his chin an inch or two, and shook his head, closing his eyes as he did so.

"Whatever," he replied, hoping Lyn would bite.

Surmising as much, Lyn did not react and waited for Ant to open his eyes. He fell for her trap as she knew he would.

"You're back with us, then?"

Lyn busied herself inspecting her nail varnish for non-existent chips while savouring Ant's tactical failure.

"But as luck and good fortune would have it, yes, I did have a chat with him."

Lyn adopted a disinterested tone, making no attempt to offer further information.

Seconds, which seemed to feel like minutes, passed as Lyn and Ant stared each other out. She knew he would give in first.

"Fair enough. You win. Now let's have the rest of it."

Lyn laughed.

"You're hopeless. Never could stare me out, even at school, could you?"

Lyn was enjoying Ant's defeat.

"How many times must I tell you, I wasn't the one who told old *Slab Head* you let his tyres down."

Hands on hips, her gaze holding firm, she had no intention of letting him off the hook just yet.

"Who mentioned the tyres? Anyway, I met our old headmaster years later. He told me he knew it was Alfie Hemmings all the time. You know, the lad who used to suck his thumb in class."

Lyn detected Ant's intrigue at the new startling news.

"He said he put me in detention because I cleaned the blackboards better than anyone else. It seemed the headmaster needed them doing for the school governors' visit the next day."

"And you let me think it was my fault all these years. You—"

"Now then. No swearing, Lord Stanton. Remember your station in life. Anyway, it serves you right for thinking the worst of me."

As the two friends squared up to each other, Lyn still held the upper hand.

"Wait a minute," said Ant.

Lyn laughed and pointed at Ant as he adopted an exaggerated gait.

"Who do you think you are? Henry VIII?"

Lyn's hilarity didn't last long as Ant hit on a connection.

"Wait a minute. That boyfriend of yours in the planning department is called Alfie, isn't he?"

Lyn blushed as Ant let out a roar of laughter.

"No wonder he's sweet on you. He thinks you took the rap all those years ago to save him from detention. I seem to remember he was always hanging around you like a puppy with his thumb stuck in his gob."

Lyn failed to see the funny side of Ant's deduction.

"Do you want to know what the man told me or not?"

Her tone confirmed she was in no mood for Ant's theatrics. Nevertheless, she had to wait for what seemed like ages before Ant had settled enough to take in Lyn's offer.

"Right. Shall I start, then?"

Lyn unfolded her arms.

"Grindle Developments has submitted an outline-planning application to build twelve executive, five-bedroom homes and four starter properties on the land behind Ethan's cottage."

She knew this information would bring Ant to his senses.

"What's more, and as you expected, the application shows road access to the development right through the cottage."

"Aha. Told you so. But answer me this. Why would Grindle invest time and money on a planning application when he doesn't own Glebe Cottage?"

Lyn frowned then shrugged her shoulders.

"Perhaps he's done a deal with someone. But who?"

"There's one way to find out, Lyn. Here's what I think we should do."

12

THE GREASY SPOON

"And what are we looking for exactly?"

Fitch failed to hide his irritation at being press-ganged into trudging through Stanton Woods.

"Do you never stop moaning?" replied Ant. "Anyway, you were the one that offered to come if I bought you breakfast."

Ant craned his neck as he surveyed the leaf-covered car park that gave access to the woods. He'd been careful to park his Morgan in the far corner of the small clearing so that he didn't contaminate possible evidence.

"Mind where you're walking, for heaven's sake."

Ant's caution caused Fitch to freeze as if he were about to step on a landmine. Turning to face his friend, he stuck both hands in his pockets and shrugged his shoulders.

"Go on, then. Give us a clue. Permission to move, sir."

Ant raised an eyebrow, unimpressed with Fitch's supposed comedy impression of a squaddie.

"Get yourself over here, and tell me what you can see."

Both men now stood side by side looking down the narrow track. Beyond, lay the spot where Ethan had been found.

"See them?"

Ant crouched as he spoke, leaving Fitch to look down at him in bemusement.

Ant's gaze veered between the trackway and the strengthening sun. His interest lay in how its rays forced their way through a tangle of branches in the tree canopy and hit the ground.

"This isn't doing my knees any good."

"Don't be a softy, Fitch. Now kneel down next to me."

Ant prompted Fitch to close one eye then the other, and tell him what he could see.

"What, you mean those parallel lines?"

Ant was impressed. He'd done much better than Lyn when asked the same question.

"Well done, Fitch. Yes, two parallel depressions leading up the track."

He pointed a finger to trace their progression into the woods.

"They're just a set of wheel marks from one of your forestry buggies, Ant. Nothing special, I'd say."

He reached forward to disturb a compressed strip of leaves in front of him.

"No, no. You're not getting it, Fitch."

Ant pointed again towards the trackway.

"Wait here, and I'll show you."

Ant walked forward in a semicircular movement. As he did so, he picked up four twigs, each about twelve inches long.

"See it now?"

Ant had laid a twig across the depressions to show their depth.

"Caused by something much heavier than one of our estate vehicles."

Ant encouraged his friend to focus on the four twigs a few feet apart, two on each track.

"Good Lord. You're right. Something bigger than a quad bike made those, that's for sure."

Ant smiled.

"There you go. The next question is, why drive something that big down this track. There's no evidence of trees being cut down, so they haven't nicked any of the estate's timber. So what else might they have been doing?"

Ant stood next to Fitch in silence for a few seconds as they focused on the tracks.

"We can say for sure whatever it was that made the tracks was heavy. But what type of vehicle do you think it was, Fitch?"

Ant turned to look at his friend.

"Judging by the width between the tyre marks and their depth, I'd say a commercial vehicle."

Ant nodded.

"And a tall one at that."

Fitch looked at his friend then back at the tracks.

"What makes you say that?"

"They do."

Fitch's eyes followed Ant's index finger.

It pointed to a neat row of snapped branches six feet above them.

* * *

LYN WAS ABOUT to give up on Ant's instruction to find Stephen Grindle and head back to work until she drove past a lay-by opposite the entrance to Home Farm. She could see Lil's greasy spoon chuck wagon was having a busy time of it.

Lyn glimpsed Grindle's gleaming sports car.

So there you are.

Pulling over, she parked her Mini in a muddy passing point on the narrow lane and headed back towards the lay-by. As she neared, Lyn spotted Grindle. He had his back to the road and was drinking from a polystyrene cup while seemingly deep in conversation on his mobile.

Keen to remain hidden from her quarry, Lyn dodged the parked lorries and made her way to the chuck wagon.

"Not seen you for a while, Lyn," said Lil.

Lyn smiled at the petite woman who wore a pristine, white apron and blue vinyl gloves.

"It's not for the want of trying, Lil. Hard to get away from school these days. May I have a coffee?"

SHE WATCHED as Lil busied herself scraping the excess cooking oil and bacon fat from a hotplate.

"You can have a china mug. The lads get the polystyrene version. It saves on the washing up!"

Lil winked as she handed Lyn her drink.

"Nice to talk to another lady for a change," added Lil with a throaty laugh.

Lyn appreciated the china mug and Lil's words.

"Get away with you. You love every minute of it. From what I've heard, the drivers think the world of you, especially when you shout at them."

In some ways, Lyn envied Lil. Twenty years her own boss. Worked when she wanted and out in the open air.

Good on you, girl, thought Lyn. She knew Lil had fought hard for the success she now enjoyed.

"Not seen anything of your ex, then, Lil?"

Lil was busy wringing out a clean dishcloth as Lyn's words hit. She let out a throaty laugh and gave the cloth an extra squeeze as if it were some part of her ex-husband's anatomy.

"No, glad to say. The best day's work I ever did was chucking that fool out. And you know what the funniest thing is?"

Lyn cupped her mug of coffee and came closer to the counter to get out of the wind. She waited in anticipation of the caterer's next revelation.

"The ratbag he left me for has got him right under her thumb. Serves the bugger right, if you ask me. He didn't know which side his bread was buttered; that was his problem."

Lyn could see Lil meant every word and spoke without a hint of regret or jealousy.

As Lyn listened, she caught a movement out of the corner of her eye. Grindle had climbed back into his car.

Hell's bells.

"Talking of bread and butter. Can you do me a bacon-and-egg bap, Lil? I'll be back in a minute."

She made off towards Grindle, greeting him with a cheery "Hello."

"Lyn Blackthorn, isn't it?"

Lyn waited for him to clamber out of the open-topped Morgan. "Thank you for doing such a wonderful job. Educating young minds is so important, isn't it?"

Lyn failed to hide her surprise. He looked dapper, sounded genuine, and had a sparkle in his eye. She could see why some women might find him attractive.

"Well, er, thank you. Yes, I suppose, well, of course I know you're right. About education, I mean."

She could feel herself blushing.

Why is he making me feel like a teenager?

An awkward silence developed as Lyn thought of what to say next without raising his suspicions.

"Now then, a few ladies mentioned they'd seen you around the village. You know what it's like in a small place like Stanton Parva. Handsome young man, posh car and all that. Now what we all want to know is, are you here to see a secret lady friend, or is it just silly business?"

Lyn hoped she'd put Grindle off the trail since he seemed to lap up her compliments like a cat having got the cream.

Grindle smiled and looked her up and down from head to foot.

I hate people who do that, thought Lyn as she endured his inspection. She was unsure if he did it out of habit or by design to unnerve his opponent.

"Oh dear. What is a man to say?"

You're a smooth one.

She noted his failure to bite on her question so tried a different tack.

"My mother thinks you're going to build them a nice big supermarket on the old petrol station site. If you do, I guess it'll make you the most popular man around here amongst us girls. It's fifteen miles and twenty minutes each way at the moment."

Lyn watched as Grindle's look intensified, and his smile morphed into a look of concern.

My my, you are a slick operator.

"Well, Ms Blackthorn, you never know." Grindle touched the side of his nose with a finger as if sharing a state secret. Speaking of which, I need to be off. You know—things to do, people to see."

Without further words exchanged, Lyn extended her

right hand. Grindle reciprocated. Seconds later he was gone, leaving her to ponder what he was really up to.

"Your bap's ready."

Lyn turned in the direction of the voice to see Lil hanging out of the chuck wagon, bacon-and-egg feast in hand.

Ten minutes later, Lyn was back in the Mini driving back into the village.

That's interesting.

Lyn had caught sight of Reverend Morton talking to a man she didn't recognise, outside Glebe Cottage. As she neared, the stranger moved off towards the village centre.

What's the vicar up to?

She pulled alongside the clergyman and wound down the window.

"Good morning, Vicar."

Lyn liked the fact that her sudden arrival had taken him by surprise. She could tell from his delayed response that he was trying to gather his thoughts.

"Oh, Lyn. There you are. Sorry if I seem a little absent minded today. I'm in a world of my own, you know."

Lyn smiled as if to give the vicar permission to compose himself.

"I just wanted to catch up with you to discuss your next talk to the children. They do love your visits to the school so much."

She watched as the vicar frowned.

"Well, yes, we can, if you wish. It's usually your secretary that finalises these things with me. The only thing is I'm a bit pushed for time just now."

Reverend Morton glanced at his wristwatch and twiddled the winder between his finger and thumb. Lyn was aware his agitation was increasing as the seconds passed.

What are you up to, I wonder, Reverend?

"Oh, I see. No problem at all. I can tell you're busy. I'll get Tina to ring you, shall I?"

Reverend Morton didn't need a second invitation to make his escape.

"People to see, you know."

Lyn waved as the reverend hurried off, still looking at his watch.

That's the second time I've heard that expression this morning.

13
NIGHT WALKING

"When you rang to ask if I fancied a walk, you didn't say I'd need my wellies."

Ant looked on as Lyn gazed at her feet.

I'm guessing rubber boots are not her idea of high fashion.

He laughed as they made their way from the back garden of Lyn's cottage onto the school field that lay beyond.

"Well, what would you rather do on a wet Monday night, Lyn? Anyway, I heard tell you were one of those women with a fetish for rubber?"

Ant put a sprint on, hoping to avoid retribution.

Clambering over the low drystone wall, Ant fell forward.

She's pushed me!

"The only fetish I've got is for the plaster you'll need when I've finished with you. Cheeky devil."

Ant let out a muffled scream as he hit the sodden ground with a dull thud.

"Are you okay?" whispered Lyn. "Ant, are you all right? For goodness' sake, say something."

Ant let out a low moaning noise. Face contorted with pain, he held a hand to his chest.

Ant fell silent as Lyn knelt over him until her face almost touched his.

"Boo."

Ant's sudden outburst caused Lyn to fall backwards and let out a strangled scream. He roared with laughter as she landed in a muddy depression with her wellington boot soles pointing to the heavens.

"That's what you get for occasioning actual bodily harm on your best mate, young lady."

His amusement continued as he scrambled to his feet, pulling Lyn up with him.

"One of these days, Anthony, one of these days."

He watched as Lyn brushed herself down and wagged a finger at him.

"Anyway, enough of this larking about. We've work to do, Lyn."

Ant caught Lyn's best head-teacher glare, shrugged his shoulders, and responded with his little-boy-lost look.

"You started it."

He gave a throaty laugh.

"Do you realise you sound just like one of your seven-year-olds?"

He watched the first signs of a smile spreading across Lyn's face.

"Whatever."

Both laughed and bumped shoulders.

Within a minute, the back of Glebe Cottage began to reveal itself as the pair trudged across the drenched ground. Set against a dark, sullen sky, Ant focused on the stark silhouette of the forlorn-looking cottage as if it were waiting to be reclaimed by the master who would never return.

"So tell me again, Ant. Just why are we getting soaked to the skin on this freezing-cold evening?"

Ant looked puzzled as his friend bent down, before spotting her attempt to loosen a small stone trapped between the ball of her foot and wellie sole.

"You have a memory like a sieve at times, Lyn. So my pathologist mate confirmed a second rope burn around Ethan's neck. If my hunch is correct, he was dead before he got anywhere near that tree."

He could see the horror of his suggestion beginning to dawn on his friend.

I wish I could take this away from her.

"You're saying Ethan died somewhere other than in the woods?"

Ant stopped and turned to Lyn and pointed to the flint-faced rear wall of Ethan's place.

"Could have happened anywhere, his cottage, for example."

The shudder Lyn gave meant Ant could see she now understood what their night caper was about.

"I know. Makes you think, doesn't it?"

Ten feet farther on, and they had reached the back gate of the cottage. Ant lifted the latch and stood to one side while Lyn passed through into Ethan's garden.

They stood rooted to the spot for a few seconds and watched shadows dance across the back wall of the humble chocolate-box building, as angry clouds first hid then revealed the moon in the gathering wind. The effect was soporific.

Could somewhere as beautiful as this really have been used to take a life? thought Ant.

"So if I'm right, there may just be something in there to tell us what happened that night."

Once they had reached the rear door to the property, Ant pulled four plastic bags from his coat.

"Here, put these on."

Ant handed Lyn two pedal-bin liners.

Lyn watched as he placed each of his booted feet into a bag.

"What on earth—"

"We don't want to tread mud all through Ethan's place, now, do we? Anyway, better no one knows we've been here."

Taking advantage of Ant's firm frame, Lyn rested a hand on his shoulder to steady herself as she pulled the plastic bags over her footwear.

Ant considered had a stranger crossed their path at that moment, they may have supposed the pair were involved in some ancient village ritual. He struggled to support both himself and Lyn as they swayed from side to side, perching on first one leg then the other and at the same time trying to tuck the plastic coverings into the tops of their wellies.

As Ant expected, once their eyes met, gallows humour took over as they collapsed in a heap against the sturdy rear door.

Got to get a grip, or we've had it.

"Come on, Lyn. No time for larking about. Someone might see us, and then we'll have some explaining to do."

His gentle reproach worked, eventually. He watched as Lyn struggled to regain her composure.

Rummaging around in his jacket pocket, he retrieved a set of keys then two short sticks made of transparent plastic.

Lyn's bemused look almost made him start giggling again.

"Here, take this," he whispered.

Ant handed Lyn one of the sticks.

"Twist it."

"What do you mean?"

"Lyn, just do it, or we'll be here all night."

A soft, thin beam of light bathed a small area of the door as Lyn complied with his instruction.

"Won't see it from outside once we're in. Clever bit of kit, eh?"

He watched as Lyn interrogated the stick light. She hadn't seen anything quite like it.

"Is this one of your spy gadgets?"

She waved the light around and giggled.

Ant fixed her with a stern look, his smile gone.

"If I tell you, I'll have to kill you."

Ant couldn't keep up the pretence for more than a couple of seconds.

"Is that so, Mr Bond?" quipped Lyn. "And those? I suppose they're some sort of sonic device for opening locks?"

Ant jangled the metal objects.

"Nope, just my house keys."

Ant noticed Lyn sigh as he put the keys back in his pocket and produced a small, stiff card.

A few seconds later, a crisp *click* pierced the silence, and Ant gently pushed the door open just enough to allow access. He smiled triumphantly.

"Impressive, eh? After you."

Passing through the kitchen and into the hallway, the pair hesitated before entering the lounge. It was as if it had been a jolly caper until now. But beyond the door, Ant expected to see the everyday things Ethan would have used and enjoyed.

He opened the oak-stained pine door. It took a few seconds for his eyes to adjust to the dark shapes in the room. He checked Lyn, who nodded to confirm all was well.

"Someone's beaten us to it."

Ant surveyed a scene of devastation. All around lay

papers that had been flung from the fitments that lined the room. Not a square foot of carpet remained free of detritus.

"What do you think they were looking for, Ant?"

He scanned the room a second time by shining his light across the chaotic scene.

"That rather depends on if whoever did this was here before or after Ethan died."

He saw Lyn shaking her head.

"It's a right mess, isn't it, Lyn?"

Ant doubted she'd taken in his words. She looked utterly lost in the moment.

"Or during the…"

Her voice tailed off.

"The murder. No, Lyn. If it helps, I don't think it happened here. This is a burglary, or it's staged to look like one. But there's no sign of a struggle—or anything else."

Ant fell silent. He knew Lyn would understand what he meant. Then a beam of light permeated the thin curtains of the front bay window.

Ant gently took hold of Lyn's arm as much to indicate she should stay still as for reassurance.

"Someone's coming," whispered Ant. "Move over to the hall door, but don't go through until I tell you."

Lyn stood rooted to the position Ant had told her to take up.

He moved towards the window. Shielding himself to the side, he slowly pulled a small section of the curtain back.

"Hell's bells. It's Riley. What the dickens is he doing here?"

It wasn't meant as a question for Lyn. If anything, he was reflecting how wise it had been, in the first place, to gain entrance to what he could plainly see was a crime scene.

Ant watched the detective inspector leave his police car and begin to walk up the front path of the cottage.

"Get ready to move... No, wait."

Just as he was about to join Lyn and escape the scene, Ant watched as something flashed in Riley's hand. The detective stopped, looked at the light, then lifted his hand to his right ear.

"He's taking a call. This is our chance to slip away. There's nothing more for us in here, Lyn."

Ant gestured for Lyn to ready herself for the short dash back through the kitchen and out into the back garden of the cottage.

He watched as Lyn ran.

Thank goodness for that. The fool's back in his car. Must have been called away to another job.

Ant let out a nervous laugh before realising Lyn re-entered the kitchen and was urging him on with an outstretched arm.

"Another lucky escape, Houdini. One of these days your luck will run out, then let's see whether being a lord makes any difference."

Ant laughed again, gave an exaggerated bow, and took Lyn's outstretched hand as she turned towards the back door.

Then came a noise that made them both freeze solid. Ant pointed his light stick at the floor. One of them had kicked something against the plinth of the kitchen units.

He crouched down.

"It's a pen. Always come in handy, do pens."

Ant stuffed it into his jacket pocket before following Lyn out of the building, taking great care to lock the back door and check that it was in the same condition in which they'd found it.

Satisfied all was well, he turned to Lyn who was pointing at her feet.

"Can we take these stupid plastic bags off now?"

He raised his index finger and wagged it at Lyn.

"Better to wear a plastic bag than spend a night in the police cells, don't you think?"

His look said it all.

"Whatever," Lyn replied.

He could see she was determined not to bite.

As the pair trudged back across the field, Ant noticed movement from a factory separated from the field by a high wire fence.

"Someone's working late."

His attention was drawn to a slim figure clambering out of a box van.

"Poor devil, I bet they're getting peanuts to work overtime," said Lyn.

Ant huffed.

"If it's their own business, I suspect they aren't getting paid at all."

14

BAD BUSINESS

"Not a job for the faint hearted, is it?"

Fitch offered a friendly smile as Brian Wilcox made polite conversation while they stood with their backs to a piercing east wind on the garage forecourt.

"You're not wrong there. That blessed wind goes straight through me."

Fitch gave an involuntary shiver while wiping a small gathering of phlegm from the end of his reddened nose.

"You'd think we'd get used to this blasted weather, being so close to sea. Well, my bones say different, Brian."

He gave a sharp tug on his woollen bob cap to provide a little comfort for his stinging ears then slammed the bonnet of a car that had seen better days.

"Come on, let's get out of this weather," said Fitch as he led the way into his office.

"Sorry about the mess, mate. Sit where you can." Fitch glanced around the tiny space, every surface piled high with car parts and oil-stained paperwork.

"I guess your place is just as bad. Us mechanical types are all the same, aren't we?"

Brian's smile provided Fitch with the response he'd expected.

"Don't include me in that. Everything in its place and a place for everything. That's what I say."

Fitch turned to see a familiar figure racing through the rickety doorway.

"Good day, Mr Perfect. Born in a barn, were you? Now shut that flaming door, so I can keep the heat in."

He gave a wry smile as his friend shook his head and pointed to a broken pane of glass in the door.

"All right, smarty pants. There's a difference between controlled ventilation and a hurricane, you know. Now what brings you out from the lap of luxury on a cold Tuesday morning?"

"If you think Stanton Hall in an easterly is a great place to be, you're welcome to it. Fancy a swap?"

Fitch knew Ant had a point.

"You must be mad. Your place is a money pit. At least all I need to do is spend ten quid on a bit of glass and it's job done." He matched Ant's smile before realising he'd almost forgotten Brian was there.

"Apologies for my friend's interruption. You know what upper-class types are like."

Fitch smiled at Brian knowing it was all the man could do to acknowledge the lighthearted exchange with a modest nod.

"Oh, you know. Just wanted to see what the real world was up to," said Ant.

Fitch gestured for Ant to sit down and smiled as his friend breezed across the cluttered space, lifted a broken steering wheel from a rickety metal chair, and plonked himself down.

"Don't believe a word he says, Brian. Although you can

eat your dinner off the floor of his workshop. That's down to his father. Anyway, you should have seen him at school. He was the most disorganised kid going."

Again, Fitch's intention was to include Brian in the banter.

Poor Brian.

Fitch soldiered on, leading an animated discussion on three subjects: the weather, how useless politicians were, and the price of diesel.

Oops, made a booby there.

"Well, I'll leave you both to it. Thanks for fixing the van."

Fitch watched as Brian looked at his invoice, folded the piece of paper into four, and tucked it into an inside pocket of his faded waxed jacket.

"Keep safe, Brian. Chin up, mate."

The mechanic couldn't help but watch Brian trudge forlornly across the yard, pulling his collar up against the biting wind before disappearing into the distance. He sighed as he turned, threw the dregs of two chipped coffee mugs onto a pile of used kitchen towels then refilled them from a grimy percolator.

"He's a proud man and as honest as the day, but he's in big trouble," said Fitch as he handed Ant the cleaner of the two mugs. He looked on as his visitor skimmed a film of something or other from its surface and commented.

"I thought he looked a bit down. Do you think he'll be okay?"

Fitch drank from his mug without skimming its surface.

"Transport's a hard game at the best of times, Ant. Did you see his face when we mentioned diesel going up in price again? I could have kicked myself."

Fitch sucked air through the gap in his front teeth to emphasise the point.

"As your dad has said to me more times over the years than I care to remember—if you run out of money in business, you're finished. Doesn't matter how full your order book is. If you've no cash to service the work, it's goodnight Vienna."

"Are you saying he's broke?"

Fitch glanced at his old friend. There were times when he thought it impossible for Ant to understand how the "other half" lived.

"That's exactly what I'm saying, Ant. When you're a one-man band, it isn't just the business that cops it. I bet he's sold his soul to the bank like most of us have to. If his removal business *does* go bust, those bloodsuckers will be on him like a pack of hounds. He'll lose everything, including his home, I bet."

Fitch spoke with an uncharacteristic bitterness. But then he'd seen what bankruptcy had done to his father and its long-lasting effects on the rest of the family.

"Are you sure you're right?"

Fitch shrugged his shoulders.

"Look, I may be jumping at shadows, but I see the signs. I hear he owes money to suppliers all over the place—including me. It's only his good name that's kept Brian going for so long. The thing is, Ant, I don't know whether we're doing him any favours."

"So you won't get paid for fixing his van?"

Fitch shook his head, more in sadness than anything else.

"At least his daughter looks after him. She dotes on the man. Mind you, after losing her mum so early, you can understand why she sticks to him like glue. You, more than most, know what losing a close family member is like."

Not quite thinking through what he'd said, Fitch gave

Ant an anxious glance, only to see his friend nodding in agreement and downing the last of his coffee, seemingly unperturbed by the comparison.

"Enough of this gloom," said Ant. "What's your next job?"

Distracted by the moment, Fitch failed to answer.

"Hello, anyone home?"

Fitch turned.

"I did hear you, you know. "The vicar's Volvo, if you must know. In a hell of a state. No pun intended, of course."

Fitch smiled even though he knew better than to laugh at his own jokes.

Quite clever that, if I say so myself.

Ant's moan, as if he'd just read a corny joke from a Christmas cracker, caused Fitch to enjoy the interlude even more.

"What's he been up to, then?"

Fitch pointed as he looked out of the office window, which was hardly fulfilling its purpose in keeping the rain out. Covered with a thick layer of greasy grime as it was, he could just about make out the vicar's Volvo.

"He's done his rear suspension in. By the look of the rubbish in the boot, he's had half of Stanton Forest in there."

"And talking about the rev's car, I'd better get on with it before I lose what little light is left."

Not giving Ant the chance to protest, he guided his friend out of the dingy office with a matey clash of shoulders and walked Ant back to his car.

"By the way, Ant, did that roof sealer do its job on your Morgan?"

He guessed by Ant's crossed-fingered gesture that it had.

"I hope so. Lyn will flatten me if this thing leaks all over her again. It's already cost me one hairdo."

Fitch laughed.

"Serves you right. I hope it was expensive."

"Have you any idea how much women spend in those places?"

Fitch raised his eyebrows and shook his head.

"You mean more than the fiver I spend with Barry the Butcher?"

Ant let go of the door handle and turned back towards Fitch.

"Lord. Is he still in business? I assumed the council had closed him down as a danger to men's necks and earlobes years ago."

Memories of several run-ins with Barry caused Fitch to pick at a small scar on his chin, inflicted when the barber momentarily lost concentration scanning *The Racing Times* instead of paying attention to Fitch's flesh.

"Let's just say they have banned him from using cut-throat razors on anyone other than himself. And the times I've been in there, and he's covered in plasters, well..."

Both men laughed.

"Well," said Ant as he climbed into the Morgan, closed the door, and wound down his window, "at least he's come to his senses."

Fitch shook his head again.

"Er, no. Since he got the shakes, his wife petitioned the council. It was her that got him banned from using anything sharp on paying customers. Couldn't get the insurance, you see."

Ant was impressed at Fitch's graphic mime of sitting in the barber's chair, quaking, waiting for Barry to strike.

* * *

"Fancy meeting for dinner tonight? My treat, so we can catch up on things."

Ant offered the invitation more in hope than expectation. It was half term, and he knew Lyn guarded her downtime jealously.

"Trust you. I've just started playing my *Midsomer Murders* box set." Ant strained to hear Lyn as her voice faded in and out.

And politicians bang on about getting us superfast broadband. I'd settle for a decent mobile signal.

He moved location a couple of feet, extended his arm as high as it would reach, and shouted into the handset.

"Is that any better? Can you hear me now?"

He could tell Lyn was having none of it.

"I said, *Midsomer Murders*. Do you understand?"

Ant chose to act dumb.

"It's a bad signal, Lyn. See you at the Wherry Arms: seven thirty okay?"

He didn't wait for an answer. He calculated Lyn's response might contain several Anglo-Saxon words that he considered unbecoming of a head teacher.

"Hello... hello. Ant, can you hear me?"

Ant could hear her well enough but chose not to acknowledge the stream of invectives that followed.

Head teacher, indeed.

15

BATTLE OF WILLS

"Fish pie and an orange squash isn't exactly what I expected when you said you'd treat me."

Ant flinched.

I'm still in her bad books.

As the pair collected their meals from the bar and settled into a corner table of the packed pub, Ant hoped changing the subject might get him off the hook.

"How was the box set?"

"Twelve strangled, thirteen poisoned, sixteen drowned, plus four killed by bow and arrow. Oh, and six decapitated, if you must know."

Not bothering to add any inflection indicated to Ant that she'd decided to make him pay for disturbing her "me" time.

"Even more dangerous than Stanton Parva, eh, Lyn?"

Better keep quiet for a minute or two, I think.

Ant decided not to bite on Lyn's shake of the head and dismissive hand gesture as she lowered her gaze to bite on a forkful of fish pie.

I hope her pie's nicer than when I had it yesterday, or I'll really be in for it.

He took a long slug of his Fen Bodger pale ale before deciding to try his luck and push on.

It was never going to end well.

"And that's another thing. Why do you always wait until I have a mouth full of food?"

He watched as Lyn spat some of the pie back onto her plate.

"It didn't go well, then?"

"Which, the fish or my meeting with Reverend Morton?"

Ouch.

"I felt such a fool. There was a woman in the church kitchen getting things ready for the weekly coffee morning. I see she's upset, so I turn on the sympathy."

Ant tried hard not to look too confused.

"And...?"

"The vicar comes in and gives me daggers. It's as if I've stolen the church silver. It turns out the woman has recently lost her husband, and he's been visiting her each day to bring God's comforts."

Ant watched Lyn pick at her meal.

Perhaps she's not hungry after all.

"Seems a bit odd."

Ant didn't feel he deserved the daggers she gave him.

"What, the fish or the vicar?"

Not again.

"The vicar, Lyn. The vicar."

She shrugged her shoulders.

"It was as if I'd invaded their privacy. It was quite creepy, actually. When I tried to placate the reverend, the woman went for me. Perhaps she thought I was having a go at him. I don't know."

Lyn stopped talking just long enough to take a sip of her orange juice

"It seems he's been delivering food and stuff to keep her going. Logs for her wood burner and the like. She said he'd damaged his car getting to her cottage, and she felt guilty. That's when *he* got agitated, so I left them to it."

"Well, well," said Ant.

"Why so happy? I thought you had the vicar in the frame for Ethan's murder. Anyhow, how did you get on with Grindle?"

Lyn's renewed enthusiasm for the case energised Ant. He guzzled the last of his pint then looked at the empty glass as if inspecting a diamond for clarity.

"To answer your second enquiry first. Yes, I eventually caught up with him by mobile. Whether he's involved or not, I can't yet say. But I did pick up a nugget of information from the call."

Now that's got you puzzled.

"As for your assertion, you're correct. I thought the vicar was up to his neck in Ethan's death. It turns out the archbishop has threatened closure. Perhaps Morton thought he could prove the parish still held title to the cottage so he could flog it off to solve the church's financial problems."

Ant saw that Lyn was itching to speak.

"Are you saying the vicar didn't have any interest in Ethan's place?"

"Oh, I'm sure it crossed his mind. A man of God he may be, but he's still human."

The two friends exchanged conspiratorial glances.

"So where do we go now?"

Ant leant in and began to whisper.

"Until I get the answer to a hunch I'm following, let's just say the jury is out... or perhaps in the case of the good reverend, the keys to the pearly gates remain just out of reach."

Suddenly a pair of hands appeared as if from nowhere to scoop two empty glasses from the table.

"What are you two up to? You look like you're planning a bank robbery or something."

Ant looked around to see Bud, the landlord, smiling at them.

"Shush, keep your voice down. We don't want everyone to know," replied Ant, winking at Bud, who tapped the side of his nose with a nicotine-stained finger.

"Fair enough. Your secret's safe with me. Now, Lyn. How was that lovely fish pie?"

Ant tried not to look at Lyn, who was about to respond when Bud scuttled off without waiting for an answer to his question.

Thank heavens for that.

"Now, what did you say? Oh, yes. What do we do next?"

Ant retrieved a long white envelope from his inside pocket and withdrew the contents. He handed a folded sheet of paper to Lyn.

"That hunch I mentioned, well, what you've just told me about the vicar clarifies one or two things. But I'm not sure it's enough to put him in the clear."

He watched impatiently as Lyn unfolded the paper and carefully placed it on the table, flattening the folds with a firm palm.

"Well? What do you reckon?"

Lyn sank back into her chair and pointed to the bottom section of the page.

"Do you mean..."

Ant focused on Lyn's finger.

"Yes, almost certainly."

"But, Ant, he's as gentle a soul as you could wish to meet!"

He could see Lyn's distress.

"He's broke, Lyn. As for murder? We're all capable. It just needs the right set of circumstances to align and... *boom*. Believe me, I've seen it too many times."

Ant's voice had a ring of sad resignation. Now he wasn't thinking of Ethan. Instead, Ant was smack dab in the middle of a war zone in some godforsaken corner of the world.

"We do have to tell the police, don't we?"

Lyn's question snapped him back to the present.

"Not on your nelly. That fool, Riley, will make two and two add up to any number he wants to fit his reading of the 'facts.'"

Ant looked at Lyn in surprise as she threw her hands up.

"You're not making any sense."

Bud appeared at their table again.

"Coffee?"

Neither answered. It was all Ant could do not to tell Bud to shove off for interrupting his flow. In any event, the landlord got the message and shuffled from the table, muttering about miserable customers.

Relative solitude restored, the pair resumed their urgent conversation.

"The problem is, Riley has also got this information. My contact at the probate office told me he'd been sniffing around. My bet is that he's come to almost the same conclusion."

"Almost?"

"Don't look so puzzled, Lyn. I've also had a tip-off from my mate in pathology that the police will pick up Brian first thing in the morning. We have to be at that yard, but I've still got a couple of phone calls to make before I can be certain I'm right."

As they left the pub, Lyn repeated her question.

"Almost?"

Ant smiled.

16

IN A KNOT

Wednesday morning broke with a cold drizzle beneath a heavy grey sky. Ant pondered how the next hour or so would develop as he waited in the Morgan outside Lyn's cottage.

He waved at Lyn as she checked the lock had engaged, gave the front door one last pull, and crossed the pavement to the open car door.

Before Ant even had time to say hi, three police cars shot past—lights blazing, sirens screaming.

"Get in, Lyn. It's about to kick off."

She did as he requested, banged the door shut, and waited.

Blast this stupid car.

Instead of the Morgan purring to life, it sat motionless, engine refusing to engage. Ant turned the key again.

No joy.

"Sod it."

A frustrated Ant flung open his door, undid the leather strap holding the bonnet shut, and bad-temperedly folded it aside. Head disappearing into the engine bay, he muttered harsh words to his beloved car.

Two minutes passed.

Nothing.

Then.

"Yes. Fixed it."

Closing the bonnet, he secured the strap, jumped into the driver's seat like a gazelle escaping its tormentor, and turned the ignition key.

The Morgan roared to life.

"Bloody distributor cap," said Ant as he pulled away from the kerb and raced towards Wilcox Removals.

Ant noticed Lyn was about to speak.

"Don't ask."

His look was nearly enough.

"Serves you right for not fixing it before. You know it's been playing up for weeks."

Why do you always state the obvious?

He knew there was little point in defending himself, since, as usual, Ant knew she was right.

By the time they arrived at the yard, pandemonium had broken out. Ant saw Detective Inspector Riley standing in the middle of the yard flanked by six officers. Brian Wilcox stood immediately in front of Riley, his arms flailing, and shouting incoherently. Fitch was also there doing his best to calm things down.

"I wondered if you two might make an appearance. Well, you're wasting your time. We have our man."

Ant remained silent. Instead, he looked over towards Fitch.

"I heard the rumpus and thought the place was being burgled."

Ant nodded.

Simultaneously, the vicar appeared out of the ether, walked across the yard, and disappeared into the yard office without comment.

Ant looked on as Riley shook.

Doesn't take much to confuse you.

"Leave it," barked Riley as one of the officers made off towards the office. "I'll deal with him later."

Riley turned back to Wilcox. His body language gave off an air of a praying mantis about to strike.

"Brian Wilcox. I am arresting you for the murder of Ethan Baldwin—"

Wilcox wore a look of horror.

"But I had nothing to do with Ethan's death. What are you talking about?"

Ant moved closer as the two men exchanged increasingly angry words.

"You found out about the housing development."

"What are you talking about?"

"You also discovered Ethan had refused to sell Glebe Cottage to Grindle Developments."

It seemed to Ant that Riley was almost spitting his words out, such was his agitation.

"No, no," replied Wilcox, placing a hand on each side of his head.

Poor soul, thought Ant.

The onslaught continued.

"You discovered you were the closest living relative to Ethan Baldwin."

"Wha... what are you talking about?"

"You are broke. You've guaranteed everything you own to the bank."

"How do you know I'm—"

"Then you found out you were first in line to inherit

Glebe Cottage. All you had to do was get rid of Ethan and sell it to Grindle Estates, and—hey, presto—in one stroke, your financial difficulties would disappear in a puff of smoke."

Detective Inspector Riley raised his right arm and flicked his wrist in Wilcox's direction. Two officers covered the short distance between Riley and the hapless man. In a second, each had secured Wilcox's arms rendering him unable to move.

Stillness descended, the quiet broken only by a trickle of water overflowing from an ancient water butt, collecting rainfall from a broken downpipe of the ramshackle building it served.

Ant thought that had circumstances been different, the water trickle might have proved therapeutic. Not so today.

It was his confident voice that was the first to break the silence.

"You're almost there, Detective Inspector."

Ant chose his words with care.

He meant to taunt Riley.

He succeeded.

Ant observed Riley contort his face with hatred.

"Brian Wilcox did not murder Ethan Baldwin. Did he, Samantha?"

The shock unleashed by Ant's assertion was palpable. It was as if time had come to a stop.

He surveyed the unfolding scene.

Riley opened his mouth but spoke no words.

Fitch shook his head as if attempting to dislodge something too complicated to process.

Lyn looked as though a light bulb had just gone off in her head.

All eyes veered towards the yard office.

"Would you like to come out now?"

It seemed like an age before he detected movement.

Samantha rushed through an ill-fitting office door and made straight for her father. She wrapped her arms around him, forcing the two policemen to give way. They looked towards Riley. He gestured for them to stand down.

"Vicar, perhaps you should also join us."

Reverend Morton complied with Ant's assertive invitation.

Ant began to speak, his voice gentle, but no less in command of the situation.

"Samantha, when I came across you in church the other day, you said that Ethan and you told each other everything. I wonder if that included Ethan telling you about his childhood, about the orphanage. Am I correct, Samantha?"

She clung to her father, face pressed hard into his chest. Brian tenderly stroked his daughter's hair. Ant could see the man was racking his brains trying to make sense of events.

Samantha didn't answer. She turned towards Ant without making direct eye contact.

"Ethan told you about his burning need to discover who his parents were. And that as an adult he'd succeeded, at least in part."

Ant scanned the yard. Everyone's attention was focused on him.

"Eventually, he traced his mother. She lived in the village, didn't she?"

Samantha remained silent, her head still buried in her father's chest.

"Well, I'll be—"

"I know, Fitch. Sounds fantastic, doesn't it?"

He watched his friend nod as he returned his attention to Samantha.

"By the time he traced her, she'd died. We can only imagine how devastating that must have been for him, yet he still moved back to the village all those years ago. It was as if he needed to be near where he was born and the memory of his mother."

Ant's flow was suddenly interrupted.

"You have proof of all this?"

"Look in the parish records, Reverend. Just as Ethan had. He discovered a burial record of someone with a name almost identical to the one the adoption agency gave him. Except it wasn't Matilda Baldwin. It was Matilda Baldwin-Wilcox."

Ant turned to Brian just as the man let out a gasp.

You never knew. What a tragedy.

"But we don't have any relatives. They're all dead. It's just Samantha and me. Just the two of us."

Ant gave Brian time to compose himself as he gave his daughter an extra squeeze.

"I'm afraid that's true... now."

He didn't mean to be cruel.

Samantha shifted position to face Ant, forcing her father to move with her, such was the grip she still had on him.

"You're a liar. I thought you were nice. But you're just like all the rest."

Ant shook his head slowly. Almost imperceptibly.

"Your dad did a good job at hiding his money problems from you for a long time. But you found out. Banks don't care who they talk to when they ring. They just want their money back."

Ant moved towards Brian and his daughter. Brian had started to cry.

I bet you've never seen him do that before.

"Ethan became obsessed with proving the link between

him and your father, and therefore to you. A fact you fully exploited when you found out about Grindle Developments wanting his cottage. You told me in church that... how did you put it, 'someone was hassling Ethan.' Well, I think you made that up to cover your tracks. The truth is Ethan refused to help. Isn't that so?"

Ant saw Samantha begin to break away from her father.

"Not just yet, young lady. I think you lured Ethan to this yard on the promise of helping him complete his family tree. Perhaps you told him your father kept the old family records in the office safe. Once you had him in the privacy of the office, you pleaded with him again to help your father pay off his debts. After all, if he sold the cottage, he would have more than enough money. When he refused again, you killed him."

Ant met Samantha's eyes as they burned into him.

"You can't prove any of this, Anthony. What are you trying to do?"

Ant shot back at the clergyman.

"A man is dead, Vicar. A man you argued with and failed to support when he needed help."

Reverend Morton recoiled at Ant's accusation. His reaction told Ant that his assumption had been correct.

"I—I thought he was just making trouble because we argued about the church pews. How was I to know that?" The vicar lowered his head.

You might well do that.

Ant turned back to Samantha, keen to get this awful thing over with.

"You strangled him and put him on the tailgate of that van. He was an old, frail man. It didn't take much effort, did it? After all, the hydraulic tailgate did all the work."

He pointed towards the van Fitch had repaired.

"When you had his body inside, you drove to the woods and staged his suicide. It was clever of you to use the same rope to string him up that you'd used to strangle him, except it left two distinct burn marks. As for the knot—well, your training with the Sea Cadets came in handy in the end, didn't it?"

He watched as Samantha's mouth turned up slightly at the edges. It seemed only Ant noticed the smirk.

Brian Wilcox interrupted.

"That's rubbish. My daughter can't drive."

Ant smiled and looked at Lyn.

"Oh, but she can. We saw her the other night moving vans around the rear of your yard, Brian. The truth is, she drove to the woods, strung Ethan up, and spent some time literally covering her tracks—but not well enough."

Ant looked over to Riley.

"Detective Inspector, I know you will have matched the broken branches and depressions in the trackway to this van, correct?"

I hope you catch my drift and go for this, Riley.

Ant watched Riley squirm but quickly catch onto Ant's risky ruse. He nodded his head, although Ant knew the detective had done no such thing.

Riley pointed at two constables and flicked his finger in the direction of Stanton Woods. They required no further instruction, leaving the yard to check Ant's theory.

"Once you'd selected the tree, it was an easy enough job to reverse the van. You pulled Ethan back onto the tail lift, tied the rope around Ethan's neck, and secured the other end around the branch. It was then just a case of lowering the tail lift until Ethan swung free. Finally, you placed a log on its side underneath the poor man, and—what do you know—we have a suicide."

Samantha grimaced.

"Like the vicar said, you can't prove anything."

Ant shook his head.

"I'm afraid I can, Samantha."

As he spoke, the remaining two officers moved towards Samantha.

"You see, you got sloppy. Perhaps you were exhausted by then, but when you cut the rope to length, some of the remnants got caught in the hydraulic mechanism of the tail lift. I've had them analysed, Samantha. They match."

Ant could see he'd once more caught Riley off guard as the detective's face flushed with embarrassment.

"Oh, and then there's this..."

Ant retrieved a small plastic bag from his coat pocket and handed it to Riley.

"Please ignore my fingerprints when you have it dusted. I'm sure you will find Miss Wilcox's prints all over it. We found that pen in Glebe Cottage."

Ant watched Riley bristle.

Here we go.

"What were you doing in—?"

He knew the detective wanted to grill him on how he came to be inside the cottage. Ant noted Riley had censored himself by thinking better of the idea. Instead, he accepted the plastic bag from Ant and read the inscription on the pen: Wilcox Removals and Storage.

"You made a right mess of Glebe Cottage looking for Ethan's will, Samantha. Then again, it was quite clever making it look like a burglary. Pity you weren't more careful about what you left behind," added Ant.

He could see Lyn itching to catch his attention.

"But what about Grindle Developments?"

"Quite right, Lyn. You recall me saying last night I had a

couple of calls to make? Well, I got back in touch with Stephen Grindle and probed our earlier conversation a little deeper. He told me a young woman contacted him to suggest a deal involving Glebe Cottage. He thought it was a hoax and didn't take things any further."

Ant looked back towards Riley.

"I'm sure he'll confirm what I've said, Detective Inspector. I have his number if it would help."

Ant sensed the irritation he was causing Riley.

He brought his attention back to Samantha.

"Now, is that enough proof?"

Hardly had he stopped speaking before the young woman let go of her father and raced towards Ant, her fists flailing. Two constables reacted in an instant to restrain her.

He found Samantha's facial expression hard to comprehend as her contorted features bore down on him. She had changed beyond all recognition as she spat her words at Ant.

"It was his fault. I tried being nice, but he wouldn't help. He could have stopped my dad going to jail. I lost my mum when I was a kid. I'm not going to lose my dad as well. Well, now he'll inherit Ethan's estate, and when Dad is released, he'll never have to worry about money again."

This time it was Ant's turn to be confused. He looked around trying to get a grip on why she'd talked about prison. Then he noticed Fitch closing his eyes and tilting his head backwards.

"I'm guessing your daughter is talking about the tachograph, Brian? When I repaired your van, I noticed something odd about the tachograph in the cab. Have you been doctoring it to extend your driving hours above the legal limit because you couldn't afford to hire a driver?"

Brian nodded then lowered his head.

"Oh, Samantha. What have you done?"

Ant looked on as Father and Daughter exchanged a final look before Samantha was placed in the back of a police Jaguar and driven away.

Didn't even look back at your father.

Ant gestured for Lyn to comfort Wilcox as he stood alone in the suddenly desolate yard. He knew that, in truth, there was little she could do or say.

At the yard gate, Ant chatted to Fitch and the vicar, each trying to make sense of the tragedy that had unfolded before them.

"Even if Wilcox has been fiddling with his driving hours, he won't get a custodial sentence for a first offence. Not that it matters. He's lost his business anyway, poor man."

Fitch nodded in agreement.

"But what about the inheritance when Glebe Cottage is sold?"

Ant was quick to respond.

"Ethan has left it all to the charity who brought him up. Isn't that right, Reverend?"

The vicar nodded.

"What?" exclaimed Fitch.

"It's true. As Ethan's executor, I met their representative the other day. They needed some information that I was able to provide."

Ant joined his two companions in a few seconds of reflective silence.

"One man dead, two lives ruined," said Fitch.

* * *

"What I don't understand is why the vicar was coming out of Ethan's place?"

Ant was distracted, hoping the Morgan would behave itself as he drove Lyn back to her place.

"Oh, you mean the papers your secretary saw him with, Lyn? Well, it seems Ethan typed the reverend's sermon each week. The vicar panicked when he realised last Sunday's was still in Glebe Cottage, so he retrieved it to be ready for Sunday."

"Who's a clever chap, then."

He basked in the reflected glory of Lyn's compliment as he felt her hand flatten the collar of his waxed jacket.

Suddenly she recoiled.

"What's the matter?"

He was aware Lyn was giving him daggers.

"I thought you said you'd fixed the leak in this stupid car?"

Ant looked at the roof seam above Lyn's left shoulder.

"I have," he answered with misplaced confidence.

"Then why have I got a wet bottom?"

END

GLOSSARY

UK English to American English Glossary

- **Back garden:** Yard
- **Bap:** Bread roll
- **Banging on:** Slang term for someone who keeps repeating point of view time after time. E.g "He bangs on about the cost of gas every time I see him."
- **Bob cap:** A knitted, woollen head covering with a "bobble" (ball shape) attached to the top
- **Bobby:** Cop
- **Booby:** Slang word, a mistake: "I made a booby of that."
- **Box van:** A truck with a hard shell to carry goods in
- **Bozo:** Slang for a stupid person: "You are a bozo."
- **Broad:** A stretch of water formed from old peat diggings. Common in Norfolk and Suffolk regions of the UK. Can take the form of narrow

- stretches of water, like canals or open water, or small lakes.
- **Buttercross:** Medieval term used to describe a standing cross, or open-sided small building, where foodstuffs and other goods were exchanged, usually in villages or small towns.
- **Car bonnet:** Hood
- **Chav:** Derogatory slang for a young person wearing designer clothes with a brash manner
- **Chippy:** Traditional British family-run, fast-food outlet selling fish (usually cod and haddock) with fries and a selection of sides including peas, gravy, sausages, pies, chicken, and burgers
- **Clocked us:** To be seen. "Quick, let's go, they've clocked us"
- **Cottoned on:** To eventually understand something, "The police have cottoned on to us."
- **Did a flit:** Ran off, or more usually, to disappear from a building without notice
- **Digestive biscuit:** Also known as a sweet meal biscuit
- **Dunk(ed):** To dip a biscuit into a hot drink (usually tea)
- **Fag:** Slang word for cigarette
- **Fine fettle:** In good order/health. "You look in fine fettle today."
- **Gob:** Street slang for a loudmouth, usually said in a derogatory way
- **Goodnight Vienna:** Slang term for "It's all over." E.g. "One more mistake like that, and it's goodnight Vienna."
- **Greasy spoon:** An affectionate term to describe a

privately owned roadside, fast-food outlet, or downtown food outlet
- **Happy as Larry:** "Larry" is thought to be of Australian boxer Larry Foley (1847 - 1917). He never lost a fight and retired at 32 collecting £1,000 for his final fight.
- **Hostelry:** Nickname for a British pub
- **Knocking Shop:** A place of ill repute: Brothel
- **Lay-by:** A safe place to pull over on the highway
- **Lorry:** A truck
- **Mint Humbug:** Black-and-white, striped, boiled candy
- **Mitts:** Slang. "Get your mitts (hands) off me."
- **Mobile phone:** Cell phone
- **Plod:** Nickname for a policeman or "the police"
- **Plonked:** Plunk(ed)
- **Postie:** A postman/woman
- **Quid:** Slang for a British pound. "Can you lend me ten quid?"
- **Scrumping:** Taking apples from a tree, usually without permission
- **Skip:** Debris box. Also known as skip boxes or dumpsters in some US states
- **Snug:** A small room in an old-fashioned British pub
- **Squaddie:** A private in the British army
- **Tallyman:** An old fashioned name for a person who sells goods and/or collects weekly cash payment by calling at the buyer's property: a form of credit.
- **Tiff:** Lighthearted argument, often between couples

- **Wellies or Wellingtons:** Rain boots. Footwear that extend to just below the knee. Usually used for walking or country sports in poor weather. Said to have been named after the Duke of Wellington.

BOOK THREE

THE BOATHOUSE KILLER

1

AFTERNOON DRINKS

Anthony Stanton's little-boy act tested Lyn Blackthorn's patience to the limit.

"What's not to like? You've got a pint of Fen Bodger, the sun's out, and the chicken burger didn't cost you a penny."

"Call yourself my best mate? You know I hate BBQs. Anyway, it isn't free. The tickets were twenty-five quid apiece."

Lyn shook her head and frowned as she scanned the lively scene in the beer garden of her favourite waterside pub, *The New Tavern*.

"I'll pay for the stupid tickets if it pains you so much, you tight devil. Anyone would think you were seven years old, not thirty-two."

She gave Ant her best head-teacher look, reserved for only the most testing of pupils.

"That's not the point. Just because you're three months older doesn't mean you can treat me like a child. I—"

Before he could finish, Lyn turned to welcome Fitch, an old friend of the pair and owner of Fitch's Automotive Services.

"Don't tell me, he's moaning about spending money again, isn't he?"

Ant frowned.

Lyn raised an eyebrow and shook her head.

"I suppose it's inbred into aristocrats like Lord Anthony Stanton here, or should I call you by your ancestral name. What is it—Norton-D'Arcy? You know what they're like, Fitch. Steal from the poor and get them to pay for your chicken burgers."

She watched as Ant refused to take the bait, stiffened his posture, and tilted his head upwards.

"Then you two should know your place in the pecking order, should you not?"

As if, thought Lyn.

Ant's cheeky reply cut no ice, and both friends dissolved into a fit of laughter.

"Oh, yes. We know our place all right, don't we, Fitch? More to the point, my lord, just at this moment *your* place is at the bar because the drinks are on you."

Lyn stifled Ant's protest with another of her head-teacher looks together with a forefinger pointing straight at the tavern's rear entrance.

"I'll have a large white wine with ice and a slice. Pint of Thatcher's Itch, Fitch?"

He nodded.

"You can have a shandy, Ant. Remember, you have a boat to sail home, and we all recall what happened the last time you had a skinful."

Lyn got the reaction she expected.

"I beg to differ. The cause of that run-in with Maynard's wreck of a boat was a faulty tiller, not Fen Bodger pale ale."

Lyn shrugged her shoulders. Fitch shook his head.

"Well, it certainly ended up a wreck when you'd finished

with it. Anyway, off to the bar you go because we're gasping for some liquid refreshment."

Shamed into paying for the round, Ant did an about turn and began to weave his way through the crowd.

Lyn caught Fitch's eye and broke out into a fit of the giggles.

"Did you sail down on *Fieldsurfer*?"

Happy as she was to continue enjoying Ant's discomfort, Lyn thought better of it and focussed on Fitch's attempt to move the conversation on.

"Yes. I took a chocolate cake to his parents. Ant suggested it might be easier to sail down Stanton Broad rather than driving through Butler's Chase. You know what it can be like at the weekend during the tourist season. Anyway, she's moored just over there."

Lyn pointed at the Earl of Stanton's, clinker-built wherry resting majestically on the Broad, standing out as she did from a line of modern fibreglass tourist hire boats.

Ant's lucky his father lets him loose with Fieldsurfer.

Just then, Lyn became aware of someone crying. Turning, she saw two women. One trying to console the other.

"None of our business, Lyn."

Men.

"Occupational habit, I'm afraid. My ears are autotuned to that particular sound."

She ambled toward the couple and sensed Fitch was close behind acting like an unhappy sibling following their mother to the dentist.

She recognised one of the women. Newly married, she'd only recently moved to the village.

"Hannah, isn't it? Can I help?"

Lyn spoke in a soft tone, making sure she gave each woman equal eye contact.

"It's fine, thank you. My friend will be okay."
She's Polish?

Lyn ignored the well-meant rebuttal and instead focused her attention on the tearful one.

"You're Hannah Singleton?"

The woman wiped a tear from her cheek.

Be careful. Don't push too hard, thought Lyn.

"Oh, don't mind me. I'm just a nosy teacher. But it does mean I get to hear what's going on in the village." Lyn smiled in a calculated move to put the woman at ease.

Hannah looked at her companion and gave a slight nod. Turning back to Lyn, she hesitated for a few seconds.

"You run the little school, yes? People have told me about you."

Lyn blushed.

"Oh dear, that bad?"

Hannah looked confused.

"No, sorry. I mean—"

Oops.

Fitch filled the awkward gap.

"No need to apologise. She's well known for being a busybody. Teachers are all the same, aren't they?"

Lyn relaxed in the knowledge Fitch's icebreaker had worked.

"This is my friend, Annabelle. We grew up in the same town. We are, how you say, best mates?"

"Just like Fitch and me."

"Am I really, Lyn?"

His smile gave the game away.

Lyn turned back to Hannah.

"I hope we yokels haven't done anything to upset you?"

Lyn's attempt at humour had the opposite effect.

Well, I got that wrong.

She watched as Hannah once more began to cry. This time, people standing nearby started to stare.

"Oh, it's not what you have said. You see, they have had their first serious argument as husband and wife, and now he is gone."

Lyn frowned, struggling to make sense of Annabelle's explanation.

"Gone? Gone where?"

Fitch fidgeted and busied himself checking his wristwatch. Lyn knew her friend didn't do emotional angst, much preferring the objectivity of cars, which either did, or did not, work. Lyn was also conscious that talk of her husband intensified Hannah's state of distress.

"I do not know what is wrong with him. Geoff said he had to go to the boathouse. I offered to go with him, but he shouted at me and rushed out of our home."

Lyn stepped closer as Hannah's voice trembled with emotion.

"Now he does not answer his mobile."

Annabelle gently placed a reassuring hand on her friend's shoulder.

"It is true. Geoff is always so patient and never loses his temper. Something is troubling him. I have noticed this for several weeks now."

That sort of talk isn't doing Hannah any good at all.

"Who's worried about what?"

The voice coming closer interrupted Annabelle's flow.

Lyn recognised it immediately.

"This brute is Anthony Stanton. You'll get used to him."

Lyn waved an arm in Ant's general direction as she introduced him. She noticed Hannah's lack of reaction, whereas Annabelle gave him a broad smile.

You're flirting with him!

"Your surname is the same as the village. Are you the earl's—"

Ant smiled.

"For my sins, yes."

Lyn gatecrashed the exchange.

"Always one for flattery, eh, my lord? If that head of yours gets any bigger, it'll explode."

"Boom."

Lyn had placed a hand on either temple to emphasise the point.

Ant looked distinctly unimpressed.

"Mock me if you wish. I care not."

The three friends giggled before Lyn turned back to Hannah, who was still crying despite their efforts to lighten the mood.

Time to sort this.

"Hannah, you bought old Kimberly's boathouse, didn't you?"

Hannah nodded.

"Ant's boat is just over there." She pointed to the wherry. "It's only ten minutes along the Broad. We can sail there to see if we can catch your husband, if you like?"

Lyn noted Ant's confused looked as she relieved him of the drinks tray and watched both men mourn the loss of their beer as if they were about to have an arm cut off.

"But—"

"But nothing, Ant. Let's get going."

Her tone was not one that anticipated being contradicted.

"Don't worry, your pale ale will still be here when we get back."

Ant took one last peek at his pint.

Hannah started to move towards them.

"No, Hannah. You stay here with Fitch and Annabelle. Don't worry, we'll be back in a jiffy."

"Don't worry, Ant. I'll keep your Fen Bodger safe."

From the look on Fitch's face, Lyn doubted that would be the case.

* * *

"Well, it looks peaceful enough," said Lyn as *Fieldsurfer* neared the boathouse.

"Not so sure that's a good sign, Lyn."

Ant brought the vessel to a smooth stop alongside a pair of wide double doors of the old wooden structure that allowed access to and from the Broad. Leaning over the side of the boat, Ant attempted to turn a large, round door handle on one of the doors. It failed to move. He then tried pressing his weight against the heavy doors. Still they stood firm.

"It's a rum do, Lyn. Push us down a bit, will you?"

She retrieved a long wooden pole from the deck and walked to the stern of *Fieldsurfer* and lowered one end into the water until it hit bottom. Using her body weight against the other end, and simultaneously pushing forward, made the wherry move just enough so that it glided without a sound six feet farther down the bank.

Ant secured *Fieldsurfer* against a thick wooden mooring post standing tall from a lush bed of Norfolk reed.

"You go to the right, Lyn. I'll go this way. Shout if you see anything."

The pair jumped from the craft and made their way around opposite sides of the old structure. Coming across a rickety set of doors that punctured an otherwise featureless façade, Ant turned an ancient Bakelite doorknob.

"Wow, what a space."

Ant stood aside allowing Lyn to pass into the cavernous interior. He watched as the loose-fitting timber-wall planks, altered by decades of neglect, allowed pencil-thin shafts of light to penetrate the otherwise darkened interior. Ant placed one foot in front of the other as if passing through a minefield, such was the building's poor state of repair. In the near distance, a gleaming vessel bobbed gently in the water.

It's made from mahogany: must have cost a fortune.

Ant steadied Lyn as she overtook him on the narrow staging. Lyn pointed at the boat.

"Well, if Geoff *is* here, he must be aboard."

Ant stepped onto the craft's immaculate deck.

"Or in the water, Lyn. We'd better check. It's sheltered in here, so he wouldn't have floated out into the Broad."

Ant could tell by her shocked response it wasn't something she wished to contemplate.

Oops, better take the heat out of this.

"I'm only joking, Lyn. I'm certain he's wallowing in some hotel or other with a whiskey until he calms down."

Lyn's frown showed she only half believed him.

"Well, that may be the case, Ant. But I think we should check below all the same. Don't you?"

For someone determined not to think the worst, Ant noted Lyn's lack of hesitation in pulling the deck cover back and launching herself down a set of steep steps.

"Watch your head on the bulkhead... Can you see anything?"

Silence.

"Is anything wrong, Lyn?"

Silence.

"You could say that."

He didn't like the pace or speed of Lyn's response.

Ant descended the steps, turned around, and rubbed his nose.

Dusty in here.

He allowed himself a few seconds to gain his bearings in the craft's dim interior.

Heaven help us.

In front sat a man of around thirty-five, resting backwards against a richly upholstered bench running along one side of the cabin. He looked in a state of total relaxation with his eyes closed and arms at rest on the table in front of him.

Poor man looks as though he's just fallen asleep.

"I'm assuming he's dead?"

Ant turned to Lyn having tried to trace a heartbeat.

"No pulse. And cold."

Ant asked Lyn to double-check.

Her look confirmed the awful truth.

"I assume it's—"

"Hannah's husband? Never met him, but who else could it be, Ant?"

How the hell do we tell his wife?

2
A POLICEMAN CALLS

"Perhaps you think I might thank you for bothering to tell us you'd found a body?"

Nothing if not consistent, Riley.

Ant expected no less from the detective inspector, who fizzed like a firecracker as he scurried into the boathouse, an open mackintosh billowing in his wake.

"Isn't it curious that whenever a corpse turns up, the terrible twosome is to be found lurking. Have a fetish for the recently departed, do you?"

On form today, aren't we.

Both stood aside as the irked policeman strutted along the unstable walkway. A police photographer and scenes-of-crime officer followed.

"And nice to see you again, Detective Inspector. Isn't that so, Lyn."

She smiled.

Riley failed to return the gesture. Ant knew the man had rumbled his sarcastic tone and might try his hand at playing the game.

"I'm surprised to find you here. I thought your sort liked going to the country for the weekend?"

Ant acknowledged the question with a lofty nod.

"Good job I'm already in the country, then, Inspector. Actually, I prefer regattas at Henley, but duty calls, and I am obliged to socialise with the working classes. You understand all about duty, don't you?"

Ant offered a benign smile.

Riley scowled.

Lyn groaned.

"When you two have stopped biting lumps out of each other, you may wish to give your attention to the dead bloke."

She pointed at the boat.

Ant caught her glare, daring him to continue. Her intervention had choked off the torrent of testosterone.

"You are a pompous ass, sometimes, Ant," she whispered.

He looked like a schoolboy about to complain that a dog ate his homework.

Riley shuffled onto the vessel and made for the deck hatch.

"Mind your..." said Ant, placing both hands on his head and crouching as if to avert imminent danger.

Too late.

The inspector let out a cry as his forehead crashed into the top of the cabin doorframe. The force of the blow knocked him backwards against the steep stairs.

Ant felt a tug on his arm as Riley tobogganed out of sight down the stairs and into the boat's interior.

"For goodness' sake, behave yourself. That must have hurt like hell."

A quick glance at Lyn told him to leave it be.

Several minutes passed as camera flashes illuminated

the cabin space, and police officers scoured the deck area. Ant could just make out Riley as he bobbed up and down.

"Watch it, Lyn. Here he comes."

"Well, no suspicious circumstances concerning the gentleman's demise as far as I'm concerned."

Ant feigned a yawn to stop himself laughing as Riley dabbed his head with a handkerchief.

"I'm certain it will comfort you to learn that violent death doesn't follow you around all the time."

Don't smirk at me like that, fool.

Ant turned towards Lyn. He knew she expected him to come out all guns blazing. Instead, he raised an eyebrow at her and nodded.

Lyn accepted the offer.

"How can you be so sure, Inspector?"

Riley checked his forehead again.

"No obvious injuries. No signs of a struggle, and no damage to the boat. In short, a man sat down, closed his eyes and died: end of story."

Ant pointed at the detective's head.

"But your poor bonce. Do you feel as bad as it looks?"

Riley instinctively recoiled as Ant extended a finger towards the eruption.

"Can't be too careful. After all, if a fit young man like that poor chap can cop it minding his own business, then an overweight policeman of a certain age needs to be vigilant when he cracks his skull."

Ant knew that the mention of the injury might encourage Riley to unconsciously touch the savage lump.

He was correct.

Riley winced.

"What my friend means, Inspector, is—"

Oh, do you, thought Ant.

"I know what he means, Miss Blackthorn, and I thank him for his concern."

Blast, he didn't bite.

Ant inwardly gave the detective due recognition for not retaliating as he watched Riley dab his broken skin and inspect his greyish-white handkerchief for blood.

I bet that doesn't half hurt.

"By the way," said Riley, doing up the buttons of his mackintosh. "You forgot to tell me how you two came to be here in the first place."

Ant began to form his response but observed Lyn would beat him to it.

"Luck? That's an odd way of describing a man's death, isn't it? As it happens, we were at a charity BBQ upriver and came across that poor man's wife. To cut a long story short, we offered to come over and see if he was here."

Ant's eyes burned into Riley.

"Turns out he is. Here, I mean, Inspector.

And I bet I know what you're going to say next.

"Did you, indeed, mister, or should I say, *Lord* Stanton? Well, we'll take it from here and get a liaison officer over to Mrs Singleton. This means there will be no need for either of you to trouble yourselves further. Do I make myself clear?"

Ant winked at Lyn.

"The name My Lord will be sufficient, Mr Riley."

Riley scowled but did not engage further as a billowing mackintosh masked the detective's bulk as he exited the boathouse, leaving the remaining officers to complete their work.

"Time to go, I think, Lyn."

Within two minutes, both were on *Fieldsurfer* making ready to cast off.

"You're quiet."

Ant considered Lyn's comment as he watched her stow the wherry's sail and give him the nod to fire up the inboard motor.

"Nothing to say, is there? I hate to admit it, but I think Plod has a point. Geoff looks as though he was just unlucky. Perhaps he had some kind of undiagnosed heart problem. Stuff happens."

Ant chose not to elaborate as he pulled the engine recoil start and pushed the tiller hard to starboard. The wherry turned on a sixpence.

He peered over the edge of the boat to see what Lyn was distracting herself with and glanced at the elongated bodies of several grey mullet skirting the vessel's timber hull.

"But you just don't sit down and die, Ant. At least not someone as young and fit as him?"

He looked up from the water and adjusted the throttle to the permitted maximum of five miles per hour for Stanton Broad.

"Ah, but you can. What about that sudden death syndrome thingy?"

Lyn moved to the centre of *Fieldsurfer* and swung an arm around the vessel's mast.

"You mean sudden arrhythmic death syndrome, Ant. You may be right, but—"

"That's spooky. The acronym spells SADS."

"Rather makes my point, Ant."

One way of finding out.

"I tell you what, Lyn. Why don't you shoot over to Hannah's place? I've got that consultant chappy coming to the Hall with his bright ideas for putting the estate on a sound footing. The police liaison officer is bound to be a woman, so you'll have no problem getting in."

Ant couldn't understand why Lyn started to apologise.

"Goodness. I forgot about your meeting. I'm happy to tag along and keep your parents entertained while you talk turkey.

Ant's look spoke of his appreciation for her concern and offer to shield his parents from what he knew would be a difficult discussion about the Hall's future.

He tried to make light of the situation.

"Bet he recommends some type of theme park. What do you fancy: safari, dinosaur, or a thousand things to make with Norfolk reed?"

Ant raised an open palm to encourage a response.

"You don't fool me, Anthony Stanton."

She can read me like a book.

* * *

As Lyn brought the Mini to a stop outside Hannah's house, she spotted a woman talking to Annabelle at the front door.

Must be the liaison officer. Do I go now, or wait for her to leave?

Events resolved themselves. The woman turned and made for her car. Once the Astra had pulled away, Lyn strolled up the brick-weave driveway and rang the doorbell.

After what seemed like an age, the door opened.

"Oh, nice of you to call, Lyn. Hannah will be so pleased to see you. Please, follow me."

Lyn noted Annabelle's reddened eyes.

"I know how horrible it must be for Hannah, but how are you coping?"

Annabelle shrugged her shoulders without making further comment.

Moving down a long, narrow hallway, Lyn followed a

quiet whimper to its source. She watched as Hannah sat crouched in a corner of the spacious lounge, weeping into the folds of a sports jacket.

Got to be Geoff's.

"I'm so sorry, Hannah. I'm sure the police will do everything they can to find out what happened."

Lyn sensed Hannah hadn't heard her. Instead the grieving young woman turned to Annabelle who sat on the arm of a leather sofa looking aimlessly out of the front window.

Poor souls.

"Now, how about a nice cup of tea?"

Neither woman answered. Nevertheless, Lyn made her way to the spacious kitchen, which stretched the full width of the house: the floorspace divided into two by a wide breakfast bar.

As Lyn first filled then flicked on the electric kettle, she couldn't help contrasting the ordinariness of the room with the extraordinary events of the day.

Cruel, but life goes on.

She pushed aside a neat pile of official-looking papers to make room on the worktop. It was as if Geoff had just popped out. Except he wouldn't be coming back.

As Lyn lifted three mugs from the wall cabinet, something fell from the top shelf.

Looks like a business card.

Lyn turned the small rectangular-shaped object over to reveal its owner.

Rufus Dean-Parker
Royal Windsor Yacht Design & Build
Bespoke Conversions

Interesting. I wonder if Geoff was thinking of selling his boat.

Still pondering her discovery, Lyn headed back into the lounge.

"Here we are."

She set a stylish melamine serving tray onto an oak coffee table.

Eventually, Hannah stirred and indicated to Lyn she might like some.

"Milk and sugar? There you are. Now you take a sip of that."

Lyn offered Hannah one of the brightly coloured mugs.

"This is your famous English tea, yes? I bought it in the village when we first moved in."

Lyn nodded and returned Hannah's smile.

Brave girl.

"Tell me about Geoff."

Lyn leant forward, encouraging Hannah to open up about her husband.

Hope this works.

Hannah responded, hesitantly at first. Her smile widened. Lyn knew she was recalling the good times.

"He was so passionate about his work you know. He refused to do business with anyone who didn't share his love for our beautiful world. Geoff worried so much about the damage we are all doing to our planet. His saw it as his mission to help develop clean energy."

Lyn sensed Annabelle moving.

"Hannah is right. He managed to run a successful business and stay true to his beliefs. That is hard to do in business, yes?"

Hannah's smile faded.

"But my husband was stubborn. His uncle and grandfather died young. I told him to see the doctor and check he didn't have the same problem, but he refused. Stupid man."

Lyn knew Hannah didn't mean to sound so angry. It was part of the grieving process.

Not the right time to ask if she knew Geoff was selling their boat.

3
CASTLE AHEAD

A wisp of cloud made lazy progress across the early evening sky like a piece of fluffed cotton as Ant and Lyn strolled around the spacious grounds of Stanton Hall.

"From the look on your face, I assume the business consultant's recommendations didn't impress?"

Lyn linked arms with her best friend by way of offering him support.

"Let's just say I've paid nearly two thousand quid for a bloke in a suit to tell me what I already know."

Ant's tone left little to her imagination.

"Let me guess. A wedding venue, opening the Hall to the public, complete with tearoom, shop stuffed with organic vegetables, and teddy bears wearing Union Jack waistcoats? Also, perhaps, suggesting you stage classical concerts during the summer months?"

Lyn's response served only to increase Ant's agitation.

"Yes, all of it. Plus, would you believe, flooding Water Meadow to reinstate the wetland that apparently existed when Adam was a lad. He says we can then turn it into a blessed bird sanctuary."

Lyn laughed.

"It's not funny."

She tugged on his arm.

"If you don't stop it, your face will stick like that, and then who'd want to visit, except at Halloween?"

His attempt to stifle a fit of giggles failed miserably.

"Actually, Ant, a bird sanctuary sounds rather exciting. And you'd be helping to save the planet."

She watched as he peered at her through narrowed eyes.

"Try telling that to the villagers in Low Road. I doubt they'd like sharing their living rooms with a flock of pink-footed geese when the damn place floods."

Lyn's eyes lit up.

"At least it would save them having to buy a bird for Christmas lunch, Ant. They're expensive, you know."

Who's the gullible one, then.

"Have you lost the plot or what? Water Meadow and Low Road are called as such for good reason. And anyway, they're protected."

Lyn let go of her friend and turned to face him.

"Protected? What, road names?"

Ant's eyes closed as he shook his head.

"The geese, Lyn. The geese... as you well know, Ms Blackthorn."

He tilted his head in mock disdain.

Her eyes flashed.

"Don't you call me—"

Ant lifted an arm and showed Lyn his open palm.

"I apologise, head teacher. Anyway, do you know what they call them?"

Lyn needed no encouragement to drop into teacher mode.

"The singular is goose, the plural, geese."

He laughed.

"No, no. Not the goose... I mean, geese. The business consultant; do concentrate, Lyn."

Unimpressed, she shrugged her shoulders.

"Shall I give you a definition of someone who charges you six hundred smackaroos a day for 'advice'?" He didn't wait for a reply. "Someone who always ends their sentences with 'but on the other hand...'"

Lyn huffed and half turned.

"Serves you right for having more money than sense."

Better move this conversation on.

"Come on, let's get going. I want to reach Stanton Broad in time for the sunset; it looks as though it's going to be a good one.

Lyn gazed at the weakening sun as it continued its inevitable submission to the horizon.

She bumped hips with Ant as they left the grazed pastures of Home Farm and progressed down a gentle slope covered in knee-high great fen-sedge.

Ant responded with a smile and bumped her back.

"Anyway, Lyn, never mind that stupid business consultant. How did you get on with Hannah Singleton?"

Lyn pulled a handful of sedge by giving the plant a sharp tug.

"She was in bits. Thank heavens she's got Annabelle there, that's all I can say. It's bad enough losing your husband, but to be in a strange country as well. That's hard."

Lyn rubbed the swelling seed heads of the sedge between her fingers.

"I get it," replied Ant. His words were spoken with a quiet dignity.

Lyn glanced at her friend, knowing the memory of losing his elder brother could still reduce him to tears.

"She's angry, Ant. It turns out he may have had a congenital heart condition that killed his father and uncle, but he wouldn't get himself checked. Too scared, I guess."

Ant copied Lyn in grabbing a handful of grass.

"Well, well. So I wasn't too far off when I mentioned that syndrome thingy. What if there was something the doctors could have done, and he didn't bother, or as you say, was afraid to find out? No wonder she's angry."

Lyn fell into a reflective mood as she shuffled through a sea of vegetation, grasshoppers springing from the tops of the sedge in response to being disturbed.

"Then again, perhaps he did find out and didn't want to worry Hannah?"

Lyn shook her head.

"I don't think so. Or if he did, he was one cool cookie to keep it from Hannah."

"What do you mean?"

Lyn stopped mid-stride.

"A question—if someone knew for certain they had a serious health condition that, without treatment, might kill them literally in a heartbeat, would they buy a new boat when they already have an almost-new top-of-the-range model?"

Lyn looked towards Ant.

"Could have been on his bucket list, I suppose. Anyway, how do you know he was in the market for a new boat?"

Lyn pulled a small card from her trouser pocket.

"Here, look at this."

Ant read the card, a smile growing as he finished examining its contents.

"Small world. I know Rufus. Geoff must have been loaded, because this guy only sells to the top-drawer crowd who don't have to ask about the price tag."

Lyn sighed.

"I should have known. The aristocrat and a rich boat builder who works for toffs."

Money always sticks together.

"Not sure I would describe some of his clients as the aristocracy, Lyn. Not in the traditional sense, anyway. He works with some dodgy people, which makes their money dodgy. Put it this way. They are most certainly not the sort of people you'd want to fall foul of."

Lyn reclaimed the business card.

"Surprising, that—I mean, given Geoff Singleton's apparent uber-ethical approach to business." She watched Ant frown. "Don't look so confused. It was something Anabelle mentioned."

"Well, there's one way to find out if our young entrepreneur was indeed as pure as the driven snow. I'll give Ruffy a ring to see if we can shoot down to his place tomorrow morning."

Ruffy.

"Ruffy? What is it with you lot that you have to give each other a nickname?"

Ant let out a throaty laugh.

"Mock ye not. It has its advantages as you will see tomorrow."

Lyn didn't appreciate the finger being wagged at her.

* * *

"I've wanted to visit Windsor Castle since I was a kid. Don't suppose I'll manage it today, either, judging by the royal standard fluttering above the round tower?"

Lyn marvelled at the immense size of the castle as Ant's beloved Morgan sports car made its way through the narrow streets of Windsor, down the steep incline of High Street and towards the waterfront.

"Have you been in there?"

Ant glanced towards the castle's massive battlements.

"Funny you should ask. I had lunch with some people a couple of years ago. It's a fantastic place. They made a great job of restoring the castle after the fire in 1992. Now it's hard to tell what's twenty years old and which bits date back a thousand years."

Lyn turned to Ant as he changed gear to cope with a tricky corner.

"I meant as a tourist, not a lunch guest of Her Majesty!"

Lyn couldn't believe what he'd just said.

"Strictly speaking, I wasn't. Although I suppose anyone who receives an official invite is, er, the queen's guest. Anyway, can't talk about that. One must never divulge such things, you know."

Lyn hung on his every word, fully expecting him to break the Official Secrets Act.

Ant put a finger to the side of one nostril and gave it a light tap.

"Hush hush and all that."

Lyn bristled, knowing he was playing with her.

Arrogant toerag.

She decided, instead, to ignore anything further he might have to say on the subject. The trouble was, Lyn knew he would expect her, at some point during the day, to demand more detail. And she would give in to temptation.

* * *

"ANTHONY, good to see you. It's been too long, old friend."

Ant had no need to remind himself what a tree of a man

Rufus Dean-Porter was. Six foot five and a dapper dresser with a penchant for Savile Row suits and tailored shirts from Jermyn Street in London. By the time Ant had turned off the purring engine of the Morgan, he realised Rufus was already holding the passenger door open and had extended a firm hand towards Lyn.

Some things never change.

Lyn didn't seem to need further invitation.

"I see you're still paying close attention to the ladies, old chap."

Good Lord, she's blushing?

"Manners maketh the man, Anthony. Isn't that so?"

Ant knew the remark wasn't aimed at him.

"That rather depends on who you ask, Ruffy." He looked towards Lyn and winked.

She is blushing!

"Are you all right, Lyn? You look a bit pink around the gills. I bet it's his driving. Always was mad in his Morgan, which just about sums up Little Lord Fauntleroy."

Didn't take you long to work your charms on Lyn.

Ant's eyes lit up.

"Such a compliment," replied Ant, enjoying every second of Lyn's embarrassment, which also meant he couldn't help noticing her angry eyes burning into him.

"Come on you two. I'll give you a tour of the boatyard before you scratch each other's eyes out."

The yard hugged the Thames shoreline and enjoyed Windsor Castle as its backdrop. The ancient scene looked magnificent in the crisp, sunny morning.

Let's get Ruffy talking.

Rufus explained the site's history, together with the intricacies of high-end, customised boat interiors. It was a story Ant had heard several times through the years. He knew his erstwhile friend would use the opportunity to further impress Lyn.

If her eyes widen any farther, they'll pop their sockets.

"It's a great spot, Rufus. Business good?"

He could see his question irritated Rufus since it forced the charmer to break off his intense gaze holding Lyn captive.

"There's always money at the top end of any market, Anthony. The trouble is getting the blighters to pay their bills. You know the type. The more money they have, the longer they hold on to it!"

Ant laughed.

"So that's the secret. Perhaps I will give it a try and see what happens."

"And if they don't pay, now that's when I send 'the boys' round."

Ant knew Rufus was only half joking.

A further ten minutes passed as their tour progressed before Ant turned to business. He watched his guide's body language as he told Rufus about Geoff Singleton's death.

"Now you've got me worried, Ant. He ran an immensely successful equity fund in London, you know. Green technology and all that. I invested a wedge of cash off the back of his sales pitch. He also placed a big contract with me for a custom job on his new boat. Looks like I'm going to get hit twice. And that I don't like at all."

Rufus' demeanour darkened as the implications of Geoff's demise sank in.

But how far will you go to get your money back, Ruffy?

"What did he want you to do?" asked Lyn.

Rufus waved an arm at a gleaming yacht inside the cavernous workshop.

"You know, Lyn. He had a very particular view on how he

wanted the interior fitted out. If you ask me, he had a thing about concealment, bordering on obsession."

Ant's intrigue intensified.

"What do you mean?"

"A concealed cupboard here, a dummy door there, all without any apparent means to opening anything, unless you had the coded remote control, of which there was only to be one. You get used to odd customers in this game, and the richer, the odder, but he took some beating. Then there were the plans for the engine compartment. We were given precise dimensions of the space required, but that was it."

Ant looked into the chasm where the power unit was to be fitted.

"So Geoff intended to fit them himself without telling you their origin? Is that usual?"

Rufus put a hand to his scalp and made as if to scratch his head.

"Good question. No, not normally, not least because of the danger if we, or the customer, gets something wrong and the engine won't fit when we hand the hull back, by which time things have gone rather too far to fix. But Geoff banged on about the power plant being experimental and a trade secret. Some new form of battery was all he would say. Anyway, it was way above my head. He signed off on the dimensions, so as far as I was concerned, that was me off the hook. If they were wrong."

* * *

"What do you make of our Rufus, then?"

Ant's question was tinged with a mix of fascination and jealousy as he accelerated away from Windsor and back toward Stanton Parva.

"He's certainly charming; I'll give you that. But there's something about him that made me uncomfortable, and I can't quite put my finger on it—"

Ant interrupted.

"You mean the flirting?"

He waited for Lyn's response, which was a few seconds in coming.

"No, I, er... Do you know, Ant, it's just—"

"Believe me, Lyn, no one crosses Rufus Dean-Porter without coming off all the worse for it. So, yes, I do know what you mean. Anyway, do you fancy a pear drop?"

The offer was Ant's attempt to lighten the conversation. Ant had seen the gruesome results of Rufus' darker side, which he had no desire to delve into with his best friend.

"Take the bag," added Ant, suddenly in need to scratch an insatiable nose itch.

Catching the sugar-boiled sweet, Lyn made her displeasure clear.

"Get your hand back on the steering wheel before you kill "us both, fool.

4

AN UNSCHEDULED STOP

Ant enjoyed stretching the speed limit of Her Majesty's highways and byways, and for the most part, their journey back to Stanton Parva remained uneventful. That was until he became aware of a particular car in his rear-view mirror.

Any closer, and you'll be in my boot.

"Damn it, where did he come from?"

Unsure of what he was referring to, Lyn looked over her shoulder to see a blue light flashing from the front grill of the vehicle.

"Unmarked police car, serves you right. I've been telling you for the last twenty minutes that you were driving too fast. You'd better hope whichever bobby is in that car is a lover of the aristocracy."

Have they nothing better to do?

"And make sure you keep your temper, Anthony Stanton. No tantrums, do you hear?"

Ant snorted an acknowledgement as he gripped the steering wheel and waited for the inevitable tap on his side window.

Here we go.

Instead of pressing the control to lower the window, he hit the switch next to it. In an instant, an electric motor sprang to life, followed by a solid "click." The Morgan's soft-top roof disengaged, lifted upwards and backwards, then descended to neatly stow itself behind the jump seat.

Ant could feel the bad vibes coming from Lyn. He knew she knew he'd done it on purpose.

He observed that to his immediate right stood a police constable whose uniform was at least one size too small. The man's overturned waistband showing the white lining of his trousers further eroded the dignity of his office as did his need for a shave.

"Trying to be funny, are we, sir?"

The bobby spoke in a low, gravelly voice.

Ant began to form his response, except Lyn beat him to it.

"I'm so sorry, Constable. That was my fault. As you can see, the two button thingies are so close together. My friend intended to let the window down, and I inadvertently nudged him, making his hand slip."

Ant continued to look straight ahead, working hard to keep a straight face.

Nice one, Lyn.

The policeman spent a few seconds pushing the tail of his shirt back into his trousers before responding. Satisfied no further mechanical surprises awaited, the burly copper leant forward, forcing Ant to crane his neck to make eye contact with the bobby.

"I see. Is that the case, sir?"

Instead of responding, he watched the towering policeman stare rather too long at Lyn for his liking.

"I'll let it pass on this occasion—"

Right. That's it.

Unable to help himself, Ant bit.

"Why, exactly, have you pulled me over, Officer?"

The policeman stiffened.

"I was just coming to that, sir."

Ant knew the officer's overemphasis of the word "sir" meant he was rattled.

Lyn will make me pay for that.

He didn't have to wait long.

Ant felt a sharp dig into his left side and winced as her blow landed.

"Something wrong, sir?"

Ant took a deep breath as he glimpsed Lyn's index finger pointing at his aching ribs. He understood her warning.

"Not at all, Officer. Just curious, that's all."

The policeman smirked.

"Just a routine traffic stop, sir. That's all. We've had reports of drunk drivers on this stretch of road. You haven't had a drink today, have you, sir?"

Not wishing for a further poke in the ribs, Ant suppressed his natural urge to aggravate the policeman.

"Not at all, Officer. Not one drop has passed our lips."

The policeman leant farther into the car, sniffing the air in an exaggerated manner, ending up inches from Ant's right cheek.

Keep your distance, pal.

He was within seconds of pushing the copper away for invading his personal space when the man relented.

The huge copper stepped away from the car, moving his attention from Lyn to glare at Ant.

"Well, I can't smell alcohol on your breath, sir, so on this occasion we will let the matter drop."

Strange he's not following police procedure by breathalysing me if he suspected I'd been drinking?

"Will that be all, Officer?"

Ant almost spat the words through clenched teeth.

Lyn flashed her index finger again. Ant glared at his friend. She blinked first and, instead, gave the policeman a broad smile.

What are you up to?

Unable to control his base instincts, the constable returned her smile as if she'd just accepted an offer of dinner for two.

"Just one last thing, sir. May I ask the reason for your visit to Windsor, today?"

He spoke without taking his eyes off Lyn.

Keep it up, girl.

Lyn succeeded in meeting her friend's unspoken challenge.

Meanwhile, Ant gripped the steering wheel with such force that his knuckles began to turn white.

This is Riley's doing. He's put us under surveillance.

"They do have some wonderful boats for sale down there, don't they, sir?"

That does it.

Ant fumed as he realised something more serious than a routine traffic stop was occurring.

He gave the official a defiant glare.

"We didn't say anything about Windsor or boats."

The policeman stepped forward so that he once again towered over Ant.

"No, you didn't, did you, sir?"

Ant took note that the man, whoever he was, spoke with a chill that would shame packed ice.

"Well, that will be all, and I apologise if I have delayed

you, sir. I know how precious time is when you're on leave, especially sick leave."

The policeman took two steps backwards, smirked, then gestured for Ant to continue his journey.

Ant was aware that his theory about Riley risked turning into a self-fulfilling prophecy as he fumed at the policeman's knowledge of their movements, and his personal circumstances.

Allowing his emotions to override caution, Ant pressed his right foot to the floor. The sports car responded immediately.

For several minutes he tore up the tarmac on the narrow, twisting country roads, lost in a world of his own.

"Time to slow down, cowboy."

Ant failed to respond. Instead, his eyes remained in a trance-like state as his grip on the steering wheel tightened still further.

Suddenly he felt Lyn's touch over his clenched left hand. Bodily contact did the trick and broke his anger.

"Cup of tea and a cake, don't you think?"

Ant turned to Lyn, offered the beginnings of a smile, and eased his foot off the accelerator.

You know how to handle me. I'll give you that.

* * *

"TWO AFTERNOON TEAS," said the young waiter as he brought a serving trolley to a stop by the side of a small square table.

"Yes, that's us. Thank you so much," replied Lyn.

Ant surveyed the elegant cake stand freshly loaded with a selection of sandwiches, cakes, and cream scones.

Leaving a pot of tea for two, the server withdrew, leaving Ant and Lyn to relax as they looked over Sheldon Broad from the spacious conservatory of The Water's Edge tearooms.

"It's all right for some."

Ant's comment summed up his view of the wildlife scurrying about on the mill's pond-like surface of the water stretching into the distance.

"Calmed down, yet?"

Ant frowned. As far as he was concerned, the moment had passed, and he was now perfectly calm.

"You know what the doctor said, Ant. Your PTSD is not going to go away without treatment."

Ant didn't acknowledge Lyn's comment or break eye contact with the water. The seconds passed as a silence descended.

Suppose I'd better say something.

"For the most part, I don't think about it. Then something sets it off and..."

Lyn didn't respond, other than to hold up the plate she'd filled for him. He looked at her, smiled, and took his food.

I know you get me.

"Anyway, what do you think about our mysterious bobby. And what was that stuff about Windsor?"

He was thankful she'd let his illness drop, at least for now.

Ant bit into a cucumber sandwich, which delayed his response by all of the five seconds it took to demolish the tiny snack.

"Odd might be one way to describe it. Riley has to be behind us being stopped. The question is why? What's he up to?"

Eyeing the selection of sandwiches on his plate, Ant selected the fresh salmon.

"So you're changing your mind about Geoff's death?"

Ant took a last lingering look at his sandwich before devouring it in one go.

"Let's put it this way, Riley wouldn't authorise one of his goons to tail us unless he thinks Geoff's death is suspicious. And if the force is interested in Geoff's demise, I suppose I should be too, don't you think?"

He could see that his reply met with Lyn's approval.

"Well, that took you long enough. So where do we go from here?"

Ant considered his options.

"Let's talk about it over dinner—my treat."

Lyn sighed as she looked at her mobile to check the time.

"Sorry. I've got a staff meeting tomorrow that I need to prepare for and a stack of marking to do. Can we give it a miss?"

Ant feigned disappointment as he grabbed the last piece of sponge cake from the stand.

"In that case, I'd better eat this lot. Tell you what. I'll do a bit of digging by giving Riley a poke tomorrow morning."

Lyn frowned and wagged an index finger.

"Make sure you behave yourself, young man, or it'll be the legal type of detention you'll be dealing with, not one of my school stay behinds."

Ant let out a roar that caused heads to turn.

"Yes, head teacher. Message understood."

Lyn nodded as if confirming the threat to one of her young pupils.

"And I'll call on Hannah after school to see how she's getting on."

5

MONDAY BLUES

Ant almost convinced himself that time had stood still as he gazed at a photo on the wall of the police station dating back over a hundred years compared to the reality of the building today.

As he leant on an old-fashioned oak countertop waiting to be attended to, he imagined the number of people, guilty and innocent, that had passed through the space he now stood over, the previous fifteen decades or so.

"Good morning, sir. How may I help you today?"

Ant awoke from his distraction as two huge hands gripped the opposite edge of the counter. He recognised their owner as Sergeant Fredrick Cummins who, as far as Ant knew, had been a policeman from the beginning of time and who had collared him more than once for making mischief as a young lad.

"Might I have a word with Detective Inspector Riley?"

Ant always felt as though he'd done something wrong and was about to be arrested when in the presence of a policeman.

Guess they must be trained to look at you like that.

Before the policeman could answer, the desk telephone rang. Ant waited patiently as the sergeant became increasingly exasperated with his caller.

"I can absolutely assure you, sir, there is no need to report running over a cat to the police. A dog, yes. A cat, no."

Several seconds passed while the policeman listened to the caller again.

"It is of no concern to the police that this Mrs Tennant you mention has threatened you with a citizen's arrest. You have committed no crime. Ruined the cat's day, yes, but executed a crime, no. You see, in the eyes of the law, a cat has no legal owner. The fact this lady bought it a toy mouse and fed the animal best-quality chicken each day counts for nothing as far as we are concerned. Will that be all, sir?"

The desk sergeant didn't wait for an answer. Instead, he replaced the handset and made a quick note of the call in the duty log.

"Now what did you say you wanted to report. It's not another cat, is it?"

Ant held his tongue, having decided any further mention of felines would be of little help to his cause.

"I didn't... want to report running over a cat, I mean."

The policeman looked confused.

"Detective Inspector Riley. Is he in?" repeated Ant.

Eventually, the penny dropped.

"That rather depends on why you want to see him, sir. He's a very busy man as I am sure you will understand."

Ant's patience had its limits.

"For goodness' sake, Fred. Is he in, or isn't he? What's up with you today?"

He watched Sergeant Cummins retrieve a pack of

headache tablets from his breast pocket, squeeze two capsules from the blister pack, and try swallowing them without liquid, which caused the policeman to pull an anguished face when they got stuck.

"That bad," said Ant as he raced the few feet to a water fountain and dispensed just enough water into a flimsy plastic cup to help Fred get his medication down.

Fred nodded his thanks and almost choked on the mixture of liquid and tablets before letting out a sigh of relief.

"Better?"

Fred nodded his head while rubbing two fingers in a circular motion to massage the pain away.

"It's him in there. In a stinking mood, he is."

Fred pointed half-heartedly at a door behind Ant.

"Perhaps the wife had a go at him for leaving his toe clippings on the floor again—he does it here as well, you know. Horrible habit. Anyway, he's been shouting at everyone since he arrived. Drives me mad, he does."

Ant smiled.

"I'm not going to let you see him if you're going to make him worse, Lord Stanton or not."

"Me?"

Ant pointed a finger at himself and offered the stressed policeman a hurt look.

"Yes, you. I know what you're like with him, so behave, understand? My head can't put up with much more today."

"Behave with who?"

Fred stiffened, immediately recognising the voice.

"This gentleman has asked to see you, sir."

The desk sergeant gave no further information. Riley started to extend his hand before quickly retracting the offer as Ant turned to face him.

"Oh, it's you."

Ant responded with a broad smile.

"And a very good morning to you, Detective Inspector. Might I have a word? I know you will be dreadfully busy, but..."

Riley scowled.

Ant's smile broadened.

"Get me a coffee, Sergeant. And you, follow me."

Both men did as they were ordered with Fred making for the staff kitchen and Ant following the detective into a small, poorly lit, windowless office.

As the detective reached the halfway point between standing and taking his seat, Ant pounced.

"Why are you having me followed?"

Ant could tell he'd unsettled him as the flummoxed policeman hovered for a few seconds before settling his ample backside into the padded leather seat of his ancient, civil service, standard-issue chair.

"What are you talking about, man?"

Now let's see what happens.

Riley fidgeted with a pile of papers and sought out his favourite fountain pen for the want of something to do.

Ant sat opposite Riley and leant into the table, closing the distance between them deliberately, before recounting events from the previous day.

Riley's facial expression changed from irritation to outright confusion.

He's a good actor; I'll give him that.

"Tall, overweight officer? Roadside stop? Have you gone mad?" Believe me, I'd have been told if one of my officers had stopped the noble Lord Stanton."

Riley's smile confirmed to Ant that the detective relished the thought of him being subjected to public indignity.

"Sounds to me like you've fallen victim to someone impersonating a police officer. We've had several such reports recently."

Ant hesitated, unsure how to respond.

Telling the truth or winding me up? One way to find out.

"A new strategy to increase the police's presence, is it? You know, if you can't put your own out, get some bloke in fancy dress to do the job for you?"

Ant counted on his words stinging Riley. They did.

"I can assure you—"

Ant pulled his usual trick of cutting the detective off in mid-sentence.

"Then how did he know about me being in Windsor? And my military background?"

Ant spoke harshly. He was in no mood to be fobbed off.

Riley stood up and paced around his dingy office.

"I have absolutely no idea, but it's not as if you are exactly anonymous in these parts, is it?"

Touched a nerve there all right.

"Let me get this straight, Detective Inspector. You're saying Geoffrey Singleton's death and me being warned off by the police aren't linked?"

Riley pulled a well-worn handkerchief from a side pocket and blew his nose into the off-white material.

"Warned off? Warned off from what? Mr Singleton died from natural causes, and the post-mortem tomorrow will confirm as much. That is, unless you have information to the contrary. Remember, Lord Stanton, I have warned you before about interfering in police work and withholding evidence. I will not hesitate to arrest you if I have the slightest evidence this is the case."

Need to be careful here.

Before Riley could interrogate Ant further, the detective's phone rang.

"Of course, sir, right away."

Riley gave no explanation as he made for the door. As he did so, the handle moved downward hitting Riley across the knuckles.

"I'm sorry, sir," said Fred while holding the detective's mug of coffee in his free hand. His smirk was unmistakable as Riley inspected the flesh covering his knuckles for damage.

"Get out of my way, man, and show this person out."

Result!

"You said you wouldn't upset him."

"I suspect the summons to his superior's office is rather more to blame for his mood than my visit... although I admit, it might be a close-run thing."

Both men laughed.

"Been doing any scrumping lately, young Stanton?"

Ant was happy to recall old times.

"I lost count how many times you walloped me across the head and sent me on my way, Fred. But thanks for never telling my parents!"

* * *

LYN PLACED a comforting arm around Hannah as they sat together on a large crimson leather sofa.

"I thought you could do with a bit of company. How are you?"

Hannah repeated how gentle Geoff was and that the success of their business meant they had no money worries.

"It's not fair. We had only just got married."

Lyn encouraged Hannah to talk before eventually managing to swing the conversation around to Geoff's boat.

"So you're saying he intended to sell it?"

"Yes, he had a new one on order." Lyn offered Hannah a tissue as she mopped tears from her cheek. "He went to the boathouse to finish off some little jobs on the yacht. Varnishing the wood, I think. I hated the smell of that stuff. It was okay for him; he had no sense of smell. Geoff loved, how you say, doing the DIY?"

Lyn nodded and offered a friendly smile.

"Yes, Hannah, that's what we call it."

"But why do you ask me this?"

Better watch how far and fast I go now.

"Oh, you know. Small village, people gossip."

Hannah frowned.

"Gossip? What is gossip?"

Lyn attempted to explain.

"Er, let me see. Well, people who talk to each other about a new bit of news. One tells another, and they tell—"

"Oh, yes. I understand. We call it plotka."

Lyn's eyes lit up.

"Well, what do you know. I've learned a little Polish today. Thank you, Hannah."

The women passed the next few minutes talking about daily life in a small village. Detecting she'd succeeded in helping Hannah relax, Lyn took her opportunity and pressed on.

"And the police. Have you heard from them?"

Lyn tried not to sound too inquisitive.

"Ah, how do you say? Er... liaison officer, yes, I have it. That lady came to the house, how you say... earlier."

Hannah broke down.

"It's okay. You cry all you want."

"No, you don't understand. They are going to cut him up tomorrow. Too horrible. His heart stopped working. Why do they have to do this?"

Lyn worked hard to keep her own emotions in check.

"Do you mean a post-mortem?"

Hannah nodded.

"Please tell them to stop. I will not let them."

6
BODY OF EVIDENCE

"Gone, what do you mean, it's gone?"

Ant knew who was complaining as he walked down a poorly lit corridor that led to the mortuary.

He's having a good day—not.

Seconds later, Ant gingerly opened one of two wide doors giving access to the cold, featureless space. It was just enough to catch a whiff of formaldehyde.

I hate that stuff.

His attention was drawn to two figures standing on opposite sides of a white ceramic autopsy slab.

Ant watched on in amusement as Detective Inspector Riley fumed as he gazed upon the surface on which Geoff Singleton's corpse should have lain.

A nervous-looking man in a white laboratory coat looked forlornly at the slab then at Riley. Ant assumed the man didn't know quite what to say.

The less you say, the better you'll come out of this.

Opening the door a touch wider so he could follow the action but still not be noticed, Ant's eyes traced Riley's progress as he prowled around the spacious room, faced with Victorian, white-glazed tiles, before coming to a halt in front of a bank of square metal doors stacked in pairs from floor to ceiling.

"Open them, every last one. He must be here somewhere."

Ant stifled a giggle as he contrasted the pale pallor and slim build of the young lab assistant with Riley's big frame and rapidly reddening cheeks.

The mortuary assistant sprang into action not wishing to incur further wrath from the scowling policeman. As he opened each door, a pair of upturned feet presented themselves, each with a paper tag attached to a big toe.

"Slide each one out. I want to see faces."

Obeying, the technician pulled a handle and walked backwards allowing the contents to extend from the flat surface like a stream of bunting pulled from a conjurer's hat.

Riley pulled back a white linen sheet from each owner's head and carefully inspected the facial features. His mood darkened as he rejected each body in turn.

Ant inwardly agreed with the young man's tactic of taking a step back and towards the exit doors each time Riley let loose a string of invective.

As the policeman looked up to check the whereabouts of the hapless man, Ant pulled his head back so he wouldn't be seen.

"Not so fast, Batman," shouted Riley as he caught the technician's attempted escape. "Please tell me how you managed to lose a dead man? I presume you checked that he was, in fact, dead and that he's not just nipped out for a coffee?"

Very good, Inspector. Not at all bad for you.

An uneasy standoff followed. Eventually, the young man attempted an explanation.

"We were just about to start the post-mortem when the fire alarm went off. We evacuated the building like we're supposed to, and when we came back, it, I mean he, had gone."

Ant had to put a fist into his mouth to stop himself laughing. It got so bad that, as he leant back against the painted wall of the corridor, he resorted to pinching an earlobe with his free hand, so that the pain might distract him from laughing out loud and being discovered.

Achieving his aim, he felt confident enough to continue peeking into the room, only to see the technician shrugging his shoulders.

No use looking for sympathy from that fool, mate.

Riley referenced a fire alarm in the far corner then at the wide entrance doors.

His eyes narrowed.

For once Riley was too quick for Ant.

"I might have known. Is there nowhere you don't manage to show up where you're not wanted?"

After struggling for a nanosecond to understand Riley's poor use of grammar, Ant threw open the door and ambled in with the air of a man out for a stroll in the morning sun.

"Good day to you, Detective Inspector. I was just in the area and—"

"In the area? So you have a fetish for dead bodies? Oh, wait a minute, you do, don't you?"

Second reasonable joke in five minutes. You're on fire today.

Ant smiled, which irritated Riley all the more, then looked at the hapless technician who seemed to be having trouble taking matters in.

"Don't worry about me, young man, I'm—"

"Yes, I know who you are, Lord—"

"Oh, let's not start all that aristocracy stuff again.

Enough. I want to know where my body is. As for you, Stanton. Get yourself out of my sight before I have you arrested."

Ant took faux offence at Riley's tone.

"Me? I didn't steal your body. A bit careless if you ask me, but—"

Ant's provocation had its desired effect.

"But nothing. I neither want nor need your contribution in this matter. Now you have a choice: leave and go back to fishing, or whatever you people do, or you can spend the day in one of my cells. Your choice."

Ant raised an eyebrow at the rattled policeman, knowing it would do the man's humour no good at all.

"Sorry to disappoint you, Inspector. I don't possess a rod or any other implement for catching living creatures. Except for a camera, of course. As for your kind offer of accommodation for the day, perhaps I'll give it a miss on this occasion. I have things to do, you know, supervising the polishing of the family silver and so forth... "

Not getting rid of me that easily, thought Ant as he made for the doors, allowed them to swing shut and waited a few seconds before opening one by the tiniest amount.

He could just about see Riley shaking his head as he returned his attention to the laboratory technician.

"And did whoever took him thoughtfully return the trolley they carted him out in?"

Riley pointed to a metal gurney that had seen better days.

With the restricted view Ant now had, he could just make out the technician turning sideways to follow Riley's index finger.

"We have two. You know, for busy shifts."

"Busy shifts? You make the place sound like *Holby City* on steroids."

Third joke of the morning, Riley. I'm impressed.

The assistant attempted to explain the ward procedures for moving deceased patients from the hospital ward. Ant could see Riley was having none of it.

"Stop. I am not interested in the finer points and progress of rigor mortis or the sensibilities of adjacent live patients. Get me the CCTV so I can watch our body snatchers go about their business."

The technician spotted Ant, froze, and looked back towards the detective without saying a word.

Good lad.

"Now will do," shouted Riley.

"There is none. Pictures I mean."

Ant watched as the young man closed his eyes as if half expecting the detective to land a blow.

"They're upgrading the system. We got an email about it the other day from the big bosses."

Ant readied himself to intervene as he observed Riley lift his right hand and clench his fist. Instead, the detective punched the mortuary slab then winced in pain.

Serves you right, fool.

"You couldn't make it up," whispered the detective inspector as he turned, cradling his injured fist into his ample stomach.

Ant realised Riley was heading in his direction. He raced to the left and hid behind a large stainless-steel trolley piled high with crisp, white, bed linen. It worked, as Riley launched himself in the opposite direction.

After a few seconds, Ant checked that the coast was clear before ambling back into the mortuary.

He smiled. The young man, reassured, smiled back.

"He doesn't half shout, does he?"

Ant grinned all the more.

"He certainly does, but well done, fella. You handled him well. I don't suppose you're used to strangers coming in here—apart from the cold ones on a trolley, of course. And they don't answer back or shout at you, do they?"

He could see his banter was having the desired effect as the young man broadened his smile, held an empty mug up, and pointed at the kettle.

"Thank you, but no."

The technician returned the mug to the sink drainer.

"I suppose that's why I like working down here. You know, for all the shouting and bad stuff people get up to, there's one thing for certain. We will all end up in one of those."

Ant nodded as the young man pointed at the bank of steel doors holding their current crop of corpses.

A wise head on young shoulders.

"And on that bombshell, I'll leave you to it. Again, well done my friend."

Ant offered the technician a "thumbs-up" sign as he exited the chilled room.

Got to catch up with Riley to see what he's about.

A few seconds later, Ant glimpsed the detective as he made his way from the building into a Victorian-walled courtyard. He was shouting into his mobile phone.

"I want this area swept and all road junctions put under covert surveillance."

Ant thought Riley would burst as he grew increasingly agitated.

Guess the news isn't good.

"A burger van, hearse, motorbike with a sidecar. In fact, a horse and cart, for all I care. In fact, anything capable of moving and concealing a corpse is to be checked. Do I make myself clear?"

* * *

"What's so funny?" asked Lyn as she entered Hammond's Bakery for her usual Tuesday lunchtime fix of fresh iced buns as a shared treat with her secretary, Tina.

"You haven't heard?"

Geraldine, the shop manager who Lyn knew had a well-earned reputation for having a macabre sense of humour, looked delighted by Lyn's ignorance.

"Them lot up there have lost someone. A body, would you believe? I mean, how do you do that?"

Geraldine cocked her head in the approximate direction of the hospital.

Lyn watched as the manager broke into another fit of laughter.

"I suppose that accounts for all those police sirens I heard. It caused havoc at school. The children wouldn't settle and wanted to know what was going on."

Lyn's question set the other shop assistants into a collective fit of the giggles.

"The bobbies are going bonkers. Checking everywhere, they are."

How odd, thought Lyn.

"Came in here about half an hour ago, they did. Asked if we'd seen anything suspicious."

The shop descended into chaos with two customers almost crying into paper tissues as group hysteria took hold.

"I told the young constable that a tired-looking bloke, who seemed a bit anaemic, got off a trolley and came in asking for a Cornish pasty. Would you believe, the lad asked if I could describe him before he cottoned on he was having his leg pulled."

Lyn shed tears of laughter as she watched Geraldine

almost bent double and holding her stomach as she delivered the punchline.

"Then we told the young bobby that if the bloke wasn't dead before he came in, he would be after eating anything we baked."

It was difficult for Lyn to know where to look. At the sight of Geraldine gasping for air, or the counter staff running for the shop restroom to deal with overexcited bladders.

Lyn worked hard with those who remained in the shopfront by not looking at each other for fear of setting themselves off again. She was thankful that after several seconds of disciplined silence, order replaced chaos.

"But that poor Polish lady. What must she be going through?"

Lyn's ears pricked up. She hadn't expected Geraldine to make such a solemn remark after their collective joviality.

"Polish lady?"

And how does she know about Hannah?

"My Ernie is a porter at the hospital. He rang me this morning to tell me what happened. All hell is breaking loose he says."

Lyn held her surprise in check. She knew any overreaction would be around the village within hours as the gossip mill churned at full speed.

"How awful," replied Lyn as she collected the paper bag containing her iced buns from the Formica counter. "Talking about your Ernie, how long have you two been engaged now?"

The shop erupted into laughter again as they anticipated Geraldine's answer.

"Twenty-two years April gone. That's longer than I would have got for murder."

* * *

"Sorry, I'm a bit behind today," said Fitch as Lyn walked onto the garage forecourt to collect her Mini Clubman.

"Not to worry, it happens to the best of us," she replied while glancing at a car bumper lying in two pieces on the yard floor.

"That looks expensive. I'm glad it wasn't my car."

Fitch smiled as he swept the plastic debris to one side with the instep of his foot.

"And Irene Chapman wasn't best pleased either. It turns out some maniac clipped her car early Saturday morning on that nasty bend near the boathouse. They didn't even stop, so that's her insurance no-claims discount up the swanny."

Lyn glanced across to a sorry-looking Nissan Micra, minus a front bumper and with a nasty dent in a wing panel.

"Ouch. I hate people who don't stop after an accident. I bet they didn't have car insurance."

"Happened to me once," replied Fitch. "Cost me a packet to fix—and that was just the parts."

Lyn nodded in sympathy.

"Anyway, I've got to get a move on. I spent too long in Hammond's bakery gossiping about missing bodies. If I don't get back to school pronto, Tina won't get her iced buns, and believe me, that's not a pretty sight."

"It's a rum do though, Lyn. How does a body just disappear into thin air: creepy or what?"

Lyn shrugged her shoulders.

"The thing is, I spent some time with Hannah yesterday. She was adamant in not wanting Geoff's body touched."

Fitch frowned.

"Well, you can't blame her for that, can you, Lyn?"

The conversation was interrupted by the wailing of yet another police car speeding through the village.

"They've been at that all morning," added Fitch.

"Same at school. A real nuisance. But this Hannah thing. You don't think she could have arranged for someone to nab the body, do you? You know, to stop the autopsy taking place?"

Fitch shook his head.

"Can't see it myself. But then I've never been in that position. What I do know is that grief can make some people do crazy stuff."

Lyn nodded then glimpsed the lit screen on her mobile.

"Got to go, or I really will be in Tina's bad books."

In seconds, Lyn was out the gates and striding along the cobbled path back towards Stanton Parva Primary.

"The Mini. It will be ready by five."

Lyn acknowledged Fitch's shout by lifting an arm and waving her hand without looking back. She was too busy concentrating on another matter.

He looks a bit odd.

She had noticed a man in dishevelled clothing and shoes with holes in their toes, shuffling towards her. As he neared, Lyn attempted to catch sight of his face. With his coat collar up and head lowered, Lyn could only see what looked like a faded scar on his right cheek.

The man brushed passed her without missing a step, knocking Lyn off balance.

Wouldn't like to meet him on a dark night.

7

ODD MAN OUT

The outer office of Lyn's room looked like a battlefield clearing station as Ant pushed aside the half-glazed door and stepped inside.

It was several seconds before Tina noticed his presence as she dealt with 3 seven-year-olds in various states of distress.

"Oh, it's you. Don't mind the noise, they'll settle down when I've dished out the stickers for being brave little soldiers."

"What on earth's been going on here?"

Tina gazed up at Ant from the crouched position in front of one of the sobbing boys.

"This one is Timmy Weston. None the worse for wear from an overzealous football tackle. That lad is Billy Lightfoot, a name not associated with his tendency to trip over the smallest of obstacles. And finally, we have young Master Hayman. He's Timmy's avowed enemy in all things football."

Ant noticed that the latter seemed the braver of the three, almost as if he were gloating at Timmy's tears and that his own injured shin had not reduced *him* to a babbling wreck.

"There you are." The voice belonged to Lyn as she breezed into Tina's casualty clearing station.

"Come in, come in. I thought I'd lost you," she said as she gave each of the boys a sympathetic look before quickly moving on to her own office and leaving Tina to tend the injured.

Ant gave the secretary a weary look in acknowledgement of Lyn's "can do" mood and nodded when Tina rolled her eyes.

"She had two cups of coffee an hour ago and hasn't come down yet," replied Tina. "You go in. I think we'll go for green tea when I've discharged the troops, or there will be no handling madam this afternoon."

Ant required no encouragement to escape the organised chaos around him.

"Where have you been? I've been trying to get hold of you since yesterday," asked Lyn as she simultaneously read a missive from the Department for Education.

When you're ready, girl.

Ant waited as it took Lyn a good forty-five seconds to realise he hadn't answered. He watched as she looked up from the briefing paper.

"Ah, got your attention, then, have I? It's no use you blinking at me like one of your pupils who doesn't want to hear he's in trouble."

"I *was* listening."

A gesture of the head and eye contact on the document did the trick. Lyn took the hint and put the briefing note down, making sure one long side rested parallel to the desk edge.

"Listening to what? I didn't say anything."

That tore it.

"Listen, smarty pants, I've got Mr and Mrs Sandown in half an hour to bend my ear about their son—again, so I'm not in the mood for your nonsense. Now, where were you yesterday?"

Ant felt as if he were back in Riley's office, except Lyn was scarier.

"Fair play, old girl. To tell you the truth... Ouch!"

Ant's explanation was interrupted by a pencil catching him square on the forehead, point first.

"How many times have I told you not to call me that?"

This is fun.

"Okay, sorry." Ant checked to see if the graphite was still attached to the end of the pencil or embedded in his flesh.

"I was only joking, Lynda."

Light the blue touch paper and stand back.

Ant watched as Lyn began to flush knowing his apology was half hearted, and the use of her full first name was a calculated jibe to wind her up even more.

Tin hats on.

"Listen, Lord Stanton, or whatever you are calling yourself today, either behave or I'll set those three little terrors in Tina's office on you. Now are you going to answer my question?"

The threat was enough for Ant to capitulate. He held his hands above his head as Lyn continued her interrogation without giving him the opportunity to respond.

"When I rang your dad to see if he knew where you were, he said you'd taken Mr Churchill's dog for a walk. What in heaven's name did he mean?"

Lyn's glare meant Ant had no option but to come clean. After a few seconds spent gathering his thoughts, he slouched back into his chair and looked at the deep-brown material of the carpet.

"Winston Churchill battled depression all his life." He watched Lyn's expression change. The penny had dropped. "It's Dad's way of explaining how I deal with my PTSD. As I've told you before, anything can set the damn thing off. As it happens, yesterday I caught a news item about the Middle East. Another time it wouldn't have affected me. Yesterday it did. I don't know why, but something went 'ding' in my head, and I broke out in a cold sweat."

Ant's eyes followed Lyn as she got up, walked around the desk and perched herself on a corner beside his chair and placed an arm around his shoulders.

"You took off, then?"

"Yes, I did. Not proud of myself but..."

His voice tailed off as Lyn stroked his hair. He could feel himself relaxing in the company and touch of someone he trusted without question.

"Anyway, the dog is back in its kennel so that's that." He gently moved Lyn's hand from his scalp and straightened his back into the chair.

"For now, anyway, Ant. For now. Anyway, how did you get on with Riley yesterday?"

He didn't get a chance to explain before a movement of the door handle and the sight of Tina's head popping through the opening told Ant the Sandowns had arrived. He sensed the change of mood and made to leave.

"I think I'll have a walk around the village. Not done that for ages. Catch up at yours tonight?"

Lyn nodded as she fumbled on her desk for the demanding parents' latest letter of complaint.

"Er, yes," replied Lyn as she looked in panic at Tina.

"Around seven thirty, and the Chinese takeaway is on you. I'll have the usual."

"It's here," said Tina in a quiet, reassuring voice.

* * *

"Haven't seen you in here for ages," said David Ingram as Ant stepped over the threshold of the family-run newsagent.

"You do too good a job of delivering the papers. She never misses a day, does she? But that means there's no need to call in except when I fancy some of your scrumptious sweets, so here I am." Ant's saliva glands worked overtime as he surveyed a wall of temptation in what seemed like a hundred old-fashioned glass candy jars.

The newsagent smiled.

"Good to hear. I'll tell young Sophie what you said. Now what can I tempt you with?"

David stood aside allowing Ant an uninterrupted view of the confectionary on offer. Suddenly his face lit up like a Christmas tree.

"I haven't seen those since I was at school. We used to call in here every day, you know."

David pointed to a glass jar of aniseed balls.

"Yep, that's them." Ant's eyes followed David's movement as he stretched to retrieve the jar from a high shelf, place it on the counter, unscrew the large plastic lid, and begin to weigh its contents on a set of scales.

"We used to ask for two ounces when I was a lad. Not sure what that is in grams or whatever they are now." Ant watched each red spherical treat fall from the stainless-steel scoop and into the stainless-steel weighing bowl.

The newsagent laughed.

"I know what you mean, Ant. Ounces sound so much better, don't they? Keep to tradition, I say."

Once David finished dispensing the confectionary into its paper bag, Ant grabbed it and plunged one of the sweets into his mouth.

"Anybody would think I've just given you a pot of gold."

Ant sucked on the hard-boiled sweet and savoured the aniseed's strong flavour.

"You've no idea, Dave."

The smile on his face said it all.

As Ant thanked the shopkeeper and turned to leave, he spotted the latest edition of *Boating World*.

"Can I take one instead of you delivering it?"

David grabbed the paper delivery book from under the counter.

"No problem. Just let me mark it in here, so you don't get another copy. That reminds me. An odd-looking chap asked if I knew where the rich Englishman with the boat lived. I didn't let on because he looked a bit shifty. Mind you, I suppose that was good enough reason to have told him where you lived."

The shopkeeper laughed.

"What, because he was odd, or I'm supposed to be the rich kid?" replied Ant joining in the light-hearted banter. "If you see him again, tell him I'm broke and have left the country for a Buddhist retreat."

Ant left David still laughing as he headed up High Street.

* * *

AFTER TWENTY MINUTES of navigating the narrow back streets of the village centre, Ant took a breather by resting against one of the village's prized Victorian, red-pillar boxes. It was just tall enough for him to rest an arm on top to support himself while he read an article from his magazine about a new form of battery technology for boats predicted to take the market by storm within the year.

Soaking in the warm afternoon sun, he noticed a familiar figure coming out of a long-closed Methodist chapel across the road. It was Annabelle.

"It's a small world; what are you up to?" said Ant as she crossed the narrow lane.

"I love your quaint villages and their beautiful buildings."

Ant followed Annabelle's outstretched arm as she waved it around to reinforce her point. "I am interested in buying this old church. I want to convert it into a nice home. The agent was kind enough to let me in. You English are always so polite."

In your dreams, lady.

"I hope you don't mind me asking, but for someone on the hunt for a property, you look a bit glum."

Ant could see he had confused her.

"What is 'glum'?"

He smiled.

"Sorry, with your English being so good, I forgot. It means looking sad."

Oops, she looks even worse now.

"Yes, I see. To be honest, I am worried about Hannah."

Ant's smile vanished as it dawned it was, perhaps, still too early for levity.

"Worried? What's the problem?"

Annabelle slouched against the pillar box, her eyes glazed with emerging tears.

"I have seen a man from Hannah's past. He is trouble. How do you say—he has a terrible temper—very jealous."

The tears began to flow. Ant knew he wasn't the most tactful of individuals at the best of times. Now he hadn't a clue what to do other than to keep asking questions.

"Well, I'm sure Hannah will be okay. After all, Poland is a long way away."

He watched as Annabelle froze.

"No, you do not understand. I have seen him here, in this village. His name is Jakub Baros, and he was Hannah's first boyfriend. Then Geoff came and took her from him. Jakub was very angry."

Perhaps the bloke David mentioned wasn't asking for me?

Ant patted Annabelle on the shoulder as if he were soothing a pet dog.

"Listen, I'll get Lyn to have a word with Hannah to keep an eye out and let us know if she sees anyone suspicious. It'll be fine, I'm sure."

Annabelle stiffened. Her face froze.

"Please, no. Do not tell Hannah he might be here. She will be very frightened. Jakub threatened Geoff when Hannah left Poland."

Before Ant could answer, his mobile rang.

"Ant, it's me. I'll have to put our meal tonight back by a couple of hours. Got to sort out my warring parents again. Meet you in the Wherry Arms just before nine instead of seven, okay?"

8

TRUE FRIENDS

"Where does everyone come from?" asked Ant as he fought his way through to a reserved table at the back of the snug.

Looking over his shoulder, he realised he'd been inadvertently talking to an elderly woman he didn't know who smiled sympathetically. Taking his seat, Ant didn't have long to wait before Sarah, one of the casual staff brought in on busy nights, approached.

"You've only just made it. The kitchen closes in ten minutes. Do you know what you want?"

Keen not to miss dinner, he looked at the specials board on the far wall and chose a main course for both himself and Lyn.

Hope she likes toad-in-the-hole.

A few minutes passed as Ant surveyed the organised chaos with staff and customers charging across the entrance to the tiny snug, most gawping at him as they passed.

Now I know what a goldfish feels like.

"Good heavens, here at last."

Ant's mood lifted as Lyn breezed into the small space,

followed by a barman carrying a pint of Fen Bodger pale ale and a white wine lemonade spritzer.

"I thought we'd be posh tonight," said Ant as Lyn settled herself into an old wooden chair opposite her friend. Sarah said they were closing the kitchen, so I ordered for you."

He waited for Lyn's inevitable response. It wasn't long coming.

"Remember last time you used your initiative to order me food? Well, if it's tripe and pickled onion again, it's going back this time—understand?"

Ant's eyes lit up.

"Aha, you underestimate me. I have a surprise."

I can see she doesn't believe me.

At that second, Sarah arrived with two steaming dishes in hand. Placing the meals on the table, she then stood back to admire the chef's work.

This isn't going well.

"Ant, since when has toad-in-the-hole and a white wine with lemonade been posh?"

He watched in silence as she eyed her plate with disdain. Ant lifted his pint and offered a toast.

"To fine food and good company."

Ant hated it when Lyn gave him a look she might offer to a six-year-old having had "a little accident."

At least I try.

Toast completed, the pair tucked into two overcooked meals. Ant made a point of commenting how good the food was. It was as if the more he said it, the more he believed his own assessment. He had the feeling the same couldn't be said for Lyn.

"Did you sort your parents out?" asked Ant, keen to move the subject away from stodgy Yorkshire pudding and sausages, which defied all but the most substantial of molars.

He allowed her the time to reply since he could see Lyn was having difficulty chewing her food sufficiently before it could be safely swallowed.

"Put it this way," said Lyn, picking a piece of gristle from her teeth. "If they were two of my young pupils, I'd sit them in a room until they saw sense."

Ant offered his sympathy. Lyn batted it away.

"They'll never change. I swear when the Grim Reaper comes, they'll accuse him of favouritism in choosing one to go before the other."

Lyn sighed before resuming battle with her meal.

Ant contented himself by emptying the last of his pint and attracting the barman's attention for a refill.

"Anyway, from the sublime to the ridiculous. Tell me about the meeting with your detective friend."

Ant playfully shook his head to acknowledge the absurdity of Lyn's comment while taking a first gulp from his new pint, then held the glass up to the light so he could admire the liquid gold.

"I refuse to ruin my pale ale by thinking of Plod in those terms," replied Ant in a lofty tone before laughing at his own pomposity.

"One thing is obvious though. He sees no connection between Geoff's body disappearing from the morgue and his cause of death. As for getting us pulled over on Sunday, nope, I don't believe it. He's either a good actor, or stupid. And I know which of the two I'll settle for."

Ant was aware of Lyn's studied look as he took another gulp of his pale ale.

"The thing is, Ant, do *you* see any connection?"

He placed his glass back onto the table with the reverence of an antiquarian mounting a precious artefact ready for close inspection.

"Let's put it this way, someone didn't want Geoff Singleton's body interfered with, which begs two questions: who and why?"

The reappearance of Sarah interrupted his flow.

"I've kept two slices of lemon cheesecake back for you, if you're in the mood?"

Ant smiled. Lyn licked her lips.

"Does that come with ice cream?" asked Ant.

"Frothy cream from a can for me," said Lyn.

Sarah touched the side of her nose.

"I'll see what I can do."

Sarah disappeared as quickly as she'd appeared, leaving the two friends to resume their analysis.

"As I see it, Lyn, there are three possible suspects: Hannah herself, though she'd have to have been a magnificent actor to carry it off, but not impossible. Then there's dear Rufus."

He could see Lyn was desperate to jump in.

"Well, you told me he knocked around with some dodgy characters. Perhaps the deal with Geoff went pear shaped, and Rufus wanted his money back—or worse?"

Ant rubbed his chin between two fingers.

"You're correct. Rufus is as mad as a box of frogs when the mood takes him. But kidnapping a body? I guess we won't know for sure until or unless he contacts Hannah demanding money for its safe return. But you know—"

"Hang on. That's two who might be in the frame. You said three?"

Ant smiled.

"Did I? Oh, yes, I did, didn't I? Well, there's Jakub Baros."

Lyn sat back in her chair and stared at her fellow sleuth.

"Who?" she said as if Ant had simply made the name up.

"Jakub Baros, Hannah's first love. Apparently, he's the jealous sort. What's more, he's been seen in the village."

Ant stemmed a flood of questions from Lyn by recounting his chance encounter with Annabelle.

"Did she describe what he looked like?"

Ant thought for a moment as he mentally ran through their conversation.

"A bit scruffy, and a scar."

Lyn banged her glass onto the table with such force that it gave Ant a start.

"I saw him yesterday, or rather, he almost knocked me over. And if he drives a four by four, we can put him at the boathouse on Saturday morning," replied Lyn as she told Ant about the damage to Irene Chapman's car.

Good eye for detail.

"You're learning, Lyn. Fabulous. All I can say is that Hannah's lucky to have a friend like Annabelle to watch her back."

Their eyes locked.

"You know what?" said Sarah, as she returned with the sweet. "The way you two look at each other, well, people might think you're an old married couple still mad about one other."

Ant frowned as he broke eye contact to engage Sarah.

"Married? That's for crazy people."

Ant turned back to Lyn and noted her gentle smile fading as she played with her glass, eyes now firmly fixed on the turning object.

9

BURNT OUT

"So there you are, Anthony. I was just talking to this young detective about the war. His father was at Monte Casino as part of the Italian campaign like me. Small world, isn't it?"

Ant couldn't disguise his surprise at finding Detective Inspector Riley in the library of Stanton Hall, let alone hear him being described as "young."

He greeted the smiling policeman politely enough. After all, that's how he had been brought up, but he felt uneasy as he tried to make sense of what the policeman was doing talking to his father.

"I mentioned to the Earl of Stanton that my dad went all the way through without so much as a scratch. Isn't that amazing?"

Ant gave a faint smile and nodded as he turned to a side table and poured a cup of coffee.

No visible scars, anyway.

"Well," said the earl, "I'll leave you two gentlemen to get on with things. I'm sure the detective has had quite enough of the ramblings of an old soldier."

Riley managed an embarrassed smile.

"Goodbye, Detective Inspector Riley, and thank you for the wonderful work your colleagues and you do in keeping us all safe."

You might well blush.

Ant escorted his father into the terrace conservatory and made sure he was safely seated before rejoining his visitor in the library.

"He's a remarkable man. Mine's the same. They don't make them like that anymore, do they?"

Ant nodded.

Maybe there's more to Riley than I give him credit for.

"His generation are certainly tough cookies, Inspector. Not surprising given the experiences they all went through."

Ant offered Riley a top-up of his coffee.

"They're all the same. War doesn't distinguish between high and low born, does it, Lord Stanton?"

Ant paused as he replenished Riley's drink, unsure if the detective had reverted to type, but gave Riley the benefit of doubt.

"As you say, Detective Inspector, war doesn't give a damn who it hurts."

The room fell into silence.

Riley glanced around his elaborate surroundings, seeming to linger on the more ornate features of a pair of bookcase cabinets.

Ant watched and waited.

Wait for it. One rule for the rich, another for the workers.

He was pleasantly surprised when the expected sarcasm didn't materialise.

"We traced the car that stopped you on Sunday."

"Really?" replied Ant, caught out that the detective had bothered to follow the matter up. "And the owner?"

"It was stolen, I'm afraid, so no trace there. We found it burnt out on an abandoned World War II airfield between Norwich and Cambridge."

Ant took a few seconds to digest the information and formulate where to go next. Taking Riley's empty china cup and saucer from his outstretched hand, he returned the delicate object to a veneered mahogany side table.

"Dare I ask about fingerprints?"

"As I said, the car was burnt to a crisp. We think a couple of local scallywags found it, took it for a spin before dumping and setting light to it."

"Then how did you come to find it?"

Riley smiled, which was not something Ant had seen him do often.

"A coincidence, and good police work. Over recent months, we've had reports of kids using laser pens to distract pilots. We asked the aviation authority to let us know about any incidents they receive from aircrew. We got one such report earlier this week. We followed it up, and hey, presto..."

It wasn't often Ant felt compelled to congratulate the detective. He felt the need to do so now.

"What can I say? But why are you going to so much trouble if it was just kids who torched the car?"

Ant's question was framed to drag as much information from Riley as possible.

"Well, as you mentioned to me the other day, whoever stopped you knew quite a bit about your background."

"Are you any nearer to finding out who he was?" replied Ant, eager for any clue the detective might unwittingly provide.

Riley took a step back, turned, and began to make his way to the door.

"We're working on that. I should also just mention that I expect you to contact me immediately should you hear anything about the whereabouts of Geoffrey Singleton's body. Do we understand each other?"

Just can't help himself.

* * *

"Anthony, Lyn is on the telephone. Don't keep the girl waiting."

The Earl of Stanton's voice carried down the long gallery of Stanton Hall without Ant's father having to raise his voice.

"Got it, Dad," replied Ant as he lifted the receiver.

"Ant, I've just taken a call from Hannah. She sounds terrified."

"What's wrong?"

"She says she's seen Jakub Baros peering into her front window. I've sent Tina round to keep her company. Shall I ring the police?"

Ant knew he had to act quickly.

"Where's Annabelle?"

"Hannah garbled something about her having to fly back to Poland to arrange finance for some building conversion project."

"Okay," replied Ant. "That makes sense. Annabelle told me she wanted to buy the old Methodist hall. I guess that's what she's on about. Don't ring the police. I'll shoot over straight away."

* * *

ANT ARRIVED to find Tina fussing over Hannah, trying to get the woman to drink tea. The traumatised woman sat in a far corner of the large room shaking like a leaf as she stared through a picture window onto the front garden.

"What's been going on?"

Tina shrugged her shoulders.

"Lyn asked me to come over, and this is what I found. I've had a quick look around outside, but I can't see anyone."

Ant noticed a short length of old wood about two inches square resting on the arm of a chair.

"Just as well you didn't find him, Hannah." Ant smiled as he pointed to the timber.

His effort to lift her mood failed. There was no reaction.

"Look at me," said Ant quietly as he knelt down beside Hannah. His persistence paid off. Eventually, she made eye contact.

"Good." His calm, gentle voice began to tease Hannah from her stupor.

"Tell me about this Jakub chap. It's safe, don't worry. We won't leave you alone."

Ant watched Hannah tense at the mention of her old flame's name.

"I promise you; I won't let anything happen to you. Annabelle told me the pair of you were fond of each other when you were younger. Yes?"

He could tell that being taken back in time had a curiously cathartic effect on Hannah. For a few seconds, her facial features relaxed. The moment soon passed.

"Yes, you are correct. He was my first serious boyfriend. We lived in a small village, and he was very handsome."

Ant smiled, urging Hannah to continue.

"But as we got older, he started to get into trouble. Small things at first then more serious. He met some bad people.

And if he thought I had looked at another boy, he got very angry. One time he hit..."

Hannah's voice tailed off, and tears began to flow.

It's okay to remember. Let it out.

"And Geoff?" Ant worked hard to help Hannah maintain eye contact.

That's it, Hannah. Come on, smile. It's okay to remember the good times with those we grieve for.

"He came to the village one day. I was down at the harbour, and he had come to look at a boat. He bumped into me. I think he did it on purpose." Hannah broke into a broad smile. "And that was it. We were inseparable. But Jakub..."

Her voice began to tremble as she spoke his name.

Ant knew he'd pushed things as far as he could.

"Listen," said Ant, getting to his feet, "why don't I have a look around while you get a few things together. I've spoken to Lyn. She thinks it might be a good idea for you to spend a couple of days at her place. It's right in the centre of the village with plenty of people around. It beats being stuck here in the middle of nowhere, don't you think?"

Ant observed a small nod. That was enough to confirm arrangements.

10

COLD COMFORT

Ant's quad bike roared to life as he pressed the engine start button and twisted the throttle. In seconds, the machine had crossed Stanton Hall's shingle courtyard and raced into the open countryside.

As he took in the view of the family's land, he remembered a time when he'd found it difficult coming to terms with the privileges he enjoyed. This was balanced by the memory of his parents' decision not to send him to preparatory school but to the local primary.

I hated being the odd one out.

Ribbed mercilessly by most of the other kids, he knew his parents had been right to ensure he experienced the real world. Some of those children now worked for the estate just as their parents had. Others left the village and went on to professional careers. His best friend, Lyn Blackthorn, was a case in point. She'd left to get away from her warring parents, worked hard for her degree, and returned to the village as a head teacher.

He, too, had felt the need to escape after the death of his older brother and the responsibilities that would eventually fall to him. As he pondered the future of the business, the finances of which didn't make for restful sleep, he watched two figures scurrying about on the roof of one of the estate's Victorian follies.

He was too far away to make out who they were. However, given the remote location, he knew they had to be locals.

Well, I'll be damned. They're stripping the lead.

In his youth he'd have jumped into the fray. Now he took a more measured approach. If military conflict had taught him anything, it was that rushing into a situation without weighing up the options usually ended badly.

Not exactly an armed threat, but here we go.

Ant cut the engine and allowed the quad bike to coast the final hundred yards down a gentle slope to the edge of a clearing from where he could keep his unwanted visitors under observation.

Two teenagers skipped across the steep pitch of the obelisk like a pair of mountain gazelles. Even though they were damaging a building of historical value, he couldn't help but admire their athleticism.

About fifteen I'd say.

Dismounting the bike, Ant crept up on their blind side until he stood at the foot of the flint-faced construction. As he heard one of them sliding down to the eaves in preparation to jump, Ant stepped back so he could confront the intruder.

"Good morning, young man. Can I help you with that? It must be heavy?"

The sound of Ant's authoritative voice caused the youth to shout in terror for his mum. Both youth and lead dropped from the eaves onto a lush carpet of long meadow grass.

Ant turned his gaze from the dishevelled youth rubbing

the hand his loot had fallen onto, to his accomplice, who was peering over the roof's edge to investigate the kerfuffle.

"Nice to meet you too, young lady. Do come and join us. Would you like a hand?"

Ant offered the girl an outstretched hand to ease her descent. Dismissing his offer, she leaped clear and landed next to her partner in crime.

"I hesitate to ask the obvious, but what exactly are you doing?"

The would-be thieves glanced at each other, then the lead, and finally at Ant.

Your faces really are a picture.

"Fair enough. I suppose that was a stupid question."

The youths scrunched their faces as if competing in a gurning competition.

"What's he on about?" muttered the boy.

"He's mad. Who is he, anyway?" replied the girl without bothering to look at the adult towering over them.

Top marks for bravado.

He remembered being their age. One which excluded adults from having anything of interest to say and whose only function was to shout and make teenagers' lives a misery.

"An apt enquiry, young lady. I'm the man whose family owns the ground you're sitting on. Oh, and the lead you kindly thought to relieve us of."

The youths turned to look at the alloy resting forlornly in the long grass, then at Ant.

"If you own this lot, you're not going to miss a bit of lead, are you?" The girl nodded in an act of solidarity with her more forward accomplice.

"True, but that isn't the point—"

"It's okay for you. You're rich, right? We've got nothing.

No money or any chance of a job. There isn't anything for us around here. My dad says the rich get richer, and the poor stay poor."

Well, that told me.

He observed the pair for a few seconds, their eyes locked on his. Neither had used bad language, given him backchat, or tried to run for it. Instead, they were standing, or rather sitting, their ground.

"Well, what *do* you want to do with your lives?"

His question met with two sets of shrugging shoulders and four eyes inspecting their respective owner's scuffed trainers.

"Nothing. You'll drop us in it with the police. They'll take us to court, and the judge will let us off and tell us not to do it again. It's always the same."

Ant's irritation surfaced.

"Is that so, young man? Then get off your backsides and do something about it. Or are you both more comfortable playing the victim, always choosing to blame others, and thinking of a dozen reasons why you can't do something to help yourselves?"

He waited and watched as the teenagers looked at their mobiles, deciding if they should bother to respond.

"Listen. I'm not interested in the police. I had my own issues with them when I was younger, so I'm hardly going to set them on you."

The teenagers looked up from their screens and frowned. Adult interest was not something they were used to.

"Let's try this again. What do you want to do with your lives?"

The girl answered first, albeit hesitantly.

"A mechanic."

I think you've just blown your mate away.
Emboldened, the boy joined in.
"Working with animals."
Now it was her turn to look surprised.
Ant smiled, careful not to appear patronising.
"Something tells me that's the first time either of you have talked to anyone about your ambitions."
Neither responded.
"Okay, give me your mobile numbers, help me put the lead back on the roof, and we'll say no more about it. I promise you; I'll have a word with one or two people to see if there's anyone that might have an opening. Do we have a deal?"
Your smile tells me we do.

* * *

FOR GOODNESS' sake Fitch, go on.

Ant stood back amused as his friend stared nervously at the half-open doors to the painted steel shipping container.

"I've been in once, remember. That was enough." Fitch began to shuffle backwards until he bumped into Ant and let out a shriek in terror.

Ant gently pushed his friend forward and shook his head.

"Don't be daft. He's dead. What do you think he's going to do? Sit up and ask you how much you charge for a full service? Anyway, since you dragged me away from watching the football, tell me again just how you ended up in the middle of nowhere with a dead bloke?"

Fitch turned his back on the container, after having one last peek at the lumpy, white shroud at the far end of the dark space.

"Well, I got a call to fix a diesel generator."

"From a bloke you'd never heard of, saying he'd pay a hundred and fifty pounds cash, which you'd find under an oil drum inside the generator room, right?"

You might well blush.

"I know it sounds daft, but I thought it was easy money for an hour's work."

Ant listened in disbelief as Fitch retold the events that had brought him to the back end of Brinton Fen on a sticky Thursday afternoon.

"Daft? That's putting it mildly. Anyway, how did you come to poke your nose in the container?"

Fitch turned and pointed to a shabby brick building twenty yards to their left.

"I turned up and followed the bloke's instructions. Sure enough, I found the generator—and my money. I got stuck in and soon found a couple of loose connections. That's all there was to it. I cleaned up the leads, tightened them, and switched her on."

Ant waited for more.

"And then what?"

"What do you mean? It started, of course. What did you expect?"

Ant pointed towards the container.

"And the corpse?"

He noticed Fitch shudder at the mention of the body.

"A bit of bad luck, really."

You're telling me.

"Bad luck? At least you're still breathing, unlike your friend covered in a white sheet, surrounded by two-dozen boxes of frozen peas in a big tin box with wonky wiring."

From Fitch's reaction, Ant guessed his friend was trying to think of anything but dead people.

"Assuming the job was done, I started to make my way back to the van when I saw a red light flashing on the side of the container and heard an alarm sounding."

Ant gestured towards the container.

"And curiosity got the better of you?"

Oops, touched his sensibilities there.

"It's not a case of curiosity. I'm a professional, I am. There was no alarm before I fixed the generator. There was one after I switched it on. I figured the freezer temperature monitor needed resetting, and I was right."

Ant scanned the side of the container for the control panel. Unable to see it, he turned to Fitch, who was wearing a wry smile.

"No, it's inside, which is how I came to find—"

"Simon the stiff."

Fitch frowned.

"If you say so."

Ant grinned, pleased at his own joke.

"Talking of whom, Fitch, we'd better have a look at the frozen one, then get the hell out of here. I wager the man who hired you won't be too pleased if he finds out we know what's in here."

Fitch once more began to step away from the corrugated steel doors.

"I've told you. I'm not going in there again. Seeing the anaemic soles of that bloke's feet last time was enough for me."

Gesturing for his friend to stand aside, Ant stepped into the container and gently pulled back a sheet covering the body.

"Good Lord. It's Geoff Singleton."

11

PARALLEL UNIVERSE

"Are you sure this is a good idea?"

Ant looked over his shoulder at Lyn as he rinsed his empty coffee cup under the hot tap.

"Listen, Fitch was the one that started this caper. If he hadn't been so keen to earn a bit of cash in hand, we wouldn't need to explain anything to 'Inspector Clouseau of Witless Yard.'"

Ant's parody of Riley speaking in a fake French accent was enough to make Lyn choke on her drink.

"Not bad for you, Anthony Stanton. Not bad at all," she said, wiping a dribble of coffee from her chin.

"And what has the corpse-finder general had to say on the matter?"

Ant could see Fitch still looked unsettled from his afternoon's work.

"Not funny, Ant."

Lyn sympathised by putting an arm around her friend.

"Never you mind the nasty aristocrat. I'm on your side. It must have been a nasty shock. But can I just ask if you managed to bring any of those peas back, only I'm a bit short."

Get in there, girl.

Having lulled Fitch into a false sense of security, Lyn's apparent afterthought did the trick. All three broke into a chorus of laughter, compounded by Ant spending the following few minutes prancing around Lyn's farmhouse kitchen doing a terrible impersonation of Peter Sellers as the famous French detective, while Lyn took on the mantle of Kato Fong, his faithful retainer, by leaping from various hiding places to demonstrate his martial arts skills on his employer.

"Where did you to learn that?" said Ant as he nursed a sore wrist from Lyn having twisted it during one of her more successful attacks.

Lyn smiled enigmatically.

"A girl can't be too careful these days, so I've been attending Cybil Dawson's self-defence classes for women. Two pounds seventy-five a session including ginger-nut biscuits and orange squash."

Ant huffed.

"Cybil Dawson? She's seventy-five if she's a day, and limps around the village leaning on a barley-twist walking stick,"

I knew it; Lyn has gone mad.

Lyn stepped slowly forward and smiled as she took hold of Ant's left hand. Confused, he smiled back, before wincing in pain as she applied one of Cybil's special restraint techniques for repelling unwanted advances.

The more Ant cried out, the more pressure Lyn applied, until he dropped to his knees and pleaded for mercy.

"Nothing to do with age or strength come to that," said Lyn as she towered above her adversary. "As a matter of fact,

Cybil took down a pickpocket in London last summer. He made the mistake of confusing infirmity with vulnerability."

"And..." said Fitch, who had been consoling himself scoffing a piece of Lyn's renowned lemon cheesecake.

"Three days in hospital with a broken arm and three months in prison for aggravated assault," replied Lyn without taking a breath.

"Who, the pickpocket, or Cybil?" replied Ant, confused and still smarting from a painful wrist.

"Funny," replied Lyn while giving Ant a sideways glance.

"I'm being seri—"

His protest was cut short by the sound of the doorbell.

"He's here," said Fitch.

Lyn broke off the conversation and headed for the front door.

"And don't say anything you know I will have a go at you later for." Ant watched Fitch frown, his confusion obvious. "Oh, don't look so daft. Just don't tell Riley anything he doesn't need to know, yes?"

Saints preserve us all.

The pair listened intently as Lyn went through the pleasantries of welcoming Riley and bidding him to follow her into the kitchen.

"Finding the same body twice. That's a record, even for you."

Ant's natural instinct was to challenge Riley's sarcastic comment, except he'd promised Lyn to be on his best behaviour.

The unlikely foursome sat around Lyn's rectangular dining table in a seating configuration that made it plain it was three against one.

"As I said, Detective Inspector, strictly speaking, it wasn't me who found Geoff Singleton's body, it was my friend here."

Riley's eyes turned toward Fitch, who wriggled on the hard seat as if he had ants in his pants.

"I don't know what else I can tell you?" said Fitch. "I went to fix a generator, saw a red light flashing and opened the container doors, and there it... I mean he, was."

Fitch shrugged his shoulders and looked anywhere except at the detective.

Riley scrutinised each of the friends in turn, lingering longest on Ant. After what seemed an age, the detective sat back in his chair.

"The police service thanks you for bringing this matter to its attention. I think that will be all for now."

Riley got to his feet.

Something not right here. What's he up to?

Ant attempted to draw Riley out.

"So what's next, Detective Inspector?"

Riley looked down at Ant.

"Next?"

You know what I mean, fool.

"It means we get the post-mortem done before some light-fingered villain nicks the body again. You don't get any prizes for finding him a third time. Unless, of course you'd like some jail time?"

Ant sensed an opportunity to wind his foe up.

"What, you mean like that bloke who Cybil Dawson took down with her barley-twist walking stick in London?"

Ant adopted a look of faux horror.

"London? Walking Stick? And who on earth is Cybil Dawson?" replied Riley in a tone tinged with exasperation.

"Don't mind my friend," said Lyn. "He's been on the

chocolate, which makes him stupid until the e-numbers wear off."

Ant noted Lyn's indifference as he attempted to stare the detective out, who, to his disappointment, soon tired of Ant's provocation.

"As a matter of fact, it's happening right now, and I'm confident it will prove Mr Singleton died from natural causes. I'm sure you are aware he had a serious health condition?"

Lyn opened her mouth as if to speak. Ant anticipated what was coming next and tapped her shin under the table.

Lyn jumped in surprise, drawing a bemused look from Riley.

"Were you about to say something, or is it your habit to make random sounds for no apparent reason?"

Lyn bit her lip to take her mind off the pain.

I'll pay for that.

"Good riddance to him, I say," said Fitch as Lyn closed the front door and made her way back into the kitchen.

"You two are nuts; you know that, don't you? One of these days Riley's going to get you."

Ant laughed.

"He's too stupid."

Lyn tossed an apple at Ant from a bowl of fruit on the worktop.

"Not so stupid that you were worried over what I was about to say to him."

Ant executed a nifty sidestep to his left allowing the Norfolk Royal to whizz past his shoulder and bounce off the bread bin onto the floor.

"If you mean hand him information on a plate, you're correct."

Lyn huffed.

"Anyway, who's for another coffee?"

"Good move, Ant," said Fitch as he handed over his empty mug.

Lyn giggled as she watched Ant trying to work out how the percolator worked. Round one went to the machine, causing Ant to leave the room in a huff on the pretext of retrieving something from his car.

Fitch took the opportunity to quiz Lyn.

"How are things between you two? I'm guessing all this shin kicking and apple throwing is displacement activity for, you know, getting it together?"

Fitch's perceptive comments took Lyn by surprise.

"What on earth do you mean?"

Fitch walked over to the percolator and prepared it for a fresh brew before switching the machine on.

"Come off it. I know I'm a bloke, but even I can see what's going on... or rather, what's *not* going on."

"Who's not doing what?" said Ant as he re-entered the room holding a small screwdriver.

Fitch brushed Ant's enquiry aside, advising his friend he had no need of the screwdriver.

"How did you do that?" asked Ant as he glimpsed the red "on" light of the percolator, forgetting about his earlier question.

"I pressed the button marked 'on.' It's not complicated, you know."

Ant peered at the machine as if it had conspired with the others to make him look stupid.

"Come and sit down," said Lyn, holding out her hand.

Ant surprised himself by gently taking Lyn's fingers while lowering himself onto a chair next to her.

"Here's what I think about the body snatcher. It seems to

me that there are only two possibilities, assuming we dismiss the notion Geoff died of natural causes."

"Go on," said Ant, keen to see if her assessment matched his own.

"Well, either Hannah arranged it to stop his corpse being cut up—"

"Or?" interrupted Ant.

"Or whoever murdered him stole the body to stop the post-mortem unearthing how they killed him."

"Exactly," added Lyn, her face beaming as she realised they agreed for once.

"And that person looks to be Jakub Baros, Lyn, yes?"

Fitch reached for the percolator and poured three coffees.

"Of course, the two could be linked," said Fitch.

Ant gestured for another sugar to be dropped into his coffee.

"That's what I've just said."

Ant wiped coffee splashes from his wrist as the sugar cube Fitch had released landed with a plop.

"No, you mentioned two people with different motives, Ant. How about if Hannah's apparent terror of her old flame is an act, and they're actually in it together?"

Ant smiled.

"Interesting. In that case it's worth me doing some digging around this Jakub fellow."

"And I'll have a chat with Hannah after school tomorrow to see if she gives anything away."

12

OLD MACDONALD

"Thank goodness that's it for another week. This term always feels the longest," said Lyn as she followed Hannah into her large rear garden. "You're nice and secluded here, that's for sure. Good to hide away from the world sometimes, isn't it?"

Lyn's line of conversation wasn't meant to offer any deep insight into the merits of privacy. Her intention was to get her to talk.

Wish I could read your thoughts.

Hannah looked pensive as they settled into a pair of matching faux bamboo chairs protected from the strong sunlight by a huge parasol.

"It's good of you to spend so much of your time with me." She spoke in a quiet voice, without making eye contact with Lyn, who rested a reassuring hand on Hannah's arm.

"Not at all. I can't begin to understand what you're going through, so I won't use the silly words most people splutter because they don't know what to say."

Hannah smiled and stole a look at Lyn from beneath her auburn fringe.

"You have a very important job, I think. Many responsibilities for all those little children."

Lyn returned the smile, pleased that Hannah was beginning to open up.

"Oh, I don't know. I have a good team of teachers and support staff. The place runs itself really. As for the children, well, they're fine. Unfortunately, I can't say the same for some of the parents."

Hannah wagged a playful finger.

"I think you are too modest."

Lyn tried not to blush.

"I'm not sure some of the parents share that view, but we all rub along together somehow."

Hannah began to frown then relaxed as she processed Lyn's line of self-deprecation.

"Ah, one of your strange English sayings, 'rub along.' Yes, I understand."

Lyn's approach was starting to pay dividends. Hannah's body language was more open now. Instinctively, Lyn mirrored it.

Time to push, I think.

"Has the detective been in touch recently?"

Hannah's smile slipped as the outside world started to once more intrude.

"No, but the, how you say, liaison officer, has. She has told me about Geoff. It is horrible, but I understand they have to find out how he died."

Lyn decided not to ask if Hannah knew the exact details of where her husband's body was found. She saw no need to add to her misery.

"You're right. Knowing what actually happened will help you eventually. We can deal with things we know about. It's uncertainty that is the hardest thing to bear, isn't it?"

Hannah nodded then stood up and headed for the kitchen door.

"I have some wonderful fruit cordial. A recipe my mother taught me back in Poland. I will fetch some."

Keep yourself busy, that's the ticket.

She returned a few minutes later with two glass tumblers filled to the brim with a colourful liquid.

"Hmm, that's superb, Hannah." Lyn licked her lips as she sampled the iced drink.

"We always made it on hot days. It was one of Geoff's favourites."

Lyn remained silent, instead, allowing the stillness of the afternoon to do its work.

"You think something bad happened to my husband, don't you?"

Better get this reply right.

"The truth is, Hannah, no one knows. But yes, it's a possibility, no matter what the police say."

Hannah nodded as she lowered her head into her hands.

Go on, give yourself permission to think the unthinkable.

"So it's important we go on until we get to the truth, no matter where it takes us. That way we're doing it for Geoff. Isn't that right, Hannah?"

A few seconds of inactivity was broken by a nod of the head. It was enough for Lyn to know Hannah understood.

"Have you heard anything from Jakub?"

Lyn waited for Hannah to react. It wasn't long coming. As she raised her head, she stiffened and stared into the middle distance.

"Do you think he did this terrible thing? He shouted at Geoff very much when we came away."

Lyn searched for the right words to move the conversation forward, trying to sound positive.

"Ant is looking for him right now, but if you can be brave enough to tell me a bit more about the man, it might just make the difference when Ant, or the police, catch up with him."

Hannah remained silent. Lyn tried a different tack.

"Tell me about when you were both young. When you first met. He was your first real boyfriend, wasn't he?"

Hannah eventually warmed to Lyn's enquiry. Her words stirred long-lost memories of happier times.

"Annabelle told you, didn't she?" said Hannah. "It's okay, yes, they were good times. It was so exciting. You know, the first time a boy kisses you."

Lyn smiled; she had her own memories.

I should remind Ant of stolen kisses on his father's wherry.

"He was very handsome and funny. He brought me flowers from the meadow each Sunday during the summer. I think many of the girls in the village were jealous, but I didn't care. I was in love. But now..."

Lyn moved quickly to stop Hannah retreating back into herself.

"Just remember you are safe, and Ant will find Jakub. He won't get anywhere near you, I promise."

Hannah offered an unconvincing smile.

Think I've pushed hard enough for today.

Lyn allowed the silence to continue for a few seconds before getting up from her chair and offering Hannah a comforting touch.

"Well, looks to me like it's time to leave you in peace to enjoy the last of the sun with your wonderful cordial. Don't forget, Hannah, if you need anything, anything at all, or something happens that you don't like the look of, call me. I can be around in five minutes. Okay?"

Hannah nodded without making eye contact as Lyn walked towards the garden gate and out into the driveway.

* * *

"How are you doing, Lil? Can I have one of your lovely quarter pounders please with all the trimmings?"

Lil greeted Ant like the old friend he was.

"A good job I don't rely on you for my profits. Haven't seen you in ages. Where have you been hiding?"

Ant smiled and deflected the question as he stood at the village institution that was Lil's greasy spoon mobile chuck wagon. The battered old van had stood in its lay-by location for more years than he could remember. Nevertheless, she still served the best roadside food for miles around.

"Beautiful day," said Ant as he sniffed the delicious aroma of beef being fried on a small hotplate and looked out across a lush landscape towards the North Sea.

"I bet the wind gets at you during the winter?" said Ant as he continued to evade talking about himself.

Lil laughed.

"Don't remind me. My bones are getting too old for those easterlies. Go right through you, don't they?"

Lil passed Ant his steaming snack, piled high with cheese and fried onions.

"I know what you mean." Ant bit into the burger so enthusiastically that clear juices began to run down the sides of his mouth.

"Good?"

"Never better." Ant grinned as he took another great bite from his brunch.

If there was one thing that stopped Ant talking, it was good food. In the case of Lil's cuisine, it meant he failed to utter a word for the five minutes it took him to polish the burger off. In that time, he'd watched Lil scraping the hotplate clean with a stainless-steel spatula, and butter two-dozen buns in preparation for the lunchtime rush.

Wiping his face with a paper towel and brushing a patchwork of breadcrumbs from the front of his jacket, his attention turned to the subject of Jakub Baros.

"I don't suppose you've come across any strangers around the place over the last week or so?"

Lil gave a broad smile.

"What, you mean more so than my regulars?"

Ant nodded and returned her grin.

"I get your point. I just—"

"Although," Lil interrupted, "there was that chap who could have done with a good wash."

I wonder.

"I don't suppose he had a scar on one cheek, did he?"

Lil's face lit up.

"How did you know that? As a matter of fact, he did. When he ordered... well, I say ordered, he just pointed at the menu and shoved a twenty-pound note at me. Never seen anyone eat a double beef burger with bacon so fast in all my life. The man disappeared before I could give him his change." Lil pointed to a shelf behind her. "It's still waiting for him."

The two old friends shared a joke about the eating habits of men, before Ant pressed Lil for more detail.

"Did you notice a car or where he seemed to head for?"

Ant's question was asked more in hope than expectation.

Lil smiled again.

"As a matter of fact, I did. It was a clapped-out Skoda campervan with foreign number plates. You should have seen the muck its exhaust chucked out, something awful it was."

"You're sure it was a Skoda and not a Range Rover?"

Lil frowned.

"I think I know the difference between the two, young Mr Anthony. Anyway, he's parked up at the old piggery on Lane End Farm. It's been abandoned for years, so I suppose the lad will get a bit of quiet. I only know because I happened to follow it for a bit on my way home yesterday."

Ant leant over the high counter of the chuck wagon and placed a kiss on Lil's cheek.

"You're a corker, Lil. I need to speak to that lad, so I'll be saying cheerio and strike while the iron's hot."

"In that case you won't mind giving him his change for me, will you?" replied Lil, reaching over to the shelf to retrieve the cash.

With that he was gone, with Lil's voice telling him "not to leave it so long next time" still ringing in his ears. Loose shingle spat from the wheels of Ant's car as he left the lay-by for the main road and took a sharp right onto a narrow farm trackway. Although plain to see the track wasn't used often, he noticed newly fallen twigs and leaves scattered on the surface of the roadway.

Something big has been down here recently to cause this damage.

A few minutes later, the overgrown vegetation gave way to a scene of dereliction. As he brought the Morgan to a halt and climbed out of the car, he realised Lil had been right to say the farm had been left unoccupied for years. As he scrambled over collapsed walls, piles of old timber, and rusted metal cladding, he scanned the area for signs of life.

Out of nowhere, a foreign-sounding voice carried across the scene of devastation.

"What you want?"
Seconds seeming like hours followed in silence.
Then the voice again. This time much, much closer.
"What you want in this place?"
Ant felt clammy breathing on the nape of his neck.

He was also aware of a sharp object resting menacingly between his shoulder blades.

13

NUMBERS

"I don't suppose your name is Jakub Baros, by any chance?"

Ant's calming tone had an immediate effect as he felt the pressure from the object pressing into his back ease off.

Turning to face the stranger, Ant knew he'd found his man.

"You police?"

Ant studied the gruff-looking man, aged around thirty, with a mop of black, curly hair and a scar on his cheek.

Lil was right about him needing a bath.

"Perhaps you would like to put your knife down, now?" Ant concentrated on looking and sounding relaxed. This was no time for sudden movements.

"How you know my name?" His eyes scanned the derelict farmyard nervously.

Rather than answer Jakub's question, Ant pointed to the old campervan, which was parked behind a half-demolished cowshed so that just the front of the rusting vehicle was visible.

"Do you have insurance for that?"

Convinced now that Ant was a policeman, Jakub dropped the knife.

"It is mine, yes. I have proof—papers. It is legal."

Ant stood aside as Jakub hurried towards the campervan and retrieved a black, imitation leather folder from the glove compartment.

"See. I have insurance." He held out a piece of paper, which Ant scrutinised closely.

A shame I can't read Polish.

"This seems to be in order." Ant's tone was polite, but officious as he returned the document to Jakub, who nervously slipped it back into the plastic folder.

He's shaking.

"You go now? I have many things to do."

Ant's body language and tone made it clear that it was he to decide when it was time to leave.

"Norfolk is a long way from, er, where did you say you came from?"

Jakub's eyes narrowed. He glanced at the knife lying amongst a pile of broken roof tiles and twisted metal. Ant followed the man's glance.

"I don't think we'll be needing this today, do you?" He bent down and retrieved the blade, admiring the quality of its manufacture.

Jakub didn't move.

"A small fishing village near Lublin."

Looks almost relieved I've taken control of the knife.

Ant suspected the man's temper had got him in trouble before. At least this time the temptation had been removed. He gestured for Jakub to follow him across the yard. As Jakub turned to see where he was pointing, Ant took the opportunity to throw the knife in the opposite direction.

"We know quite a lot about you. Do you know a woman called Hannah Singleton?"

Jakub bristled at the mention of her name.

Is he going to run for it or stay to find out what I really know?

"Do join me," Ant said, inviting Jakub to sit with him on a set of stone steps leading to the upper floor of what was once a sizeable grain store. His quiet voice did the trick.

Looks like he isn't going anywhere.

Jakub sat down, his body odour making Ant wonder if he been a little too accommodating in his offer.

"Tell me about Hannah. She was your girlfriend, yes?"

Jakub shrugged his shoulders.

"You know this already. Why do you ask?"

Ant pressed his point.

"Because, Jakub, her husband was murdered a few days ago. Then again you already know that, don't you?"

Jakub attempted to get up. Ant placed a firm hand on the man's arm to dissuade him.

"Hannah called me saying she was in trouble and for me to come. She needed my help. So I come." Jakub shrugged his shoulders again as he submitted to Ant's firm restraint. "And now, nothing. I call. She does not answer. I go to house. She is not there. What am I to do?"

What on earth is going on?

"You're telling me you came all the way from Poland because of a telephone call, and now the woman who rang you won't see or speak to you? Sorry, that doesn't make sense."

Ant felt Jakub tensing.

He's either going to hit me or make a run for it.

"I have told you; Hannah is in trouble. You say you know

everything about me. So you know how special that lady is to me, okay?"

One of them is a very good liar, but which one?

Jakub picked up a small shard of rusty metal and began twisting the material. Ant quickly understood what the man's actions might lead to.

Better keep him talking.

"Listen, I'm here to help you. We know you were jealous when Geoff took Hannah away. Who wouldn't be? Most men have had those feelings. But Geoffrey Singleton is dead, and you have suddenly appeared out of nowhere. I don't think you had anything to do with his murder, but you must help me. Do you understand?"

Oops, shouldn't have mentioned 'murder.'

Ant made no attempt to stop Jakub as the man sprang from the steps and put ten feet between them. He knew the next few seconds would end in one of three ways:

Jakub would launch an attack.

He would run for it.

He'd see sense and stay put.

That was a close-run thing, mused Ant as Jakub paused, turned to look at the campervan, then back at Ant and put his clenched fists in the pockets of his work-worn, black leather jacket.

"Hannah called me on Tuesday. She was crying. It was hard to understand her. She said they had been arguing for weeks and were breaking up, but then Geoff died." He allowed his shoulders to rest forward and stared at the debris beneath his feet.

Good man. Stay where you are.

"She said she was being blamed for his death, and the police were going to do something to his body, then take her away."

Ant remained seated. He spoke in a calm, measured tone.

"Didn't that seem strange to you?"

Jakub frowned.

"But it was Hannah. If she said something is so, then it is so."

Love is a terrible thing sometimes.

"She said I should hide his body until she could prove her innocence."

Ant got to his feet and closed the distance between them.

"You mean Hannah told you where his body was, how to get Geoff out of the mortuary, and where to hide him?"

Is she taking us for mugs?

"You said she called you? Then you will have her number saved on your mobile?"

Jakub rummaged through the pocket of his coat. From the time it took him to retrieve the phone, Ant assumed the lining had perished.

"It is always the same; she never answers," replied Jakub as he handed an ancient mobile over.

Ant looked at the call log. Baros seemed to be telling the truth. He also noted a long list of unanswered calls the other way.

He's certainly been persistent.

"And you still don't think it's a bit funny?" said Ant as he tried the number twice without success.

Jakub screwed up his face. Ant realised his error.

"Sorry, I didn't mean it like a joke. What I meant was it's a bit strange. Do you understand?"

Jakub's facial features relaxed.

"But I love her. What she asks for, I do."

Is love that blind, or is he having me over?

"She still loves me. I know this. She told me to be careful because the police were watching. You are here. She tells me the truth."

Time to check a few things out.

"You will stay here until I send for you Jakub. Do you understand?" Ant slipped Jakub's mobile into his pocket. He was relieved the stranger made no attempt to stop him.

"Understand?" repeated Ant.

Jakub nodded.

Right, let's get to the bottom of this.

14

NO HIDING PLACE

Saturday morning broke with a fine drizzle, which left the grasslands of Stanton Hall glistening against a shy sun peeping out from a huge bank of dark grey clouds.

"You're out and about early," said Ant as he watched Lyn cover the last few yards from the lawn in front of the Hall and across the gravel driveway to the double front doors.

She handed Ant a round tin as she scrubbed her wellington boots on the coconut doormat before stepping into the majestic hallway.

"Thought it would be good exercise since I sit at a desk for most of the week. And by the way, don't pinch any of that chocolate cake before your mum and dad have had some. Your butler told me what you did last week."

Ant adopted his best schoolboy "it wasn't me" look as he gently shook the tin to check how big the cake might be.

"To be fair, the cook thought the tin was empty and put it in the pantry."

Lyn seized her opportunity.

"Since when does a fully qualified cook store empty tins in the larder?"

Ant tried to rebuff Lyn's logic.

"I was hungry."

Lyn shook her head.

"What, to scoff enough Victoria sponge to start a cake stall?"

The banter continued as the two friends passed into the morning room of the Tudor building.

Time to change the subject, I think.

"Anyway, enough about cake, how did you get on with Hannah yesterday?"

Lyn took the bait as the pair settled themselves into a matching pair of Chippendale chairs.

"She told me all about this Jakub Baros chap. It seems he has a temper and mixed with some dodgy types when he was younger. Hannah said he'd been in trouble for violence, and she was frightened of him."

"Interesting," replied Ant as he rubbed his chin in the style of Sherlock Holmes.

Lyn's look of irritation told Ant he needed to expand.

"Well, Hannah may not be as innocent as she makes out. In fact, there's a good chance she's one of the best actors either of us has come across."

Lyn shook her head.

"If you're thinking she had anything to do with her husband's death, you're on the wrong track. I've spent a lot of time with her over the last few days, and I can tell you her grief is genuine."

Ant offered Lyn a mint from a small silver dish on the veneered mahogany coffee table, which separated their chairs.

"I accept her tears may be genuine. The question is, for whom is she weeping. Geoff or herself?"

Lyn took the mint and popped it into her already open mouth.

"You clearly know something I don't, so out with it, clever clogs."

Ant spent the next few minutes filling Lyn in about his run-in with Jakub the previous day.

"You see, either he's a fantastic actor, or she's been manipulating him. Believe me, two minutes in his company is enough to convince anyone he's not the sharpest chisel in the toolbox."

Lyn leant forward in her chair to pick up a second mint from the small silver dish.

"So we have a jealous ex-boyfriend, with known violent tendencies, showing up just when the body of his love's rival gets himself bumped off. Have I missed anything?"

Got it in one.

"Congratulations, Lyn. You've won our Sleuth of the Month competition, and first prize is as many mints as you can eat in five minutes."

"The only problem is," said Lyn, ignoring his attempt at humour and beginning to suck on the sugar treat, "Who's setting whom up, because if we're right, one of them could be next for the chop?"

Ant flicked a mint into his mouth and jumped to his feet.

"Time to revisit the crime scene. Come on, pull your wellies on. We're off to the boathouse."

* * *

"WILL you stop fiddling about with your nose," said Lyn as the pair hopped onto Geoff Singleton's boat and made their way into the cabin of the luxury cruiser.

Ant huffed as he gave his left nostril a final scratch

before settling himself down on a leather-covered bench seat next to the galley.

Lyn remained standing and scanned the immaculately fitted-out interior.

"What are we looking for?"

"I don't know until we find it, Lyn. I'm certain there's something here that will tell us what really happened. And if we're lucky, why he was killed."

There has to be something in here that will tell us what happened.

"It's not as if there's anywhere to hide anything, that's for sure," said Lyn as she opened various cupboards and inspected their interior.

Yes, got it!

Ant let out a triumphant cry and clapped his hands.

Lyn jumped at the sudden noise.

"What on earth's the matter with you. Have you gone mad?"

Ant beamed at her.

"You said it."

"Said what, Ant?"

"A hiding place."

He could see Lyn was none the wiser.

"Rufus, remember? He said Geoff had been very particular about wanting concealed storage in his new boat."

"And?"

"Well, if he wanted that kind of stuff in the new boat, it makes sense he's got one or two hidey-holes in this one. Don't you see?"

Lyn's changing body language told Ant his theory had clicked.

"So maybe he hid something in the cabin that his murderer wanted?"

Ant's smile broadened.

"Absolutely. All we have to do now is find it."

"If it's still here, Ant—whatever 'it' is."

Ten minutes passed. The banging of doors and knocking on timber panels became louder as their frustration grew.

"This is a waste of time," said Lyn as she knocked her knee on the corner of the dining table for the umpteenth time. "I've had enough; let's see if Jakub has anything else to say for himself. Perhaps he's been here?"

Just one more thing to try.

"Wait a minute." Ant pushed a narrow strip of wood under a low shelf, recessed to the point it was hidden from view. Straining to get a firm hold of the narrow facia, Ant first pressed then pulled the strip of teak. Nothing moved. In a final effort to prove his theory, Ant pushed the strip of wood upwards toward the shelf it was supposed to be supporting. Ant was rewarded by a satisfying "click."

"Yes."

"Have you found something, Ant?"

Now that the wood strip was free, he gently pulled it toward him.

"You can say that again."

Ant pulled the panel back to reveal a concealed compartment around three inches high and twelve inches deep.

"What's that?" asked Lyn as Ant removed a spiral-bound document of around fifty pages and glanced through the index page before quickly turning several pages, until he came across a table of figures.

"The reason Geoff Singleton was murdered, I suspect." He spoke slowly as he digested the mass of information.

Lyn strained to see what Ant was so engrossed in.

"Let me have a look."

Ant handed it over allowing Lyn to also scrutinise the figures. She shook her head, trying to make sense of the numbers.

"It's a new type of marine electric propulsion system, according to the title," said Lyn, "but it's not making any sense to me."

Ant moved closer so that they could both see the table of figures.

"Nor me. But Geoff certainly understood. See, look at his notes here, and here." Ant pointed to the pencil markings in the page margin.

"I think he discovered that whoever undertook the research into the new battery technology knew it didn't work then tried to massage the research results to hide the evidence."

It's as if his notes were meant for us.

"Perhaps he was about to go public."

Ant nodded at Lyn.

"Remember Rufus saying how Geoff always insisted on an ethical approach to business and his investment fund, Ant? What if these results compromised his reputation in some way?"

Ant's face lit up. Lyn's assessment sparked an idea.

"Who wrote the report?"

Ant gestured for Lyn to close the document and reveal the author's name on the front cover.

"Some outfit called EMGEN, Ant. And you know what? I've come across that name before."

15

NOSE TROUBLE

The centre of Stanton Parva was unusually quiet for a Saturday afternoon as Ant and Lyn sat on an old bench by the village pond. On the far side of the water, the Wherry Arms pub welcomed the occasional visitor, while the newsagent next door had to content itself with a delivery of soft drinks.

"I was reading the village magazine the other week. It seems we're not supposed to feed the ducks with bread," said Ant as he tossed the last of his wholemeal sandwich to a gaggle of wildfowl. The prospect of a free meal resulted in a terrific din as the birds scurried towards him to nab the best position.

"I read that too," replied Lyn as she watched the ducks being cheated of their treat by half a dozen seagulls, swooping down from the roof of a nearby thatched cottage. "I hate those things. If Phyllis Abbott and Betty didn't insist on feeding the things each day, they'd disappear back to the coast in a jiffy."

Ant did his best to wave the seagulls away. They were

having none of it. In protest, one left a chalky deposit on the shoulder of his coat.

"You're not the only one, I'd shoot the damn things if there wasn't a law against it. All I can say is, whichever civil servant in London came up with the ban has never had their clothes bleached by guano."

Ant glanced at Lyn just as what looked like a sympathetic smile dissolved into laugher.

"Oh, very funny," said Ant as he dabbed the glutinous white liquid from his coat.

"Don't be such a baby. It's a waxed jacket, isn't it? It'll wipe off easily enough."

Ant muttered a string of invective better suited to the army.

"Language, Ant."

He muttered some more as he focussed on the glint in Lyn's eye.

"That's not the point," he moaned as he gathered up the last of the guano with a paper tissue.

Ant watched as Lyn's smile turned to disdain.

"What?'

"What indeed, Ant. The tissue?"

Ant followed the tip of her index finger which was pointing at the scrunched-up mass in his right hand. He thought better of dropping the soggy tissue between the wooden slats of the bench. Instead, he trudged to a nearby waste bin before resuming his seat and glowering at the seagulls as they waited for the next titbit with a menacing look in their eyes.

"So," said Lyn as she encouraged a plain-coloured hen and its ducklings to move closer, while a more brightly coloured drake observed from a distance, "have you discovered anything else from the EMGEN report we found this morning?"

Ant stretched out his legs as if relaxing. In truth it was a tactic to discourage the wildfowl from getting any closer to him. Lyn's withering look soon made him change his mind.

"As a matter of fact, I think I have. It was something Dad said over lunch. He still dabbles in the stock market and has been tracking the performance of Geoff Singleton's investment fund; seems it specialised in investment for new technologies in the marine industry, which my father is still crazy about."

"Has he invested in Geoff?"

Ant shook his head.

"Now that would be a coincidence too far. No, it's just a hobby of his. Anyway, it turns out the report we found yesterday is the third in a series of updates produced for investors. Dad reckons that each time an update is released, which is, apparently, always more positive than the previous iteration, more people invest in his fund."

Lyn bent down to feed the hen. Ant wanted to shift the animal aside but decided discretion was the better part of valour.

"Let me guess, Ant. Once you've hyped the results once, you have to keep doing it. A small fib becomes a big lie, and so on."

Ant nodded.

"My guess is that once Geoff cottoned on to what was happening, it put him in a heck of a dilemma. Go public to save his reputation, or stay quiet and try to fix the problem —and keep his fortune."

Lyn shrugged her shoulders.

"Risky whichever way he jumped. Could the stress have brought on that heart attack?"

Ant raised an eyebrow.

"It's possible. But I guess if he was going to tell anyone he was in trouble, it would have been Hannah."

Lyn watched as the wildfowl deserted them for a new snack offered by a couple and their young child on the other side of the pond.

"I suppose she had a lot to lose as well. You know, brought up in poverty but enjoying all the trappings of wealth since meeting Geoff. Posh cars, fancy clothes, and the rest of it. I guess it would have been easy enough for her to bamboozle Jakub into bumping Geoff off before her world crashed?"

Ant rummaged in his jacket pocket as he digested Lyn's theory.

"Don't expect me to understand the workings of a woman's mind. I suppose the same might have applied to Geoff last Saturday. Perhaps he told her they were facing ruin. She hit the roof, so Geoff kept out of her way by re-varnishing his boat?"

Ant produced a tatty paper bag half full of manky-looking boiled sweets.

Lyn flinched as she peered into the discoloured bag.

"Just how long have you had those things in your pocket?"

Ant failed to understand the fuss she was making.

"Pear drops don't have a 'use-by' date. The trick is to keep them dry and away from daylight. Anyway, do you want one or not?"

Some people are really hard to please.

He watched as Lyn retrieved the cleanest-looking sweet she could find then spent several seconds picking it clean of fluff and bits of paper tissue.

Ant didn't bother to check the condition of his selection.

He sniffed the essence of the sweet by holding it close to his nostrils before popping the treat between his lips and sucking hard. His nostrils started to itch.

"For goodness' sake. What is it with you and those silly sweets? First you have a finger up your nose standing over Geoff at the boathouse, then you almost crash your precious Morgan scratching your snout."

Ignoring Lyn's protests, Ant wallowed in the fleeting pleasure of easing his itch, acutely aware of the pain which would follow.

Something clicked. It was if a light bulb had gone off in his head.

"What did you say?"

She gave him a puzzled look.

"Not to talk with your mouth full."

Ant shook his head, took the sweet from his mouth, and placed the sticky lozenge into his jacket pocket.

Lyn gave him a look that meant he was for the naughty chair had he been one of her pupils.

"No, no. You said *body* and *crash*."

Judging by the funny "ugh" sound Lyn was making, he knew she was still focussing on his eating habits.

"I think, Ant, that there were some other words in between those two that made my sentence grammatically correct, which is more than I can say for your conversational skills these days."

Ant's face lit up at his epiphany.

"And there we have it, Lyn."

"Have what?"

"How they did it and then skedaddled. Very clever. That is if my schoolboy chemistry is any good."

Lyn's bafflement continued as Ant sprang to his feet.

"I'm off to the boathouse. There's a couple of things I

need you to check while I have another shufti around. Give me a ring in about an hour, Lyn."

* * *

ANT STOOD in the eerie silence of the boathouse, with only the gentle wash of water audible as an occasional pleasure boat passed in front of the old wooden building. He knew exactly what he was looking for. Making his way into the cabin of Geoff's boat, he pulled open one of two exquisitely veneered cupboard doors beneath the stainless-steel sink.

Knew I'd seen it.

Ant retrieved a small paint brush. Opening the second door, his face lit up with a quiet sense of satisfaction as a bright steel tin, with its contents written on a lozenge-shaped, green paper label came into view:

Water-based Yacht Varnish
Wash brushes out in warm, clean water

He even used environmentally friendly varnish.

Ant imagined Geoff Singleton purposely making the decision to use the slower-drying liquid rather than a solvent-based alternative.

Picking up a dish cloth from the worktop, he lifted the tin from the cupboard and placed it onto the draining board.

Better keep my fingerprints off this.

Carefully, he levered the lid off the tin with a blunt knife and immediately felt his nostrils go into spasm.

An overpowering smell of pear drops filled the tiny cabin. It was too much. Ant quickly replaced the lid and ran for the open doors of the boathouse.

No water-based varnish gives off a vapour like that.

He gulped fresh oxygen like a blue whale scooping up krill. Just as his breathing began to settle, his mobile rang. He recognised the number as Lyn's.

"I've remembered where I saw the name EMGEN the other day. It was at Hannah's. I tried to get to her, but one of the neighbours said she'd seen her leave with Annabelle. Seems they drove away like a bat out of hell."

Ant wasted no time in responding.

"I'm certain now how Geoff was murdered. She's been very clever. Listen, stay there, and I'll pick you up on my way."

The line fell silent for a few seconds.

"To where?"

"See you in ten minutes. And ring Fitch for me, will you?" added Ant before briefing her on what to say to him. "And don't take no for an answer. Tell him there's two pints of Thatcher's Itch pale ale on me every night for a week, *if* he comes up trumps."

16
FLIGHT OF FANCY

Ant's Morgan roared down the A11 out of Norwich towards Cambridge taking little account of the speed limit.

"For goodness' sake, man, is she worth killing us both?"

Ant wasn't listening. His eyes focussed on a familiar shape in the distance as he pushed the sports car close to its limit. He couldn't make out the colour, but he knew it was a Range Rover 4 x 4.

"We'd better get Riley on the phone," said Ant, pointing to the mobile sitting in the centre console. Lyn did as he asked, and seconds later, a ringtone sounded through the car's speaker system.

Riley didn't bother with the usual pleasantries.

"And why exactly have you decided to interrupt my Saturday evening?"

Silence.

"Are you there? What is it you want?" The detective spoke in a loud, slow voice, articulating each syllable like a British holidaymaker in a foreign country.

Ant looked across to Lyn, who was glaring back at him.

"Enough, Ant."

He smiled.

"Good evening, Detective Inspector. How are you today?"

Ant could hear Riley trying to formulate a coherent response and assumed the detective's bad temper prevented him from doing so. Eventually he got the words out.

"I assume there is a point to your call?"

Ant dropped a gear as he engaged the car's right indicator, pressed the accelerator, and propelled the Morgan past a lorry with a full load of sugar beets.

"As a matter of fact, there is," replied Ant as he settled the Morgan back into the nearside lane.

Ant briefed him on developments, assisted by Lyn, who leant towards the car's microphone more than once to add details her co-sleuth had omitted.

"I didn't know you were so fond of me," said Ant as Lyn pressed into his side to make herself heard."

"Be assured that is most definitely not the case, Lord Stanton."

The two amateur detectives fell into a fit of laughter leaving Riley hanging on the phone until Ant had recovered sufficiently to respond.

"I'm hurt, Detective Inspector. Have you no feelings for me at all?"

Riley now knew he was having the rise taken out of him. Instead of trying to match Ant, he got down to the business at hand.

"So why haven't you said anything before now? I've warned you both before about withholding information from the police."

He's like a broken record.

"Because, Detective, until one hour ago, there was nothing to tell you other than a bunch of ideas Lyn and I had. Are you seriously telling me you'd have listened?" Ant's tone hardened. Gone was his "hail fellow, well met" persona. Now he spoke with the gravitas of a battle-hardened army intelligence officer. "One request, Detective Inspector Riley. Keep your traffic officers in their cages. I have no time to waste being pulled over and booked for speeding."

Ant didn't need to ask twice.

"You don't need to worry about that. Are you sure she's heading for the old airstrip at Fendham?"

Some common sense at last.

"No, but that's the direction she's driving in. I can't think where else she'd be going."

The mobile fell silent again, then Ant's car speaker rang out with the sound of a door being banged shut.

"I'm on my way now and about ten minutes behind you."

So he can make a decision when it suits him.

Twenty miles and fifteen minutes had elapsed since his call to Riley as Ant thundered along the A11. He could now see the 4 x 4's distinctive colour scheme, but not its occupants.

"Better ease back, Ant. We don't want her to see us."

Ant nodded and brought the Morgan back within the speed limit.

"Look out!" squealed Lyn as a roe deer jumped onto the carriageway from the thick field.

"Hellfire," shouted Ant as he caught a glimpse of the animal as it stopped and turned. Not knowing whether he had hit the beast or not, Ant struggled with the steering wheel to keep the vehicle upright and on the road.

Shouldn't have tried to avoid the stupid thing.

In a second it was over. Looking in his rear-view mirror, Ant could see the still outline of the deer as it looked aimlessly at the car from the safety of the grass verge.

"Damn those things. That was close." Adrenaline still surged through his body.

Lyn instinctively touched Ant's left arm and pressed gently to let him know it was okay.

"There's a lay-by up ahead. I'd better pull in and check for damage—and get my breath back."

Ant slowed, indicated, and brought the Morgan to a stop.

"It's that time of day, Ant. I hate driving early in the morning or sunset. It's like a scene from *Watership Down* around here sometimes with so many animals out and about."

Ant failed to hear Lyn's assessment of Norfolk wildlife. Instead, he gave the car one last check before clambering back into the Morgan.

"Lucky it turned just in time. Even though those things don't have any weight on them, they can still cause a right mess."

Lyn shook her head.

"Wouldn't have been particularly therapeutic for Bambi either, eh?"

Ant was already back on the hunt for the 4 x 4, dismissing Lyn's observation with a grunt.

"We're losing the light, and they've disappeared, damn it," said Ant as the Morgan shot back onto the carriageway and sped towards Cambridge. "This is hopeless. Listen, give Riley a ring and see if he can give us directions."

Lyn grabbed Ant's mobile and tapped in the detective's number, looked across to Ant, and waited for Riley to respond.

"Blast it, the signal's dropped out."

Ant's attention was suddenly elsewhere. He let out a sudden whoop of excitement, making Lyn jump.

"Doesn't matter, there she blows." He pointed towards a clump of trees to their right about a mile ahead.

"What?"

"Laser light. That green thing. Can't you see it?"

Now that she knew what she was looking for, it stood out like a sore thumb.

"Good heavens. Riley said some kids had been using a laser light to distract local aircraft, except—"

"Except," interrupted Ant, "we're not talking about kids distracting the pilot, are we? If I'm right, whoever is holding that light is doing the exact opposite."

Lyn nodded.

"So she's guiding an aircraft onto the old landing strip. Tricky to land on something that was last used in 1945?"

Ant smiled as he took a right turn across the carriageway and propelled the Morgan up a dusty trackway. Ahead, lay a small gap in a thick clump of trees.

"I guess if you're desperate enough, you'll try anything." Ant turned the Morgan's engine and headlights off and allowed the car to coast to a stop.

"Come on, Lyn. Quietly does it. Stay within the treeline with me, so we can get as close as possible without spooking them. We need that plane to land."

Ant put his military training to good use as he navigated through the close columns of pine trees that held sentinel between friend and foe.

"I can see them," whispered Lyn. "Look, over there."

Slowly, slowly does it.

Barely twenty feet now stood between them and two women, their backs to Ant and Lyn, with one holding a laser pen pointing to the star-filled night sky.

One more push.

Ant signalled for Lyn to stay close as they crept forward and closed the final few yards.

"Good evening, ladies."

Hannah and Annabelle visibly jumped and look stunned as they turned from the rear corner of the Range Rover to face the intruders.

Got you.

"You took some catching," said Lyn.

Hannah attempted to distract Lyn, while Annabelle pointed a pen-like laser back into the darkening sky.

Ant ignored the woman's actions as he inspected the front of the 4 x 4. He found what he expected. The corner of the vehicle showed signs of damage with paint residue etched into its surface.

Hannah looked at Annabelle, who continued to scour the sky for signs of an aircraft. Her face lit up as she caught a first glimpse of a moving light in the heavens. Ant noted Annabelle was pointing the laser slightly below its source.

Don't want to blind the pilot, do we?

Seconds later, a four-seater plane touched down on a short strip of concrete that had remained intact from its wartime use. The plane's propeller was still running with the engine over-revving.

Not the first time he's done a quick turnaround.

He turned to Hannah, who wore a look of desperation.

"It's my only chance. The police blame me for stealing Geoff's body. They think I murdered my husband. Annabelle has arranged all this for me. Please, let us go."

Before either Ant or Lyn could respond, the two women ran towards the aircraft's open passenger door and started to clamber aboard.

As Ant chased after them, the sound of a police car siren

outdid the roar of the plane's engines as it turned and started to taxi. Its progress was halted as Riley's car pulled up a short distance in front of the plane, effectively blocking any escape.

Detective Inspector Riley sprang from his police Jaguar.

"So you were right," he said to Ant as the policeman pulled open the passenger door, shouted at the pilot to cut the engine, and peered inside at the two passengers.

"Hannah Singleton, I arrest you for the murder of—"

Ant interrupted Riley as Hannah looked forlornly at the floor.

"It wasn't Hannah, Detective Inspector. Annabelle Emms murdered Geoff Singleton." Ant's voice lacked any sign of emotion as he glared at Annabelle.

Riley frowned.

"You said—"

"I," interrupted Ant, "said *she* was responsible, and that I could prove it. I didn't say *which* of them murdered Mr Singleton."

Hannah protested as Riley ordered both women to leave the plane.

"No, no. You have it wrong. Annabelle is helping me to escape. She did not kill my husband. Why would she?"

Annabelle's shocked look reinforced Hannah's plea.

Ant allowed stillness to descend. For a few seconds, the only sound came from leaves rustling in the light breeze of a cool evening.

"We were all together in the pub garden the day Geoff died. How could I have anything to do with the death of my dearest friend?"

Who's the cool one, then?

Ant smiled.

"Geoffrey had a heart problem; everyone knew that," Annabelle continued. "Hannah knows what happened. His heart gave out, just like his uncle. Why do you make these things worse for her? You are a cruel man."

Ant noticed Riley giving him a stern look and guessed he had no intention of being made to look a fool again.

"Correct on both counts."

Annabelle started to smile.

"But," Ant continued, "there are many ways to make a heart stop. Sometimes the body does this itself. Other times something is done to make it stop. And that's what you did, wasn't it, Annabelle?"

Ant looked deep into her eyes to determine if his hypothesis held up. Hannah shook her head.

"No, no... you are wrong, mad."

Lyn held out a hand to Hannah.

"I've told you. I was at the BBQ. You saw me. Jakub must have killed Geoff. I told you how jealous he was and that I'd seen him in the village."

"Ah, yes. Well, I spoke to that gentleman. He maintains Hannah rang him to say she needed his help."

Hannah pulled away from Lyn.

"I did not speak to him. Why would I do this?"

Riley's neck swivelled from side to side like a spectator at a Wimbledon tennis final.

Ant changed tack.

"Is that your Range Rover, Annabelle?"

"What are you talking about?" she replied as she turned to look at the aircraft.

"It's okay, Annabelle. I've already checked. The car is yours. Unfortunately for you, you hit a car in your haste to get away from the boathouse after you placed chloral hydrate into the tin of varnish Geoff was using to spruce up his boat before selling it."

"Chloral hydrate?"

Ant ignored the policeman's parrot-like repetition.

"You see, Annabelle, pear drops make my nose itch. Isn't that right, Lyn?"

Lyn nodded, her amusement obvious for all to see.

"And as it turns out, chloral hydrate also smells of pear drops. Lucky, really. Well, perhaps not for you." Ant moved closer to Annabelle to press home his dominance of the space between them.

"You don't have any proof of this nonsense. You are just making this up."

You can look as angry as you like, lady.

"Oh, I think I have. I'm sure your fingerprints will be all over that can. You got sloppy, Annabelle. Were you running out of time to pick Hannah up and get to the BBQ? I think you were, so you couldn't get the tin away from Geoff after you spiked it, to get rid of your fingerprints. Or perhaps you just assumed the police would think he died of natural causes, and you didn't need to bother. After all, poor Geoff would have innocently used the varnish then put the tin away. He was tidy like that, wasn't he? All the time he was in that cabin, the fumes were doing their work; Geoff was unaware it was killing him. I assume you knew he had a poor sense of smell, so he didn't notice anything wrong. In the end, he just sat down and died—but only because you poisoned him."

Annabelle stood rooted to the spot.

Hannah's gaze burned into her.

The temporary silence was broken by a ringtone.

"I think that's for you, Annabelle."

Annabelle looked at Lyn, then the handset gave off an eerie halo in the darkness.

Lyn held up a second handset, its screen also illuminated.

"This is Jakub's phone, Annabelle. You know, the one you rang to get him over from Poland. The one you dialled to fool him it was Hannah ringing, and the one you used to get him to move Geoff's body."

Hannah cried out as if in physical pain. Lyn walked her away from the group, giving what comfort she could from the relative quiet of Ant's car.

Ant noticed Annabelle's demeanour change. When Fitch pulled up with Jakub in tow, it broke completely.

Almost there.

"That report was written by your husband's research company, wasn't it?"

Annabelle gave the faintest of nods to acknowledge Ant's question.

"Geoff told you he'd realised what had been going on, and that he wasn't prepared to ruin his reputation. He realised your husband had got his findings wrong, yes?"

A tear rolled down Annabelle's cheek.

"My husband knows nothing of what I have done. We would have been ruined. Twenty years of work gone in a second, along with everything we own."

Riley started to move forward holding a pair of handcuffs in his right hand.

"I told Geoff we could fix things. He didn't believe me. He said one lie would lead to another and he couldn't allow that. Well, I couldn't let him ruin us."

Ant took a step away from Annabelle.

"And so you did your own research. You found out chloral hydrate had been used as a sedative, but if administered in a big enough dose, it could stop the heart, especially where a weakness already existed."

Annabelle nodded again. The rest of her body hung limp.

"Pretending to be Hannah to ensure Jakub came was a clever touch, I'll give you that. As was arranging for me to be pulled over by that bogus copper. One day I'll find out who told you so much about me to make it so convincing. And who knows, if my mate, Fitch, hadn't been called out to fix a generator, Geoff's body would have vanished forever. Hey, presto, no autopsy results to show traces of chloral hydrate. Just Hannah's spurned lover with a history of violence.

"But you got sloppy when you gave me all that guff about buying the old chapel and having to fly back to Poland to sort out your finances. Did you not think I would check with the estate agent? It took us five minutes to discover the building wasn't for sale after all. Instead, it was Jakub you had just met when I came across you on Wednesday, wasn't it? As for your flight, well, you never left the country, did you?"

Annabelle sobbed and gazed down at the leaf-strewn concrete without answering.

"Over to you, Detective Inspector." Ant vacated the scene and turned to see Jakub leaning into the open-topped Morgan. His arm provided a protective blanket around Hannah's shoulders as they exchanged warm smiles.

"Oh, I have something for you, my Polish friend."

Jakub turned towards Ant.

"A certain young lady asked that I give you this." Ant held out the change Lil had given him for Jakub. "I know food is expensive in the UK, but even we don't charge twenty pounds for a burger!"

Nice to see you smile.

* * *

"You did say two pints of Thatcher's Itch every night for a week, my Lord Stanton?" Fitch reinforced his point by pointing at the wooden beer pump handle at the bar of the Wherry Inn.

"Yes, he did," interjected Lyn.

I give up.

Ant reached into his trouser pocket to retrieve his wallet.

"Watch out for the moths," quipped Fitch.

"Very funny," replied Ant as he drew the attention of the barman and handed over 5 twenty-pound notes. "Put this behind the bar for my friend. If there's anything left by the end of the week, pop it into the lifeboat collection box. Never let it be said I don't pay my debts."

Ant was amused to watch Fitch and Lyn exchange confused glances knowing shelling out cash was not something either of them were used to seeing him do that often.

"What are you up to?"

Ant looked furtively at Fitch as he shuffled from one foot to another.

"As a matter of fact, I need a favour."

"I knew it," moaned Fitch.

"Out with it," demanded Lyn.

Ant played for time by taking a large gulp of his Fen Bodger pale ale.

"I came across a couple of teenagers stripping lead off Hill Rise Folly earlier in the week. The upshot is I said I might be able to help them find a job."

Don't look so suspicious, Fitch.

"What, as plumbers, or demolition experts?"

Having just taken a gulp from her glass, Lyn laughed then coughed as the bubbles from her white wine spritzer hit the back of her nose.

"Er, not exactly. The lad wants to work with animals, so I got him a placement with the vet."

"And the other one." Ant hesitated as Fitch's eyes narrowed.

"She wants to be a mechanic."

Fitch froze.

"*She*—a mechanic? Don't tell me you—"

Ant looked nervously towards the pub's front door then ran.

"I've told her to pop along to the garage first thing on Monday. Is that okay?"

Fitch was up in a flash.

"Lord or not, you come back here before I..."

END

GLOSSARY

English (UK) to US English Glossary

- **A rum do:** A strange or surprising occurrence
- **Bakelite:** Early type of plastic
- **Boiled sweet:** Candy mainly made from sugar and flavourings boiled into a hard treat
- **Bonce:** Street slang for head. "I hit my bonce on the shelf."
- **Broad:** A stretch of shallow water formed from old peat diggings. Common in Norfolk and Suffolk regions of the UK. Can take the form of narrow stretches of water like canals, or open water like small lakes.
- **Car boot:** Trunk
- **Cottoned on:** Finally understood something
- **Fobbed off:** Street slang for not being taken seriously
- **Folly:** A building with no practical use. Traditionally constructed by wealthy landowners on their estate as a symbol of their power and

prestige. Can be a simple tower or obelisk, or more ornate faux castle ruin, for example.
- **Gawping:** Old-fashioned English word for looking obtrusively at something or (more usually) someone
- **Gurning:** A traditional British pastime in which individuals pull a grotesque face by projecting the lower jaw as far forward as possible then covering the upper lip with the lower lip. The head of the competitor is usually placed through a horse's harness as a "frame"
- **Jiffy:** A word to describe doing something almost immediately—"I'll be with you in a jiffy."
- **Lay-by:** A safe place to park at the side of a highway
- **Holby City:** Eponymous UK soap opera based in a hospital
- **Manky:** Something, or someone, who smells of a bad odour. Often used to describe something that is falling to bits
- **Mackintosh:** A eponymous waterproof coat or jacket
- **Newsagent:** A shop which sells newspapers, magazines, tobacco and candy
- **Plod:** nickname for a policeman or "the police"
- **Pillar box:** A Royal Mail postal box sited in public places and usually painted bright red (pillar-box red)
- **Quid:** Pound sterling
- **Shandy:** A mixture of roughly 50% or more of beer and 50% lemonade (soda)
- **Shufti:** Street slang used to describe having a look at something. Often said in jest

- **Sixpence:** A UK coin used until 1971 and worth approximately two US cents today
- **Snug:** A small room in an English pub. Old-fashioned and not designed for pubs today
- **That's the ticket:** Showing courage or willing to do something with a good heart
- **The City:** London's financial district and stock exchange
- **Tight:** Does not spend money easily—penny-pincher
- **Toad-in-the-hole:** British food dish first described in 1762 as a pastry dish containing a small piece of beef. Used to make meat go further in poor households. The modern version consists of sausages cooked in with a Yorkshire pudding and is a popular pub meal.
- **Toerag:** Street slang to describe someone who cannot be trusted
- **Toff:** Slang word for upper-class or rich person generally seen to be "looking down" on other people
- **Turned on a sixpence:** turned on the spot
- **Trolley:** A gurney used in hospitals
- **Wherry:** A traditional sailboat used for carrying goods and passengers on the Norfolk & Suffolk Broads
- **You're a corker:** Old-fashioned description of something excellent in a thing or person

READERS' CLUB

Join My Readers' Club

Getting to know my readers is the thing I like most about writing. From time to time I publish a newsletter with details on my new releases, special offers, and other bits of news relating to the Norfolk Murder Mystery series. If you join my Readers' Club, I'll send you this gripping short story free and ONLY available to club members:

A Record of Deceit: 17,000 word short story

Grace Pinfold is terrified a stranger wants to kill her. Disturbing phone calls and mysterious letters confirm the threat is real. Then Grace disappears. Ant and Lyn fear they have less than forty-eight hours to find Grace before tragedy strikes - a situation made worse by a disinterested Detective Inspector Riley who's convinced an innocent explanation exists.

Character Backgrounds: A 7,000 word insight

Read fascinating interviews with the four lead characters in the Norfolk Cozy Mysteries series. Anthony Stanton,

Lyn Blackthorn, Detective Inspector Riley and Fitch explain what drives them, their backgrounds and let slip an insight into each of their characters. We also learn how Ant, Lyn and Fitch first met as children and grew up to be firm friends - even if they do drive each other crazy most of the time!

You can get your free content by visiting my website at www.keithjfinney.com

I look forward to seeing you there.

Keith

AFTERWORD

Did You Enjoy the Compilation?

Reviews are so important in helping get my books noticed. Unlike the big, established authors and publishers, I don't have the resources available for big marketing campaigns and expensive book launches (though I live in hope!).

What I *do* have, gratefully, is the following of a loyal and growing band of readers.

Genuine reviews of my writing help bring my books to the attention of new readers.

If you enjoyed this book, it would be a great help if you could spare a couple of minutes and kindly head over to my Amazon page to leave a review (as short or long as you like).

All you need do is head back over to the Amazon and search your order history for this purchase, then click 'write a product review'.

Thank you so much.

For Joan who is always there for me.

ACKNOWLEDGMENTS

Cover design by Books Covered

Edit & Proofreading: Paula.
paulaproofreader.wixsite.com/home

PUBLISHER INFORMATION

PUBLISHED BY:

Keith Finney - Author

Copyright © 2020

All rights reserved.

No part of this publication may be copied, reproduced in any format, by any means, electronic or otherwise, without prior consent from the copyright owner and publisher of this book.

This is a work of fiction. All characters, names, including business or building names are the product of the author's imagination Any resemblance that any of the above bear to real businesses is coincidental.

www.keithjfinney.com

Printed in Great Britain
by Amazon